She had almost reached the Acura when a figure stepped out of the shadows. Abbie held back a cry of alarm. It wasn't until the stranger took another step forward and came to stand directly under the lamppost that she recognized him.

The man from the ballpark.

With a sinking feeling in her stomach, she looked around her. The parking lot was deserted. She was alone.

"Who are you?" she asked, trying to keep her voice from shaking. "What do you want?"

The obvious answer was money, yet she sensed this was more than a robbery.

"What's the matter? You look nervous." As he talked, the stranger reached inside his shirt pocket and took out a cigarette and a Zippo lighter. "You're not scared of me, are you, Abbie?"

He knew her name. Was that good or bad?

Acting braver than she felt, she inspected him closely, trying to remember when and where she might have run into him.

"I'm afraid you have me at a disadvantage, Mr....?

With an amused expression, the man stuck the cigarette in his mouth. "Nice place you've got there," he said, nodding toward the restaurant. "How much do you gross a night? Five grand? Ten?"

"How much I make is none of your business." As she spoke, she took her cell phone out of her purse. "So why don't you do yourself a favor and get out of my way? Or would you rather I call the police?"

Unfazed, the man took a deep drag of the cigarette and exhaled the smoke slowly, blowing it toward her. "Now, now, Abbie, is that any way to greet your big brother?"

Also by CHRISTIANE HEGGAN

MOMENT OF TRUTH
BLIND FAITH
ENEMY WITHIN
TRUST NO ONE
SUSPICION
DECEPTION

CHRISTIANE HEGGAN

DEADLY INTENT

MIRA

ISBN 1-55166-648-0

DEADLY INTENT

Copyright © 2003 by Christiane Heggan.

Visit us at www.mirabooks.com

Printed in U.S.A.

This book is dedicated to the International Book Club of South Jersey and Pennsylvania. It's my way of thanking you for your support over the years, the wonderful luncheons, the lively discussions, the laughter and, above all, your friendship. To all of you,

Danke
Tack
Spasibo
Mange Tak

Thanks
Merci

Prologue

May 18
Allen Correctional Center
Lima, Ohio

On his forty-third birthday, which nobody gave a crap about, Ian McGregor decided he'd had it with prison life. He came to that realization as he and nine other inmates walked from Cell Block 11 to the prison rec room, dragging their feet and shoving each other, for no other reason than to piss off the guards.

Ian had spent half his adult life in and out of prison. While most of his offenses had been minor—drunk and disorderly, attempted burglary, bad checks—this last stint, sixteen months for breaking and entering, had been the pits. Thank God, ten days from now he'd be a free man, and this time, by God, he would stay free. No more stinking cells, no more pervert inmates and no more prison riots, the last of which had left him with four ugly puncture marks on his arm where some goon had stuck him with a fork.

Unfortunately, freedom was about all he had to look forward to. He had no money, no job prospect and no place to call home, unless his longtime, on-and-off girlfriend, Rose Panini, took him back. He wouldn't blame her if she didn't. With his track record over the last twenty years, he wasn't exactly what women called a catch. Simply put, Rose was fed up. She had made that plain the morning of his last sentencing, swearing she never wanted to see him again. So far, she had kept her word. His pleas for her to visit him had remained unanswered, as had his letters. But Ian was optimistic. Once she saw him standing on her doorstep, repentant and oozing with charm, she'd take one look at him and forgive him. Rose was no prize, but she had a big heart. Not to mention a steady job.

His second problem was a little more serious. And it came with a name: Arturo Garcia, one of the meanest SOB's he'd ever had the misfortune to know. Ten years ago, Ian had worked for the man, delivering meth and cocaine to nightclubs throughout the Toledo area. The job had been fairly easy and the money good until the cops, who had been watching Ian, had apprehended him in the middle of a delivery and hauled him off to jail.

But just when he thought he'd be spending the next decade behind bars, the D.A. had offered him a deal that was almost too good to be true—his freedom for the goods on his boss. Ian hadn't thought twice. He should have, because in addition to ratting on Arturo, Ian had walked off with thirty thousand dollars of his money, and that had made the drug distributor even more enraged.

On the day of his sentencing, which Ian had been dumb enough to attend, Arturo had to be dragged out of the courtroom kicking and screaming as he fired a volley of obscenities at Ian.

"This ain't over, you lousy snitch," Garcia had shouted. "When I get out I'm gonna find you and gut you like a fish."

Fortunately, by the time Arturo was getting out of prison, Ian was going in for the B & E job, a twist of fate that

saved him from a sure and painful death. The word was that Arturo had returned to his native town of El Paso, where he and his younger brother, Tony, helped their widowed mother run the family grocery store. But who could tell if that was really true. For all Ian knew, Arturo could be cooling his heels outside the prison gates right now, waiting for a chance to kill him.

Ian's thoughts were interrupted by a vicious whack behind the knees. "Move it, McGregor. What do you think this is? A funeral procession?"

Ian was tempted to yank the guard's baton out of his hand and shove it up his ass. The thought, satisfying as it was, went no further. That kind of behavior would only get him a week in solitary and suspension of his TV privileges. He didn't mind the solitary part, but he hated to be deprived of his nightly hour of television, especially now that *Baywatch* had gone into syndication and was being shown every night. There was nothing like a bunch of stacked babes in tight bathing suits to get a man's blood pumping.

As always, the recreation-hour crowd was divided into two groups—the hard-core poker players, who never got the game out of their system, even when they played with fake money, and a handful of TV aficionados. Tonight, Ian and his tube-addicted buddies were in for a treat. Instead of a full hour of their favorite program, they had elected to watch the last half hour of a local beauty pageant, followed by the last thirty minutes of *Baywatch*.

Taking a seat in the first row, Ian kept his eyes glued to the screen where six shapely girls, all finalists in the Miss Columbus Pageant, pranced across the stage in skimpy bikinis, their boobs bobbing up and down and threatening to spill out of their tops. Ian and his friends clapped and cheered every time a contestant got close to the camera and

gave them a mouthwatering view of her firm round ass. Even the guards joined in, whistling and ogling the girls as if they'd never seen skin before.

"Hey," the inmate next to Ian said when the pageant was over. "Somebody tape that?" Larry Warmath made a goofy face and wiggled in his seat like an idiot. "I'd like a replay at my next jammy party."

Laughter erupted, but Ian was no longer paying attention to the banter. Remote in hand, he was flipping through the channels in search of *Baywatch*, when two women on the screen, a skinny blonde with too much makeup and a brunette in a white apron, caught his eye. The slim, rather petite brunette wasn't exactly his type, but he had to admit she was a looker. She appeared to be in her mid-thirties until she smiled, then she looked much younger. Her dark brown hair was pulled back from her face and held with a white ribbon at the nape of her neck. The eyes were very nice, big and gray and unwavering, but it was her mouth that drew his attention. It was full, lightly tinted and conjured up all kinds of fantasies.

The two women appeared to be in a restaurant, empty at the moment. His eyes on the brunette, Ian listened.

"Today," the blonde was saying, "we are talking to Abbie DiAngelo. Ms. DiAngelo is the owner and executive chef of the French-country restaurant Campagne, right here in Princeton."

Ian sat up. Abbie DiAngelo? He had known an Abbie DiAngelo once. His stepsister. She was eight the last time he'd seen her, so he couldn't be sure it was her, but how many Abbie DiAngelos could there be?

"Gimme this!" Warmath tried to take the remote from Ian, but Ian kept it out of the man's reach. "We ain't interested in no news, man. We want *Baywatch*."

"This ain't the news, so chill out, Larry, okay?"

"Then what the fuck is it?"

"Two good-looking broads. You don't have a problem with that, do you?" He winked at the others, who were already snickering. "Casanova?"

"Hell, no." Warmath, who wasn't too bright, wet his lips and settled in his chair. He didn't have much of a choice, anyway. Ian had the remote control and he wasn't about to let it go. The other three men didn't seem to mind watching the two women.

"Ms. DiAngelo," the reporter continued, "is a graduate of the New York Culinary Institute and is well known to Princeton-area residents. Prior to opening her restaurant, she owned and operated a popular catering service, aptly named DiAngelo Catering."

She turned to the young woman. "And now you have just returned from Lyon, France, where you were awarded one of the world's most coveted culinary prizes—Le Bocuse d'Or. This is an incredible accomplishment for an American chef, isn't it? Until now, no one from this country had ever received such an honor."

Leaning against one of the tables, Abbie DiAngelo ignored the camera and focused her attention on her interviewer. "No, and frankly, I never thought I'd be coming home a winner. I would have been happy enough to place in the top ten, especially since this was my first time as a competitor."

"How did the French react when they heard you had won?"

Abbie DiAngelo laughed, and there, in her left cheek, Ian thought he recognized a dimple. "The same way they reacted when Lance Armstrong won his first Tour de France." Feigning a shocked expression, she cupped her cheeks with both hands. *"Une Américaine? Mon Dieu! C'est pas possible."*

The reporter laughed but Abbie quickly turned serious again. "Actually, they couldn't have been nicer, before, during and after the competition. A local reporter nick-named me *La Petite Américaine*—the little American. Somehow, the name stuck and when it was all over, all the contestants were thrilled for me."

"What does winning this award mean for you, Abbie?"

Abbie's eyes lit up. "Well, for one thing, it's doing won-ders for my ego."

"I'm told you don't have one."

She laughed again. "Don't be so sure. A chef without an ego is like a soufflé without air. It will never rise to the occasion. Seriously," she continued, "for me, the real re-ward is to have been part of such an elite group for an entire week. Working with world-renowned chefs, sharing tips with them, comparing techniques and then cooking un-der such pressure for three days, convinced me that no matter what challenge comes my way now, I'm ready for it."

"The menu you prepared for the judges was impressive. Will you be adding any of those dishes to your current menu?"

"I already have. All have been a big hit."

Leaning toward Abbie but winking at the camera, the reporter said, "Is that the reason it's so difficult to get a reservation at Campagne these days?"

"Oh, I don't know," Abbie replied with a smile. "You might try using your connections."

Next to Ian, Warmath jabbed him in the ribs. "Hey, what's with you and that broad, man?" He wiggled again and said in a singsong voice, "You in love, McGregor?"

Ian kept his eyes on the screen. "No, I just think I know her."

"Oh, yeah?" The inmate barked out a laugh. "Well,

then, why don't you introduce us? We'd like to know her, too." He turned to his buddies. "Ain't that right, fellows?"

"Shut up, will you?" Ian tuned them out, fascinated by what he was hearing, almost certain the woman on the screen was his stepsister.

"Did you always want to be a chef?" the reporter asked.

Behind her, a waiter in black pants and a white, short-sleeved shirt moved from table to table, placing silverware beside each plate. "Actually, I wanted to be a ballerina."

It's her, Ian thought, remembering the ballet posters in Abbie's room, the dancing lessons she had taken twice a week, the recital he and his sister Liz had been forced to attend. It's really her. Son of a bitch.

The blonde's gaze followed the waiter for a couple of seconds before returning to Abbie. "When did you change your mind?"

"I'm not sure. My mother was, and still is, a wonderful cook. That had a lot to do with my decision to go into the food business."

So Irene was still around. That wasn't surprising. She had only been in her mid-thirties when she had married Ian's father.

"Thank you, Abbie, for taking time from your busy schedule to talk to us. And again, congratulations on your award." The reporter turned to the camera and flashed her pearly whites. "We've been talking to chef Abbie Di-Angelo, the new recipient of the prestigious Bocuse d'Or. For CBS, this is Loraine Grant."

Warmath gave Ian another jab. "Maybe we should get that broad to come here and cook for us. That prison grub they're feeding us is carving a hole in my stomach the size of the Grand Canyon."

But Ian wasn't listening. He was thinking. Though not religious by any stretch of the imagination, he believed that finding Abbie after twenty-eight years was no accident. It was a sign from up above—one he couldn't afford to ignore. A moment ago he had been wondering where his next buck would be coming from and now everything had changed. Yes siree, at long last the gods were smiling on Ian McGregor. And he owed it all to a twist of fate—or in this case, a punch of the remote.

Who said miracles were only for the believers?

May 28
Stateville Prison
Akron, Ohio

The first person Ian went to see when he walked out of Allen Correctional Center ten days later wasn't Rose, but an old buddy of his, a death-row inmate who had been awaiting his fate at Stateville for the last six years.

Ian and Earl Kramer had met in San Francisco more than a decade ago. Both men had been partners in a venture to bring in illegal aliens from China—men and women so desperate for a better way of life, they were willing to pay ten thousand dollars each for safe passage to the United States. Before Ian and Earl could make a single penny from their investment, however, the third partner had split with their money.

Broke and bitter, Ian and Earl had drifted apart, each looking for the next get-rich-quick scheme. A couple of years later, Ian heard Earl was back in jail, this time for killing a cop, and had been sentenced to die.

Ian wouldn't have given Earl a second thought except that he had hatched up a clever little plan regarding Abbie, and he couldn't put it into action without his old buddy. Getting in to see him, however, hadn't been easy. Even though Stateville wasn't a maximum-security prison, only immediate members of the family were permitted to visit death-row inmates. It wasn't until Earl's wife, Anna, had told prison officials that Ian was an old friend, practically one of the family, that he had been allowed in.

After a thorough search, both of his body and his belongings, he was escorted down several narrow corridors and into a room with two booths separated by a pane of thick glass. A telephone hung on each side of the partition. Choosing the far booth, Ian sat down and looked nervously around him. The atmosphere was different in this wing, quieter and more somber. You could almost hear a clock ticking, even though he didn't see any. Maybe the eerie feeling came from knowing that somewhere on this floor was the death chamber, patiently waiting for its next occupant. Ian shivered.

He had begun to sweat profusely, when he heard the rattle of chains approaching. A few moments later, Earl walked in, escorted by two guards. Surprisingly, in spite of six long years on death row, the man had held up remarkably well. His hair had turned a dull gray and was sprouting out of his head in spiky clumps. He was also heavier than Ian remembered, more solid under the faded, blue prison suit.

His hands and feet shackled, he shuffled to the booth and sat down. That's when Ian noticed the small black book Earl had brought in with him and laid on the table. A bible. He had heard that some death-row inmates turned to God when all else had failed, but he had never pegged nasty, foulmouthed Earl as a believer. Worried his hopes for some quick and easy money would collapse like a deck of cards, Ian searched the man's face for a moment, waiting to hear the words *fooled you* coming out of Earl's mouth. But if Kramer sensed his old partner's anxieties, he didn't let on.

Ian waited until Earl had picked up the phone with both hands before speaking into it. "How're you doing, buddy?"

Earl glowered at him. "I'm on fucking death row. How do you think I'm doing?"

Ian relaxed. Now *that* was the Earl he knew. "I guess that was a stupid question."

The halfhearted apology seemed to go over Earl's head. "What the hell you doing here anyway? I thought after what Garcia threatened to do to you, you'd be halfway across the country by now."

"I will be, soon." Ian glanced at the two guards standing by the door. They were watching him but looked more bored than suspicious. He lowered his voice. "I have a proposition for you."

"You're gonna spring me?"

Ian laughed. "I thought a man with your connections would have already figured a way to get out of this place."

"Connections don't come cheap."

Ian grinned. "In that case, you're definitely going to like my proposition."

Trying to appear as though they were having an ordinary conversation, Ian lowered his voice another notch and laid out his plan.

One

"Way to go, Ben!"

Abbie DiAngelo sprung to her feet and clapped vigorously as the ball her nine-year-old son had just hit sailed over both the infield and the outfield, before falling two feet short of a home run.

"Go, go, go!" The crowd whooped and cheered as two runners came home and Ben reached third base in a spectacular slide.

The umpire threw his arms flat out, signaling Ben safe.

Grinning, Ben got to his feet and took a congratulatory hand slap from his third-base coach before glancing toward the bleachers. Abbie gave him the thumbs-up sign. In reply he tugged the brim of his helmet, but she knew that beneath all that composure, he was elated. His batting had been off lately, but thanks to Brady Hill, Campagne's young sous-chef who had once dreamed of playing for the Yankees, Ben's technique had improved dramatically in the last two weeks, and so had his batting average.

Fifteen minutes later, the undefeated Princeton Falcons were making their way toward the stands and their proud parents. As Ben stopped to say a few words to one of his teammates, Abbie watched him for a moment, feeling the familiar knot in her stomach. She was so proud of him, of the way he had turned out, warm, open and good-hearted. For a while, the fear of raising a child on her own had been so overwhelming she had actually questioned her decision to divorce Jack. But, as her mother had been quick to point out, staying in a bad marriage was often more detrimental for a child than going through a divorce. And if anyone knew how devastating a bad marriage could be, it was Irene.

Funny how her life had paralleled her mother's in so many ways, Abbie thought. Both had made some bad choices, yet both had survived, concentrating solely on their child, and emerging from their respective ordeals stronger than ever.

His bat bag slung over one shoulder, Ben ran toward her. Except for his sunny disposition, which he had inherited from her, the nine-year-old was his father's spitting image. He had Jack's flaming-red hair and big blue eyes and the same sprinkle of freckles across his nose.

"Did you see that triple, Mom?" His eyes filled with youthful excitement. "And the double before that?"

Abbie's first impulse was to give him a big hug. Just in time she remembered that now that he was nine, hugs and kisses were reserved for home, so she contented herself with tousling his hair. "I sure did. I'm proud of you, sport."

"Jimmy says my three RBIs won the game."

Not wanting to dampen his spirits, Abbie chose her words carefully. "You were awesome out there, but you remember what we talked about the other day? Baseball is a team effort. All the players contributed to tonight's win."

Ben nodded, if somewhat reluctantly. "That's what the coach said."

Abbie smiled as she savored this moment with her son; even though the dinner hour at Campagne was well under way and she ought to be getting back, she didn't rush him. Brady would cover for her. "I think that triple deserves a special treat. What do you say we stop at Flo's for an ice-cream cone before I drop you off at the house?"

"Before dinner?"

"Let's live dangerously."

Ben rewarded her with another happy grin. "Cool."

Forgetting the "no touching in front of his friends rule," Abbie draped an arm around his narrow shoulders and together they headed toward her red Acura SUV. Just then, a feeling she hadn't had since her ex-husband had threatened to take Ben from her skittered across her skin. Mildly alarmed, she glanced around. A man stood a few feet away, one shoulder against the wire fence that partially circled the ball field. Although he wore jeans, a polo shirt and sneakers—the standard clothing for Little Leaguers' dads—something about him didn't quite fit. Maybe it was because he was alone. Or it could be the unsettling way he kept looking at her. Common sense told her he could be completely harmless, a fan of youth baseball. But in this day and age, with so many predators roaming the streets, it wouldn't hurt to be cautious. If she saw him again at the next game, she would point him out to Ben's coach.

Trying to shake her uneasy feeling, Abbie tightened her hold on her son's shoulder, and didn't let him go until they had reached the SUV.

Ian watched Abbie get into her car, a bright-red SUV, pleased to see that he had made her nervous. He loved to rattle people. It made whatever little surprise he had in store for them so much more gratifying.

From the restaurant, he had followed his stepsister to the

ball field and had quickly realized she had a son on the Falcons, the team currently in first place. Picking him out, however, had proved a challenge since none of the players had the name DiAngelo written on their shirts. It wasn't until he heard Abbie cheer and call his name that he had finally spotted him, a freckle-faced, redheaded kid with a big, toothy grin. The back of his shirt bore the name Wharton in big black letters.

The boy had been a surprise. Abbie hadn't mentioned him in the interview, and nothing Ian had read on the restaurant's Web site before leaving Ohio had suggested she had a child. Or that she was even married. That thought didn't thrill him. A man in her life would complicate things. On the other hand, he hadn't seen a wedding ring on her left hand, so maybe she was divorced. Or widowed. Or maybe she was one of those flaming feminists who had gotten herself inseminated, just to show the world she didn't need a man to raise a kid.

Either way he wasn't complaining. So far, everything had gone pretty much according to plan. Even Rose, good, dependable Rose, had come through for him. She hadn't exactly welcomed him with open arms, though. In fact, it had taken some doing on his part to keep her from slamming the door in his face, but in the end, she had let him in.

"I'm turning my life around," he had told her with all the sincerity he could muster. "I'm getting out of this crummy town and starting fresh." He had given her a long, sober look. "And I want you to come with me, Rose."

He'd proceeded to tell her how he had located his stepsister and was hoping she would loan him some money— enough to rent a decent apartment and buy some new clothes so he could start looking for a job. He hadn't told her anymore than that. Rose was funny that way. She was too much of a straight arrow, and the less she knew, the better off he was.

At the word *job,* Rose had looked doubtful, and for good reason. In the past, his inability—or, as she put it, his *un-willingness*—to find a job had been the subject of endless arguments between them.

But even though he felt he was deserving of an Oscar for his performance, it had taken a while for Rose to warm up to the idea of leaving Toledo, where she was born and raised. It took her even longer to agree to finance their trip to Princeton, New Jersey.

"Look at it as an investment," Ian told her as he rubbed her leg in that slow, sexy way she liked. "An investment in us."

Those last words had worked magic. Rose had melted in his arms, and two days later, she had given notice to her landlord and to her boss at the beauty shop where she worked as a manicurist.

The bad news was that Rose didn't have as much of a nest egg as he had hoped. And since he didn't know how long it would take Abbie to come up with the money, they would have to watch their pennies. Even that crummy motel on Route 27 was a rip-off.

After checking in earlier today, Ian had borrowed Rose's Oldsmobile and taken a drive to Palmer Square for a close look at Abbie's restaurant. He had been impressed. The square was one of those fancy-shmancy shopping centers designed around a small park the locals called the Green, and surrounded by trendy boutiques and expensive restaurants.

From the restaurant, he had gone to the tax assessor's office in search of his stepsister's address, as well as Irene's. Realizing he was from out of town, a helpful clerk had taken out a tax map and showed him the location of both streets.

If success could be measured by the size of a house, then Abbie had done all right for herself. Her house was twice the size of the McGregors' house in Palo Alto and was surrounded by several acres of land, most of it heavily wooded. Irene, on the other hand, lived in a well-maintained but modest two-story home in a working-class neighborhood.

Pulling away from the fence, Ian walked toward the Oldsmobile. He had heard enough of Abbie's conversation with her son to know that she was taking him for an ice cream and then home. She hadn't said what she planned to do afterward, but his bet was she'd be going back to the restaurant for the dinner crowd.

With nothing to do, he drove back to Palmer Square, found a parking space in the small lot in back of the restaurant and waited. Sure enough, half an hour later, the red SUV pulled in.

Pretending to be reading a road map, Ian watched his stepsister get out of the car and hurry toward the restaurant. It would be a long wait until she closed up the place, but he didn't mind. Ian was a patient man—when the stakes were high enough.

Two

"No, Arturo." Tony Garcia put himself between his older brother and the duffel bag on the bed. "You're not going after McGregor."

Arturo, a whole foot taller than Tony and a hundred pounds heavier, shoved him aside. "Who's gonna stop me?"

"Me."

"Lay off me, Tony, okay?" Arturo threw a handful of clothes into the bag. "I waited ten long years to make that son of a bitch pay for what he did, and by God, he's gonna pay."

"He's not worth going back to prison for."

"I ain't goin' back to prison."

"You will if you kill him."

Arturo came to stand in front of Tony. He was a huge man, with the strength of a bull and a temper to match. He looked even more menacing now that he had shaved his head and grown a goatee. "What I do to McGregor is my business, brother."

Unfortunately, it wasn't just Arturo's business, Tony thought with a sigh. Not that he wanted to be his brother's keeper, but he had no choice. Six months ago, he had made a promise to his dying father to keep Arturo out of trouble and he intended to make good on that promise.

"Arturo, be reasonable," he said, appealing to a side of his brother that didn't exist. "It's been ten years. Time to forgive and forget."

Arturo glared at him. "If I did that, the whole barrio would laugh at me. I'd lose my edge."

"So that's what this is all about? Saving face?"

"It's about getting my money back." Arturo brought his face close to Tony's again. "Thirty grand that little vermin took from me. I want it back, man."

"Are you telling me all you want is your thirty thousand back?"

Arturo threw a pair of scuffed boots into the duffel bag. "That's a start."

"Then give me your word you won't kill him."

"That depends on McGregor. If he gives me no shit, maybe I'll let him live. If he does…" He shrugged.

"And then what? You get caught and you go back to prison. What will happen to Ma if you're sent away again? That last time almost killed her."

"She'll be okay. She's got you."

"No, she doesn't."

Arturo stopped, one hand on a T-shirt. "What the fuck you mean by that?"

"I mean that I'm not going to be here, Arturo. If you insist on going after McGregor, then I'm going with you."

"I don't need a fucking baby-sitter!" Arturo bellowed.

"Get used to it, because I'm going to be right there." He punched the air with his index finger repeatedly, each time coming within an inch of Arturo's nose. "In your face, keeping you on the straight and narrow. You got that, Arturo?"

Before Arturo could get a chance to close his mouth, Tony stormed out of his brother's room, wishing he could just keep on walking and leave Arturo to his fate. But the truth was, Tony loved that big jerk. And he owed him for sticking up for him when they were kids, always coming to his defense and scaring the shit out of whoever had the audacity to throw a punch at the younger Garcia.

Raised in the barrio, both boys had been talked into joining a street gang at an early age. Tony had been fourteen and Arturo nineteen. Four years later, disgusted with all the violence, Tony had left the Blades and gone to work at his parents' grocery store. He had even started taking a few courses at the local college. Arturo, on the other hand, already had his sights on becoming the gang's next leader. Shortly after his initiation as the Blades' new *jefe*, a well-dressed, smooth-talking man had approached Arturo and told him he was a powerful drug kingpin and was looking for someone with balls to run his distribution center in Toledo, Ohio.

Worried his brother was headed for a life of crime, Tony had tried to stop him from taking the offer. Arturo had just laughed at him.

"Are you nuts, Tone? Just look at me." He had spread his arms wide, determined to make his point. "Here I'm just another gang leader, an ugly, badass spic with no money and no future. There ain't much I can do about the ugly spic part, but I sure as hell don't have to stay penniless all my life."

His vision had been right on the money, because within a month Arturo was making a thousand dollars a week, tax free, and living the good life. Business was so good in Toledo that he had taken a partner, a man by the name of Ian McGregor.

Two years later, during a sting operation, McGregor was

arrested, then later released when he had handed Arturo to the D.A. on a silver platter.

Although Arturo had sworn to get even with McGregor someday, Tony had prayed his brother would forget his former partner's betrayal and go on with his life. No such luck. As soon as Arturo had learned from the prison grapevine that McGregor was out, he had started packing.

Cursing under his breath, Tony walked into his room, took out his own duffel bag from the closet and threw it on the bed. Keeping Arturo from killing McGregor wasn't a job he looked forward to, but if he didn't do it, who the hell would?

Abbie called Campagne's kitchen the restaurant's nerve center, and anyone who had ever been there would agree. It was a busy, noisy place where the frantic pace was enough to make first-time visitors count their blessings they hadn't chosen the restaurant business.

Abbie felt exactly the opposite. No matter how many hours a day she spent in this kitchen, or how worn-out she was at the end of the day, she never tired of the sights, sounds and challenges that had become such an integral part of her daily life.

Glad to see that the kitchen was running with the efficiency and precision of a well-oiled machine, she took her apron from a hook and smiled as Brady walked over to her.

"How did it go?" he asked eagerly.

Her sous-chef was a personable young man with movie-star good looks, short, spiky blond hair à la Brad Pitt and an engaging smile. A broken elbow had ended a promising baseball career and forced Brady to examine new options. On a dare from his buddies, who loved his cooking, he had enrolled in a local cooking school, and upon his graduation had landed the job of second assistant to the chef de cuisine in a Philadelphia restaurant. Three years ago, when Abbie had opened Campagne and was looking for a sous-chef, she had come upon his résumé and had immediately set up an interview. After the first ten minutes together, Abbie knew she had found her man. Their compatibility was such that they quickly broke the barrier of employer/employee relationship, and became good friends.

Brady had spent hours with Ben, helping him with his batting, so Abbie gave him a detailed replay of the game, knowing he expected nothing less. When she told him about Ben's spectacular triple in the final inning, and the three RBIs, Brady beamed.

"He's a shoo-in for the all star team," he said with a confident nod.

Abbie tied the apron around her waist. "Don't tell him that, okay, Brady? I don't want him to be disappointed if he's not picked."

"If he's not picked, I'll have a little heart-to-heart with his coach."

Abbie let out a groan. "Oh, no. You're turning into one of those Little League fathers who thinks his kid is so much better than the others."

Brady laughed. "All right, all right, I'll shut up."

The young man by her side, Abbie started walking around the large room filled with stainless-steel appliances, glancing at the order slips clipped to a rotating rack, lifting lids, smelling, tasting, peeking in the oven where four individual cassoulets bubbled gently in their little clay pots.

"Anything unusual happen while I was gone?" She moved to the shoulder-high swinging doors and glanced into the crowded dining room.

"The president of the university and his wife are at table

three. They're celebrating their twenty-fifth wedding anniversary.''

Abbie recognized the silver-haired academic. Both he and his wife were regular customers and generous sponsors of the yearly food festival, the proceeds of which went to a local women's shelter. ''Send them a bottle of champagne, will you, Brady? Compliments of the house. And tell them I'll be by later to wish them a happy anniversary.''

Brady immediately snapped his fingers at a passing waiter and repeated Abbie's instructions. ''Oh,'' he added with a twinkle in his eyes. ''I almost forgot. Your admirer is here.''

Abbie raised a quizzical eyebrow. ''I have an admirer?''

''Oh, don't play innocent with me, you wench. You know darn well I'm talking about Professor Higgins. He couldn't make it for lunch today, so he came for dinner. And of course, he insisted on sitting at his usual table. I had to do a little reshuffling, but I figured it was worth the trouble, being he's such a good customer.''

Abbie had no difficulty spotting the dapper, retired professor sitting in the small alcove. Oliver Gilroy, who had left his native England fifteen years ago to teach English literature in the U.S., was a charming man with an appreciation for fine food and everything that made life pleasurable. In a roomful of people, he didn't particularly stand out. He was small and slender with neatly combed gray hair and the kind of features that were quickly forgotten. He was, however, somewhat eccentric, always arriving at the restaurant at the same time every day—twelve noon—requesting the same table and always ordering the same wine, an Australian chardonnay, regardless of what he ate.

It was true that he seemed to have grown fond of Abbie, but she suspected that this show of affection stemmed more from her resemblance to his daughter, whose picture Abbie had seen, than a romantic attachment. It was his good manners as well as his refined British accent that had prompted Brady to nickname him Professor Higgins, the unforgettable character in *My Fair Lady*.

"I think he brought Ben another present," Brady whispered.

Abbie's gaze stopped on the miniature wooden rail car beside the professor's wineglass. Now that he was retired, Professor Gilroy was able to devote more time to an old passion—trains, which he painstakingly built from prefabricated kits. After finding out Abbie had a young son, he had brought Ben a Big Boy locomotive he had just completed. He had followed that present with a log buggy, a livestock car, a gondola and several freight cars.

Although Abbie had tried to discourage him, he continued to add to Ben's collection, claiming he would do so until Ben had a complete set of the Southern Pacific Railroad, one of the professor's favorites.

She would stop by his table during her rounds later on, and since she knew he was fond of cream puffs, she would ask Brady to fill a box of his favorite pastries to take home with him.

Brady let out a chuckle. "Nothing like buttering up the child to impress the mother, eh?"

"For God's sake, Brady, will you stop it? The man is old enough to be my father."

"So what? He's well educated, not bad-looking, wealthy, from what I heard. And it's not like you couldn't use a little romance in your life."

Abbie made a face. "Thanks for reminding me."

"You know what I mean."

"Yes, you think I lead a dull life." She gave him a playful tap on the arm. "Let's put that creative mind of yours on something that will really pay off—like that roast duck for table one.''

By eleven o'clock, the last satisfied diner had finally left, the staff was gone, and the kitchen was as immaculate as it had been that morning. Alone in the empty dining room, Abbie stood at the cash register, counting the day's receipts. Fourteen thousand dollars. Not bad for a Monday night.

Reaching under the register, she took out the pouch she used to make her daily deposits at the bank. As she slid the money into it, her gaze swept over the deserted room. Even now, after three years as the owner of Campagne, she always experienced a feeling of pride at the realization of all she had accomplished in such a short time. Circumstances, rather than choice, had dictated the path her career had taken. As a wife and mother of a new baby, she had been satisfied running a catering service that allowed her to set her own hours. But after her divorce from Jack, she had realized that in order to make some serious money, she had to set higher goals for herself. And that meant opening her own restaurant, a dream she'd had since her first day at the Culinary Institute.

At first, the thought of taking such a risk had been overwhelming, but little by little, as she took inventory of her talent, her determination and her finances, fear turned to excitement. She could do this. She *would* do this.

Using the money from her divorce settlement plus what she had managed to save over the years, she financed part of the venture and convinced her banker to loan her the rest. The first year hadn't been easy. Or the second. With so many well-established restaurants in the Princeton area, Campagne was slow in catching the attention of the public. But thanks to a few good reviews and word of mouth,

Campagne was now one of the hottest eateries within a twenty-mile radius.

Unlike some owners of French-country restaurants, she had resisted the temptation to clutter the dining room with the expected terra-cotta pots, lavender sprays and other country artifacts. Instead, she had gone to France and brought back several bolts of *souleiado,* a Provençal cloth that came in tones of blue, red, green and yellow, and had turned them into tablecloths. The dishes, brilliant ocher pottery, were also from the south of France, as was the bubble-glass stemware. Except for an antique tapestry she had unearthed in a local flea market years ago, she had left the saffron-colored walls bare. The effect was nothing short of spectacular.

"All right, girl," she said, stuffing the money pouch into her purse. "That's enough gloating for one night. Time to go home."

Humming softly, she walked from the dining room, through the kitchen, turning off the last light switch before going out the back door.

She had almost reached the Acura when a figure stepped out of the shadows.

Abbie held back a cry of alarm. Holding her purse against her chest, she reminded herself that Princeton was one of the safest communities in New Jersey. In the three years she'd had the restaurant, she had never had a reason to be afraid, even at this late hour.

It wasn't until the stranger took another step forward and came to stand directly under the lamppost that she recognized him.

The man from the ballpark.

With a sinking feeling in her stomach, she looked around her. The parking lot was deserted. She was alone. A true gentleman, Brady had repeatedly offered to stay with her until closing and walk her to her car, but she had always turned him down. Now she wished she hadn't.

"Who are you?" she asked, trying to keep her voice from shaking. "What do you want?"

The obvious answer was money, yet she sensed this was more than a robbery. If money was all he wanted, what had he been doing at the ballpark? The thought she might be raped brought a quick burst of panic, but did not render her helpless. If that's what he was after, he would have one hell of a fight on his hands. Thanks to a course in self-defense she had taken after her divorce, she knew how to take care of herself.

"What's the matter? You look nervous." As he talked, the stranger reached inside his shirt pocket and took out a cigarette and a Zippo lighter. Without taking his eyes off her, he tapped the cigarette gently on the lighter's flat side. The gesture was vaguely familiar but she couldn't place it. Or the man. "You're not scared of me, are you, Abbie?"

He knew her name. Was that good or bad?

Acting braver than she felt, she inspected him closely, trying to remember when and where she might have run into him. At the restaurant, perhaps? Back during her catering days? Now that he was closer, she saw that his eyes were either dark brown or black. His hair was the same color, a little too long for her taste, and combed back, exposing angular features and a narrow forehead. She estimated him to be about forty.

She was certain she had never met him before, but apparently he knew her. Or maybe he had caught the interview she had done for the CBS network a couple of weeks ago. That could be it. People she didn't know now stopped her in the street, or at the farmers' market where she shopped, to congratulate her on the award.

Curious, and not wanting to offend a potential customer,

even a peculiar one, she said, "I'm afraid you have me at a disadvantage, Mr....?"

With an amused expression, the man stuck the cigarette in his mouth. "Nice place you've got there," he said, nodding toward the restaurant. "How much do you gross a night?" He talked with the cigarette clamped between his teeth. "Five grand? Ten?" The Zippo flared, and as he brought the orange flame to the tip of the cigarette, she saw his gaze drift to her purse. He chuckled again as if he knew exactly what was in it. And what she was thinking.

Yet instinct told her he was not a robber. He was too chatty, too preoccupied with the shock value of his remarks to be truly frightening. That thought gave her a small burst of courage. "How much I make is none of your business." As she spoke, she took her cell phone out of her purse. "So why don't you do yourself a favor and get out of my way. Or would you rather I called the police?"

Unfazed, the man took a deep drag of the cigarette and exhaled the smoke slowly, blowing it toward her. Then, leaning against the SUV, he said, "Now, now, Abbie, is that any way to greet your big brother?"

Three

Abbie's first impulse was to dial 911. But even as her finger stood poised over the keypad, she stopped. Something about the man—maybe the unconcerned way he kept looking at her—made her wonder if he could be telling the truth.

She rejected the thought even though the first hint of doubt had begun to gnaw at the pit of her stomach. Ian McGregor had been fifteen the last time she had seen him, which would make him forty-three. He'd had dark curly hair and dark eyes that always lit up with a malevolent gleam—as they did now—when he was about to play a prank on someone.

"That's right." Ian took another drag of his cigarette. "It's me. Ian McGregor. In the flesh. I bet you didn't think you'd ever lay eyes on me again, did you?"

She didn't know how to answer that question. When she and her mother had left California following the devastating fire at the McGregors' house, Ian and his sister, Liz, had stayed in Palo Alto with their aunt Lucinda. Eight-year-old Abbie, who had had to put up with Ian's querulous disposition and Liz's lofty indifference for two long years, had quickly put the teenagers out of her mind.

"What's the matter, Princess?" Ian asked, using the nickname he had given her years ago. "Cat got your tongue all of a sudden? Or are you too overcome with emotion to speak?''

"How do I know you are who you claim to be?"

Silently, he pulled out a wallet from his back pocket, opened it and held it in front of her, tilting it toward the light so she could read it. The expired driver's license, made out to Ian McGregor, had a Toledo, Ohio, address, and the photograph resembled him enough to erase her last doubts. Now she knew why his earlier gesture had seemed so familiar. His father had also tapped his cigarette against his lighter in much the same way.

With a flick of the wrist, he snapped his wallet shut. "I would have looked you up sooner, but your mother didn't bother to leave a forwarding address."

"You knew perfectly well where to get hold of her if you had wanted to," Abbie snapped. "And she did leave a forwarding address—with your aunt Lucinda."

Ian tucked the wallet back in his jeans pocket. "How is my dear stepmommy?"

"How did you find me?"

"I saw that TV interview you did. Me and my fellow inmates were flipping through the channels—"

"Fellow inmates?" she repeated as his words sank in. "You've been in prison?"

"Don't look so surprised. Isn't that the fate Irene had predicted for me?" He shook his finger in a mock imitation of a scolding parent. "'I swear, Ian McGregor, if you don't shape up soon, you'll end up in juvenile court.' Well, guess what? She was right. Somehow I got myself mixed up with the wrong crowd and before I knew it, I was in the slammer.

"I shouldn't complain, though, should I?" A slow grin spread over Ian's face. "Something good came out of my last stint. I found you."

"And why would you want to do that?"

"Why not? We're family, after all."

"Since when? If I recall, you always treated me like an intruder."

He chuckled. "I can still tell when you're pissed, you know that? Your eyes narrow just like they did when you were little, although I wouldn't have recognized you if it hadn't been for the DiAngelo name. You've changed, little sister." He let his gaze travel up and down her body. "For the better, I must say."

"What do you want, Ian?" She heard the impatience in her voice but didn't care. She was tired and she wanted to go home.

He didn't seem to have heard her. "So you became a famous chef. I can't say I'm surprised. You and Irene were always in the kitchen, cooking those great meals. It was quite a change after the kind of slop my mother used to feed us when she was alive."

"Then why couldn't you have shown a little gratitude to my mother instead of always being rude and critical?"

"For God's sake, Abbie, give me a break, will you? I was a thirteen-year-old kid when you guys moved in. All of a sudden, my life was flipped upside down. I didn't just have to put up with a new stepmother but a bratty stepsister as well. It was one hell of an adjustment."

"And now, out of the blue, you want to renew family ties?"

He pulled on the cigarette again, and this time, he had the courtesy to blow the smoke toward the night sky. "They say people turn sentimental in their old age. Maybe that's what's happening to me. I'm turning sentimental."

She'd had enough. Whatever his game was, she wasn't playing. "Good night, Ian." She tried to walk past him but he blocked her way to the SUV.

"Not so fast, Princess. You and me have a little unfinished business."

As badly as she wanted to get out of here, she had no choice but to wait for him to continue.

"You remember the fire, Abbie?"

His question, though unexpected, brought an instant image of the McGregors' house in flames, and of Irene, dragging Abbie and Ian out of the inferno. She had watched in horror as her mother had ran back inside to save her husband and Liz, terrified she'd never see her mother alive again. Thankfully, the firemen had arrived in time to stop her. Liz had survived, but it had been too late for Patrick McGregor.

Oh yes, she remembered that night. Next to her dad's death when she was just five, it was one of the darkest moments of her entire childhood.

"I remember," she said quietly.

"Do you remember how it happened?"

"Why are you bringing this up now?"

"Just humor me, Abbie. Do you remember how the fire happened?"

"I remember what the fire chief said happened. Your father was in bed, smoking, and as usual, he had been drinking. He fell asleep with the cigarette in his hand." She didn't care if her accusatory remark upset him. He had started this.

But Ian didn't look upset. He looked smug. "That's what Irene *wanted* the fire chief to believe. That's what she wanted everyone to believe, but that's not what happened."

Abbie felt suddenly sick. She wanted to blame the feeling on the long day, but she knew she was only kidding herself. Ian was the reason for the tightening of her stomach. Seeing him after all these years brought a foreboding she couldn't shake. Without being sure why, she knew this

unwelcome little reunion was about to change her life forever. She wanted to push past him, get in her car and pretend this visit had never taken place. Yet an unknown
force, something close to a premonition, kept her rooted
where she was.

"What are you talking about?" Her voice was barely
above a whisper.

"That fire was no accident," Ian said. "It was the work
of an arsonist." He paused, obviously for effect. "An arsonist paid by your mother."

Four

Abbie's mouth went dry. For a few seconds, she couldn't fully comprehend what she had just heard. Then, as the words slowly sank in, she slapped Ian's chest with both palms. "You're a sick man, Ian. I had hoped the past twenty-eight years had changed you, but I see they haven't. You're still as twisted as ever, and if you think I'm going to stand here and listen to your lies, you're sicker than I thought."

She shoved him out of the way with more force than she'd ever thought herself capable of and opened the SUV's driver's door.

"What if I told you I had proof that your mother paid someone to set fire to my father's house? Would you believe me then?"

She was shaking so hard, it was a wonder she could talk at all. "If you had proof, you would have gone to the police long ago."

"I found out about it just before I left Ohio. Seems I wasn't the only inmate who saw you on TV that night, bragging about your fancy award, your successful restaurant, your good fortune. My friend remembered Irene's former name—DiAngelo—and put two and two together."

"An inmate?" Abbie let out a brittle laugh. "That's your proof?"

"Inmates are people, too."

"They're criminals who lie as easily as they breathe."

"Some, maybe, but Earl Kramer is telling the truth about Irene."

"How would you know?"

His lips twisted in a half smile. "I've been around liars long enough to know when I'm being conned. And if Earl says Irene hired him to kill my father, then I believe him."

"How long have you known this man?"

"Twelve, thirteen years."

"And he waited all this time to tell you he burned down your father's house?" She laughed, even though she found nothing amusing about the situation. "Come on, Ian. Even you can see the holes in this story."

The mockery in her tone didn't seem to faze him. "He would have been a fool to admit to a crime while he was still a free man. Now that he's on death row and has exhausted all his appeals, he has nothing to lose by telling the truth."

"But he may have a lot to gain by fabricating the story."

"What would he have to gain?"

"Money, Ian." Still holding the SUV's door, she turned around to make sure he heard her but also to show him she wasn't afraid. "Inmates need money, don't they? To support their families, to give to the guards who might make their lives a little easier. How much did it cost you to convince this Earl Kramer to lie?"

Ian did a good job of looking shocked. "You've got it all wrong, sis. Earl sent for *me*. He knew I was getting out, so he figured it was time for him to level with me."

"Why this sudden urge to confess?"

"Earl found religion. That's right, he's a reformed man." He shrugged. "Won't do him any good now, but that doesn't bother him. He wants to cleanse his soul before he meets his maker."

"And he chose you to help him do that?"

"That's right."

She gave a slow shake of her head. "Do you have any idea how phony that sounds?"

"You don't believe me?"

"You're a self-admitted grifter, Ian. Your whole life has been one big sham. So, no, I don't believe you."

"I'm not a grifter anymore. I want to turn my life around, start a business maybe."

"Doing what? Conning little old ladies out of their pension money?"

He let the sarcastic remark pass and took a puff of his cigarette, holding the smoke in before releasing it in a long, slow stream. "Maybe you should talk to Earl, Abbie. You should let him tell you how Irene contacted him through the classifieds, where they met and how she explained that she wanted my father killed but it had to look like an accident."

"He must have agreed to do the job for free, then, because we both know my mother didn't have any money."

"Wrong again, sis. She still had money left over from the insurance policy on your dad. That's what she used to pay Earl. Twenty-five hundred dollars up front and the other twenty-five hundred after the job was done."

"You expect me to believe that my mother would know how to get in touch with a hired killer?"

He shrugged. "I'm sure she didn't. That's why she put that ad in the newspaper. It's done all the time. Take a look when you get a chance."

"I don't know who's lying here, you or your prison buddy, but one of you is."

"You know something? At first I didn't believe him either. Then it hit me that Earl was telling the truth. The bastard was actually responsible for my father's death. I wanted to kill the son of the bitch,'' he continued in a thin, angry voice Abbie was sure was a put-on. ''I wanted to end his miserable life right there and then. I wanted him to pay for killing my father, for all the misery I had to endure after Irene abandoned Liz and me.'' His voice dropped a notch. ''Unfortunately, he was protected by two inches of safety glass and two armed guards. And even if I could have killed him, I wouldn't have. I wasn't about to risk going back to prison for a vermin like him.''

She had to admit, it was a good act, but not good enough. ''Sorry, Ian,'' she said with a smile she hoped looked as condescending as she intended it to be. ''I may have been gullible as a child, but I'm all grown up now and I'm not buying your pathetic tale. If you were as smart as you think you are, you would have realized that before you came here and made a fool of yourself.''

This time, her words seemed to strike a chord. His mouth compressed to a thin line and his eyes went flat. ''Oh, I'm smart all right,'' he said harshly. ''Smart enough to know that if I went to the Palo Alto police with my story, as *pathetic* as it sounds, they'd listen. And what do you think they'd do next?''

He didn't wait for an answer. ''They'd go and question Earl, and then they'd come and question Irene. No matter how much she denied Kramer's accusations, they'd dig into her past, and her relationship with my father. That wouldn't be too good, would it, Abbie?'' He looked smug again. ''From what I remember, those two were fighting all the time—loud, nasty rows that could be heard all over the neighborhood. Irene even threatened to leave my father once and that sent him into a rage. You remember that night, don't you, sis? Sure you do. You ran into your room in tears. Oh, yeah, the cops are going to love hearing all that dirt. And since there's no statute of limitations on murder, my guess is that Mommy Dearest is going to find herself in deep shit.''

Abbie fought back the panic that threatened to shatter her composure. Whether or not Ian was lying, he was right about one thing. If Earl had even one ounce of credibility, the police would have no choice but to check out his story. And turn her mother's quiet life into a living hell.

"The way I see it, sis," Ian continued, "I'm entitled to some kind of compensation for losing my father, for Irene leaving me with an aunt who only wanted our inheritance, for my life turning shitty when yours turned out so right. I would have gone to Irene for the money, but from the look of her place, she doesn't seem to have much. You, on the other hand, seem to have a lot—probably more than you need.''

The realization he had gone to her mother's house made her angry enough to shout. "You stay away from my mother, Ian, do you hear me?''

"The whole world can hear you, sis.''

"And stop calling me sis.'' She looked around her, annoyed that she had allowed him to get to her, and took a deep calming breath. "Let go of the door," she said between clenched teeth, "or I swear I'll—''

"A hundred thousand dollars, Abbie.'' He was dead serious now. "That's what I want for my silence. I'll give you time to think about it, and while you do, take a look at this.'' He pulled a sheet of paper from his pocket and handed it to her. "It's just a copy, so don't think tearing it to pieces is going to do you any good.''

It was a letter, written a week or so before the Palo Alto fire. It was addressed to her grandfather and signed by her mother. In the letter, Irene told her father how badly Patrick was treating her. "I hate him so much, Daddy,'' she had written at the end, "there are times I look at him when he's sleeping and all I want to do is kill him."

"Where did you get that?" Abbie asked in a shaky voice.

Ian's smug expression had returned. "From the kitchen table where Irene left it for a minute, not knowing I was there. She had threatened to tell my father about the pot she had found in my room, see, so I took the letter and made your mother a deal. I wouldn't show my dad the letter if she kept quiet about the pot."

"And she agreed?"

He laughed. "Of course she agreed. She knew damn well what my father would do to her once he saw that letter."

"How did one sheet of paper survive the fire when everything else in the house burned to the ground?"

"I buried it in the backyard, along with some of my other stuff. After the fire, I went back and dug it out. I don't know why I hung on to that letter all those years. With my dad dead, it had become useless, but for some reason I kept it. Then a couple of weeks ago, out of the blue, my good buddy Earl Kramer calls, and I knew that letter would come in handy."

Abbie's tone turned skeptical. "You had it with you, in prison, all this time?"

"No. It was in a suitcase I left with a friend. When I got out, I went to claim my things and there it was, exactly where I had left it, tucked in a book."

"This proves nothing," Abbie said, shaking the letter and hoping she sounded more convincing than she felt. "People make threats all the time."

"Yes, but how many carry them out?"

"I've already told you, my mother did nothing wrong! She risked her life to—"

"Tell it to a jury."

He let go of the door and Abbie slammed it shut, afraid of what she might do to him if she listened to one more word. She tried to insert the key into the ignition, but her hand shook so badly, she had to try three times before she finally made the connection. Then the powerful engine came to life and she tore out of the parking lot.

Five

Her white-knuckled fingers gripping the steering wheel, Abbie drove down the familiar route home on auto mode, unable to stop thinking about Ian's ridiculous demands. A hundred thousand dollars. Was he out of his mind? She didn't have that kind of money. Except for thirty thousand dollars in zero coupons she had earmarked for her son's education, and her prize money from the Bocuse—thirteen thousand dollars she had invested in a bank CD—she had nothing. Not even an IRA.

A cold fear settled in the pit of her stomach. Whether or not Ian's accusations were true, and she was certain they weren't, he had the upper hand and he knew it. Just as she knew that he would have no qualms about carrying out his threats. The man had no conscience. The question was, would the police believe Earl Kramer? A man on death row? They might if they started questioning the Mc-Gregors' neighbors, provided they were still around, and found out about Irene's unhappy marriage, the countless arguments they had heard over those two years.

But why should that matter? Abbie reasoned as she turned onto Elm Road. All married couples fought. She and Jack had had their share of bitter arguments during their stormy, five-year marriage. But she hadn't killed him, just as Irene hadn't killed Patrick McGregor. How could she? Abbie's mother was the most gentle soul she knew. She was kind, considerate and caring. And she had loved Abbie with all her heart. Why would she risk her little girl's life in a blazing fire just to get rid of her husband? It didn't make sense.

If only there wasn't that letter. Alone, it wouldn't be enough to convict Irene, but together with the neighbors' possible testimony and Earl Kramer's so-called confession, it spelled disaster.

At last, the two-story farmhouse with its stone facade and sloping roof came into view. The downstairs lights were on, a beacon of reassurance and safety. Tiffany, the baby-sitter, would be watching TV with the sound turned low, while upstairs, Ben would be sound asleep, his beloved bat and glove at the foot of the bed.

Pressing the remote control clipped to her sun visor, Abbie waited for the double doors of the two-car garage to open. Once inside, she stuffed the letter in her purse and took a couple of seconds to collect herself before going into the house.

Tiffany, an avid fan of 1940s films, was in the family room, watching an old black-and-white movie from Abbie's extensive collection. Always alert, however, she turned her head at the sound of Abbie's footsteps and stood up. She was a lovely nineteen-year-old college sophomore, with long blond hair parted in the middle, expressive hazel eyes and a quick smile. The older sister of three rambuctious boys, she knew exactly how to handle Ben without him being the least bit suspicious that he was being outsmarted.

"Hi, Ms. DiAngelo."

"Hello, Tiffany. Sorry I'm so late." Abbie dropped her purse on a chair. "Everything all right?" She rarely asked that question, but tonight she felt uneasy and needed to be reassured.

"Just fine." Tiffany laughed as she gathered her school-books from the coffee table. "Ben was so hyped up about his game, he didn't even balk at the sight of the green beans on his dinner plate."

Abbie smiled. Ben's aversion for green vegetables was legendary; her best friend, Claudia, had once told him, "I don't trust, much less eat, anything that's green," and thanks to her, he now assumed he could do the same.

After Tiffany left, Abbie turned off the lights and went upstairs for one quick look at her son before going to bed herself. The night-light was on, casting a soft golden glow on the room, which she had redone the previous year in a baseball theme. On the walls were posters of Ben's favorite big leaguers—Mark McGwire, Sammy Sosa, Barry Bonds, and of course, Scott Rolen, the Philadelphia Phillies' star third baseman.

Ben was curled up on his side, his hands tucked under his cheek, his red hair mussed. Abbie was filled with a new fear. If Ian carried out his threat, Ben's life would be affected, too. This was a small town, and thanks to that award she suddenly wished she had never won, the word would spread quickly. Would she be able to protect her son from the ugly publicity that was bound to erupt once an investigation was launched?

He had gone through so much already, she thought—the constant tension in his parents' marriage, the eventual divorce, the acrimonious custody battle. How could she stand by and watch him be hurt again, see his happy, orderly life thrown into shambles.

For the first time since divorcing Jack, she wished she had a husband to talk to, someone strong and wise who could not only comfort her, but advise her and help her confront the enemy.

A bitter laugh caught in her throat. That definitely left

out Jack. He had never been the knight-in-shining-armor type. He didn't even care that much about Ben. The only reason he had threatened to take him from Abbie was to get back at her for leaving him. Now that he had moved his law practice to Edison in northern New Jersey and had a girlfriend, he hardly came down to see Ben, preferring to talk to him on the phone or send him expensive presents.

She could talk to Claudia. Wonderful, dependable Claudia, who had seen her through some tough times. And there was Brady, her perennial problem solver. The temptation to turn to both in this time of need was strong, but she resisted it. This was something she couldn't afford to share with anyone—not even her two dearest friends.

Come on, DiAngelo. She gave herself a mental shake. *Snap out of this funk. You've been in worse situations than this.*

Had she? Or was she just kidding herself?

Pulling the bedspread over the sleeping boy, she bent down and kissed his forehead. Then, without a sound, she tiptoed out of the room.

Back in her bedroom, where she had always felt so safe, the uneasy feeling she'd had since Ian had approached her refused to go away. It was as if her stepbrother's bad karma had followed her home, impregnating the walls and threatening to engulf her.

She took her mother's letter from her purse and read it again. Irene's spirits must have been at an all-time low that day, because the letter was raw with despair. "I feel trapped," she had written. "If I leave Patrick, I'll be left without a dime. If I stay, I may lose my sanity." And then that last line. *"There are times I look at him when he's sleeping and all I want to do is kill him."*

Slowly, Abbie folded the letter and slid it way back into her nightstand drawer, under a stack of old pictures. Then, as if to reassure herself that she could protect those she loved, she walked over to the French armoire against the wall and opened it. The left side concealed a hanging rack that was filled with winter clothes, while the right side consisted of six shelves and four upper drawers. Only the top drawer was locked, its key hidden behind a stack of towels. Abbie slid her hands into the hiding place, found the key and opened the top drawer. Her hand quickly found the gun.

Even though it was not loaded and the ammunition was hidden under her mattress, the sensation of cold metal against her skin was at once reassuring and revolting. She hated guns. The only reason she had bought one was because Jack had threatened to take Ben from her.

"No damn judge is going to keep me from being with my son," he had told her outside the courthouse the morning of the court's ruling on the custody case. "Do you hear me?"

She had not only heard him, she had taken him very seriously. From the courthouse, she had gone straight to the police station and applied for a gun permit. Two weeks later, permit in hand, she had gone to a gun shop and taken a long look at the array of weapons in the display case. Sensing her indecision, the shop owner had recommended a 9 mm Walthers PPK. The German-made pistol was light yet sturdy and fitted her hand perfectly.

Once she felt comfortable holding it, he had showed her how to remove the magazine, how to load it and how to work the slide. Then he had demonstrated how to release the safety so the gun was ready to fire. At that point, he had added, all she had to do was pull the trigger.

Her next step had been to go to the firing range and learn to shoot the damn thing. She had been awful at first. And scared to death. But she hadn't given up, returning to the range day after day until she was able to consistently hit the target. She had even surprised herself once or twice by hitting the bull's eye.

She let the PPK sit inside her palm for a moment, conscious of its weight, glad she could look at it without feeling as if it was going to bite her. When she felt calmer, she put it back, went through the ritual of locking the drawer and hiding the key, then closed the armoire.

If anyone came after her or Ben, she was ready.

Six

"Well, well, well. Look who's finally decided to drag his miserable tail in."

Rose stood in the middle of the motel room, her fists on her hips and an angry scowl on her face. In spite of the late hour, she was fully dressed in lime green slacks and a white, oversize T-shirt with the words Elvis Lives printed on the front. On the table beside her, a dozen tarot cards were spread out, predicting inescapable gloom or great happiness, depending on Rose's mood and interpretation of the moment. These days, the gloom won out every time.

She had been a looker once, but hard times and a fondness for chocolate cannolis had taken their toll on her looks. At forty-two, she was twenty pounds heavier than when Ian had first met her, and the bags under her eyes made her look closer to fifty than forty. Her hair had changed over the last two decades, going from black to brown to blond before finally settling on red—not a subtle red, but a bright carrot color you could spot from a mile away.

She was also tougher than she used to be. The docility Ian had once appreciated had been replaced by an "I don't give a shit what you think" attitude that had taken him by surprise. He wasn't totally turned off by those changes. He liked a woman with a little backbone, but there were times, like now, when he wished she'd just keep that big mouth of hers shut.

"Not now, Rose, okay?" He walked to the Styrofoam cooler, which he had stocked with beer, lifted the lid and took out a Coors.

"Yes, now," she replied, coming to stand in front of him as he drank from the bottle. "I've been cooped up in this damn room for the last eight hours and I'm sick of it. Not to mention that I'm starving."

"You should have gone out to dinner. You knew I'd be a while."

"You had my car, Einstein. How could I go anywhere?"

He pointed a finger toward the window. "There's a Burger King just down the road. Why didn't you walk there?" He was about to add that a little exercise wouldn't hurt her, but realized he'd be asking for trouble.

"I don't want Burger King, dammit!" She gave the cooler a savage kick. "I financed this gig and I expect a little more than a greasy hamburger and a container of fries, which is all we've been eating since we left Toledo."

"And I explained that until my sister comes through with the loan, we'll have to be frugal. If we start spending what's left of our money on fancy meals, we'll be broke by the end of the week."

"Money should be the least of your worries." She threw a meaningful look toward the tarot cards. "You've got more serious problems."

Ian rolled his eyes. "Not that again, Rose. Please."

"Look at the cards, Ian. Just look at them for a minute." She pointed a finger. "This one is called the Lovers. That's us. The reemergence of an old relationship."

Ian brought the bottle to his mouth. "What's so bad about that?"

"We are surrounded by negative forces, such as partings,

the end of an affair, an impossible choice. Even a *wrong* choice. And this one—'' she picked up a card and shook it in front of his nose ''—is from the suit of Wands. It spells disaster, loss, separation.'' She paused and fixed him with a dramatic stare. ''And death.''

''Stop it, will you? You know I don't believe in that bullshit.'' The truth was, all that psychic stuff gave him the willies, but he would never tell her that.

''The cards don't lie, Ian,'' Rose continued. ''I had bad feelings about this trip before I even picked up a deck of cards and I still have bad feelings.''

Ian went to sit in the easy chair by the window. ''You're just spooked because of Arturo Garcia. I shouldn't have told you about him.''

''You didn't have to.'' She picked up another card. ''The Four of Swords. This represents violence and battle, people with an attitude all coming to a nasty end.''

''You may want to get yourself a new set of cards, sugar, because Arturo is nowhere in sight. All is well and going according to plan.''

That last remark seemed to pacify her. ''You saw your sister?''

''That's right.''

''She agreed to give you the money?''

''She agreed to *loan* me the money.''

Rose gave him a suspicious look. ''This woman hasn't seen you in twenty-eight years. Until tonight, she didn't even know if you were alive or dead, and just like that, she's going to loan you money.''

''That's my sister, generous to a fault.''

''I find that hard to believe. Unless there's something you're not telling me.''

Rose was a lot smarter than she looked. That's why he had to be careful how much he told her. ''I don't keep anything from you, Rose. Not anymore." He took another long pull of his beer. "I admit Abbie was reluctant at first, but when I told her I was turning over a new leaf and would repay her every cent, she agreed to help me."

"The woman must be a saint. If I were her, I'd have given you a swift kick in the ass and told you to hit the road."

"Really, Rose?" He yanked her onto his lap and slid his hand under her T-shirt. "The way you told me to hit the road when I showed up on your doorstep last week?"

Apparently, she wasn't in a playful mood, because she slapped his hand away. "When exactly are you going to get this loan?"

"In a few days."

"And what are we supposed to do in the meantime? Or did you forget that my credit card is maxed out."

"How can I forget it when you keep reminding me every minute of the day?"

But Rose was like one of those mechanical toys—once she was wound up you couldn't stop her. "Maybe we should look for jobs."

She jumped up and went to pick up a newspaper she had folded at the classifieds page, and turned it so he could see what she had circled in black ink. "I already checked out a few ads. Lucky for us, there's no shortage of work in this town."

Just the thought of work of any kind gave Ian the chills. "I can't look for a job now. I don't have any clothes."

"Strickland Orchards on Cold Soil Road is looking for help. They don't care how you're dressed. They just want someone to repair the fencing, weigh and pack strawberries, that sort of thing. They pay six dollars an hour."

"Christ, Rose, that's barely minimum wage."

"It'll pay for the room and a couple of decent meals. Not to mention what it'll do for our self-esteem."

Propping his feet on the other chair, Ian picked up the TV remote. "Look, Rose, if picking strawberries for a pittance is your idea of self-esteem, you go right ahead, girl. I'm not stopping you." He turned on the TV, wondering if they had *Baywatch* in this burg. "Personally, I've done enough hard labor to last me a lifetime."

A storm front had moved in from the Delaware Valley overnight, leaving the roads wet and the air heavy with morning dew. Abbie left the house as soon as Ben's bus pulled out and was now driving north on Route 27, heading for her mother's house in neighboring Kingston. Thanks to Brady's offer to go to the produce market every morning, Abbie was free to visit Irene for an hour or so each day without feeling as if she was neglecting the restaurant.

These private moments with her mother were more precious now than ever. Last year, Irene DiAngelo had been diagnosed with Alzheimer's, and although the symptoms were still mild, Abbie had begun to notice longer periods of forgetfulness and confusion and greater mood swings. So had Marion, the devoted housekeeper who cared for her.

Abbie had been warned that a progression of the disease, no matter how slow, was inevitable, but for the moment, Abbie was grateful for any quality time she spent with her mother. Her only regret was that Irene, who fiercely valued her independence, had turned down Abbie's offer to come and live with her and Ben.

"I may be a little forgetful," she had told Abbie in a tone that left no room for argument, "but I can still take care of myself. And under no circumstances will I become a burden to my daughter."

Maybe in a few years, when her condition worsened, she

would feel differently. For the time being, Irene still lived in the house she had occupied for the past twenty-seven years, a modest but well-kept two-story on Shaw Drive. As a compromise, she had agreed to let Abbie hire a companion, someone who could watch over her, run errands and do light housekeeping duties. So far, neither Abbie nor Irene had regretted the arrangement. Marion, a widow with two grown children, was a gem in every way.

"Mom!" Abbie called as she let herself in. "Marion! Anybody home?"

"In the kitchen!" her mother replied.

Abbie found her wiping the kitchen counter with a dish towel, while on the stove a partially covered cast-iron pan let out a delicious aroma. Petite and delicate, Irene looked more like a dainty southern belle than a woman of Italian descent. Her eyes were a startling color—a blend of gray and green—and her skin was as flawless as a twenty-year-old's. This morning, she wore the pretty blue dress Abbie had bought her for her sixty-fourth birthday last week. She looked lovely in it.

Knowing how much her mother appreciated compliments on her cooking, Abbie made a big deal of sniffing the air. "Lamb meatballs?"

"Polpette d'agnello," her mother corrected. "Have you forgotten your Italian?"

"And risk your wrath? Never." Abbie kissed her mother on the cheek. "It smells wonderful, Mom. Can I have a taste?"

Beaming, Irene handed her a wooden spoon. Abbie dipped it into the rich brown sauce, scooped up a little on the tip of the spoon and brought it to her mouth. "Mmm." She closed her eyes. "This is incredible. Are you sure you won't come to work at Campagne? I'm willing to pay top dollar."

Irene laughed, looking delighted. "No, thanks. You're too bossy."

Abbie shook her finger. "You've been talking to Brady, haven't you?" She dropped the spoon in the sink and looked around her. "Where's Marion?"

"She went to the store for some milk."

Abbie nodded, glad that her mother was still at a point where she could be left alone for short periods of time, especially on a good day, as she seemed to be having now. How long that stage would last no one knew. Not even the doctors. The course the disease took and how rapidly changes occurred varied with every patient.

Abbie waited until Irene had turned down the heat under the simmering pot before taking her mother's hand. "Come sit down, Mom. I need to talk to you about something."

She led her into the familiar living room with its beige tweed sofa and chairs and brown wall-to-wall carpeting. Through the large picture window that overlooked Shaw Drive, Abbie could see old Mr. Winters bending down, with some difficulty because of his arthritis, to pick up the debris left in the wake of last night's brief storm.

Abbie remembered the day she and her mother had moved into this house as if it were yesterday. She had been wild with excitement, running from room to room, trying to decide which one would be hers, while her mother beamed as she admired the well-equipped kitchen. Life hadn't been easy in those days. In order to support herself and her daughter, Irene had had to work two jobs—one at the local hospital as a daytime nurse's aide, and the other cleaning office buildings at night while a friend watched Abbie. Despite the fact that she was an attractive woman, Irene had never remarried.

"From now on, it's just you and me, pumpkin," she had

told Abbie that first night in their new house. "And that's the way it's going to stay."

Abbie often thought about those days, and the many sacrifices her mother had made for her, the nights she had come home exhausted but smiling, never too tired to read Abbie's favorite bedtime story to her. Oh, yes, there had been some wonderful moments spent in this house. It was up to Abbie now to make sure her mother stayed happy here as long as possible.

"What do you want to talk to me about, dear?" Irene plumped a decorative pillow before settling into an easy chair, across from Abbie. "You look so serious all of a sudden. Is something wrong at the restaurant?"

"No. Thank God, Campagne is running smoothly." Abbie clasped her hands and leaned forward. "I had a rather unexpected visitor last night."

"Oh. Who?"

"Ian McGregor."

Irene's expression registered instant shock. "Ian? What is he doing here?"

"He said he was passing by."

"I don't understand. How did he know where to find you?"

"The TV interview. He saw it, heard I lived in Princeton and decided to look me up. Thanks to the Internet, tracking me down wasn't too difficult." She paused, knowing how little it took these days to get her mother distraught, but knew of no other way to learn the truth than to speak frankly. "He wanted to know if I remembered the fire."

Irene's back went rigid. "Why ask you? If he has questions, he should come to me."

"I didn't want him upsetting you."

"And I don't want him upsetting *you!*"

"He didn't, Mom," she lied. "He was a little annoying,

which, as I recall, is pretty typical of Ian, but that's all." Glad to see that her mother was taking the news without any dramatic change in behavior, Abbie forged ahead. "What exactly did happen that night, Mom?"

"You know what happened. Patrick fell asleep with a cigarette in his hand. It was a nasty habit he had and it scared me to death. That's why I started sleeping in the next room."

Another detail the authorities would find interesting. "Ian claims he heard one of the firemen say something about arson," Abbie said cautiously.

Irene's eyes seemed to cloud over for a second or two. "He said that?"

"Is it true? Did the authorities initially suspect arson?"

"They may have."

"You don't remember?"

"No, Abbie," Irene snapped. "I don't. Who can remember every detail of something that happened so long ago?"

"Don't get upset—"

"I'm not upset! I'm angry. We haven't heard one word from that boy, or his sister, in all these years, and now you're telling me he's here, stirring up trouble?"

"No, he's not. Mom, please—"

"Tell him to leave us alone, Abbie." She sprung out of her chair. Her face was pale, her eyes bright. "Tell him to go away."

Before she had a chance to answer, Abbie heard the sound of footsteps hurrying across the foyer. A moment later, Marion walked in, a grocery bag in her arms. She was a small, round woman with tightly permed gray hair, chubby cheeks and sharp brown eyes.

Looking alarmed, she glanced from Abbie to Irene. "What's going on? I can hear the two of you all the way from the street."

"It's all right, Marion." Abbie stood up and walked over to where Irene stood, kicking herself for having let the situation get out of hand. "Mom got a little upset with me, but she's all right now." She wrapped an arm around her mother's shoulders. "Aren't you, Mom?"

Irene nodded. She appeared calmer, but the expression in her eyes said otherwise. Why had she become so distraught at the mention of the fire? Were the memories of that night so vivid and painful that she couldn't talk about it? Was it simply because of the Alzheimer's? Or was it more than that?

Abbie spent the next half hour trying to bring Irene back to her earlier state of mind. As badly as she wanted to know the truth about the fire, further questioning would have to wait. Nothing, not even Ian's threats, was worth getting her mother in such a state of agitation.

While Irene filled a Tupperware container with generous servings of polpette, Abbie chatted about the new dishes she was planning to add to her summer menu, and Ben's now-famous triple. She also told her about the new Al Pacino movie that was coming out next Friday. Irene was crazy about Al Pacino.

As Irene began to relax, so did Abbie. Maybe she had made too much of her mother's behavior. Why shouldn't she get upset at the mention of a fire that had killed her husband? In her condition, emotional outbursts were commonplace and certainly not a reason to jump to conclusions.

A little after ten o'clock, Abbie got ready to leave. "I'd better go," she said, "before Brady sends out a search party for me."

Irene handed her the Tupperware container. "Give Ben

a hug for me. And tell him to come and see me. It's been ages since I've seen that boy.''

Abbie felt a pinch in her heart. The three of them had had dinner together only two nights ago.

Seven

When Abbie returned to Campagne, Brady was waiting for her. "Someone's here to see you," he said in a low voice. "A man. He says he's your brother."

Abbie bristled. Was that what Ian had meant when he had said he'd give her some time? Less than twelve hours? "Where is he?" she asked.

"I took him to your office, although what he wanted was to be seated in the dining room and be served lunch. His exact words were, 'Bring me something expensive and free.'" That Brady and Ian had not hit it off was obvious. "You never told me you had a brother."

"He's a stepbrother, actually. I'll tell you about him later." She headed toward her office. "I guess I'd better see what he wants."

She found him standing at her desk, a framed photo of Ben in his hand. "Put that down," she said sharply.

At the sound of her voice, Ian turned around. "Good-looking boy. Doesn't look like you, though. Must take after his daddy."

She crossed the room, snatched the photo from his hand and put it back on her desk. "I don't want you coming here, Ian."

"Would you prefer if I came to your house?"

"What I would prefer is for you to disappear."

His nose up in the air, Ian started walking around the

room, stopping every now and then to look at one of the many photographs scattered about. This glimpse into her private life made her wish Brady had let him sit in the dining room after all. There was nothing about herself or her family she wanted to share with this man.

"No can do, sis," he said, turning around. "As I said last night, we have unfinished business." He laughed, a good-natured sound, as if this visit really was an innocent family reunion. "I don't see any pictures of your hubby. You do have a husband, don't you?"

"I've already told you my private life is none of your business."

He raised his hands up in the air, palms out. "Okay, okay, don't blow a gasket. I was just curious." He waited a beat before adding, "So, did you give some thought to our…little arrangement?"

"You're blackmailing me, Ian. I'd hardly call it an arrangement."

"And I'd rather call it a payback—for all the misery your mother put me through."

"She didn't do anything! However your life turned out is your doing, no one else's."

He brushed her remark aside with a wave of his hand. "I don't really care about that. All I want to know is, did you ask her about the fire?"

"No." Abbie hoped he wouldn't see through her lie. "I didn't see any point in upsetting her by bringing up such bad memories."

"You didn't even tell her I was here?"

"No, Ian, I didn't, for the same reason I just stated."

He gave her a long, probing look, as though trying to decide if she was telling him the truth. Uncomfortable to be under such scrutiny, she spoke again, this time forcing a confidence in her voice she was far from feeling, "And frankly, I don't know why *I'm* still here, listening to your nonsense, when I have a million things to—''

"Because you know damn well you have no choice in the matter." His eyes had hardened, and all cheerfulness, phony as it had been, was gone from his voice. "I'm holding the trump card here, Abbie. So either you come through with the money, or I call the Palo Alto P.D. and tell them your mother is a cold-blooded killer."

Go ahead, Abbie, call his bluff. Who are the police going to believe? Two con men or a respectable, law-abiding citizen?

For a moment, she felt as though she could do it. If she stayed strong and showed him she wasn't intimidated, he would back off. But although the words were just on the tip of her tongue, she remained silent. She and Ian just stood there, measuring each other, waiting to see who blinked first.

"Tell you what." Ian reached inside his shirt pocket and took out a cell phone. "Since you still have doubts, I'll put you in contact with Earl. He'll convince you."

She started to protest but he was already dialing. As he waited, he winked at her, looking supremely confident. "Anna," he said when the call was answered, "this is Ian McGregor. Please have Earl call the phone number I'm going to give you as soon as possible, and tell him to ask for Abbie DiAngelo. You have pen and paper?"

He waited another few seconds before giving the restaurant number, which he seemed to have memorized. "Can you get word out to him today? It's urgent." He smiled. "Super. Thanks, Anna."

He flipped the phone shut and tucked it back in his pocket. "That was Earl's wife. She said that unless he has already used his three allowed phone calls for the week, you should hear from him sometime today."

"How will I know the call is coming from the prison?"

"He has to call collect. The operator will tell you the call is from Stateville."

He had covered all his bases, anticipated all her questions. Was that part of a well-engineered bluff? Or was he telling the truth?

He placed a scrap of paper on her desk. "I wrote down my cell-phone number for you. Call me after you hear from him."

"I'm not at your beck and call, Ian. I have a business to run."

Before he could answer, there was a knock at the door. Without waiting for an answer, Brady stuck his head through the opening. One look at them and he seemed instantly aware of the tension in the room. "Abbie, we have a crisis in the kitchen. Can you come right away?"

There had never been a crisis he couldn't handle and she doubted there was one now. But she was grateful for the interruption. "I'll be right there."

She looked at Ian, who gave a slight bow. "I'll go." Then, leaning toward her so his mouth almost touched her ear, he whispered, "But I'll be back."

As he walked by Brady, who was holding the door open for him, he added, "I'd lose the attitude if I were you, kid. Nobody likes a wise guy."

"You should know," Brady fired back.

He and Abbie followed Ian into the empty dining room and watched him make his way around the tables. Once he was gone, Abbie turned to the young sous-chef. "Tell me there is no crisis, because I don't think I could handle anything more serious than burned toast right now."

He shook his head. "I used that as an excuse to see if you were all right."

"How did you know I needed rescuing?"

"I've seen his kind before." He glanced at her. "How did you end up with a character like that for a stepbrother?"

Brady deserved to know as much as she could afford to tell him. "After my biological dad died, my mother remarried a man by the name of Patrick McGregor, a widower with two children. Two years later, Patrick died and my mother and I moved to Kansas to live with my grandfather who was ill. Ian and his sister stayed in California with their aunt. I haven't seen either one of them in twenty-eight years."

"What does Ian want?"

She started toward the kitchen. "A loan."

"I hope you told him you're not the Bank of America."

"Not in so many words, but he got my drift. I think."

"If he didn't, let me know. I'd love to wipe that smirk off his—"

Brady was interrupted by the sound of shouting voices coming from the kitchen. One of them belonged to Sean, one of Campagne's two kitchen helpers.

"I told you, Abbie is tied up at the moment," Sean was saying. "You'll have to come back."

"Look, punk," the other man replied, "I was in this business when you were still in diapers, so don't tell me what to do."

"That's Ken!" Brady on her heels, Abbie hurried to the kitchen, slapping the swinging doors open.

Ken Walker stood in the middle of the kitchen, his face an angry red, his hands balled up into fists as though he was ready to strike. In his mid-thirties, Ken had the sturdy, muscular build of a wrestler and a volatile temper. Six weeks ago, after a year in Abbie's employ, Brady had caught the kitchen helper stealing money from the cash register. Abbie had fired him on the spot and later found out he had a gambling problem she hadn't been aware of.

"What's going on in here?" she asked, glad the restaurant hadn't yet opened for business. "Ken, what are you doing in my kitchen?"

"Hello, Ms. DiAngelo." He removed his baseball hat and held it in front of him. "I came to see if I could get my old job back."

Brady started to say something, but Abbie stopped him. "I'll handle it, Brady." Then, motioning Ken into the utility room, she said, "You know that's not possible, Ken. First of all, my policy hasn't changed. You stole from me and that's not something I can easily forgive. Secondly, as you saw, we've already replaced you, with Sean. I couldn't give you your old job back even if I wanted to."

"I don't gamble anymore," Ken said as though he hadn't heard her. "And I go to Gamblers Anonymous three times a week. I know it's working because I haven't set foot in Atlantic City in over a month."

"I'm glad to hear that, Ken, but I still can't give you a job."

"Are you sure? I've been watching the restaurant. It's busier than ever now that you've won that award. You probably could use some extra help in the kitchen. I'd even be willing to settle for a lesser position, until I earned my old one back."

His stubbornness was one of the reasons they'd had problems with him from the start. At the risk of sounding like a broken record, she repeated, "I can't do it, Ken. I'm sorry."

His tone turned belligerent again. "You like kicking a man when he's down, don't you, Ms. DiAngelo? That's all part of that power trip you're on."

Abbie stiffened. "You're out of line, Ken."

"Maybe *you're* out of line. I came here in good faith and admitted I had a problem. I even told you what I was doing to fix it, but none of that matters to you."

Brady came out of nowhere and grabbed the man by the arm. "That's it, buster. You're out of here."

"I'm not finished!" Ken shouted.

"Oh, yes, you are." Brady shoved him out the back door. "Ms. DiAngelo didn't press charges against you the last time because she felt sorry for you, but if you ever show your face in this restaurant again, I'll call the police myself." He shut the door and locked it, cutting off the man's ranting.

"I don't like the way he's acting," Brady said to Abbie. "Why don't we call the police and ask them to keep an eye on the restaurant."

Abbie shook her head. "I don't want to get him in trouble. Or hurt his chances of finding a job elsewhere. Let's just wait and see what happens."

She glanced out the window. Ken was gone, but somehow that failed to soothe her already frayed nerves. She wondered what else this day had in store for her.

Eight

Ian sat in Rose's car, no more than a hundred feet or so from the small blue house, wondering if he should go ring Irene's doorbell.

Something about Abbie's reaction earlier, when he had asked if she'd talked to her mother, hadn't set right with him. Abbie had never been much of a liar, and when he had caught a slight hesitation in her voice and the way she had averted her eyes, he had known she was hiding something. And he wanted to know what.

He was still wondering how to approach Irene, when the front door opened and a woman stepped out, looking hesitant, almost fearful.

Although close to thirty years had passed since he had last seen her, he recognized her right away. Irene DiAngelo. Most of her dark hair had turned gray, but other than that, she hadn't changed much. She was still the same petite, attractive woman he had known way back when. Something about her was different though. She was acting weird, like she didn't know where she was, which didn't make sense since she had just walked out of her own front door.

He kept watching her, one elbow resting over the edge of the open car window, waiting for her to do something. She just stood there, looking uncertain. Then, before Ian could duck, she turned in his direction and stared right at him, not moving or blinking. Ian cursed under his breath. Jesus, that's all he needed, for her to call the cops and report a Peeping Tom.

Quickly, he grabbed the Mercer County road map from the passenger seat, unfolded it and held it in front of him while watching Irene from the corner of his eye. The ruse seemed to have worked because she was no longer looking at him, but walking toward a rose bed along the front of the house.

As he watched her, a blue van turned the corner of Shaw Drive and pulled into the driveway. A teenage boy, no more than seventeen or eighteen, jumped out and waved at the woman.

"Hi, Mrs. DiAngelo."

She looked at the boy as if she had never seen him before. Weird, Ian thought. Really weird.

"I'm here to cut the grass," the kid said. Apparently her strange behavior didn't seem to bother him as much as it bothered Ian.

As the kid chatted about the weather, he dragged a lawn mower out of the back of the van and set it on the driveway. But when he started wheeling it toward the front yard, Irene's expression turned into one of sheer panic. As if she had just seen the devil himself, she spun around and ran back inside the house.

Ian sat there for a moment, his mouth gaping. What the hell was going on? What was wrong with Irene?

Well, he thought, opening the car door, there was only one way to find out. He got out of the Oldsmobile and approached the house at a fast pace, like a man on a mission. The boy had just returned to the van to get his Weed Whacker and was watching him.

"Hi," Ian said affably. Then, still holding his map, he gestured toward the house. "Maybe you can help me. I'm a real-estate appraiser. I was sent here by my company to take a look at the houses on this block, but when I rang Mrs. DiAngelo's bell a while ago, she acted strangely and wouldn't let me in. She has a problem or something?''

The kid shrugged. ''Mrs. Di's all right. Her memory comes and goes, that's all. Drop back in an hour or so and she should be fine.''

''What do you mean, her memory comes and goes? What's wrong with her?''

The teenager unscrewed the cap of a gasoline can and started to fill the lawn mower. ''She's got some disease that affects the memory. I forgot what's it called.''

''Alzheimer's?''

''Yeah, that's it. Alzheimer's. Most of the time she's okay. And real nice. Other times, like now, she can't remember who you are.''

Ian could barely hold his jubilation. Irene had Alzheimer's. That's why Abbie had acted so peculiar earlier. And why she hadn't mentioned the fire or his accusations to her mother. What would be the point if Irene couldn't remember anything about that night? And if she couldn't remember, how could she deny the accusations?

If that wasn't a stroke of pure luck he didn't know what was. He had been concerned that Abbie would know he was lying and call his bluff, but all that bravado on her part had been a bunch of bullshit. The girl was scared, much more so than he had expected. And now he knew why.

The lunch hour at Campagne was almost over and the kitchen activity starting to slow to a more manageable pace when the call came. Abbie was standing a few feet from the wall phone when it rang. After making certain the staff was too busy to eavesdrop, she picked up the receiver.

"You have a collect call from Earl Kramer at Stateville Prison," a nasal feminine voice recited. "Do you accept the charges?"

Abbie turned to face the window, aware that her throat had suddenly gone dry. "Yes." She swallowed. "Yes, I do."

"Abbie DiAngelo?" The voice at the other hand was rough and uneducated. "That you?"

"Yes." She cleared her voice. "But I'll have to take this in my office. I'll only be a few seconds."

The man laughed. "I ain't goin' nowhere."

As Brady passed by, she handed him the phone. "Brady, would you mind hanging up when I tell you to?"

"Sure."

Aware his curious gaze was following her, Abbie hurried to her office, locked the door behind her and went to pick up the extension on her desk. Her heart pounded in her chest, but not from the short sprint. "I've got it, Brady. Thanks."

"No problem."

"Mr. Kramer?"

"Yeah."

Holding the phone, she circled her desk and sat down. "Do you know why Ian asked you to contact me?"

"Sure I do. You want to know if what I told him about your mother is true." He paused. "It's true."

She closed her eyes and forced herself to count until five. "You know it's not. Why are you doing this? Did Ian offer you money?" Stupid question. Did she actually expect him to admit it if he had?

"Money ain't much use where I am, missie. Besides, Earl Kramer ain't for sale."

That she didn't believe. "Why are you coming forward

now? Why didn't you tell your story to Ian after you were convicted?"

"Because I still had a chance to beat the death sentence on appeal. Now, after two tries, they tell me that's it, I'm done, so I might as well confess to *all* my sins, not just those that got me on death row."

"Why?"

"Because I've been blessed with God's forgiveness, Miss DiAngelo," he said with a reverence that sounded as phony as the rest of his claims. "And confessing to all my crimes is my way of repaying His kindness."

Abbie fell back against her chair. Who was she talking to? A religious convert? Or a shrewd con man? "Ian said you'd be able to convince me, so go ahead. Convince me."

"How do I do that?"

"What did my mother look like twenty-eight years ago?"

"She was a looker. Great ass."

"Stick to her facial features, please."

"All right, let's see." He was silent for a moment. "She had dark hair, shoulder-length, wavy. And light-colored eyes. Gray or green." He paused. "And she had a beauty mark above her upper lip."

All true, but Abbie still wasn't convinced. Ian could have given him a description of Irene. "What about the house?"

"It was on El Camino Lane—half a mile or so from the center of town. A big house with a basement and an attic."

That, too, he could have found out from Ian. She had to ask some pertinent questions, something not everyone knew. But what? She wasn't exactly an expert when it came to interrogating hard-core murderers. "How did you get into the house?"

"Your mother left the back door open. She told me which room your stepfather slept in, so I went up and made sure McGregor was sleeping soundly. There was an empty bottle of bourbon on the nightstand and the place reeked of booze, so I knew there wasn't much chance he'd wake up.''

"Didn't it bother you that three children were also asleep in that house?''

"Your mother was awake. She wasn't going to let you kids die.''

Yet by the time Irene had reached Abbie's room, the upper half of the house was already in flames. If she was awake, why had she waited so long before getting everybody out?

"How could you be sure? Did you wait around to find out?''

He laughed again, a cynical, condescending laugh, meant to make her feel stupid. "What and get caught? You've got to be kidding.''

"Ian said my mother contacted you through the classifieds?''

"Yeah. Lots of people do it that way, even now. For the average Joe out there, with no connections, a classified ad, worded just right, is about the only way of finding what you want. All you have to do is say something like…'' He paused for a second, "'Looking for an exterminator to do specialized work.' Or 'handyman to do demolition work.' You'll get lots of calls, but if you're patient, sooner or later, you'll get just the person you want.''

"What did my mother's ad say?'' Maybe she could check the newspaper archives. These days most newspapers kept copies on microfiche.

"Oh, Christ, how am I supposed to remember that?''

"What about the name of the newspaper then? And the date the ad ran? Surely you remember those?''

"Sorry. I was reading more than a dozen papers in those

days, from all over the country. I can't remember which one Irene used, or the date she contacted me.''

''How convenient.''

This time he heard the sarcasm in her voice, because he reacted. ''Hey, don't blame me if that's not what you wanted to hear. It don't change what I know.''

''You mean, what you're making up, don't you, Mr. Kramer?''

''That's for the cops to decide, missie.'' He let a second pass. ''Are we finished? My fifteen minutes are almost up. You wouldn't want me to get in trouble, now, would you?''

Abbie felt drained. She wasn't sure what she had expected from this conversation, or if she had even expected anything at all. ''Yes,'' she said. ''We're finished.''

''Then will you join me in a prayer, Ms. DiAngelo?''

Startled, Abbie started to say something, but he was already talking. ''My Lord, Jesus, you gave your life for me and now I want to give my life for you. I offer you my death, oh Lord, as I offer you my body and my soul—''

Abbie slammed the phone down. What kind of sick monster was this? Did he actually think she was buying his act? And what man made up such outright lies without an ounce of remorse, then prayed for his soul all in the same breath?

She covered her face with her hands and remained in that position, until Brady buzzed her on the intercom to tell her he was leaving.

Maybe all was not lost, she thought as she rose from behind her desk. Maybe there was a way out of this nightmare—a *legal* way. She didn't know what it could be, but Claudia's brother was an attorney. Although he lived in Philadelphia, he and Claudia got together often, and whenever he was in town, Abbie made sure they stopped at

Campagne for lunch or dinner. More important, she knew she could trust him.

With that thought in mind, she grabbed her purse and ran out.

Nine

Thirty-five-year-old Claudia Marjolis and Abbie had met seven years ago, when Abbie had catered the grand opening of Claudia's first one-woman show. The younger child of an old-money Philadelphia family and a self-admitted rebel, Claudia had astounded her family when she had dropped out of medical school to become a sculptor.

Although her parents had eventually recovered from the shock and supported her wholeheartedly, they still didn't know what to make of their daughter's free spirit, a spirit that was reflected not only in her work, which some critics had labeled revolutionary, but in her lifestyle, in the way she dressed and even in the food she ate.

Home and studio shared space in a second-story loft that had once been a candy factory. A bank of windows along one wall offered an unobstructed view of Princeton University's Holder Tower, one of the most recognized landmarks in Princeton. Half the loft space was taken up by her work, an eclectic assortment of clay and bronze sculptures of every shape and size. The rest of the space featured a combination living area and kitchen, all done in various shades of red and black. The bedroom was concealed behind one of Claudia's most intriguing creations—a glass tower made entirely of empty jars. At night, a golden light angled just right lit up the display, making it appear as though it was on fire. Ben loved coming here, partly because Claudia spoiled him rotten and partly because she often took him to the salvage yard where she bought metal scraps for her work.

She was grunting loudly when Abbie walked in, attempting to move a six-foot-long sculpture of a reclining woman across the slate floor. At five foot three and no heavier than a hundred pounds, Claudia didn't look as though she could budge a feather. Waitressing in a busy SoHo cafeteria during her two years at the Lower Manhattan Art Center, however, had given her an upper-body strength few women her size possessed.

With her mass of red curls that were presently speckled with gray plaster, her big round blue eyes and granny glasses, she looked like a prettier version of Raggedy Ann. Smart and successful, she had never married, although she had come close—three times. All three expectant grooms had been left at the altar, victims of the bride's now-notorious jitters. Abbie often teased her that the movie *Runaway Bride* was based on Claudia's life story.

At the sound of the door closing, Claudia turned her head, then straightened, one hand on the small of her back. "About time you got here. This thing must weigh a ton."

"It looks it."

Abbie gave the sculpture a second appraisal, her gaze lingering on the woman's conical breasts, mammoth thighs and tiny feet. She had followed the progress of Claudia's new endeavor over the last six months, but it wasn't until four weeks ago that she had realized the block of plaster was becoming a woman.

"Well, what do you think?" Claudia asked, looking like a proud mama.

Her lips pursed, Abbie walked slowly around the statue, taking in every detail. Two black-beaded eyes had been encased into the face and seemed to follow Abbie's every move. "Hmm, I'm not sure. When did you decide on the pointy breasts?"

"I knew you were going to ask that." Claudia picked up a feather duster from the floor and gave the woman's torso a light brushing. "I got the idea last week after seeing a biography of Josephine Baker. Her breasts were the rage of Paris, you know. They inspired me."

Abbie slanted her friend an amused look. "Why, Claudia, is there something about you I don't know?"

"I meant, smart-ass, that I was inspired in an artistic way. Now give me a hand, will you." She set the duster down and flexed her fingers. "And make sure the rug stays underneath. I don't want to scratch the floor."

Abby tossed her purse on a chair. "Where do you want her?"

Claudia pointed at a spot in front of the window. "Over there, so everyone walking down Nassau Street will see her."

Following Claudia's cue, Abbie took her position, placing her hands on the statue's broad back. She started pushing slowly and steadily until it stood at its designated space. The movement must have attracted passersby, because a few pedestrians stopped and looked up, mouths open, which was the exact reaction Claudia had aimed for.

She backed off to admire the effect, nodding approvingly. "Perfect."

"Did you name her yet?" Abbie asked, knowing how much Claudia hated to title her work. Most of the time, they ended up being called "Untitled."

"No, but my dealer is starting to pressure me to come up with something. Any ideas?"

"Sorry, my creativity begins and ends in the kitchen."

"In that case, a cup of coffee might just be what you

need to stir up your creative juices. And I've got some muffins I want you to taste. It's a new recipe.''

"What's in them?'' Abbie asked suspiciously.

"Flaxseed, corn and a pinch of jalapeño. Don't make that face. You'll love them.'' She walked toward the kitchen. "And then you can tell me what's going on.'' She picked up the glass carafe from a black coffeemaker and filled two mugs. "And don't tell me nothing,'' she added, her keen eyes on Abbie's face. "Because, my dear friend, that troubled look in your eyes, which you're going to great pains to conceal, is a dead giveaway.''

At first, Abbie hadn't intended to confide in Claudia, not only because the matter was so personal, but because it would have been unfair to put her best friend in such a compromising position. But once Abbie had made up her mind to ask Dennis Marjolis for help, she knew there was no avoiding taking Claudia into her confidence.

"It's complicated,'' she said, not sure where to start.

Claudia set a plate of fragrant muffins on the counter and climbed onto a red, lacquered stool. "You're looking at the person for whom the word *complicated* was invented. So, come on, talk to me.''

Abbie told her everything, from the moment she had spotted Ian at the ball field the previous day, to her telephone conversation with Earl Kramer less than ten minutes ago.

"Oh, for God's sake!'' Claudia exclaimed when Abbie was finished. "I've never heard of such nonsense. Those two clowns are nothing but flimflam men who engineered that story to make a quick buck. And that letter was written in a moment of desperation. It doesn't mean a thing.''

"That's what I was thinking.'' Abbie broke a piece of her muffin and chewed it slowly. It was surprisingly good.

"Then why haven't you told Ian to go find himself another patsy?"

"I would have if my mother hadn't acted so suspiciously."

"Honey, your mother was just having a bad day. Maybe the memories of that night were too painful for her. Or maybe they triggered something inside her head and she became confused. Didn't Dr. Frantz explain she would have days like this?"

"Yes, but…"

"But what?" Claudia pressed.

"What if it was more than that? What if she was unconsciously suppressing the events of that night? Or what led to them."

Claudia shook her head. "You're letting that rotten stepbrother of yours get to you. You want my advice? Here it is. Call the police. What Ian is doing is called extortion. That's illegal, Abbie. Don't let him torture you a day longer than you have to."

Abbie wasn't surprised at her friend's reaction. For all her unconventional ways, Claudia had always been a strong supporter of the justice system. "I can't go to the police until I've had some sound legal advice. That's why I'm here. I need to talk to Dennis."

"Why didn't you say so?" Claudia picked up a cordless phone from the kitchen counter. Abbie watched her intently as she identified herself to her brother's secretary and asked to speak to him. At the disappointed look on Claudia's face and her next few words, Abbie's shoulders sagged. Dennis was away on a business trip.

But Claudia's expression brightened almost immediately. "He'll be back tonight? Terrific. Please ask him to call me, will you, no matter how late he gets in. Thanks, Sylvia."

Claudia hung up. "Is it all right if I give Dennis a run-down of your situation when he calls? Or do you want to do it yourself?"

"No, go ahead. I'll fill in the blanks later."

The gentle bong of the grandfather clock in the foyer struck once. One o'clock in the morning and Dennis Marjolis still hadn't called. Maybe his flight had been delayed, Abbie thought, or he didn't feel right giving her advice on something so complicated and perhaps hopeless. Abbie had just about given up on him, at least for tonight, when the phone rang.

Lunging toward the kitchen counter, she answered it on the first ring. "Hello?"

"Abbie?"

She let out a sigh of relief. "Dennis." Too worried to waste time on small talk, she came straight to the point. "Were you able to make any sense out of what Claudia told you?"

"Pretty much." The attorney paused and she could hear the rustling of papers. "Let's take first things first, and please stop me if I start to confuse you. I do that some-times."

He didn't, but it was sweet of him to say that rather than make her look stupid. "All right."

"First, let's take Kramer's claim. Death-row inmates routinely confess to fictitious crimes, intending to generate enough interest to earn a stay of execution. The police are aware of such tactics and therefore would need something a little more convincing before they took Kramer's confession seriously."

"Would the letter my mother wrote be convincing enough?"

She heard Dennis's sigh and guessed his answer. "That

letter is damaging evidence, Abbie. Like it or not, it shows that the desire to kill Patrick was there. Even if Irene denies ever intending to kill her husband, the prosecution will introduce that letter as proof that your mother was not only entertaining thoughts of killing her husband, but was desperate enough to carry out those thoughts.''

''Are you saying there could actually *be* a trial?''

''I'm afraid so. The letter, along with Kramer's detailed statement incriminating Irene, will be enough for a prosecutor to seek a grand jury indictment against her.''

''But what about Earl's convenient memory loss? He seems to remember everything except the name of the newspaper where my mother supposedly put that ad, the date of the ad or the wording of the ad. Doesn't that prove he's lying?''

''Not necessarily. Those are small details. And twenty-eight years is a long time.''

This was not what Abbie had wanted to hear, but there was still an angle they hadn't discussed. ''All right,'' she said. ''Let's assume the worst possible scenario—that charges are brought against my mother. What about her illness? Wouldn't having Alzheimer's rule out the possibility of a criminal trial?''

''Whether or not your mother is deemed to be mentally competent to stand trial will be determined by a court, after conducting a competency hearing. Irene will have to submit herself to a mental examination conducted by the State's doctors, whose job it will be to determine whether she is capable of understanding the charges brought against her. The legal standard for mental competence to stand trial is not whether her Alzheimer's has impaired her ability to remember past events, but whether she is capable of understanding the gravity of the charges brought against her.

If I recall, the last time you and I talked, your mother was in the early stages of Alzheimer's?''

"She still is," Abbie said, already knowing where he was leading to.

"So she's alert and fairly competent most of the time?"

Abbie felt her earlier hopes drain out of her. "Yes."

"You see the problem, don't you, Abbie?"

Abbie leaned against the kitchen counter as images of Irene being questioned by the police and then made to stand trial for murder unfolded in her head. The wonderful, peaceful life her mother had led until now would be forever shattered. Her days would become a succession of accusations, blaring headlines, humiliation and fear. If that didn't kill her, a prison sentence certainly would.

"Abbie?" The attorney's voice was filled with concern.

"Yes, I...I heard you, Dennis. I'm trying to..." She felt her voice break and stopped.

"I'm sorry, Abbie. I wish I could have given you more encouraging news."

"Me too."

"Do you have any questions? Anything that needs clarifying?"

"No. You were painfully clear."

"I'm sorry," he said again, and she knew he meant it. "Please call me if you need further help. Oh, and put a dollar in the mail, will you?" he added as an afterthought. "That way you'll be guaranteed client/attorney confidentiality."

"I'll do that."

Ten

Abbie sat at her kitchen table alone, her morning cup of coffee growing cold. A gusty wind had chased away the clouds, leaving the Princeton skies a cerulean blue, but the balmy weather did little to lift her sinking spirits. She had spent a restless night. Her phone conversation with Claudia's brother had left her more depressed than she had been previously. Short of going to the police, as Claudia had suggested, and taking her chances that the truth would prevail, she saw no way out of this mess.

And what was the truth, anyway? All Abbie knew for certain was that during Irene's two-year marriage to Patrick McGregor, her mother had been a very unhappy woman. Even now, after all this time, Abbie could still remember the violent arguments between her mother and Patrick. Hidden under the covers, Abbie had prayed for the shouting to end, while wishing her stepfather could be more like her real dad—warm and caring and fun to be with. Abbie had loved her dad. She'd loved the way he looked and smelled and laughed. She only had to close her eyes to remember the way he used to scoop her off the ground and perch her on his shoulders so she could watch the Thanksgiving Day parade, and the fun she'd had learning to ride a two-wheeler on her fifth birthday, with her dad running beside her and shouting words of encouragement.

Then that terrible accident at the construction site had

happened, killing Joe DiAngelo and three other workers. Life had never been the same after that.

Abbie couldn't blame her mother for remarrying. She was only thirty-six, with no work experience, and not at all prepared to raise a daughter on her own. When a friend had introduced her to Patrick McGregor, a widower and successful businessman, Irene hadn't stood a chance. On their first date, Patrick had told her about his big house on El Camino Lane, and his two terrific kids who were bravely trying to cope with the death of their mother.

It hadn't taken long for Irene to succumb to the Irishman's charms and good looks. A few weeks later, the couple was married and Abbie had a new brother and sister, although Ian and Liz were more like the siblings from hell than the great kids Patrick had portrayed.

The truth about Patrick's drinking hadn't surfaced until several weeks later. It had seemed harmless at first. Some men unwound from a day's work by reading the sports page, listening to the news or playing with their kids. Patrick drank.

Soon, however, the nightly habit grew into a problem Irene was unable to control. The arguments multiplied and their intensity escalated to such an alarming level that Irene began considering leaving her husband. One night, Abbie heard Irene on the phone, talking to her father in Kansas about Patrick's drinking. Unfortunately, Patrick heard the conversation as well and flew into such a rage that a neighbor had come to the door and asked them to tone it down or he would call the police.

Ian was right. If the authorities decided to question their old neighbors—those who were still around—they would find plenty of reasons to suspect foul play.

So what was her option? Abbie wondered, holding back a hopeless sigh. She didn't have a hundred thousand dollars to give to Ian. But assuming she did, would she allow herself to be blackmailed? What if a hundred thousand dollars wasn't enough? What if Ian came back a year from now, asking for more?

The mere thought of sinking to such a level made her sick to her stomach. Until now, her life had followed a very straight path. The values she believed in and lived by were the same ones she tried to instill in her son—integrity, respect and consideration for others, honesty, self-esteem.

If her mother was well right now and in possession of all her faculties, Abbie knew exactly what Irene would say. "We fight him, honey. Truth versus lies. Good against evil. We'll win. You'll see."

But her mother was not well, and although she didn't know it yet, she was about to be crushed by the very evil she would have defeated in better times.

Unless Abbie did something about it.

After gazing into her mug for a long time, as though seeking an answer from it, Abbie stood up and carried her cold coffee to the sink. Considering the turmoil she was feeling, her hands were remarkably steady. She was glad, because from now until this nightmare was over, she would need nerves of steel.

"I won't let anything happen to you, Mom," she murmured as she poured her coffee down the drain. "I promise."

Her stride long and sure, Abbie walked toward Princeton National Bank on the north side of Palmer Square. Her decision to borrow the hundred thousand dollars hadn't been made lightly. Although the restaurant had started to make money, an additional loan at this time meant that she had to increase her revenues. And the only way to do that was to start opening Campagne on Sundays, at least for dinner.

Getting the loan shouldn't be a problem. Senior loan officer Ron Meltzer, whom she considered a friend, had been instrumental in getting the board to approve Abbie's two previous loans. She was confident he would help her again. Why shouldn't he? She was never late with her mortgage payments, kept all her accounts at this one bank, and considering Campagne's growing popularity, she could only be regarded as an excellent investment. The only problem was that she would have to lie to Ron about the reason for the loan.

After a short hesitation, she pushed the glass door and walked in, spotting the banker at his desk in the back.

"Abbie!" Ron Meltzer, a tall, almost bony man with rimless glasses and a friendly smile, circled his desk and came halfway across the lobby to meet her, holding out both hands. "What a lovely surprise," he said, kissing her cheek. "The only times I get to see you these days is when Lori and I come to Campagne for dinner." He waited until she was seated across his desk before returning to his chair. "And that's not nearly as often as I'd like."

"Thank you for saying that, Ron."

"So." He folded his arms and assumed his serious-banker expression. "How can I help you today, Abbie?"

She cleared her throat, more nervous than she had realized. "I need a loan, Ron. A rather large one."

He leaned back in his chair. "How large?"

"A hundred thousand dollars."

He raised an eyebrow. "Did you decide to expand the restaurant? I remember you said something to that effect the last time Lori and I were there."

"No." Abbie shifted in her seat. "Actually, I need the money to remodel my mother's house."

This time, both eyebrows went up. "The house in Kingston?"

Abbie nodded.

"What kind of remodeling did you have in mind?"

"Well—" she moistened her lips "—as you know, my mother has Alzheimer's. She also has arthritis, and I thought if we could build a bedroom and bathroom downstairs, it would make her life much easier." *Forgive me, Mom, for using you this way.*

"Have you had the house appraised?" Ron asked.

Abbie began to feel uncomfortable. This wasn't going the way she had anticipated. "Not recently."

"Well, it so happens that I'm familiar with the homes on Shaw Drive, and what they are selling for." He gave a light shake of his head. "The kind of improvements you're talking about would make your mother's house the most expensive property in that neighborhood. And that, as you know, would greatly diminish her chances of selling it later."

"My mother has no intention of moving."

"Maybe not now, but she'll have to eventually, right?"

"I suppose so."

"Let's put the resale value aside for a moment and tackle another problem—your ability to take on a new loan." As he talked, Ron's fingers moved across his computer keyboard. Once Abbie's account was on the screen, he turned the monitor around so she could read the display.

"As you can see, you have two jumbo loans already, one for the restaurant, the other for the house. If you recall, it took quite a bit of persuasion on my part to convince the board of directors to approve that second mortgage."

"And I haven't let you down," Abbie was prompted to say. "I've made my payments every month, on time."

"Indeed you have, but this would be a considerable burden on your budget.'' He looked sincerely regretful. ''I wish I could help you, Abbie. You're a hard worker and an important member of our community, but to approve such a large loan at this time would be unwise. My advice to you is to keep your mother's house as it is, and when she can no longer manage the stairs, which I hope is a long way from now, encourage her to move in with you. Or into a retirement community.''

Abbie remained silent. What could she say? He was right. She had been so desperate to get this loan, she hadn't seen the obstacles in her way. Barely able to force a polite smile, Abbie rose, thanked Ron and hurried out.

Oblivious to the crowds that jostled her, Abbie walked slowly back toward the restaurant. Now what? Ron had turned down her request for a loan and taking her chances elsewhere was pointless. Every financial institution she approached would tell her the same thing. She was overextended.

Short of robbing the damn bank, she wasn't going to get her hands on a hundred thousand dollars anytime soon.

She could call Ian's bluff. She could simply tell him she had been turned down for a loan and had no money. Nada. If he wanted to go through with his threats, so be it.

But was that a risk she was willing to take?

The answer was all too obvious. She had never been much of a gambler. No, that wasn't entirely true. She had taken a huge chance when she had decided to open her own restaurant. But the food business was her field. Crises didn't scare her off. Neither did difficult customers or a temperamental staff. She could deal with the daily ups and downs of her trade, but what did she know about bluffing a blackmailer?

She kept thinking, refusing to give up, until a possible

solution found its way through the haze of despair. She could cash in her zero coupons and her certificate of deposit. With a penalty for early withdrawal and interest computed in, the total would come close to fifty thousand dollars. It was a huge cut from what Ian had hoped to get, but if he was as hungry as Abbie thought he was, he might just take the money and run.

Considering Ian's low level of patience, she had expected to find him waiting in front of the restaurant when she returned from the bank, but he wasn't. Instead, he showed up in the middle of the lunch hour, this time making his grand entrance through the back door, surprising the staff, especially Brady, who looked as though he could strangle him.

Without a word, Abbie led Ian toward her office. Once there, she closed the door and leaned against it. "Is this some kind of emotional harassment, Ian? Coming here at all hours, disrupting my work and my staff."

"I call it protecting my investment." He sat down behind her desk and leaned back in her chair. "So, you heard from Earl?"

"Don't look so smug. The man sounds like a complete phony."

"But he can make a lot of trouble for dear Mom."

That he could do. "It doesn't matter," she said flatly. "I don't have a hundred thousand dollars."

Ian's arms came down. "What kind of shit is that? You're loaded."

"I don't know what gave you that impression, but the truth is, the restaurant didn't start making money until a few months ago."

"That's not my problem—"

"Let me finish." She fixed him with a hard stare, and to her surprise, Ian's mouth snapped shut. "All I have is thirty thousand dollars plus interest in zero coupons and a thirteen-thousand-dollar CD that doesn't mature until three years from now.''

Ian remained perfectly still. ''I can cash both,'' she continued in the same commanding tone. ''I made some calculations and the total should come to approximately forty-eight thousand dollars.''

She saw him wince.

''Take it or leave it.'' She offered no apology, made no request for mercy. Both would have been useless.

''What about a loan from your bank?'' he said at last. ''You're somebody in this town. You've got clout, collateral.''

''I went there this morning. They turned me down. With my business loan and the mortgage on the house, I'm over-extended.''

She folded her arms and watched him, feeling a perverse pleasure at the look of disbelief and disappointment on his face. It felt good to have the tables reversed for a change. How long that would last, however, was anyone's guess.

When Ian spoke again, his voice was surprisingly subdued. ''How soon can I have the money?''

She fought back a sigh of relief. She would not give him the satisfaction of seeing how frightened she had been that he would turn her offer down. ''I'll have to check with the bank, but probably no later than Friday afternoon.''

''I'll be here at four.''

''No.'' Her sharp tone made him cock his head. ''You've caused me enough trouble by coming here. Just tell me where you're staying and I'll bring the money over.''

He hesitated as though suspecting she might pull some kind of trick.

''Don't worry,'' she said. ''Unlike you, I'm a person of

my word. If I tell you I'll be there with the money, I'll be there. Just make sure you have my mother's letter—the original—with you.''

He took another two or three seconds to answer. ''I'm staying at the Clearwater Motel on Route 27.''

She nodded. ''I'll be there at three-thirty. I'll call if there are any changes.''

''What kind of changes?''

''I don't know,'' she said impatiently. ''My schedule doesn't revolve around you, Ian. Problems occur.''

He stood up and walked around the desk. ''See that they don't.''

Eleven

Ian got behind the wheel of Rose's Oldsmobile and glanced at the dash clock. Shit, he was late again. True to her word, Rose had started making the rounds of beauty salons in search of a job and had asked him to bring the car back by one. Well, let her stew. He didn't give a fuck. His sweet deal was beginning to turn sour and he didn't know what the hell to do about it.

Finding out he'd be getting less than half what he had expected had been a huge disappointment. At first he hadn't believed Abbie. Forty-eight grand. She had to be shitting him. But the more he thought about it, the more he realized she wasn't lying. She was what you called house poor. In her case, house and business poor.

Forty-eight thousand dollars was still a lot of money. More than he'd ever had in his life. And since he had never intended to split it with Earl, it was all his. But his bad luck hadn't stopped there. Earlier today, he had learned through Rose's cousin in Toledo that Arturo Garcia had showed up at her house, put a knife to her throat and demanded to know where Ian was. Marie, who was afraid of her own shadow, had claimed to have had no choice but to tell him the truth.

Ian had almost pissed in his pants. Now that Arturo knew he was in Princeton, he'd call every fricking motel in the area until he found him.

Common sense told him to get the hell out of Dodge. Hanging around until Friday wasn't healthy. On the other hand, how far could he get on fifty-nine dollars? He pulled the money from his pants pocket and counted it again. The small roll hadn't magically fattened overnight. Count it any way you want, it still came to fifty-nine stinking bucks. Even if Rose found a job today, she wouldn't be getting a paycheck until next week.

As always when he was in a bind and needed some quick cash, he thought of his sister, Liz. Like Rose, she had come through for him before, but Liz was unpredictable. And so damn judgmental. That ice-princess stare she gave him every time he asked for money always made him feel like a beggar. Unfortunately, at the moment, she was his best bet. Hell, she was his *only* bet, so maybe he should swallow his pride, buy a round-trip bus ticket to New York and look her up.

It was either that or starve until Friday.

By splitting up the driving and stopping only to buy food and to shower, Tony and Arturo had made the eighteen-hundred-mile trip from El Paso to Toledo in thirty-nine hours. In Toledo, Arturo had quickly located Rose Panini's cousin and found out that Ian and his girlfriend had left for Princeton, New Jersey, on June second. But although Marie Panini was scared out of her mind, she couldn't tell Arturo any more than that. Rose hadn't left a forwarding address and she hadn't heard from her. Arturo didn't seem worried, though. The name of the town was all he needed. The rest would be easy.

Finding a place to stay so far away from home would have been a challenge for most people, but not for Arturo, who had connections in half of the fifty states. After a few calls, a friend of his had put him in contact with Enrique

Soledad. Enrique owned a garage in the south side of Trenton and occasionally rented the small apartment above it. Judging from the conversation between Arturo and the mechanic, Tony had concluded that Enrique wasn't too keen on harboring two strangers, but after a little coaxing, he agreed to let them move in, for free, provided they were out of there before his next renter moved in, two weeks from now.

As they were about to cross the Pennsylvania–New Jersey border, Tony made one last attempt to convince Arturo to turn around and forget Ian McGregor had ever existed.

"He can't repay you anyway," Tony pointed out. "You heard Rose's cousin. The man is broke."

"I know a loan shark in the Bronx." Arturo gave Tony a nasty grin. "I'll be glad to give McGregor a recommendation."

"And how is he supposed to repay the loan shark?"

"That ain't my problem, little brother."

Tony knew only too well what happened to people who didn't repay loan sharks, but maybe Arturo was right. That wasn't their problem. If McGregor was stupid enough to go that route, then he ought to be ready for the consequences.

They arrived in Trenton at 5:00 p.m. on Wednesday and easily found the garage. As Tony had expected, Enrique's greeting was just a shade warmer than icy, but when Arturo handed him a bottle of Johnny Walker Black—Enrique's favorite—the man mellowed considerably. Half an hour later, the whiskey still burning their bellies, the three men walked up the stairs to the garage apartment, which was small but clean. It even had a working TV, which made Arturo happy.

"Call me if you need anything," Enrique told them before leaving. "After hours, all calls to the garage are forwarded to my house. If I'm not there, my grandfather will take a message.''

As soon as Enrique was gone, Arturo didn't waste another minute. He took the Mercer County phone book from the bookcase and sat down. Using Tony's cell phone, he began calling the area's motels.

Twelve

It was a little after five o'clock when Ian stepped off the bus at New York Port Authority, and already the streets of the Big Apple were thick with commuters hurrying to catch their rides home. This was a great city to get lost in, he thought as he joined the throng of people for the walk uptown. Arturo would never find him in this maze, and since that big bully was still a threat, maybe he should consider moving here. Liz might even let him crash at her apartment until he found his own place. He didn't need much, just a couch, a shower and a six-pack.

The Manhattan Towers was a seventy-two-story hotel that catered mostly to businessmen and women, judging from the busy lounge at the far end of the lobby. The fact that it was the middle of the week didn't seem to stop New Yorkers from one of their favorite pastimes—conducting business over chilled martinis.

After a few minutes' wait, Ian found a table, ordered a beer and watched his sister behind the bar, serving drinks with a smile that would have melted Antarctica.

He had to admit she looked a lot better than the last time he'd seen her. She had finally lost those fifteen pesky pounds, and though she was far from the size six she used to be in her younger days, she looked trim and fit. The narrow black pants and the snug white shirt even made her look sexy. Her blond hair was now slick and blunt cut and styled in a way that hid that ugly scar on her right cheek. Why she had kept that damn thing when her rich rocker husband could have paid to have it removed was beyond him.

She wore little makeup, just some blush and a hint of lip color. The results made her look younger than her forty-five years. She had never needed makeup anyway. She was one of those fortunate women who looked great the moment she woke up and only got better as the day went on. That's why she had been such a hit with the guys at school.

He kept watching her, chewing on the trail mix the waitress had brought him, and wondered how Liz would react once she realized he needed money again. Knowing her, she'd probably laugh in his face and remind him of all the other times he had borrowed from her and never paid her back.

But then again, she might surprise him. Liz was a strange bird, a loner who didn't talk or complain much, not even when their father had married Irene DiAngelo. Ian had had plenty to say about that, but Liz, though not pleased, had taken it all in stride. She just wasn't the type to get emotional about stuff like that.

On her eighteenth birthday, Liz had pocketed what was left of her share of their father's inheritance and moved to New York City. There she met and married Jude Tilly, the lead singer of a band so hot at the time, all five members had become instant millionaires. Liz and Jude had lived the high life for a while, jet-setting around the world, entertaining in their Manhattan penthouse and spending, spending, spending.

And then one day, the band broke up, and Jude's hopes of staying on top of the charts on his own fell flat. Hit hard, he started drinking and doing drugs, and within a couple of years, the guy was broke. Desperate to help him get his life back on track, Liz decided that a baby was just what her husband needed. Then came more bad news. Liz couldn't have children.

Instead of comforting his wife, Jude chose that time to file for divorce. After ten years together and more abuse than she deserved, all Liz got from her marriage to the famous rocker was a summerhouse in upstate New York. Or was it in the Berkshires? Ian wasn't sure because he had never been invited.

Without Liz to keep Jude out of trouble, the singer's life began to spin out of control. Three months after the divorce, he died of an overdose.

For a while, Liz had been inconsolable, but eventually, her survivor instincts had kicked in and she had rejoined the living.

Looking at her now, the way she mixed, shook and poured, he would have sworn she had done that all her life. But then, why should he be surprised? Liz was the type of person who could do anything once she set her mind to it.

And if she was so good, she was probably raking in tons of tips.

He took another sip of his beer, then, reaching into his pocket, he brought out a piece of paper and a pencil, wrote a short message and signaled the waitress.

"Another beer, sir?" she asked.

"Not yet." He handed her the note and gave her his most charming smile. "Do me a favor, will you, doll? Give this to the barmaid." When she hesitated, he handed her a five-dollar bill. The tip was a little outrageous, but what the hell. Like the saying went, you had to spend money to make money.

He watched as the waitress handed Liz the note, pointing in his direction. His sister showed no reaction when she saw him, no sign of recognition, or irritation. She simply took the note, slid it in her shirt pocket and took the next order.

He had to wait another hour, until another bartender came to relieve her, before she finally made her way to Ian's table, carrying a glass and a bottle of mineral water.

"What are you doing here?" she asked, taking the chair across from him.

"Hello, Ian," he said. "Good to see you. You're looking swell."

Ignoring his sarcastic tone, she poured half the water into her glass and took a thirsty gulp. "When did you get out of prison?"

"A couple of weeks ago." He looked around him. "Nice place. Not like that dump you worked in years ago."

"I'm glad you approve."

"Hey, I'm just happy you're doing so well."

"I bet you are." She took another sip. "How much do you want this time?"

"Why do you always think I want something? Why can't I be here to visit my sister? You know how long it's been since we've seen each other?"

"Three years. I believe that's when you came to my apartment asking to borrow—*borrow*," she repeated with greater emphasis, "two thousand dollars. Or was that the time you borrowed three thousand dollars and told me I'd double my money in a week's time?"

"Hey, the deal fell through for me, too. I lost a lot more than you did."

She kept sipping her water, looking completely disinterested.

"The truth is," he continued, "I do need money, sis. Not much, just enough to tide me over for a few days."

"Have you tried to earn it like the rest of us do? By working?"

He sensed a lecture coming and prepared himself for it. Everything came with a price. "I've done nothing but try to find work since I arrived in New Jersey," he lied. "Problem is, nobody wants to give an ex-con a job."

"Or maybe you're not trying hard enough."

"Look," he snapped, a little put off by her snotty attitude. "You haven't walked in my shoes, okay? And until you do, you'll never know what it feels like to be an outcast."

She gazed into her glass, a small smile on her lips, as if she was having a private joke with herself or something. Then he got it. She must feel like an outcast all the time, with that scar of hers, but dammit, keeping it had been *her* choice.

It took her forever to look up. "Why New Jersey?"

"Because there's an opportunity there I can't afford to pass up."

"Where did you find the money to get there?"

"Rose Panini."

Liz laughed. "That poor woman is still carrying a torch for you? After all you put her through?" She shook her head. "She must be nuts."

"She loves me, Liz. Is that so hard to understand?"

"Yes, but that's only my opinion."

He let the remark go. Getting Liz all riled up wouldn't help his case. "I know I've done some dumb things in my life, but those sixteen months at Allen changed me. God, Liz, you can't imagine how bad that place was," he said, figuring a little exaggeration wouldn't hurt. "You hear about it, you read about it, but when you see it, when you're actually part of that hell, it's a lot worse than what you could ever imagine. I was even in therapy for a while. I bet you didn't know that."

She brought the glass to her lips. "No. You seem so grounded."

"Go ahead, be sarcastic. It won't make me mad. I don't get mad anymore."

"Next you're going to tell me you're a changed man."

"I am. Ask Rose." He looked around him again before lowering his voice. "I'm turning over a new leaf."

"Prove it."

Jesus. He had forgotten what an overbearing bitch she could be. "I'm thinking of starting my own business."

"What kind of business?"

"I don't know yet."

Liz set her glass down. "If you think I'm going to finance a new venture, forget it. The bank is closed, buster. Permanently."

He shook his head. "No, that part is covered. All I need from you is four or five hundred bucks to get me by until the deal comes through."

"Ah, yes, another one of your deals."

"Don't look so skeptical. I'm about to make some serious money. Don't you want to know how?"

"All right, I'll admit I'm curious. What is it this time? You're selling tickets for a trip to the moon? Or maybe you've discovered a gold mine somewhere and you're looking for investors. Go ahead, Ian, tell me. Who's the next sucker?"

He leaned back in his chair, looking forward to the expression on her face. "Abbie DiAngelo."

Liz's aloof smile faded. "Irene's daughter?"

"Do you know any other Abbie DiAngelo?"

"Where is she?"

"Princeton, New Jersey. She owns a fancy restaurant there and is doing very well." He snorted. "Although if you listen to her, she's barely making ends meet."

"And she's going to give you money to start your own business?" Liz laughed. "Give me a break."

"She's going to give me the money," he said in a low voice, "because she has no choice. I know something about Irene that can destroy her."

"What are you babbling about?"

He had her attention. Good. Now all he had to do was be as convincing as he had been with Abbie. "Irene killed our father," he stated calmly.

Liz's expression turned stony. "What did you say?"

He told her everything he had told Abbie, almost word for word, and how it had been sheer luck that his old buddy, Earl Kramer, had seen Abbie's interview on TV.

Liz listened quietly, her features tight, the tip of her tongue popping out from time to time to moisten her lips. He could tell the news had hit her hard. When he was finished, she lowered her gaze, staring into her glass and holding it in both hands.

"How come you never told me about that letter?" she asked at last.

"I forgot I had it," he said truthfully. "And then when Earl called, I thought if I could find it, it'd make my case that much stronger."

But Liz was shaking her head. "It won't. Everyone knows Dad caused his own death with that disgusting habit of smoking in bed. It's a wonder he didn't set fire to the house sooner."

"That's not what happened."

"How do you know your friend didn't make that story up?"

"Because I know Earl."

"And he's willing to confess to the crime?"

"If it comes to that, but it won't."

Liz looked into the distance, her face devoid of expression. "Irene," she said quietly, as if talking to herself. "Sweet Irene. Who would have known?"

"I did. Under all that sweetness, I knew the woman was a bitch. You had to know, too, Liz."

Liz played with her glass, turning it around and around on the small table. He could tell she was still skeptical. "You and your friend are criminals," she said as if in answer to his thoughts. "Irene DiAngelo is a respectable woman. When she denies the accusations, who do you think the cops will believe? Two con men or Saint Irene?"

"But that's the beauty, Liz. Irene is not in a position to deny anything. She's *loco*."

"What?"

"The old lady is a couple of slices short of a pizza pie." He paused before delivering the next bomb. "She's got Alzheimer's."

Liz poured the rest of her mineral water into her glass. "I see you haven't changed. You still have the morals of an alley cat."

"Oh, and you're just a paragon of virtue, aren't you?"

"No, but I wouldn't take advantage of a sick woman."

"Well, I guess we're different in that respect."

"You're going to end up in prison again, Ian."

"How do you figure?"

"What if Abbie turns you in?"

"She won't. That letter really shook her up. She isn't about to put her mother through such a nightmare. Or her son."

Liz's thin blond eyebrow went up. "She has a son?"

"His name is Ben. He's nine years old. Don't you see? She's got too much at stake. That's why she agreed to give me the money."

Once again, Liz fell silent. Ian wasn't sure what she was

thinking because she was so damn hard to read. "Why are you doing this?" she asked suddenly.

"Doing what?"

"Blackmailing Abbie."

He rolled his eyes. "Are you spacing out on me, too, girl? Irene killed our father. Christ, Liz, aren't you mad, knowing what she did? How she wrecked our lives?"

"If revenge is all you want, call the cops and turn Irene in."

"Revenge is not enough. I want to be compensated."

"So you're blackmailing Abbie."

"Hey, I'm not fussy. I'd gladly take money from Irene, but the old broad's got zip." He scooted to the edge of his chair. "So, are you going to help me out? With the money, I mean. I spent all I had on a bus ticket to come up here. Rose will kill me."

Liz sighed and glanced at her watch. "I get off at seven. Stick around and we'll walk to the ATM together. Right now, I've got to go back to work."

Ian grinned, already thinking how he and Rose would be celebrating tonight. A nice juicy steak maybe, a bottle of wine—the kind that came with a cork—and a nice romp in the sack.

Life couldn't get much better than this.

Thirteen

Ian felt on top of the world. He had returned from New York yesterday five hundred dollars richer, thanks to Liz's generosity, and he was now only an hour away from pocketing an additional forty-eight thou. His pinching-pennies days were over.

Humming softly, he stood in front of the mirror in his motel room and tugged a thick gray wig in place, making sure none of his hair showed on either side. Satisfied, he picked up the matching mustache, the back of which was covered with a thin coat of theater glue, and patted it gently above his upper lip.

He pulled back to admire his handiwork. The New York shop owner who had sold him the wig yesterday hadn't exaggerated. The transformation was uncanny. Even his own mother, rest her soul, wouldn't recognize him. And neither would Arturo Garcia, if and when that son of a bitch found him. The odds of this happening had diminished considerably in the last twenty-four hours, thanks to another of Ian's brilliant ideas—bribing the motel clerk. With a wink and fifty bucks held between two fingers, Ian had mentioned a jealous husband hot on his trail. The clerk had returned the wink to show he understood, and pocketed the money.

The disguise was extra insurance, just in case Arturo was roaming the streets of Princeton in search of his prey.

Feeling more excited than he had been in weeks, Ian chuckled. Even the minor setback of having to settle for less money didn't seem important anymore. What mattered was to get out of here and put as much distance as possible between him and Arturo. New York City still sounded good, or maybe L.A. Or Chicago. Once he reached his destination, he'd send Rose some money. She didn't really need it now that she had found a job, but it was the decent thing to do. She might come in handy someday, though he doubted she'd ever forgive him for bailing out on her that way.

He glanced at his watch, feeling a little jittery. Abbie wouldn't be here for another hour and the wait was killing him. He hoped nothing would go wrong on her side. But why should it? Her stakes were just as high as his. She wasn't about to screw up now. Maybe he should start packing. The activity would quiet his nerves.

Whistling the tune of "Happy Days Are Here Again", he walked over to the closet and took a quick inventory. He didn't have much, just the clothes Rose had bought him before they left Toledo, but that would soon change.

He was debating whether to pack now or later when a strong arm suddenly clamped around his throat, cutting off his air supply.

"Going somewhere, *amigo?*"

Arturo. Ian felt as if his bowels might let loose at any moment. He clutched at the man's steely arm, trying desperately to loosen its grip. He opened his mouth to talk, but the only sound that came out of his mouth was a strangled *aargh*.

The arm relaxed a fraction of an inch. It was enough for Ian to take a gulp of air.

"What did you say, McGregor?"

"Pl-please," Ian gasped. "You're...killing me."

"And that's gonna break my heart?"

Ian tried to wiggle out of the viselike grip but only managed to wedge himself in even tighter.

"Quit squirming, will ya, or I'll really hurt you." To show he meant it, Arturo jabbed him in the back with his knee, hard enough to make Ian groan. "You're gonna be still?"

Eyes closed, Ian nodded.

"And what's with this getup, anyway?" With the tip of a nasty-looking blade, Arturo plucked the wig off Ian's head and dangled it in front of his nose. "You thought you could fool me with this? Or with that motel registration under your girlfriend's name? What the fuck you take me for, McGregor? An idiot?"

That lousy, double-crossing clerk.

Ian got another hard jab. This one was on the kidney and brought out a cry of pain. "Arturo, please," he said when he could talk again. "Let me explain."

With a shake of his wrist, Arturo let the wig drop to the floor then brought the switchblade to Ian's throat. "Okay, explain. You've got one minute."

Ian's mind worked furiously, trying to come up with a way to get that ape to let go so he could make a run for it. Unfortunately, at this moment, Ian wasn't in a particularly creative mood.

"I...I know you're pissed off about...what happened in Toledo, but it's been a long time, man." The sharp point dug deeper into Ian's skin. Something warm trickled down his neck. Christ, he was bleeding. The bastard had cut him. Ian held his breath, afraid the slightest move would be fatal.

"Not long enough, you miserable piece of shit." Arturo's breath was hot against Ian's ear. "Not long enough for me to forget how you ratted on me ten years ago. Or how you stole my thirty grand."

Ian licked his lips. Maybe, just maybe, there was a way out of this death trap. "Arturo, look…about the money. You can get it back, man. Every penny."

"Yeah?" The blade didn't budge. "How?"

"My sister is going to loan me some money. That's why I'm here."

"Liz?"

"No, not Liz. Abbie DiAngelo. My *step*sister. Her mother was married to my dad a long time ago. She owns a restaurant here in Princeton."

"Are you fucking with me, McGregor? I don't know nothin' about a stepsister."

"I'm not fucking with you, man, I swear. Abbie's agreed to loan me some money so I could get back on my feet— forty-eight grand. You can have it all."

"You owe me a hundred."

"A hundred! Are you nuts? I only took thirty from you. You said so yourself."

"A hundred with the juice. And I'm giving you a break. You know what the rates are."

"All right, all right. I'll…get you the rest…somehow."

The hold around Ian's neck relaxed some more. "When are you getting the cash?"

Ian's mind started working double time. He had a chance to get out of this alive after all. In fact, if he played it cool, he'd be able to run *and* take the money with him. But he couldn't do much in this motel room, where Arturo clearly had the advantage. He had to draw him out in the open.

"Tonight," he said in answer to Arturo's question. "At ten o'clock, after Abbie closes the restaurant."

"She's coming here?"

"No. We're…meeting at the pier," he improvised, remembering walking along the lake a day or so ago.

"Where the fuck is the pier?"

"At Lake Carnegie. It's close by, maybe three blocks from here. That's why I picked that location, so I could walk to it. Rose waits tables at a local diner and she needs her wheels." He figured the more details he gave, the more credible his story sounded. How he'd find an opportunity to call Abbie and tell her the plans had changed was something he hadn't worked out yet. But he would. He had to.

Arturo laughed. "Your old lady works and you're here, playing dress-up. That's real manly of you, McGregor." The smile faded as quickly as it had come. "When is Rose coming back?"

"Midnight."

Arturo was silent for a moment. "All right," he said suddenly. "Here's what we're gonna do. We'll go to the pier—together. Once your stepsister shows up, you get the money, wait until she leaves and hand it over. You got it?"

That was exactly what Ian had hoped he'd say. He nodded. "And then what?"

"If you don't give me no trouble, I'll let you live."

Yeah, right, Ian thought. Like he was going to believe that.

Arturo pressed his mouth against Ian's ear again. "But if you cross me, *amigo,* I'm gonna make you regret it—in a bad way. *Comprende?*"

"*Sí.* I mean…yes."

"Good." Arturo let him go and Ian turned around, taking his first look in ten years at the man who had come almost two thousand miles to find him. Christ, he was even bigger and uglier than Ian remembered. He had shaved his head, exposing an uneven skull and disgusting warts, and had grown a goatee. He still wore multiple earrings in his left ear, one of them in the shape of crossbones. He had dark, beady eyes that didn't exactly sparkle with intelligence, but when a man was as large and as mean as Arturo

Garcia, brains didn't much matter. He wore frayed jeans, a grungy T-shirt cut off at the shoulders and scruffy boots. Naked mermaids and fire-spitting dragons were tattooed on his beefy arms.

Ian glanced at the door he knew he had locked. "How did you get in?" He immediately realized that was a stupid question.

Arturo laughed, showing the gap between his two front teeth. "With my trusted pick." He grinned again. "Never travel without it."

He snapped his switchblade shut. "Now. I'm gonna sit right there until it's time for us to go," he said, pointing at the chair by the window with his knife. "If you try anything, you're a dead man."

"We've got to stay in here for seven hours?"

"You got a problem with that?"

Being cooped up in a motel room with a madman? Yeah, he had a problem with that. Was he going to admit that to Arturo? Hell, no.

Ian shook his head. "If you don't give a shit, why should I?"

Arturo went to sit in the chair, stretching his long legs in front of him, and turned on the TV. After flipping through several channels, he finally settled on a Power Rangers cartoon. Ian rolled his eyes as he laid on the bed. The man's intellect never failed to amaze him.

While the action heroes did their stuff, Ian's mind tried to work out a plan. He had to contact Abbie before she left the restaurant. A few more minutes and he wouldn't be able to get hold of her.

His gaze swung toward the nightstand and Rose's cell phone. If he could get it without Arturo noticing, half the problem was solved.

He waited until his unwelcome guest was lost in the

antics on the screen, then, slowly, he extended his arm, palmed the small phone and slipped it into his pocket. The easy part was done. Now for the hard part—making the call.

Ian waited another minute, swung his legs off the bed and stood up. "Okay if I go take a leak?"

Without moving, Arturo looked at him, then at the bathroom door, which was ajar. He stood up, and without a word, headed for the john.

Ian laughed. "What? You're afraid I'll escape through the toilet drain?"

"No, but you're dumb enough to try the window."

"There ain't no window, man."

In the bathroom, Arturo glanced around him, chuckling when he saw Rose's undies and a pink baby-doll nightgown hanging on the shower rod. Apparently satisfied there was no way out, he nodded. "Make it quick."

Ian closed the door, simultaneously taking the phone from his pocket. He dialed, his mouth tight, his whole body tense with the fear Abbie wouldn't be there.

Come on, come on.

One of the kitchen workers—not the wise-mouthed kid—answered, and within seconds, Abbie was on the line. Ian spoke fast and in a furious whisper. "Abbie, it's me, Ian. There's been a change of plan. Do not come to the motel. Meet me at the Lake Carnegie pier instead, at ten o'clock tonight."

"Why? What happened?"

"I don't have time to explain. Just do it." He repeated the time and place, then hung up.

Estimating he had been in the bathroom about thirty seconds, he flushed the toilet, washed his hands and dried them. He looked at his watch again. That had taken ten more seconds. He'd have to remember that.

When he walked out, Arturo gave him only a cursory glance before returning his attention to the TV screen. Ian took his position on the bed again, his back resting against the headboard. An idea had occurred to him while he was drying his hands, but its execution would require a second trip to the bathroom.

At six o'clock, as Ian woke up from a nap, he yawned loudly while studying Arturo, who was now watching *The Three Stooges* and laughing like an idiot. "Hey, Arturo," he said casually. "I'm getting hungry. How about we order some chow? A pizza maybe? Or I could go and pick up some Chinese."

Arturo slanted him one of those looks. "Yeah, right." He pointed at the motel phone on the coffee table. "Order a pizza, large, sausage and pepperoni. And extra cheese." And just to make sure Ian wouldn't do anything stupid, he took out his knife again and snapped the blade open. "What the fuck you waiting for?"

A half hour later, there was a knock on the door. With the knife, Arturo motioned for Ian to answer it while he slipped out of sight, staying close enough to ram the blade into Ian's back if necessary.

It took no more than ten minutes for Arturo to devour enough pizza to make a bull burst at the seams. He also downed three of Ian's beers and smoked two cigarettes. The man was much more relaxed now but no less watchful. If Ian had had any hope his captor would doze off, they evaporated quickly.

Still, this was as good a time as any to put phase two of his plan into action. He stood up and started to head for the bathroom.

"Where the fuck you think you're going?" Arturo demanded.

"To the can, man."

"You just went. What's the matter with you? You got a problem or something?"

"No, I don't have a problem. It's been five hours since I went. Don't you ever take a piss?"

Arturo waved the knife. "Okay, okay, stop whining. Go."

Back in the bathroom, Ian checked the time, then yanked Rose's nightgown from the hanger. Working quickly, he unwound the hanger, the way a buddy of his had showed him once, until he had one long piece of wire which he fashioned into a garrote, with two loop handles on each end.

He tested his new weapon for flexibility a few times, then, satisfied it would do the trick, he slid it into his pant leg and went back to the bedroom.

He was ready.

Fourteen

Abbie had stuffed the forty-eight thousand dollars, all in hundred and fifty-dollar bills, into an old leather satchel, which now sat on the Acura's passenger seat. The money had been waiting for her when she had arrived at the bank earlier, and a teller Abbie knew had escorted her to a private room where the bundles were counted.

Abbie was glad Ron Meltzer hadn't been at his usual post. It saved her from telling another lie, although she was certain he knew about the withdrawal. Not much went on in that bank without him being aware of it. Maybe his absence from his desk was intentional after all. It was entirely possible that he had wanted to spare them both an embarrassing moment.

Now, as she drove home in the rain, she kept thinking about Ian's phone call. This sudden change of plan had unsettled her. It was clear from the way he had whispered his instructions that someone had been standing nearby. But who? And more important, how would this silly cloak-and-dagger game affect her? Was she in some kind of danger? With Ian's track record and the company he had kept over the years, that wouldn't surprise her.

A few minutes later she pulled into the garage and got out of the truck, leaving the satchel on the passenger seat where it would be safe. Then, when the garage door was once again closed, she walked into the house.

The sight of Ben and Tiffany sitting at the kitchen table, one doing homework, the other cramming for exams, brought a sense of normalcy back into her life. "Hi, guys."

She gave Ben a quick kiss. He didn't mind if she kissed him in front of Tiffany because he had seen the baby-sitter do the same with her brothers. "How was your day?"

"Good." He reached between the pages of his math book and pulled out a sheet of paper. "This is from the summer-camp director," he said. "You need to fill it out and sign it."

Joining them at the table, Abbie glanced at the form, almost identical to the one she had filled out the two previous years. *Almost.* "Ben, this isn't for day camp."

"I know," he said nonchalantly. "I'm too big for day camp, Mom. That's why I signed up for Camp Kettle Run this year."

"But you'll be gone for two whole weeks!"

"So?"

So, she wasn't ready for this. She wasn't ready to be in this big house for fourteen days and nights, all alone, worrying about him. Only a year ago, he hadn't wanted to hear anything about Camp Kettle Run. He had been happy enough to be dropped off at his regular day camp at nine and come home at four, ready to swim or go to Jimmy Hernandez's house and play catch.

She caught a flicker of worry in his eyes. "It's okay, isn't it, Mom? I can go?"

He's nine years old, Abbie. This is how you raised him to be—independent, confident and adventurous.

She smiled as she caught Tiffany's amused glance. "Of course you can go."

"Don't forget to sign the form, then. The camp is filling up fast."

"I won't forget." She stole another kiss, then quickly got out of her chair. "Sloppy joes okay for dinner?"

"With fries?"

"Fries it is."

An hour and a half later, while Ben and Tiffany were eating dinner, Abbie ran upstairs, locked the bedroom door behind her and walked straight to the armoire where she kept the PPK. This time, however, she didn't put it back. Then, reaching under her mattress, she took out the box of ammo. Her hand shook slightly as she loaded all seven bullets into the magazine, but she lost none of her concentration. Her nerves steady, she checked the safety, as she had done dozens of times, and put the gun in her purse.

Then, feeling remarkably calm, she hooked the strap around her shoulder and walked back downstairs, where she found Claudia waiting for her.

"Claudia." The bag around her shoulder seemed to suddenly weigh a ton. "Did I know you were coming?"

"No." Her friend's concern was apparent. "I was worried about you," Claudia whispered as they hugged. "We haven't talked since Wednesday."

Abbie let out a nervous laugh. "There's nothing to worry about. I've been busy, that's all." Before Claudia could reply, Abbie went to kiss Ben goodbye, promised Tiffany she'd be home early for a change and ushered Claudia toward the garage.

"What is the matter with you," Claudia said once they were out of earshot. "If I didn't know better, I'd say you were not only avoiding me, but trying to get rid of me as well."

Abbie pushed a button on the wall and the garage door slid open. "Don't be silly. Why would I do that?"

"I don't know. Maybe because I disagreed with you the other day about handling Ian on your own?"

"That's nonsense. You know how much I value your opinion."

"Good, because whatever course of action you choose to take, I'm here for you. You know that, don't you?"

Abbie wondered if Claudia would still feel the same way if she knew about the loaded gun in her purse, a gun she intended to use if Ian so much as lifted a finger against her. "Of course I do. It's just that..." She hesitated. "I don't want to get you involved."

"I'm your friend! I *want* to be involved."

The sincerity in Claudia's tone gave a huge boost to Abbie's spirits and made it easier to tell her the truth. "I'm going to pay him off, Claudia."

Claudia didn't seem surprised. "When?" she asked simply.

"Tonight. I was supposed to drop the money off at his motel at three-thirty, but he called just before I left the restaurant and told me there was a change of plan. I'm meeting him at the Lake Carnegie pier at ten o'clock, with the cash."

"A hundred thousand dollars? I thought you said you didn't have that kind of money."

They started walking toward Claudia's van. "I don't. I cashed in all my savings and came up with forty-eight thousand dollars. Ian agreed to take it."

"And he'll leave you alone after that?"

"He gave me his word."

Claudia made a derisive sound. "What's the word of a con man worth these days?"

"Not much, I suppose, but I have to trust him. I have no choice."

"He'll be back for more, Abbie. You know that, don't you?"

"I don't believe he will. He knows I don't have any more money."

Claudia gave a firm nod. "All right, end of lecture. I have one request, though. Let me come with you."

Having expected the offer, Abbie gave an emphatic shake of her head. "Absolutely not. I told you, I don't want you involved. And anyway, Ian would freak out if he saw I brought someone with me."

"He won't know. I'll hide."

Despite the seriousness of the situation, Abbie smiled. "I think you've seen too many reruns of *Magnum*. Thanks for the offer, but the answer is still no."

"Then promise me you'll call when you get back and let me know all went well."

"I will." Abbie kissed Claudia's cheek, aware that her friend hugged her a little tighter than usual. "Now, let me go," she said in a teasing tone. "Some of us have to work for a living, you know."

Ian knew that for his plan to work, it was essential that he and Arturo walk to the pier rather than drive.

"I know it's raining," he had told Arturo, "but Abbie knows I'll be on foot. If she gets there first and sees a car anywhere in the vicinity, she'll just keep on going."

Arturo had given a grunt of disapproval, but offered no other protest.

Halfway to their destination, Ian began to put his plan into action. Trying to be as inconspicuous as possible, he removed the wire from inside his pant leg and held it casually by his side. His friend had explained the garrote was no weapon for amateurs. It required precision, speed and great strength. An untrained killer could easily miss the mark—the intended victim's neck—and get the wire caught on the nose, or the chin, making it possible for the victim to grab the weapon and turn it against his attacker. While Ian had never killed anyone or even attempted to kill anyone with a garrote, he had seen the weapon demonstrated enough times, once in prison, to feel fairly confident he could do the job. Arturo may be a big man, but Ian had the element of surprise on his side. And one major incentive—survival.

It was a dark, cloud-filled night, illuminated only by the high beams of an occasional car as it traveled up and down Route 27.

"That it?" Arturo pointed at a car that had slowed down.

"I don't know. I can't see. Is it a red SUV?"

As if on cue, Arturo turned his back to Ian, bending a little to peer through the trees.

Ian sprang into action. Holding the wire by the handles, he looped it over Arturo's head, wrapped it around his neck and pulled tight. At the same time, he positioned his knee in the small of Arturo's back for balance.

As expected, Arturo twisted and clawed, trying to get his fingers under the wire. Ian held on tight, his face contorted with the effort it took to keep that oversize beast from wiggling free.

But instead of falling to his knees as he should have by now, Arturo stumbled back, knocking Ian off his feet. His head slammed against a tree with enough force to stun him for a few seconds.

When he opened his eyes again and tried to shake the dizziness away, Arturo had ripped the garrote from around his neck. For a moment, he just stood there, his long arms hanging at his sides, looking like a big, nasty ape.

"You son of a bitch," he muttered just before he lunged at Ian.

The two men rolled around on the wet leaves, shouting and cursing, but it was soon obvious that Ian was no match for the bigger man. In less than ten seconds, Arturo had Ian flat on his back and was straddling him.

"You made a big mistake, *amigo*," he said, holding him between his powerful thighs.

Ian never saw him pull out his switchblade, but all of a sudden, there it was, looking more lethal than ever. Arturo held it like a small sword, between the thumb and index finger, while the other fingers were wrapped around the handle.

Ian couldn't think of anything helpful to say, so he threw a couple of punches, but Arturo kept dodging his head, laughing at him, enjoying the moment.

"You thought you could fuck with me, punk? You thought you could take me on? Are you out of your fucking mind?"

Ian started to plead, but Arturo shut him up with a hard backhanded slap. "I warned you, didn't I? I told what I'd do to you if you played games."

Ian never had a chance to reply. With a look of sheer pleasure on his face, Arturo plunged the blade into Ian's gut. Not once or twice, but in a succession of vicious stabs, each followed by a grunt.

Pain exploded throughout Ian's entire body. He no longer felt the rain, or the fear. Just the pain, hot, raw, unbearable.

Above him, the trees began to tilt, first to the right, then to the left. Ian lifted his head off the ground in a desperate attempt to call for help, but he couldn't find the strength to utter a single word, so he let his head fall back to the ground with a dull thud.

A large shadow stood over him, out of focus. Arturo? He wanted to talk to him, but he was having a hard time forming words. The trees began their crazy dance again, spinning faster and faster.

His hands clenched his belly, from where the pain radiated. He needed help, someone to stop whatever was happening to him. His lips moved as his lungs fought for air, yet strangely, as he grew weaker, so did the pain. That had to be a good sign. Maybe lady luck had decided to shine upon him one more time after all.

He wanted to laugh. He had always been a lucky son of a bitch.

From somewhere in the distance, he heard the sound of a car engine. Someone was coming for him. He would be fine. All he had to do was keep still, conserve his energy, and everything would be all right. The pain was almost gone now. And the trees had stopped spinning.

Relieved, he closed his eyes.

Fifteen

The pace in Campagne's busy kitchen hadn't let up once, but for Abbie, who was a nervous wreck, the evening had gone excruciatingly slow. More than anything, she wanted this day to be over and for her life to go back to normal.

At nine forty-five, she removed her apron and tossed it in a straw basket marked Laundry, trying to appear as casual as possible, considering her heart rate had almost tripled in the last few minutes.

"Leaving early?" Brady asked.

"Yes." She didn't meet his gaze. "Tiffany is studying for finals and I told her I'd be home early. You don't mind closing up, do you?"

"Of course not." He glanced at the leather satchel she had hooked around her shoulder along with her purse. "That looks heavy. Want me to carry it to the car for you?"

"No, I'll be fine." But she wasn't fine at all. She was scared, and breathing so fast she thought she'd start hyperventilating any minute.

As Brady continued to scrutinize her, she gave his arm a quick squeeze and wondered if he could see how nervous she was. Brady had always been intuitive. Until now, that sixth sense of his had been the subject of happy banter between them. Tonight, she found it unsettling. Rather than answer any more questions, she tossed a quick good-night to the rest of the staff and walked out.

Thank God, the nightmare was almost over. Twenty minutes from now, she would be back home, kissing her little boy on the forehead as she did every night, and Ian would be on a bus to wherever.

The rain had intensified, hampering her visibility and forcing her to drive slowly. But even with the reduced speed, it took her no more than eight minutes to reach Lake Carnegie. During the day, this section of Route 27 was heavily traveled, but tonight, due to the rain and the late hour, it was relatively quiet.

Several large boulders marked the entrance to the parking area. Abbie made the wide turn, brought the Acura to a crawl and peered through the wet windshield in search of Ian. To her left was the boathouse where the university rowing team kept their gear, and straight ahead was a densely wooded area that extended from the water's edge to the road.

Ian was nowhere in sight.

She inched the truck closer to the trees and stopped. With one hand on her purse so she could quickly get to her gun if she had to, she pressed a button on the door panel. The window on the driver's side slid down noiselessly. She stopped it halfway and stuck her head out. "Ian," she called out. "Are you there?"

No answer.

Her mouth dry, she glanced at the clock on the dash. She was a few minutes late, but surely he would have waited.

A pair of headlights suddenly appeared around the bend, and for a moment she thought the car was slowing down. Worried it might be a state trooper in an unmarked car, she turned off her lights. She didn't want to have to explain to a police officer what she was doing here at this time of night and in this weather. She waited until the car drove off before calling Ian's name again.

Nothing.

She was debating whether or not to stay, when a man lunged at her truck. His right hand gripped the window, while the left held a knife.

Abbie's heart lurched in her chest and she let out a scream. As she pulled back, her fingers searched frantically for the window button.

"Where's the money?" The man tried to open the driver's door and became even more enraged when he realized it was locked. "Give me the fucking money!"

Abbie finally found the button, but her attacker held the window down with such force that it didn't budge an inch.

The gun, Abbie. Get out the gun.

Her right hand went inside her purse and found the PPK. "Get away," she screamed as she released the safety. "I have a gun and I will use it!"

"Give me the money, you bitch!" The man stuck the knife through the window, slashing it in the air, back and forth. With each stroke, the blade seemed to get closer to Abbie's face.

Pull the trigger!

The words her instructors had said to her over and over flashed through her head. "Never pull out a gun you don't intend to fire—your opponent will see your fear, take your gun and use it against you."

She could do this. She would not be a victim.

Her attacker's arm was inside the car, trying to snatch the gun from her. With a scream, Abbie yanked her hand back. She threw the weapon on the seat next to her. Fighting this maniac was out of the question. Her priority right now was to get out of here.

Slapping the gearshift into drive, she slammed her foot on the gas pedal. The Acura shot forward and she started to swerve right and left in an attempt to get her attacker to let go.

But he held on. "Give me the money!" This time the blade whooshed by her cheek and grazed her hair.

She screamed again, but didn't lose her hold on the steering wheel. She kept swerving, and although she could see the man's body being jerked around, he wouldn't let go. At one point, she almost drove into the water, then quickly realized where she was and brought the SUV back onto firm ground.

The rain beat furiously now, running down from the man's bald head onto his face, making him look more like a beast than a human being. Desperate to get away from him, Abbie gunned the engine, pressing her foot to the floorboard as far as it would go and sped across the length of the parking area. Then, just as suddenly, she jammed her foot on the brake, bracing herself for the snap of the seat belt around her chest.

She saw the look of surprise on the man's face as the jolt knocked him off. Not waiting for him to get back on his feet, she put the Acura into reverse, then drive, and took off. Before exiting the parking area, she glanced back and saw her attacker sprawled out on the ground, motionless.

Dear God, had she killed him?

She kept on driving, heading for home, but by the time she reached the traffic light at the corner of Nassau Street and Vandeventer, the adrenaline that had kept her going through the past few minutes had drained out of her, leaving her trembling from head to toe.

She couldn't go any farther. The thought she may have killed a man was almost paralyzing. But he had attacked her! With a knife. Given the chance, he would have killed her. So why was she worrying about his fate instead of counting her blessings that she was still alive?

The light turned green, but instead of heading toward home, she made a U-turn and headed back toward the lake. She had to see if he was dead, although she had no idea what she would do if he was. Hopefully he would only be hurt, in which case she would call for help and hang up before anyone had a chance to ask for her name.

This time she kept her window rolled up. No matter how badly the man was hurt, she would not allow herself to get within striking distance of him. She stopped the car and scanned the area, staring at the spot where he had fallen. It was empty.

The man had vanished.

Leaning back against her seat, she heaved a sigh of relief. If he had walked away of his own free will, then he must be all right. She hadn't harmed him.

Thank you, God.

Shaken but relieved, she turned the truck around, retraced the route she had taken a moment earlier and drove home, this time without stopping.

"You killed him?"

Tony stared at Arturo in total disbelief. "You killed McGregor?"

Dripping wet from the heavy rain, Arturo threw the truck keys on the bed. "What the fuck did you want me to do? The son of a bitch tried to kill me first. Take a look at this if you don't believe me." He yanked down his T-shirt.

Tony saw the raw red gash around Arturo's neck. "How did he do that?"

"The bastard had a garrote with him. Can you believe it? He was planning to kill me all along."

"So you killed him? Couldn't you just have knocked him out or something? How hard could that be? You're twice his size."

Arturo started to pace the small room, his giant stride covering the width of the living area in just a few steps. "He tricked me! He made a fool out of me, man, pretending he had to take a piss, and the whole time he was making that damn garrote."

Tony sank into a chair, wishing he'd had the foresight to go to McGregor's motel room with Arturo. He should have known something would go wrong. It always did with Arturo. Trouble had a way of following him like a lost puppy.

But murder?

He watched his brother walk over to a cabinet, uncap a bottle of rum and take a long drink, right out of the bottle. "That woman." Tony spoke calmly, reminding himself he was the strong one, the sensible one. "McGregor's sister. Did she have a good look at you?"

"Hell, yes. The bitch pulled a gun on me."

"So she can identify you."

Arturo took another swig of the liquor and didn't answer.

"What about the truck?"

"What about it?"

"Did anyone see you drive out of the motel parking lot?"

"How the hell should I know?"

"Did you see anyone?" Tony asked patiently.

"I wasn't paying attention. I had other things on my mind."

Tony picked up his cell phone, remembering what Enrique had said about his calls being forwarded to the house. Hopefully he'd be home.

Arturo gave him a dark look. "What are you doing?"

"Calling Enrique. We have to get the truck off the street, just in case someone saw it."

"Enrique ain't home."

Tony flicked his phone off. "How do you know?"

"Because I'm not as stupid as you think I am. I knew I'd have to hide the truck, so I called him. His grandfather said he was out on a date and wouldn't be back until late."

"You stopped to make a call after you killed McGregor? Are you nuts?"

"I didn't stop. I used this." He took out a cell phone from his pocket and set it on the table in front of Tony.

"What's that?"

Arturo laughed as if he had just done something incredibly clever. "McGregor's cell phone. I took it from him." He pulled a wad of bills from his pocket. "And this. Four C's and some change, man. The bastard wasn't as broke as we thought."

But Tony wasn't looking at the money. He was looking at the cell phone. "You used McGregor's phone to make a call?"

Arturo gave him a blank look.

"Don't you get it? The call can be traced. Once the police find out the phone is missing, they can get hold of the phone records."

"And who's gonna report it missing, bright boy? A dead man?"

"How about Rose? She had to know Ian had a cell phone."

Arturo fell silent. Without a word, Tony took the phone from the table and wiped it clean. Then he walked over to the closet and dropped it in his duffel bag.

"I'll get rid of it in the morning. In the meantime, don't touch it. And don't answer it if it rings. You hear me?"

Looking relieved now that Tony was handling all the details, Arturo meekly nodded.

"I'll call Enrique in the morning," Tony continued. "Right now, take the truck off the street and park it behind the garage."

"You're not going to tell Enrique I killed a man, are you?"

"No. I'll make up a reason why we need to hide the truck."

"And then what do we do?"

Funny, Tony thought, now that Arturo was in serious trouble, he used "we" instead of "I."

"We lay low and wait for the heat to cool. When it's safe to leave, we'll leave."

"I ain't goin' nowhere until I get my money."

Tony felt like grabbing that bottle from Arturo's hand and using it to knock some sense into that thick skull of his. "And how are you going to do that? You plan to kill McGregor's sister, too?"

"I'll do what I have to do to get my money back."

"It's not your money!"

"She was going to give it to McGregor, wasn't she? Now she can give it to me." He brought the bottle to his mouth again. "And she will, if she knows what's good for her."

Abbie stood on rubbery legs and waited until Tiffany had driven away, before closing the door and leaning against it. The events of the last thirty minutes kept replaying in her head in vivid, frightening details, and although her heartbeat had finally returned to normal, she was still filled with too many conflicting emotions to think clearly.

Something had gone terribly wrong at the lake, but

what? Where was Ian? Who was that man who had attacked her, demanding the money? Obviously he had known about the payoff or he wouldn't have been there. He may even have been the reason Ian had called her in that urgent tone earlier, whispering new instructions. Yet, a man she knew nothing about had ended up at the meeting place instead of Ian.

She ruled out the possibility the man was Earl Kramer. The death-row inmate was as likely to have escaped from prison in the last twenty-four hours as she was of jumping off the Stony Brook Bridge.

But if not Kramer, then who had been willing to kill her just to get his hands on that money? And how was she going to find out?

Sixteen

Homicide Detective John Ryan had to circle FitzRandolph Academy three times before finally finding a parking space. He could have double-parked, the way most cops did when they needed to get somewhere in a hurry, but this was his son's school and it wouldn't bode well for an advocate of law and order to break the rules.

Hands in his pockets, he stood for a moment, gazing at the sprawling three-story brick building with the well-known logo above the entrance—the profile of Nathaniel FitzRandolph, an eighteenth-century landowner and one of the town's early benefactors.

Although the school was indisputably one of the best learning establishments on the East Coast, John hadn't been in favor of sending his son to a private institution. Old-fashioned by nature, he was a strong believer that a well-rounded education could only come from a public school. But his wife—ex-wife, now—had been adamant that Jordan needed structure and discipline, something she claimed public schools did not provide. The problem was, Jordan wasn't happy here, and it was beginning to show. This was John's second visit to the headmistress this year. The first, in January, had been in regard to Jordan's failure to turn in his homework. And now, the energetic nine-year-old had apparently punched a classmate in the nose. Clarice had been notified as well, and would call him as soon as she could get a moment. God forbid she should leave in the middle of an important meeting.

John started toward the main entrance. In spite of what Clarice thought, Jordan was not a difficult boy. He was a little more passionate than most about the things he cared about and that occasionally got him in trouble, but other than that he was a good kid.

Knowing that children of divorced parents needed more attention than most, John spent as much time as possible with Jordan. He took him fishing, picked him up after school on his days off and coached his baseball team whenever he could squeeze in a couple of free hours between shifts.

For a while after he and Clarice had agreed to split up, he had considered filing for custody, partly because he liked the idea of having Jordan with him full-time, and partly because Clarice's schedule wasn't much better than his. In fact, it was worse. As the newly appointed vice president of a pharmaceutical firm, her life was a series of meetings, seminars and sales conferences that often took her out of town for days.

Those absences had been the subject of constant bickering between the two of them. John had felt she should spend more time with Jordan, and Clarice accused him of not understanding how important her career was to her. "Every bit as important as yours is to you," she had told him, missing the point entirely.

In front of the glass door, he took a moment to check his appearance, in anticipation of Mrs. Rhinehart's own eagle-eyed inspection. He ran a hand through his black hair, glad he had remembered to get a haircut. He was so busy these days that he often let that part of his grooming go until his captain gave him a stern reminder. His gaze drifted down. The navy blazer and gray trousers were just out of the cleaner's, and the open-neck white shirt crisp enough to please the most discriminating of headmistresses.

Satisfied he wouldn't embarrass his nine-year-old son, he pushed the door open and walked in. Although school would be out at ten today due to a teachers' conference, the halls were empty when John walked through the glass-domed entrance. Remembering the location of the head-mistress's office, he turned right and headed toward the administrative wing, wondering what could have prompted Jordan, a relatively gentle soul, to hit a classmate. Well, he'd know soon enough.

Mrs. Rhinehart was at her desk, sorting through a stack of correspondence, when John knocked on her door, which she had left ajar. She was a fairly attractive woman whose rather dour expression and stiff demeanor discouraged the slightest pleasantry.

She waved him in. "Come on in, Mr. Ryan. Please have a seat." She had made it a point, from the very first visit, not to call him "detective," explaining that the philosophy at FitzRandoph was to treat all parents as equals. That was fine with him; he had never been big on titles.

"Thank you." The words "What has he done now?" almost slipped out, but he stopped himself in time, allowing her to speak first. He was beginning to get the hang of that private-school stuff.

Mrs. Rhinehart pushed her papers aside and rested her arms on the desk surface, looking at him above the center line of her bifocals. "Do you box, Mr. Ryan?"

Since she had obviously meant it as a serious question, John tried to keep an appropriate demeanor. "I did, in my younger days." At her slightly disapproving look, he added, "But I haven't put on a pair of gloves in at least twenty years."

His attempt at a little humor seemed to make matters

worse. "I was wondering where Jordan had learned his technique." She surprised him with her next remark, although it was delivered with the utmost gravity. "To quote one of your son's friends, who was an eyewitness to the incident, 'Jordan's got a killer right hook.'"

John felt an involuntary rush of fatherly pride. During the first six years of his life, Jordan had been painfully thin and the object of many cruel jokes, in and out of school. One day, unable to take the humiliation any longer, he had lunged at one of the boys who had called him "bread stick," only to have the boy retaliate mercilessly. When Jordan had come home sobbing and bloody, John had taken him out in the backyard and taught him a few moves. Soon afterward, the same bully, certain he'd score an easy victory, had instigated another fight. This time, he was the one who had run home crying.

That's when Clarice had decided her son was turning into a bully and it was time to put him in a private school.

The expression on Mrs. Rhinehart's face, however, reminded John this was no laughing matter. "May I ask what brought on the fight?"

"Some silly argument about baseball icons." Her tone made it clear she didn't think much of baseball. "I didn't go into it, Mr. Ryan. The reason for the fight is not important. I must mention, however, that the other boy threw the first punch, which is the reason I'm not suspending Jordan. But he did hurt his classmate, and for that I must put him on probation. One more incident like this one, regardless of who starts the fight, and I *will* suspend him."

Although John had turned thirty-nine two months ago, under that unyielding gaze, he felt ten years old. "How's the other boy?" he asked.

"In pain, although I'm glad to say his nose is not broken." She paused, her eyes still on John. "I know you and

Mrs. Ryan have been divorced for a couple of years now, but I was wondering if there had been any changes in Jordan's life recently. I'm not prying,'' she added. ''I'm just trying to find a reason for the boy's sudden aggressiveness.''

John sighed. There was no avoiding responsibilities here. He was just as guilty as Clarice. ''His mother is out on the road a lot,'' he said. ''And I've been working long hours.''

''Where does Jordan go when his mother is away?''

''He stays with me. Or his mother makes arrangements with a neighbor who has a boy his age.''

Mrs. Rhinehart nodded. ''Has he expressed displeasure over those arrangements?''

''Not to me.''

''A lack of active parenting could be the base of the problem,'' she continued, sounding more like a psychologist than an educator. John's reaction must have shown, because she immediately raised her hand. ''I'm not accusing you or Mrs. Ryan of being bad parents. I'm merely suggesting that children of Jordan's age need their parents much more than a teenager would. Jordan could be lonely, or homesick for the life he used to have when both you and your former wife lived together. The symptoms may not be apparent at first, but sooner or later, they manifest themselves. In your son's case, I believe they already have. He wants attention, Mr. Ryan, and if he can't get it the standard way, he'll get it any way he can.''

''By fighting with a classmate?''

Mrs. Rhinehart gave a light shrug. ''It got you here, didn't it?''

She had a point. ''I'll talk to him, Mrs. Rhinehart. And I promise you this will not happen again.''

''Good. In the meantime, perhaps you and your wife could reevaluate your respective schedules? See how you might be able to fit in an extra hour or two each day for your son?''

It was as close to a reprimand as he had ever gotten, but she had driven her point home. Changes would have to be made.

When the bell rang at ten o'clock sharp, Jordan was the first one out of his classroom. Tall for his age, and still slender, he had filled out nicely in the last two years, gaining the kind of confidence he had so desperately needed. His thick black hair was a little mussed, maybe from the fight, but by some strange miracle his navy-blue uniform didn't have a spot or a tear in it. Either the fight had been stopped at an early stage, or fighting was not what it used to be when John was a boy.

Looking sheepish, Jordan raised a tentative hand in a wave, but instead of running toward his father the way he usually did, he walked slowly, studying John's expression with a look of apprehension in his big blue eyes.

''Hi, Dad.'' He stopped in front of John, gave a tug to the straps of his backpack and looked up. One thing about Jordan, no matter what trouble he got himself into, he was never afraid to look John in the eye. ''You talked to Mrs. Rhinehart?''

''I just left her.''

''Am I suspended?''

''No, but there better not be a repeat of this incident, kiddo, or you will be. And we don't want that, do we?''

''No.''

They didn't say anything more until they were inside John's car, a black Plymouth he used on and off duty. Once Jordan was buckled up, John turned in his seat. ''So, you want to tell me what happened?''

''Well—'' Jordan swiveled to face his father ''—there's

this kid in my class who thinks he knows everything about baseball.''

John felt a tug at the corner of his mouth. "I thought that title belonged to you."

"I know a lot more than he does, Dad."

John didn't doubt that. Jordan lived and breathed baseball. And when it came to facts, he was a walking encyclopedia. "What did he say that ticked you off?"

"He said that Lou Gehrig still held the record for consecutive games played, when everybody *knows* that Cal Ripken now holds that record."

"And that's what you fought over?"

"I wasn't going to, but he hit me first, so I hit him back. That's what you told me to do, right, Dad?" Serious eyes studied John's face. "You said I could defend myself."

"Yes," he said, not sure Mrs. Rhinehart would approve. "I did tell you that, but did you have to hit him so hard?"

"I didn't, Dad, I swear. I can't help it if he's got a glass nose. Besides," Jordan added with a touch of scorn in his voice, "he made a big deal out of nothing. His teacher told him to tilt his head back so the blood wouldn't gush out, but Tim wouldn't do it. He let it run all over his mouth, making it look a lot worse than it was." Jordan made a disgusted sound. "He wailed like a girl."

John wasn't sure how he managed to keep a straight face. "He was probably in a lot of pain," he offered, starting the car. "Apparently you hit him with a pretty solid right hook. It's a wonder you didn't break his nose."

Jordan, who didn't have a malicious bone in his body, nodded as he looked out the side window. "I know. When I heard him scream and saw all that blood coming out, I felt bad."

John reached over and tousled the boy's hair. "Just promise me you won't let something like that happen again. The moment you realize a fight is coming, you walk away.''

"But wouldn't that make me a coward?"

"There's nothing cowardly about walking away from an argument, especially if you know you can hurt the other person."

Jordan swung his head from one side to the other, which was his way of saying he didn't like the suggestion but would give it some thought.

At that moment, John's cell phone rang. "That will be your mom," he said, taking the phone from the cradle beside the gearshift. "Hello?"

"John, what's going on?" Clarice said in an agitated voice. "What did Jordan do? Where is he? Is he hurt? Mrs. Rhinehart only said he had been in a fight."

"Jordan's fine, Clarice. He's right here with me in the car." Before she could embark on a new string of questions, he added, "I'm taking him to my place. Why don't you meet us there?"

As John hung up, Jordan threw him a worried look. "Is she mad?"

"More worried than mad. Expect to be grounded, though. You know how your mother feels about fighting."

Ten minutes later, as he approached his town house on Terhune Road, he saw Clarice waiting by his front door. Though she had just celebrated her thirty-eighth birthday and complained her looks were quickly vanishing, she was still a beautiful woman. She had wide green eyes that could go from friendly to frosty in a microsecond, blond hair she always wore neatly clipped at the back of her neck, and a figure she kept trim and fit with regular visits to the gym.

"Well, Jordan," she said as father and son approached. "What do you have to say for yourself?" The look she gave John left no doubt that she would somehow find a way to blame him for today's incident.

"Please, Clarice, let's not give the neighbors a free show, okay?" John opened the door to the town house and moved aside to let her in.

As usual, the place was a mess. Standing on the threshold, Clarice let her gaze sweep across the living room, furnished with contemporary, comfortable furniture. She took in the newspapers scattered on the coffee table, the empty coffee mug next to it and the pile of shirts John had meant to take to the laundry but hadn't gotten around to because he'd been called on a homicide in the middle of the night.

To her credit, she said nothing. She only let out a small resigned sigh, as though she had finally accepted his lifestyle, now that she was no longer a part of it, and folded her arms. "Now can I find out what happened?"

John repeated what Mrs. Rhinehart had told him, stressing the fact that Jordan had not started the fight but had merely defended himself.

"And that makes it all right with you?"

John turned to Jordan. "Why don't you go to the kitchen and get started on that homework, kiddo. If you're hungry, there's a pack of Oreos in the cupboard. And milk in the fridge. But smell it first," he added as an afterthought.

He glanced back at his ex-wife in time to see her roll her eyes. John's eating habits, which she deemed deplorable, were another pet peeve of hers. "Now," he said, pointing to a brown leather sofa, "why don't we do this the civilized way and sit down."

Her high heels clacked on the hardwood floor as she marched toward the sofa. She sat on the edge, as if afraid to get too comfortable, her legs pressed together, her hands folded on her lap. She was ready for battle. "This is your fault, you know," she said, breaking all previous time records in the "blame John" category. "You taught him that in order to survive, one had to resort to violence."

In the old days, he would have snapped a sharp reply, but he had learned that tit for tat accomplished little. And Jordan was in the next room, probably listening to every word. "I taught him how to defend himself," John said patiently, even though he had said those same words a million times. "Which is what he did today."

"He could have broken the boy's nose."

"Would you prefer if *he* had been the one with the broken nose?"

"I would prefer if he used words instead of his fists."

"Words don't do much good when you're being pounded on. Believe me, I've been there."

Clarice was silent for a while, as though weighing what he had just told her. When she spoke again, the frost in her voice matched the one in her eyes. "I want to send him to military school. I've been meaning to discuss—"

John sprang out of his chair then sat back down, aware that an outburst would be heard from the kitchen. "Over my dead body," he said between clenched teeth.

"Jordan needs structure, John. He needs discipline and focus. He needs to learn how to follow rules and get along with others."

"He gets along with others just fine. As for structure, discipline and rules, he doesn't have a problem when he's with me. All he needs is to know he's loved."

"I do love him. You know that."

"Then show him you do, Clarice. Spend more time with him. Take him to a movie once in a while, or to one of his games. Grab a handful of his friends and take them all out for a bike ride. How hard can that be?"

Color rushed to Clarice's cheeks. "I'm doing the best I can, John," she said stiffly. "I have a job, too, you know."

And I'm paying you enough money to stay home, dammit. But he didn't say that. Why start World War III?

"Look," she continued, determined to settle the matter here and now. "I've already checked out several schools. Brandywine Military Academy in Philadelphia comes highly recommended. The tuition is high, and I don't expect you to pay all of it—"

"Stop right there. You know I don't care about the money. I'll gladly double the child support payments, if that's what you want, but military school is out of the question. The boy is nine years old, for God's sake. These are his formative years. He needs his parents not a drill sergeant."

Clarice's thin lips tightened. An authority in marital discord, she was smart enough to know when a battle had been lost. Not one to take defeat gracefully, however, she would simply retreat and rethink her strategy before attacking again. For the time being, she just averted her eyes and called out Jordan's name to let him know they were leaving.

John walked them to the door, an arm around his son's shoulders. "See you at the game on Sunday?"

Jordan looked up, his expression only half-hopeful. "I thought you were working this weekend."

"I am, but I'm planning to take the afternoon off so I can come and watch you play."

The grin on his son's face was all the reward John needed. Maybe General Rhinehart had more insight into this parenting thing than he had given her credit for.

Clarice's BMW had just pulled out of his driveway, when his phone rang. It was Officer Wilcox of the township police. The officer got straight to the point.

"We found a body."

Seventeen

Since its opening date in 1906, Lake Carnegie had been the sight of many aquatic sports—canoeing, sailing, windsurfing, and of course, intercollegiate rowing. John's great-grandfather, a graduate of Princeton University, had been one of the school's first rowers to use the long-awaited boathouse after it was built in 1913. Never in the lake's ninety-seven-year history had it been the scene of a murder.

A light rain had begun falling again, turning the June morning damp and dreary. The inclement weather had kept boaters away except for a lone sculler, a college sophomore practicing for an upcoming race. The university student, whom John had already questioned, had just taken his scull out of the boathouse when he had spotted the body at the edge of the woods.

The area had been cordoned off with yellow police tape. On the road, a uniformed officer was trying to move motorists along and keep gawkers at bay. Two crime scene techs were already at work, walking inside the sealed off area in search of evidence, tagging things and not paying attention to John.

"What can you tell me about the victim?" John asked the uniformed officer standing beside him.

Dave Wilcox was an eighteen-year veteran and as shrewd as any detective in the department, which was the reason John had encouraged him to take his detective test next fall.

"Caucasian male by the name of Ian McGregor," Wilcox replied without looking at his notes. "Forty-three years old, according to an expired driver's license issued in Toledo, Ohio. Cause of death seems to be multiple stab wounds to the abdomen. A clothes hanger shaped into a garrote was found near the body, along with a key from the Clearwater Motel. That's down the road a ways."

John nodded. He knew the place. "Found the murder weapon?"

"Not yet, but there are tire tracks and footprints all over the place." They started walking toward a large area of the parking lot where one of the CS techs had started to spray the tire tracks with a special fixative.

The man looked up when John approached. "Looks like an SUV, Detective." He pointed at the tracks going in all directions. "Some kids showing off. Or maybe someone tried to run the victim down."

John studied the tracks spread over a circumference of twenty to thirty feet. The tech's last assumption made more sense to him than the first, but if someone had tried to run the victim down, how had McGregor ended up in the woods, stabbed? On the other hand, if kids had been here, they may have seen or heard something. Ditto for the houses along the road, he thought, looking up at the handful of homes overlooking the lake.

"Let me know what you find out."

"Sure thing, Detective."

Ignoring the nagging drizzle, John walked toward the medical examiner kneeling over the body. Frank Wang was a small, almost frail-looking Chinese-American, with sallow skin, graying brown hair and tired eyes that had seen too much. He and John had been together the previous night, when both had been called to the scene of another homicide.

"What's up, Frank?" John asked.

Wrapped in a yellow rubber poncho, the ME looked up. "Don't you ever sleep?"

"I could ask you the same question."

Frank gave a disapproving shake of his head. As a doctor, he was a strong advocate of the eight-hours' sleep doctrine, even though he seldom took his own advice.

John looked at the victim lying on the wet ground, the sharp, almost angular features, the straight nose, the dark hair that formed a widow's peak at the center of his forehead. He wore a navy polo shirt that was now stained with blood and blue jeans. Black sneakers completed the outfit. "Dave says the victim was stabbed?"

The ME nodded. "Multiple wounds to the abdomen. Massive internal bleeding. Time of death estimated between eight last night and midnight. I can't come any closer than that until I do an autopsy because of the body's exposure to rain and the drop in temperature."

"Any clues on the killer? Male? Female?"

"Probably male. The wounds were inflicted at an upward angle and in rapid succession. A female attacker, as you know, would have held the knife with a fist grip, like an ice pick, and stabbed in a downward motion."

John nodded. He knew from past cases that women who chose to kill with a knife held their weapon differently from the way men did. They simply didn't have the kind of strength that was required to strike in an upward motion, over and over, as was the case here. "How soon can you schedule an autopsy?"

"Two-thirty soon enough?"

John smiled. "You're an amazing man, Frank. I'll see you then."

As he walked away, he glanced toward the row of houses that bordered this section of Route 27 and made a mental note to question their occupants before the end of the day.

Right now he had to find out if Ian McGregor had a wife and kids waiting for him at the Clearwater.

The Clearwater Motel, no more than three blocks from the crime scene, was a one-story concrete building with a road sign advertising free cable TV and in-room coffee.

The desk clerk was reading the sports section of the *Princeton Packet* when John stepped into the small lobby. A freestanding reception desk, a green plant, a vending machine and a color poster of Princeton University were the room's only accessories. At the sound of footsteps, the clerk looked up. "Can I help you?"

John held out his badge. "Is the manager in?"

The man's attitude improved quickly as he folded his newspaper, almost snapping to attention. "I'm the manager. Name's Rudy Walsh." He smiled, showing a chipped front tooth. "What can I do for you, Detective?"

"You have a guest registered here, a man by the name of Ian MacGregor ?"

The manager hesitated. "McGregor?" he repeated.

"That's what I said. Is he registered?"

"Name doesn't ring a bell offhand, but let me check." He turned to the computer monitor on the right side of his desk and hit a few keys. "Nope. No one by that name."

John held up a small plastic bag with the motel key in it. "Why don't you see who's in room 11?"

Looking increasingly nervous, Walsh punched two more keys. "Here we are. A double room, but it's registered to a Ms. Rose Panini." As he talked he swung the monitor around so John could see the entry.

John read the registration with Rose Panini's name on it. "Anyone come in asking for either of those two?"

Walsh's Adam's apple moved up and down. "No."

"Why don't I believe you?"

The man, so relaxed a moment ago, shot a nervous look at the door, even though there was no one there. "I don't know. I told you the truth."

"Look, Mr. Walsh," John said patiently, "I'd rather save time and talk to you here, but I can just as easily talk to you at the police station. Which one is it going to be?"

Walsh swallowed again, with greater difficulty this time. "I don't want to get in trouble with...anyone."

"By *anyone,* you mean someone other than the police?"

He gave a faint nod.

Realizing the man was scared, John spoke in a gentler tone. "Did someone come here and asked for Ian McGregor?"

"Yes."

"Did he give a name?"

"No. He just said he was an old friend of Mr. McGregor's."

"Describe him, please."

"He was big, maybe six-five. Two hundred and fifty pounds. Or more. His head was shaved and he had tattoos on both arms." Beads of perspiration had formed above his upper lip. "He said he'd kill me if I didn't give him his friend's room number."

"Did you see him go into Mr. McGregor's room?"

Walsh shook his head. "He told me to stay put and not say a word to anyone, and that's what I did."

"When was that?"

"About two-thirty yesterday afternoon."

"Did you happen to see what he was driving?"

"No. I was reading the paper when he came in. I looked

up, and there he was, big as a house." He wet his lips. "Will I have to...you know...testify about this?"

"We're not there yet, but if the time comes for you to testify, we'll make sure you have adequate protection." He gave a reassuring smile. "All right?"

Some of Walsh's color returned to his cheeks. "Yes. That's what I wanted to know. Thank you."

John put the bag with the key back in his pocket. "Is Ms. Panini in her room?"

"I don't know. She came in earlier to get a soda." He pointed at the vending machine. "I haven't seen her since." Relief made him suddenly gabby. "What's going on, Detective? What have they done?"

"Where is room 11?" John asked, ignoring the man's question.

"Last one at the end of the building."

An old but well-maintained Oldsmobile with Ohio plates was parked in front of it. John knocked and a couple of seconds later, the door was flung open. A rather flamboyant-looking woman stood looking at him, an angry expression on her face. She was in her mid-to-late forties, with bright-red hair and a voluminous bosom. Her eyes would have been unnoticeable were it not for the frosted turquoise shadow and the dark liner around them. She wore tight jeans and a vibrant-red blouse knotted at the waist.

"Ms. Panini?"

"That's me."

"I'm John Ryan of the township police." He held his badge long enough for her to verify his identity and was surprised when she let out a long-suffering sigh.

"All right, where did you find the bum? Drunk in some gutter? Because if that's the case and he wants me to bail him out, tell him to forget it. He can stew in jail for the rest of his life for all I care."

"May I come in?" he asked gently.

Rose Panini's expression immediately went from angry to worried. She moved aside and quickly closed the door. "What happened?" There was a slight tremor in her voice.

John's gaze swept quickly over the room, his trained eye picking up the Styrofoam cooler against the wall, an empty pizza box folded in two and shoved into the wastebasket, the Diet Pepsi on the nightstand. Next to it were two other items—a man's gray wig and a matching mustache. "Are you Ian McGregor's wife?" he asked.

"Girlfriend." Her expressive face was beginning to show signs of alarm. "Where is Ian? Has something happened to him?"

In spite of her flashy makeup and no-nonsense attitude, there was something touching about this woman, a vulnerability that contrasted sharply with her outside persona. "I'm afraid so, Ms. Panini."

Her hands went to cover her mouth. "Oh my God, what?" she asked, talking through her hands. "Is he hurt? How bad?"

There was no easy way of saying this. There never was. "His body was found half an hour ago in a wooded area bordering Lake Carnegie."

"Body?" She whispered the word as though she had never heard it before. "You mean…"

"I'm sorry, Ms. Panini—Rose. May I call you Rose?"

She didn't answer. She let herself plop down on the bed, and looked at him with a dazed expression. "It's not true. It can't be true." She searched John's face as though she expected him to concur.

"Can I get you anything?" he said instead. "Some water?"

She shook her head, then, with a small cry, she covered her face with her hands and sobbed quietly. John had seen that kind of despair time and time again during his thirteen years on the force. Each time the raw, uncontrollable grief hit him hard. In his early rookie days he had even considered changing careers, and put to good use that master's in criminal psychology he had worked so hard for. Each time he had talked himself out of it. Law enforcement was as much a part of who he was as his DNA.

As Rose Panini's sobs began to subside, he took a crisp, white handkerchief from his pants back pocket and handed it to her.

"Thanks." She blotted her eyes, sniffed a couple of times. "How did he die?"

"He was stabbed."

For a moment, he thought she would start sobbing all over again, but she didn't. Making what looked like a valiant effort to hold herself together, she gave a sad, almost fatalistic shake of her head. "He got him," she said simply.

John's ears perked up. "You know who killed him?"

She looked up. Her eyes were red, her cheeks already blotchy, her lipstick smeared. "Arturo Garcia. Ian had just found out he was looking for him."

John had never heard of Arturo Garcia, but that didn't mean anything. "Do you know what this Arturo Garcia looks like?"

She shook her head. "I've never had the pleasure," she said sarcastically. "But Ian said he was big and mean."

Walsh's visitor. "Why would he want to kill Ian?"

"Because Ian ratted on him in exchange for immunity. His testimony sent Arturo to prison for eight years."

"What was their connection?"

"Ian worked for Arturo in Toledo." She hesitated before adding, "He was a courier."

"Courier?"

"He delivered drugs for him for about two years, until

he was arrested and offered the immunity deal in exchange for the goods on Arturo, who ran the drug distribution center. Arturo swore that when he got out, he'd hill him. Ian was scared to death of him. That's why he used my name on the motel registration.'' She walked over to the nightstand and picked up the wig. ''And probably why he bought this stupid thing. And the mustache to go with it.''

John took the wig and turned it around in his hands. ''If he was so scared, why wasn't he wearing the disguise when we found him?''

''I don't know.''

John remembered the expired driver's license in the man's pocket and the absence of other identification. ''Was Ian in prison recently?''

Rose nodded. ''He just got out after serving sixteen months for breaking and entering.'' A small laugh turned into a sob. ''Ian and I were going to start a new life together, get jobs, find a place to live.''

''Here in Princeton?''

''We hadn't decided that. Ian came to reunite with his stepsister. He hadn't seen her in twenty-eight years.''

''What's his sister's name?''

''DiAngelo. Abbie DiAngelo. She has a restaurant on Palmer Square.''

John knew the name. He had never met the restaurant owner, but she had been the talk of the town a few weeks ago when she had returned from France with a culinary award. Other details such as her marital status—she was divorced—had been supplied by Jordan, who played in the same baseball league as Ms. DiAngelo's son, Ben, and was good friends with the boy.

''You said they hadn't seen each other in twenty-eight years. Why is that?''

''When Ian was thirteen, his father married a woman by

the name of Irene DiAngelo—Abbie's mother. Two years later, a fire destroyed the McGregors' home in Palo Alto, California. Ian and his biological sister went to live with their father's sister, and his stepmother and stepsister moved back to Irene's home state—someplace in the Midwest, I think.''

''How did the reunion with the stepsister go?''

''Not well,'' Rose admitted. ''At least at first. From what Ian told me, Abbie wasn't too pleased to see him.''

''Why not?''

''Probably because he wanted to borrow money. Although, in the end, she agreed to help him out.''

Help out a stepbrother she hadn't seen or talked to in twenty-eight years? That was something worth checking into. ''Do you know where Ian's other sister is?''

''New York. She bartends at the Manhattan Towers. Ian went to see her on Wednesday.''

Ian McGregor had been a busy man in the short time he had been in town.

Rose's eyes filled again. ''What about the...body?''

''It will be released to you once we're done with the autopsy. But before we do that, you'll need to make a formal identification.''

She blanched at the thought. ''When?''

''How about two o'clock? I'll be glad to send someone to pick you up and bring you back.''

''That's when my shift starts, but I'll ask for today off. I don't much feel like going to work anyway.'' Then in a small voice, she asked, ''Will you be there? When I identify the body?''

John nodded. ''Where do you work, Rose?''

''I'm a waitress at the Golden Diner on Route 1. I just started a couple of days ago. I took the 2:00 p.m. to midnight shift to make some extra money.''

"So, when you came home last night, Ian wasn't here."

"That's right."

"Didn't you find that unusual?"

"No. Ian hated to be cooped up. Did too much of that in prison. He liked to go out and have a few beers, but he's never stayed out an entire night. When I woke up this morning and saw he still wasn't here, I thought he had gone on a binge. That's why I was a little short with you a while ago." She sniffed into the handkerchief. "Sorry about that."

"That's all right." John lay his notebook on the dresser. "There was no sign of struggle in the room?"

"No, although..." She stopped.

"What?"

"In the bathroom." Her gaze swung back in that direction. "I had left my nightgown hanging on the shower rod to dry. When I got home, the nightgown was on the floor and the hanger was gone."

That explained the garrote Dave had found near the body. It was possible McGregor had meant to use it as a weapon, but against whom?

He pointed at the wastebasket with the pizza box in it. "His dinner or yours?"

"His. I eat at the diner."

Using a tissue, John took the box out of the trash and wrote the name and phone number of the pizzeria in his notebook. "Pretty large pie for just one person," he commented. "Was Ian in the habit of eating a whole pizza all by himself?"

Rose frowned. "Heavens, no. Three slices at the most." Her eyes opened wide, registering instant fear. "Oh my God, you think there was someone here with him? The killer?"

"We'll know soon enough." He took out his cell phone

and dialed Max Castelano, the CS tech he had talked to at the lake. "Are you almost done there?" he asked when Max answered.

"Just about, why?"

"I need you and the other tech to come to the Clearwater Motel, room 11 and dust for prints."

"I'll be there in five."

"Thanks, Max." He folded the phone and saw that Rose was watching him. "Something wrong?"

"My phone," she said, meeting his gaze. "I had a cell phone Ian was using. Did you find it?"

John took out his notebook again. "No." He started writing. "Do you know the number?"

She recited it from memory and he wrote it down before snapping his book shut. "I'll check it out. And I'll send someone to pick you up at two."

"Thank you."

The two CS technicians arrived a few minutes later, and John quickly got out of their way. Back in the car, he checked his watch. It was almost noon and he hadn't had anything to eat since that burger at three o'clock the previous afternoon. No wonder that pizza box in the wastebasket had made him salivate. Normally he'd content himself with some form of fast food and eat at his desk, but not today. Today, he would treat himself to something different, something special. And since he was a lovable kind of guy, he would take Tina with him.

Eighteen

Abbie was an emotional wreck. And looked it, she thought, catching a glimpse of herself in the mirror of Campagne's utility room. Small wonder. Once in bed, she had tossed and turned for hours, going over last night's events a hundred times, wishing she had done things differently—like never agreeing to meet Ian at the lake.

By morning, exhausted and sick with worry, she had turned on the TV in search of local news, but there had been no report of a man being either killed or injured at Lake Carnegie.

And no news of Ian.

Claudia had already called twice—once at home, where she had left a message, and once at the restaurant. She was probably on pins and needles, anxious to hear how the delivery of the forty-eight thousand dollars had gone. Unfortunately, Abbie was in no condition to talk to anyone right now, not even Brady, who must have sensed her mood and was leaving her alone.

She had kept busy, concentrating on the many tasks at hand, supervising the staff and refusing to second-guess herself. Afraid people would pick up on her state of mind, she thought of bypassing her daily rounds today. But as the restaurant began to fill, she changed her mind. Taking the time to go into the dining room and welcome her guests was something her customers appreciated and looked forward to. Depriving them of that pleasure wouldn't be right. Besides, the distraction would be good for her.

John's stomach was growling by the time he pulled into the parking lot of the Princeton Township Police Department on Witherspoon, and the thought of enjoying a scrumptious meal for a change made him even more ravenous.

Detective Tina Wrightfield was just ending a phone conversation when he walked into the detective bay. The sixteen-year police veteran was a forty-something brunette with intelligent brown eyes and a sharp mind. The widow of a state trooper who had been killed in the line of duty, she was raising three daughters on her own and doing one hell of a job. She was also one of the most dependable partners he'd ever had.

This month, however, due to two retirements and one long-term illness, the PTPD was seriously understaffed, making it necessary to split forces. Tina had been assigned to a gruesome murder—the strangling of a young boy whose body had been found in the park along Herrontown Road. It was the third such murder this year, although the other two had occurred outside the Princeton jurisdiction. The case was proving more difficult than Tina had expected. The killer had left no clues—except that he strangled his victims with a rope. Since all three boys had been raped prior to being killed, the evidence pointed to a pedophile, one who knew how to cover his tracks. Not a speck of DNA had been found. No sperm, no hair, no skin residue, no fingerprints. Nothing.

Tina had been working non-stop and looked as tired as John felt, although she would never admit it. As the only female detective in the department, she wasn't about to elicit sarcastic comments from her male colleagues by wimping out.

"Yo, Wrightfield," John called from across the room. "Want to go to lunch?"

"No, thanks," Tina replied with a straight face. "I still have heartburn from that last place you took me to. What was it called again—as if I could forget? Hot Tamale?"

"Hey, that wasn't my fault. Grover in vice recommended it."

"That should have been your first clue."

John assumed a smug look. "Too bad. I heard Campagne serves the best food in—"

Tina looked up. "Did you say Campagne? On Palmer Square?"

"Yes, ma'am."

She gave him a suspicious look. "Since when do you eat at fancy French restaurants? Didn't you tell me once that bœuf bourguignon was just another name for stew?"

"That's why I'm inviting you to come along. I was hoping you'd keep me from making a fool of myself." He started for the door. "But since you're not interested, I guess I'll go alone."

"Who said I wasn't interested?" She grabbed her purse, almost knocking her chair over in her haste. "Lead the way."

Campagne was nestled between Ann Taylor and Banana Republic, overlooking the Green, where the locals played croquet on weekends and added to the area's air of gentility. The rain had finally let up and dark clouds were slowly making way for blue skies, although the air pushing behind last night's storm was cooler now, not at all typical of a June afternoon.

"How did you manage to get a last-minute reservation?"

Tina asked as they walked across the square. "This place is harder to get into than Fort Knox."

"Charm, my dear Watson. Try it sometime."

"I will, but right now I want to know why you're taking me to Campagne when it's common knowledge that your tastes lean more toward Wendy's and McDonald's."

"Oh, come on, Tina. I'm not that bad. I know my forks."

"Barely, but you didn't answer my question. Why this particular restaurant?"

"An out-of-towner by the name of Ian McGregor was found stabbed to death at Lake Carnegie this morning."

Tina took a compact from her bag, opened it and checked her make-up. "So?"

"The victim is Abbie DiAngelo's stepbrother."

She looked at him, wide-eyed. "The owner of Campagne?"

"That's right." He stopped in front of the restaurant and held the door open for her. "They hadn't seen each other in twenty-eight years. McGregor was just released from prison, and when I heard he came to Princeton to visit his stepsister, I got curious."

After their reservation was verified by a pretty hostess in a slinky black dress and black clogs, they were led to a small window table overlooking the two-hundred-and-forty-five-year-old Nassau Inn, known to locals as "the Nass."

"This is even nicer than I had imagined." Tina's observant gaze swept across the room. "It's elegant, but still warm and colorful. And the aroma…" She closed her eyes and inhaled deeply. "This lunch is going to cost you, partner."

"It'll be my pleasure."

Tina smiled as a waiter handed them a menu with a

watercolor of Van Gogh's famous irises on the cover. The drawing was a perfect match for the single iris on each table. John looked around him, hoping to see the boss lady, but she was nowhere in sight.

"So are you planning to question Abbie DiAngelo?" Tina asked. "Here? Today?"

John continued to study the menu. "I see no reason to put it off, do you?"

"No. Not that I'm complaining, but why the lunch? Why didn't you just go and question her, the way you do with all your witnesses?"

"Because I wanted a chance to observe her when she wasn't on her guard, see what she's all about in her own environment."

"How will you do that when she's in the back, cooking?"

"I happen to know that she comes out halfway through the lunch hour to greet her customers." His gaze stopped on an item in the menu. "What's a *fougasse?*"

Tina rolled her eyes. "Oh, Ryan, you are so not au courant. *Fougasse* is a flat Provençal bread studded with either olives or herbs, or both. It's very good."

After another few minutes of indecision, Tina finally settled on the baked bass with fennel. John, being a meat-and-potato man, ordered the roast lamb. A glass of wine would have gone nicely with the meal, but they were both on duty, so John ordered a bottle of Evian.

They had just finished their entrée when Abbie DiAngelo came out of the kitchen and began circulating from table to table, saying a few words to her customers and accepting compliments with a smile.

John's first reaction was that the newspaper photograph he had seen in the *Princeton Packet* hadn't done her justice. Her eyes, which he had thought were brown at first, were in reality a stunning, smoky shade of gray, and sparkled when she laughed. Her hair was a warm chestnut brown and looked as if she, or someone else, had just raked her or his fingers through it. She was shorter than he had expected—five-four at the most—but perfectly proportioned. She wore tailored slacks the color of expensive cognac and a tan blouse neatly tucked in.

She stopped at a table occupied by a well-dressed, older man who handed her an object John couldn't identify. She thanked him and gave him a gentle squeeze on the shoulder before moving to the next table.

He was still staring, when Tina kicked him under the table. "Stop drooling, will you. You're giving me a complex."

He pulled his gaze away just as Abbie reached their table. He could see the item in her hand now—a model railroad car.

"Hello, I'm Abbie DiAngelo." She smiled at both of them, then glanced discreetly at the remains on their plates. "Did you enjoy the bass?" she asked Tina.

"It was incredible. Made me want to get on a plane and fly to the French countryside."

"Careful, you might not want to come back." She turned to John. "And the lamb?"

Under her friendly gaze, John found himself as tongue-tied as the day Jeanette Smokley had asked him to the third-grade dance. Another discreet kick snapped him out of his trance. "Excellent," he managed to say.

"I'm glad you both enjoyed yourselves." Perhaps assuming he and Tina were husband and wife, she asked, "Is this your first visit to Campagne?"

He and Tina said yes in unison.

"Then you must come back and see us soon." With a nod, she moved on to the next table.

"Charming." Tina took a sip of her Evian, studying John above the rim of her glass. "And you're disgustingly smitten."

An embarrassing flush crept up John's neck. "I am not," he protested.

"Are too." Tina put her glass down. "Tell me something. How in the world are you going to conduct an investigation and remain objective if one of your suspects has already gotten under your skin?"

"She's not a suspect and she has certainly not gotten under my skin. Jesus, Wrightfield. Give me some credit, will you?"

Tina started to reply, but the waiter had returned, this time with the dessert menu. On his recommendation, both ordered the lavender-flavored crème brûlée and coffee.

Half an hour later, the meal finished and the bill paid, John rose and handed Tina his keys. "Why don't you take my car back and ask Bernstein to pick me up here in a half hour."

Tina took the keys. "I should really walk off this meal, but I'm expecting a call from the DMV, so I'll take you up on the offer."

She leaned toward him and whispered in his ear, "Try not to embarrass the department."

Nineteen

Her rounds finished, Abbie returned to the kitchen, feeling much more relaxed than she had been twenty minutes earlier. Agonizing over a man who had apparently vanished from sight was stupid and nerve-racking. Whoever had attacked her was gone, and so was Ian. Good riddance to both.

A blowtorch in her hand, she was putting the finishing touches to a crème brûlée, the restaurant's most popular dessert, when Brady gently touched her arm. "Joel just told me that a homicide detective from the Princeton police is in the dining room and wants to have a few words with you."

Abbie's fingers curled tightly over the torch handle. There could be only one reason a homicide detective was here. Her attacker hadn't disappeared after all. He had been found—or rather, his body had been found. And somehow the police had linked him to her.

"Did he say what he wanted?" she asked.

"No." Brady's eyes were filled with concern. "Abbie, are you all right?"

"Yes." Feeling shaky, she started to shut off the torch, but Brady took it from her. "Here, let me finish this."

"Thanks." Fear tightened in Abbie's stomach like a knot. How could she have been foolish enough to think

something as serious as what had happened last night would simply go away?

"What's the detective's name?" she asked, already untying her apron.

"John Ryan."

John Ryan. Why was the name familiar? Then she knew. He was Jordan Ryan's father. She had seen him at the baseball field a few times when Ben had played Jordan's team, the second best in the league. That's why the man at table six had looked familiar. She hadn't recognized him without his jeans and baseball cap. The woman, however, was definitely not Clarice Ryan.

With little time to speculate, Abbie tossed her apron aside. "Tell Joel to take him to my office." As soon as he was gone, she walked into the utility room for a quick glance in the mirror. Could she look any more guilty? Her skin had turned a putty color, and thanks to a sleepless night, there were dark circles under her eyes. She gave her cheeks a few quick slaps, hoping to restore their original color. The sudden flush made her look a little better, but for how long? Well, there was nothing she could do about that. Squaring her shoulders and hoping for the best, she walked briskly toward her office.

He stood with his back to her, studying her most recent award, which was prominently displayed on the wall behind her desk. "Detective Ryan?"

He turned around, a smile on his face. Abbie returned the smile, taking in the tall, athletic physique, the watchful, compelling brown eyes, the short black hair so much like his son's and the strong square jaw. Something about him—she couldn't say what—told her that in spite of his good looks and easygoing manner, he was not a man to be underestimated.

Realizing her inspection had lasted longer than was nec-

essary, she covered her sudden embarrassment with a question she hoped would break the ice. "Did you have second thoughts about the lamb?"

This time when he smiled, a deep dimple creased his left cheek. "None whatsoever. My partner and I agree this was the best meal we've had in years."

So the woman with the kind smile was his partner. Had they come here on official business?

"Good." She closed the door and walked across the room, trying to appear at ease.

"Actually I'm here about your stepbrother, Miss Di-Angelo."

Her composure dropped like a rock. He knew about Ian. Praying her voice wouldn't betray her panic, she asked, "What about my stepbrother?"

"You don't know?"

"Know what?"

"He was killed last night. Stabbed. His body was found at Lake Carnegie about four hours ago."

Abbie took a moment to absorb the news. Ian was dead. She should have felt something, some regret at the loss of a human life, maybe a little sadness because, for a short while, he had been part of her family. She felt nothing except immense relief.

"Do you know who did it?" she asked.

"Not yet."

She, on the other hand, had a pretty good idea. She thought of the man who had jumped on her car, his face contorted with rage, hacking away at her with that knife. He had known about the money and had been willing to kill for it. And now he was on the loose, perhaps looking for her.

"That's why I'm here," Detective Ryan continued. He was watching her but in a rather relaxed, unthreatening

way. "I'd like to collect as much information about Ian McGregor as I can. It would make my investigation a lot easier."

She felt the tension gradually ebb from her body. "I'm afraid you're asking the wrong person, Detective. I haven't seen my stepbrother in twenty-eight years. I know next to nothing about him." She paused, then asked, "How did you find out about me?"

"His girlfriend, Rose Panini, is here, too. She told me that Ian came to Princeton with the specific purpose of reuniting with you."

A girlfriend. Why hadn't Ian mentioned her? How much had he told her? More important, how much had the woman told Detective Ryan? Abbie leaned against her desk and folded her arms, studying the policeman. She had heard enough from other Little League mothers to know that he was divorced, a great dad and one of the best investigators in the police department.

"Nothing goes by him," a single mother had cooed not too long ago. She had laughed. "I wish *I* didn't."

Abbie chased the intrusive thoughts away. "What exactly did Ms. Panini tell you?"

"That your stepbrother was recently released from prison and needed some quick cash. That's why he came here. He was hoping to borrow money from you."

She wondered if Rose had really told him that or if he was baiting her. Lying wasn't something that came easily to her, and knowing that the forty-eight thousand dollars she had withdrawn from the bank sat in her safe, waiting to be reinvested first thing Monday morning, didn't help matters.

But right now, lying was a necessity, so she took a stab at it. "She told you the truth. Ian was here. He approached me on Monday evening and said he needed money to get back on his feet, maybe to start a business of his own.''

''What kind of business?''

She wasn't sure exactly when he had taken a small black book from his jacket pocket, but suddenly he was writing. ''He didn't say and I didn't ask. It wouldn't have mattered anyway. I couldn't help him. I'm a single parent, with a business to run and a mortgage to pay. I don't have the kind of money he wanted.''

''How much was that?''

''A hundred thousand dollars.''

The detective let out a slow whistle. ''That's a lot of money.''

''He saw a TV interview I did a couple of weeks ago, found out I own a restaurant and figured I was wealthy, which couldn't be further from the truth.''

He looked at her with an unblinking gaze. ''How did he take it when you turned him down?''

She shrugged. ''He wasn't happy, but there wasn't much he could do about it.''

''Yet he hung around,'' he remarked. ''Why do you think that is?''

Her stomach flip-flopped. ''I beg your pardon?''

''You said he approached you on Monday. He was killed on Thursday night. Why was he still here?''

Her hands were beginning to feel clammy. She groped for a logical answer and couldn't think of one. ''I don't know. I suppose he was exploring other avenues. From what I gathered, Ian was a scam artist, always looking for the next deal. Or maybe he decided he liked it here, not that I can blame him.'' Too late she remembered one of her favorite TV mystery series—*Columbo*—and how the culprits always talked too much, offering solutions to the seemingly bumbling detective, unaware that he was actually trying to trip them up.

"Was Monday the only time you saw your stepbrother?"

She thought quickly, wondering if there was any harm in mentioning Ian's return visit the following day. "Actually, no. He stopped by again on Tuesday, hoping I had changed my mind."

"But you hadn't."

"No."

His gaze was steady, a little unnerving. Not accustomed to this kind of questioning, Abbie glanced out the open window overlooking a small herb garden, while John Ryan made another entry in his book. A blue jay was perched on the birdbath, his watchful eye surveying the surroundings. She tried to focus on the pastoral scene and absorb its soothing effect, but already she could feel a dull ache press against her temples.

"What time do you close the restaurant at night, Miss DiAngelo?"

She forced herself to maintain eye contact. "Around eleven. Sometimes later if we're exceptionally busy."

"Was last night one of those exceptionally busy nights?"

"No, but I still didn't leave until after eleven." Worried she had spoken a little too defensively, she quickly added, "May I ask *you* a question, Detective?"

"Certainly."

"Am I a suspect?"

"In your stepbrother's murder?" His mouth curved into a smile. "Hardly. Ian McGregor was viciously attacked, and died as the result of multiple stab wounds. As adept as you must be in the kitchen, I doubt you could have handled a man that size, and stabbed him repeatedly."

She gave a nervous laugh. "Well, that's a relief."

He flipped a page in his notebook. "What do you know about a man by the name of Arturo Garcia?"

She shook her head. "I've never heard of him. Who is he?"

"According to Rose Panini, he used to run a drug distribution business in Toledo, Ohio, and your stepbrother worked for him. Ian was caught during a delivery and turned state's evidence in exchange for immunity. As a result, Arturo Garcia went to prison for eight years, but not before he swore to kill Ian the minute he got out. Your brother didn't mention him to you?"

Abbie couldn't hold back a little sigh of impatience. "Detective Ryan, you seem to be under the misconception that Ian confided in me. He didn't. The two conversations we had were brief and to the point. I didn't even know he was here with a girlfriend, or where he was staying."

Why had she said that? Why was she compounding lie upon lie?

"The Clearwater Motel on Route 27." The detective glanced at his notes again. "Ms. Panini said something about a fire destroying your Palo Alto home twenty-eight years ago and that the tragedy was the reason you, Ian and his sister Liz were separated."

Abbie felt her pulse quicken. That was more information that she wanted him to have. "That's right."

"Would you mind giving me a little background on you and the McGregors?"

"Is that relevant to the case?"

"It could be."

She sighed to show she was humoring him, and hoped she wasn't overdoing it. "All right. My father—that is, my biological father—died when I was five. A year later, my mother married Patrick McGregor, a widower and the father of two children, Ian and Liz. Two years later, our house caught fire and burned.''

''What started the fire?''

Knowing any change in demeanor would give her away, she resisted the impulse to swallow, even though her throat was as dry as an Arabian desert. ''My stepfather had been drinking that night, and was smoking a cigarette when he fell asleep.''

''The rest of the household was asleep as well?''

''Yes. My mother was awakened by the sound of her own coughing. Somehow, she managed to save Ian and me, then a fire rescue team arrived and pulled Liz out. By the time they found my stepfather, he was already dead.''

''But how could that be? Wasn't he in bed, next to your mother?''

''No.'' She slid her hands behind her and gripped the desk, afraid he would see them shake. ''Because of my stepfather's habit of watching TV in bed, she had moved into the guest room.''

''I see.'' His gaze held hers for a long second. ''So, after the fire, you and your mother moved away?''

''To Kansas. My grandfather was recovering from a stroke and my mother wanted to be there and take care of him. After he died, we moved here.''

''But Ian and Liz stayed in California.''

''Yes.'' God, was this ever going to end? ''My mother had intended to keep her stepchildren with her, but when their aunt showed up, saying she was a blood relative and they should be with her, there was nothing my mother could do.''

''And there was no further contact?''

''No, none. Until this past Monday.''

''Finding Ian McGregor on your doorstep after all this time must have been quite a surprise.''

"It was a shock," Abbie admitted. "And so was finding out Ian had been in prison."

"Did he visit your mother while he was here?"

"No."

"Why not?"

"He didn't ask to and I didn't encourage him. My mother isn't well," she continued, seeing no point in hiding something he could so easily find out. "She has Alzheimer's. His visit might have upset her. I didn't want that."

She glanced at her watch again, looking for an excuse to end the conversation, especially since it had begun to steer toward her mother. "If that's all, Detective. I really need to get back to work."

"Of course." He flipped his notebook shut. "Thank you for your time, Ms. DiAngelo. I'll let you know what I find out."

She walked with him to the now-empty dining room. It wasn't until the detective had disappeared from sight that she allowed herself a sigh of relief.

Or was that a little premature?

Twenty

Abbie was lost in thought as she watched the detective walk away, and didn't notice Brady standing beside her until he spoke.

"Nice man. Where have I seen him before?"

"The ball field. He coaches his son's team sometimes—The Princeton Cardinals."

Brady nodded. "That's it. I didn't know he was a homicide detective, though." He gave Abbie a casual glance. "What did he want?"

There was no longer any reason to hide the truth from him. The news of Ian's death would be out soon enough. "Ian McGregor is dead."

Brady's face showed only mild surprise. "Your stepbrother? What happened?"

"Someone stabbed him. His body was found at Lake Carnegie this morning."

"I hope you don't expect me to be all broken up about it."

She smiled. "No. You've made your feelings for him perfectly clear."

"Did they catch who did it?"

"Not yet." She repeated what Detective Ryan had told her, but did not mention Ian's blackmailing scheme. Hopefully no one would ever find out about that.

"Are you all right?" Brady asked when she was finished. "I mean, you're not in trouble or anything?"

"No, of course not."

"Well, like I said, I'm not sorry." He draped an arm around her shoulder. "The man came here with only one goal in mind—to sponge off you. It's too bad he had to die, but at least now you won't have to put up with him anymore."

As always, Brady seemed to have read her mind, because his words reflected exactly how she felt about her stepbrother's death. They had just stepped into the kitchen when Claudia, apparently tired of waiting for Abbie to return her calls, flew into the room, a worried expression on her face.

Abbie waited until Brady had returned to his station before drawing her friend into a quiet corner. "I know, I know," she said, cutting short Claudia's string of questions. "I should have called."

"Yes, you should have. I was frantic. All Brady could tell me was that a homicide detective had come here to talk to you."

Abbie brought her up to date and could see the effect each of her words was having on her friend.

"Dear Lord." Claudia's eyes were filled with disbelief. "No wonder you're wound up so tight, and I walked in here like gangbusters. I'm sorry, Abbie."

Abbie smiled. "You should be. You scared Brady."

"Nothing scares Brady, but I'll make sure to apologize." She went to the industrial-size refrigerator, found a small bottle of Perrier and twisted the cap off. "So who do you think killed Ian? That ape who attacked you?"

"Who else? He was there. He knew about the money." She paused, reliving the ordeal. "And he had a knife."

"You should have told Detective Ryan."

"And admit Ian was blackmailing me?" Abbie shook her head. "I won't do that. I won't put my mother through a murder investigation."

"That's assuming John Ryan would notify the Palo Alto authorities."

"He's a police officer. He would have no choice."

"And what are you going to do about this maniac who attacked you? He's still out there, you know."

"You don't need to remind me."

"And what about Earl Kramer? What if he decides to 'confess'?" She made quotation marks in the air. "Or blackmail you himself?"

"That thought has also crossed my mind."

"Then talk to Detective Ryan. Tell him the truth. From what you told me about him so far, he sounds like a decent man. He might just decide to help you."

"He would have to believe me first."

Claudia gave her a teasing grin. "That part is easy. I bet you've already charmed the pants off him." She leaned against the refrigerator and took another sip of Perrier. "Didn't you say he was divorced?"

"What does that have to do with anything?"

Claudia rolled her eyes. "Do I need to draw you a picture? A handsome, available man, a beautiful, available woman. Sparks fly. Get it?"

She got it. And she would be lying if she didn't admit, at least to herself, that Detective Ryan's good looks and undeniable charm had not gone unnoticed. But Claudia, who was a hopeless matchmaker, didn't need to know that.

"There were no sparks," she stated flatly. "And how do you know he's handsome?"

"Brady told me." She leaned forward, scrutinizing Abbie. "So, is he right? Is John Ryan a babe?"

"I suppose you could say that."

"Sexy?"

"I wouldn't know."

"Oh, come on," Claudia teased. "It hasn't been that long, has it? You still know a sexy man when you see one."

"For heaven's sake, Claudia. Must you measure every male/female encounter on a sexual level?"

Claudia laughed. "Of course. I'm an *artiste*, remember? I deal with touch, emotions, sensations."

"Well, don't expect inspiration from me. My mind is not on romance these days, and even if it were, I'd never be so stupid as to fall for a man who could turn out to be my worst enemy."

Abbie sat across from Ben at the kitchen table and watched him devour the chocolate chip cookies she had baked earlier, knowing they were his favorite. Between bites, he told her about Bobby Talbot, who had been sent to the principal's office for throwing paper balls at one of the girls in the front row. One ball had missed its target and hit Miss Simmons instead.

Elbows on the table, chin resting on her folded hands, Abbie laughed with Ben, wishing she didn't have to put a damper on her son's perfect day. But she knew that if she didn't tell him about Ian, someone else would. Or he would hear it on TV and wonder why she had kept something this important from him.

She waited until he had drunk the last of his milk before saying, "I need to tell you something, too, sport, although my story won't be nearly as funny as yours."

Serious blue eyes focused on her. "Is Grandma okay?"

"Grandma is fine." She wasn't surprised that his first thought had been for his grandmother. Ben adored Irene and had become very protective of her since finding out about her illness.

Abbie spoke quietly and honestly, trying to be truthful without being morbid. She told Ben Ian had been in prison and why, and how he had found her. Once again, she said nothing about the blackmail or Detective Ryan's visit. Ben and Jordan were friends and she didn't want him to feel awkward in front of the detective's son. She simply said the police had questioned her because she and another sister in New York were Ian's only living relatives.

Ben listened until she was finished, then looked at her, his expression solemn. "How come you never told me I had an aunt and uncle?"

"Because I lost touch with both of them."

"But they were your family, right?"

"For a short time."

He bobbed his head a few times as though he understood, then asked abruptly, "Are you sad your brother is dead?"

The question took her by surprise, and for a moment she didn't know how to answer it. She had always made it a point to be honest with Ben, and the thought of lying to him now in order not to appear heartless sounded too hypocritical to even consider.

Instead, she opted for diplomacy. "It's always sad when someone dies, but I hardly knew him. Twenty-eight years without seeing or hearing from someone is a long time. And remember, he wasn't my real brother."

"How come I didn't meet him? Didn't he want to see me?"

Another difficult question. She wouldn't dodge it this time. "I'm the one who didn't want him to meet you."

"Because he was in prison?"

''That had a lot to do with it.'' And so did the fact that he was a louse, she almost added.

''What about Liz? Will I get to meet her?''

Abbie winced inwardly. Another question she hadn't expected. ''Do you want to?''

He hesitated. ''I don't know. Maybe. All my friends have aunts and uncles and cousins. It's kind of neat.''

''You have Aunt Claudia.''

''It's not the same thing. I like Aunt Claudia a lot, but she's your friend, not my real aunt.''

''Liz is not your real aunt either. She is your *step*aunt, related to you only by marriage.'' She was aware that her tone had turned brittle, almost defensive, which was not how she had intended it to be. Ben was a little boy, and given his kind, considerate nature, those questions were only natural.

''It's complicated, isn't it?'' She smiled as she brushed a red strand from his forehead.

''Not really.'' He reached for another cookie, but only twirled it in his hands. ''You don't want me to meet her.''

Abbie bit her lip. This wasn't turning out the way she had expected. It was true she had no intention of bringing Liz into their lives. Why should she? The woman had never made any attempt to find her, and her attitude toward Abbie during the two years they had spent together under the same roof had been downright unpleasant. But was she being fair keeping Ben from her?

''I don't know where she lives, but I'm sure I could find out.'' She dreaded it already but would do it, for Ben. And hope he didn't end up disappointed.

He seemed satisfied with that answer. ''Does Grandma know Uncle Ian is dead?''

So, it was Uncle Ian now. ''Not yet. I'm planning on telling her today.'' Before he could ask another question, she reached across the table and covered his hand with hers. "Ben, the reason I told you all this is because the story of Ian's death will probably be in the papers, maybe even on TV. If you read or see or hear anything you don't understand, I want you to come to me. Will you do that?"

He nodded again, but obviously, his curiosity hadn't been fully satisfied. "Is there going to be a funeral, like when Joey Barfield's uncle died?"

Why hadn't she anticipated this third degree? How could she have imagined that he would take the news placidly and then go about his day the way he always did? "I don't know, Ben. Ian was here with his girlfriend, so she'll probably make the arrangements and bury him in Ohio where they live."

"When will you know?"

"Know what?"

"Where the funeral will be."

She had never expected a conversation with her nine-year-old son would be this stressful. "I suppose I could talk to Ian's girlfriend and see what she has planned."

In fact, a visit to Rose Panini was first on her agenda, not because she was anxious to know the details of her stepbrother's funeral, but because she needed to find out how much Ms. Panini knew, and whether or not she should worry about her.

And there was the letter. Somehow, she had to find it.

"Why don't you get started with your homework. Tiffany will be here any minute." Not quite ready to field any more questions from her inquisitive son, she stood, half expecting Ben to ask if he could attend the funeral. To her relief, he didn't.

Twenty-One

The Clearwater Motel was a one-story building with light green siding and a small patch of grass in front of the canopied entrance. It was a ten-minute ride from the restaurant and an easy walk from Lake Carnegie where the murder had occurred.

Aware that Ben had been doing his homework and watching her at the same time, Abbie had called Rose Panini, introduced herself over the phone and asked if she could stop by. Far from being reluctant, the woman had told her she wanted very much to meet her, and had sounded as though she meant it.

"I don't have to be at work until five," she had added. "We'll have plenty of time to talk."

That last part, about not having to go to work until five, worried Abbie. Why had Rose bothered to find a job when Ian had planned to leave Princeton as soon as he had the money? Maybe she knew about the blackmailing scheme. Maybe she was just as greedy and ruthless as Ian, and intended to pick up where he had left off.

Abbie tried not to speculate or worry unnecessarily. There were a number of reasons Rose Panini might want to stay in Princeton. She could have friends here, or relatives. Or maybe she had fallen in love with the area. Many visitors who came here for the first time developed an instant liking for the university town, finding it both cultured and hip.

The woman who opened the door of the motel room was not what Abbie had expected. It was obvious she had been crying, and when she saw Abbie, fresh tears started rolling down her cheeks again.

"I'm sorry if this isn't a good time," Abbie said, feeling bad for intruding.

Rose shook her head, then, unexpectedly, threw her arms around Abbie, enveloping her in a cloud of Obsession. Quiet sobs shook the woman's shoulders for about half a minute, during which Abbie felt totally helpless.

At last, Rose pulled away to let her in. "Don't mind me. I just came back from the morgue." She took a tissue from the box on the dresser and blew her nose, sounding like a foghorn. "Seeing Ian lying on that cold slab hit me hard. If I didn't believe he was dead before that, I certainly believe it now." She pressed the balled-up tissue against one eye then the other.

Abbie was a little thrown off by this show of grief. It was inconceivable to her that someone as despicable as Ian could have inspired love. Either he had cleverly concealed his true nature from his girlfriend, or she was a very tolerant woman.

"I'm sorry, Miss Panini." Oddly, she meant it.

"Call me Rose, okay?" Rose sniffed. "I'm glad you called. I wanted to meet you, but didn't know how to go about it." She sat on the edge of the bed, her tight black skirt riding up to reveal chunky thighs. A white blouse and black, open-toed sandals completed the outfit. Abbie guessed Rose was waitressing.

"I didn't know Ian had a girlfriend until Detective Ryan told me." She sat on the chair by the window and cast a quick glance around, wondering if her mother's letter was anywhere in this room, or if Ian had taken it with him to the lake. What if the police had found it on his body? Either way, getting her hands on it would not be an easy task.

"Is there anyone you can call?" she asked, turning her attention back to Rose. "A friend? A family member?"

Rose shook her head. "I just have a cousin in Toledo, and my friends have enough problems of their own without having to worry about mine." She shrugged. "I'm kind of a loner anyway."

Abbie was glad to hear that. A loner didn't have anyone to talk to. "You said something about having to go to work. Does that mean you're planning to stay in Princeton?"

Another shrug. "I don't know. Maybe. I like the people at the Golden Diner where I work. Kat, one of the waitresses there, said I could move in with her and split the expenses. It'll be a little cramped, but anything's better than this room, where all I do is think of Ian." She gave her nose a few more swipes with the tissue before tossing it in the wastebasket. "I feel so damn guilty."

"What happened isn't your fault."

"Yes, it is. I shouldn't have given Ian the money for the trip."

"Why did you?" Now that it was out, the question seemed a little too forward, but Rose didn't seem to mind.

"I could never say no to him. And he painted such a nice picture of the two of us starting over, having our own business. I let it go to my head. I should have known better. I should have remembered all the ventures Ian started that went sour."

Abbie found herself liking the woman. "Where did you and Ian meet?"

"Vegas. I was a showgirl." She may have seen the surprise in Abbie's eyes, because she added, "I was twenty years younger then, a size six and had legs that wouldn't quit. Ian was quite a looker, too. And boy, did he know how to charm a girl.''

That, too, was hard to believe. ''What was he doing in Las Vegas?''

''He knew people there—dangerous people. A year after I moved in with him, we had to skip town in a hurry. Seems like someone was always after Ian.''

''Like Arturo Garcia?''

Rose looked surprised. ''Ian told you about him?''

''Detective Ryan did. He wanted to know if I had heard of him.''

''I hope the police find him.'' She shivered. ''I wouldn't want him to show up here.''

''Why would he?''

''Detective Ryan didn't tell you?''

''I know Ian turned in state's evidence against Arturo, but how would that concern you?''

''That's not all Ian did. He also ran off with thirty thousand he had just collected on Arturo's behalf. The man's going to want his money back, and if he thinks *I* have it, which I don't, he could come after me.''

''After all this time?''

''Men like Arturo Garcia don't like unsettled scores. It's bad for their reputation, if you know what I mean.''

Abbie remembered the fierce look on her attacker's face and knew exactly what Rose meant.

''He sounds dangerous,'' she said, fishing for information.

''Oh, he is that. That's why Ian was so scared of him.'' She blew her nose again. ''Did Detective Ryan tell you Arturo may have been here the afternoon of the murder? In this room.''

''No.''

"He won't know for sure until he gets fingerprint results from the lab, but I don't need a crime scene expert to tell me that brute was here. I *know* he was." She gave a sideways glance. "It's all in there."

Abbie followed her gaze and saw large, colorful cards laid out on the table by the window, some in pairs, some in a cross pattern. She smiled. "You read tarot."

"I've been reading tarot cards since I was a teenager. My folks and I lived next door to a psychic and I used to spend more time at her house than at mine. She taught me how to read the cards and how to interpret them."

"Are you pretty good at it?"

"Never made a wrong prediction yet." Her voice dropped. "Ian used to say it was a lot of bullshit, but he was wrong. Everything I ever saw in the cards came true." She looked at Abbie. "You're in there, too."

Abbie didn't believe in psychics or anyone with special powers, but felt compelled to ask, "What did you see?"

"Troubles, worries, danger. Someone wants something from you." She walked over to the table and tapped a card picturing a man standing behind a woman and putting a necklace around her neck. "I can't tell what because cards can be interpreted many different ways, but I see money. A repayment for a debt." She looked back at Abbie. "Maybe that's the money you were going to loan Ian?"

Loan. She had said loan, so it was possible that she didn't know about the blackmail. "He told you about that?"

"Yes. At first, I didn't want to believe him. Why should a stepsister he hadn't seen in twenty-eight years hand over twenty thousand dollars?"

So that was the amount he had told her. It made sense. A hundred thousand would have alerted Rose—who was far from stupid—that he had more in mind than a loan.

"Actually, you were right in your assumption," Abbie said. "I had no intention of loaning Ian any money. I couldn't have, even if I had wanted to. All my assets are tied up in the restaurant and my house."

"But he told me…" Rose studied Abbie for a few seconds, as if she was trying to decide who had deceived her—Abbie or Ian. "You really turned him down?"

Abbie nodded.

"Why didn't he tell me that? Why did he let me believe you had agreed to help him out?"

"I don't know." And for some inexplicable reason, Abbie felt terrible about lying to this woman. Maybe it was best if she steered the conversation in another direction. "Will you be taking Ian's body back to Toledo?"

Rose looked down at her hands. "No. I'm going to bury him here, in Princeton. I don't have the money to ship his body back, and I can't ask Liz to foot the extra expense. She's already paying for the funeral."

That was a surprise. "You've been in touch with Liz?"

Rose stood up, walked over to the table and started gathering the cards. "I called her as soon as I found out about Ian. She tends bar at the Manhattan Towers in New York City."

"I see." A thought suddenly struck Abbie. "Did Ian talk to her while he was here?"

To her dismay, Rose nodded. "He took the bus to New York earlier this week. It was my first day on the job and he was here alone, so he decided to touch base with his sister."

"How did that visit go?"

"Fine, I guess, for a sister and brother who saw each other once in a blue moon. He didn't say much about it."

"How did she react when you told her about Ian's death?"

"She didn't seem too worked up about it, or maybe she didn't want to show her feelings over the phone. Ian told me she was kind of a cold fish." She turned a card, studied it for a moment. "But she surprised me by offering to pay for the burial, just when I was wondering where I'd find the money. She'll be here in a couple of days."

She flipped another card. "Did you know she was married to a rock star once?"

Abbie remembered reading about it. Irene had insisted on sending a card, in care of Jude Tilly's publicist, but like all the other correspondence she had sent, it had remained unanswered. "Yes, I did."

"Abbie?" Rose put the card down. "About the funeral. I don't really know what to do or where to go. I was wondering if you could come with me, help me pick out…you know…a casket." As she said the word, a small sob caught in her throat.

Thrown by the unexpected request and the sadness in Rose's eyes, Abbie searched for the right words. But what could she say to this grieving woman, all alone in a strange town, burdened with the saddest task of all—burying a loved one.

"Me?" It was all she could come up with.

"Liz can't come down just yet and you're Ian's only other relative, so I thought…" She pressed another tissue to her eyes, unaware that all that crying had ruined her makeup and given her racoon eyes. If anything, she looked even more vulnerable than she had before.

Abbie found herself nodding. "I'll be glad to go with you, Rose. Just tell me when."

Rose sighed with relief. "Would tomorrow morning be all right?" she asked hopefully. "Detective Ryan said I could have the body back by then."

She would have to make a few changes in her schedule,

Abbie thought, and ask Claudia to take Ben to baseball practice, but it could be done. "Could we start early?"

"The earlier the better." Rose gave her a shaky smile.

"I'll pick you up at eight-thirty, then."

"Thank you, Abbie. Thank you so much." After a slight hesitation, Rose hugged her again. This time Abbie returned the embrace.

"Hello, Marion." Abbie set her purse on the kitchen counter where Marion was mixing a pitcher of iced tea. "How's Mom today?"

Marion beamed. "See for yourself." Abbie followed her gaze and understood why Marion was so cheerful. Irene sat in the living room, perfectly groomed, flipping through the pages of *Good Housekeeping.*

"She's only had one tiny outburst and that was because she misplaced her reading glasses."

"She's been misplacing her glasses ever since I can remember."

Marion chuckled. "That's what I told her." She set the pitcher on a tray. "Can I bring you some iced tea, too?"

"I'd love some, Marion. Thank you."

Abbie strode into the living room. "Hi, Mom."

Irene looked up, her smile bright, her eyes clear. "Abbie, darling, I didn't hear you."

"I didn't want to disturb you. You seemed so absorbed." She sat beside her on the sofa and peeked over her shoulder. "Brownies?" she said when she saw the recipe Irene had circled. "Those wouldn't be for Ben, by any chance?"

"You know they are."

"Make plenty. I like them, too."

Irene studied her for a moment. "Are you all right, honey? You look a little frazzled."

Abbie ran her fingers through her hair. "Do I?"

"And you're pale. Are you working too hard again? And not sleeping enough?"

Abbie laughed. "Probably, but didn't you used to tell me when I was growing up, there could be no success without sacrifice?"

"Did I really?" Irene's beautiful eyes filled with mirth. "I must have sounded like a preacher."

"No, just a caring mother."

"And you are stalling, young lady."

"Yes, I am." Abbie folded her hands on her lap. "I have disturbing news, about Ian." She hesitated, all too aware that the wrong word could send her mother into one of her moods. But how many ways were there to say someone had died? "Something happened to him."

Irene's smile quickly faded. "You mean…he's been hurt?"

"It's worse than that. He's dead, Mom."

Irene's hands flew to her mouth and her eyes filled up. "Oh, no. When did that happen? How?"

She told her, using the same gentle tone she had used with Ben, glad that this time there was no sign of panic in her mother's eyes, no confusion—just sadness.

When Abbie was finished, Irene fell back against the cushions. "That poor boy. I prayed he'd find the right path someday, but how could he, when his own father had already given up on him?" She put the magazine aside. "Do they know who did such a terrible thing?"

"Not yet. But the police are investigating." She took her mother's hand in hers. "The detective in charge of the case is John Ryan. He was at the restaurant earlier, questioning me."

A look of mild alarm shadowed Irene's eyes. "Why? What do you have to do with Ian's murder?"

More than I'd like to, Abbie thought. "Nothing." She avoided looking directly into her mother's eyes. "But Detective Ryan is trying to put together a complete profile on Ian. He says it will help his investigation."

"But you hardly knew him. If this Detective Ryan wants information, why doesn't he talk to Ian's girlfriend? What did you say her name was?"

"Rose. He did talk to her, Mom. She was very helpful."

Irene's keen eyes kept studying her. "Does she know who might have killed Ian? In a town where he doesn't know a soul?"

"No. She's just as puzzled as I am."

"Is she nice?"

Abbie smiled. "As a matter of fact, she's very nice, not quite what I imagined, but nice."

"And you said Liz is making all the arrangements?"

"She's asked me to help. I said I'd do it."

"That was nice of you, honey." She was silent for a moment before adding, "I'd like to go to the funeral, Abbie. Ian and I were never close, and I did find his visit here a little suspicious, but nonetheless, I'd like to pay my last respects. It's only right."

Abbie nodded. Although she had hoped there would be no contact between her mother and Liz, especially since she didn't know how much Ian had told his sister, the request didn't surprise her. From the very beginning, Irene had treated Liz and Ian like her own children, shielding them from Patrick's drunken outbursts, even covering for them so they wouldn't get in trouble. Abbie had no idea if Irene remembered the incident with the letter, but either way she had no intention of bringing it up. Or Ian's more recent extortion plan. She had made that decision the night Dennis Marjolis had laid out the cold facts for her. With any luck, Ian had taken his accusations to his grave, and that's where they would stay.

Twenty-Two

John stood under the hot, powerful shower spray, unable to decide what bothered him most—knowing that Abbie DiAngelo had lied to him, or that he couldn't get her out of his mind.

The cop in him wanted to believe the former, but who the hell was he kidding? In the last twenty-four hours, he had behaved like a complete idiot. Dialing Abbie's restaurant and then hanging up at the first ring because he couldn't think of an excuse for the call. Or driving around Palmer Square in the hope of catching a glimpse of her. Or logging on to Campagne's Web site to see what else he could learn from the enigmatic Ms. DiAngelo. He had even caught himself fantasizing about her, wondering if her skin was as soft as it looked, or if she tasted as good as she smelled. Teenager stuff. Ridiculous stuff a sensible, grown-up man ought to be ashamed of.

But the truth was, he couldn't remember the last time a woman had affected him that way.

Not that he hadn't had his share of good times with members of the opposite sex. On the contrary. Thanks to his well-meaning pals at PTPD, there had been a steady flow of blind dates over the last two years, some interesting, if not promising, others downright scary. Why was it that so many women felt that cops were lost souls who needed saving?

John loved his job. In fact, he had almost alienated his entire family when he chose law enforcement over a career in the military, as had all the previous Ryan men. So when a woman expressed regret that a mind such as his was being wasted and that he ought to do something a little more gratifying, like heading a corporation or running for office, he had no qualms about ending the relationship, often before it even began.

His friends had nicknamed him Picky John. But they were wrong. It wasn't that he was picky. He just didn't like anyone putting down what he did for a living. No matter how smart and beautiful the woman was.

So why, to use Tina's words, was he so damn smitten with Abbie DiAngelo? Other than what Jordan had told him, he didn't know anything about her, except perhaps that she wasn't a very good liar. As soon as she had walked into her office, he had realized that the woman he was looking at was different from the one who had greeted him in the dining room earlier. Her complexion had been a shade paler, her breathing irregular, and a few minutes into the conversation, a sheen of perspiration had appeared on her forehead.

But in spite of that, there was something exciting about her, an energy, an undercurrent he found both startling and seductive. Foolishly, he found himself wishing someone else was investigating Ian McGregor's murder.

He poured a capful of shampoo into the palm of his hand, then rubbed it vigorously onto his head. As he scrubbed, he tried to concentrate on the possible whereabouts of Arturo Garcia, since, at the moment, the man was his prime suspect.

He only succeeded in bringing Abbie DiAngelo into sharper focus.

Combing his fingers through his hair, he pushed the wet

strands from his face. What the hell was he doing? Had he been sleeping alone so long he was now having erotic thoughts about a woman he hardly knew?

Was that all it was, then? Lust? If so, he could handle it. It was the other aspect of attraction that scared the hell out of him—the falling-in-love part. The big L, as Tina liked to call it, followed by the big C—commitment.

Half muttering to himself, he dried off, tucked the towel around his waist, and padded to the kitchen for a much-needed cup of coffee.

He'd find a way to see Abbie DiAngelo again, but until then he couldn't lose sight of another equally important part of this puzzle—Liz Tilly. Maybe sister number two would be more forthcoming with what she knew than sister number one.

To Abbie's surprise, Rose had remained stoic and collected during their visit to Patterson's Funeral Home. After selecting a modest casket and making the proper arrangements for the funeral director to pick up Ian's body from the morgue, Rose settled the bill and agreed to bring back a suit in which to bury him.

"Did Ian have a suit?" Abbie asked as they walked out of the white stucco building.

"No." Rose's cheeks colored. "I only said that because I was too embarrassed to admit he didn't. I don't think Ian has ever owned a suit in his life."

"Did you go through his things? There may be something suitable."

Rose shook her head. "He only had the few pieces I bought him before we left Toledo—jeans, a couple of shirts and sneakers." She took out her wallet and counted the few bills in it. "I have enough to buy him a pair of pants, a shirt and shoes."

"Didn't you say Liz was paying for everything?"

"Not everything. She only sent me money for the casket and the cemetery plot. I told her I'd take care of the rest." She looked up, a worried expression on her face. "Would fifty dollars do it? For the clothes?"

Abbie squeezed her arm. "I know just the place. Come on."

Half an hour later, they walked out of Carlton's, a discount store on Route 206, with a pair of navy pants, a white shirt, a navy tie and a pair of black loafers. At the cash register, as Rose had started to take her wallet out, Abbie had told her to put her money away, and paid for the purchases herself. "It's a small contribution," she had told her. "Please let me do it."

The gesture had surprised her more than it had surprised Rose, and the thought that Ian was about to be buried in clothes *she* had paid for seemed so ludicrous, she wondered if she had lost her mind. But Ian wasn't the reason she had picked up the tab, she reminded herself. Rose was.

From the department store they drove to Hillside Cemetery to choose a small plot and then to Abbie's church where Reverend Barfield had agreed to perform a short graveside service.

As Abbie drove Rose back to the motel, she was tempted to ask her if she had come across a letter written by her mother years ago, while going through Ian's things. If Ian had had the letter with him, as he claimed, then it must be there, at the motel. It couldn't have been on his person at the time he was killed or Detective Ryan would have said something.

But as she brought the car to a stop in front of room 11, she remained silent. Mentioning the letter, and then explaining why Abbie had to have it, was just too risky.

She would have to take her chances that it would never

surface, or hope an opportunity would arise for Abbie to go through Ian's effects herself.

Sitting beside her, Rose reached for the two shopping bags in the back seat. "I can't thank you enough for all you've done," she said to Abbie. "I would have been lost without you."

"I'm glad I could help." She motioned to the bags in Rose's arms. "Do you need help with those?"

"I'm fine. And you have to get back to work."

"I'll see you at the cemetery on Wednesday morning, then."

Rose nodded, but made no movement to get out of the car. Instead, she opened the large tote bag at her feet and started digging into it, obviously searching for something. "When I was going through Ian's clothes the other day, I found something."

Abbie held her breath.

"A letter." Rose pulled out a folded sheet of stationery, yellowed by age. "Your mother wrote it a long time ago." She kept her tone matter-of-fact, as if the letter held no importance. "I'm not exactly sure what it is, or why Ian had it." She finally looked up and handed it to her. "But I thought you should have it."

Lost for words, Abbie took it, feeling both relieved and scared at the thought that she was now holding the one piece of evidence that could further implicate her mother in a cold-blooded murder. "Thank you," she said in a whisper.

She thought of giving Rose an explanation she would buy, then changed her mind. Rose wasn't stupid and she had just done a very nice thing, no questions asked. To make up a phony story at this point would be both insulting and unfair.

"Rose—"

"You don't have to tell me anything," Rose said. "It's none of my business."

"Just this one thing." Abbie dropped the letter in her purse before looking up. "I didn't kill him, Rose. You have to believe me."

Rose smiled, a gentle, totally trusting smile. "I do."

Then she opened the door, struggled a little with her packages and got out.

As Abbie had expected, the press had quickly picked up the scent of a titillating story and ran with it. By the time the *Mercer County News* hit the stands on Saturday morning, news of Ian McGregor's death and his connection to Abbie DiAngelo had made the headlines with a caption that made Abbie wince: Local Celebrity Chef Connected To Murder Victim.

The article went on describing Ian's life of crime, his recent release from prison and his hopes of reuniting with a sister he hadn't seen in twenty-eight years. Just what she needed in a community that placed respectability and good breeding above everything else.

Thank God, Brady had talked to the staff; by the time Abbie arrived at the restaurant, each worker was doing his or her best to treat the day like any other. Not so in the dining room, however, where the atmosphere was charged and the glances openly curious. Acting as naturally as she could under the circumstances, Abbie made her rounds, greeting first timers and habitués with a smile, grateful the headlines had not kept customers away.

The only exception was Professor Gilroy. The moment Abbie approached his table, he stood up, looking as saddened as if *he* had suffered a loss.

"Abbie," he said, taking her hands in his. "I am so sorry about your brother."

"Thank you, Professor." Gently, she pulled her hands free. "But as I'm sure you've heard, I hardly knew him." If that sounded cruel, she didn't care. She refused to put on a show and pretend to be grieving when she wasn't.

"Yes, I did hear that." Professor Gilroy sat down. "But the shock of being reunited with a long-lost relative and then hear he had been brutally murdered must have been a terrible shock. How is Ben?" he added. "Does he know?"

"Yes, I talked to him. And he's fine, really." She couldn't quite keep the impatience out of her voice. "Ian McGregor was a stranger to him."

The professor's face took on a pained look. "I've offended you. I'm sorry."

Great, Abbie. You've just insulted your best customer. "No, Professor, I'm the one who is sorry. My nerves are a little frayed today. It's been a difficult twenty-four hours. Please forgive me."

"No need to apologize. I understand perfectly." He was smiling again. "And perhaps you'll allow me to be of some help."

She frowned, not understanding.

"I'm accompanying a group of young boys from FitzRandolph Academy and four teachers to Northlandz next Saturday. I was wondering if Ben might like to join us."

The name rang a vague bell. "Northlandz?"

"The railroad display just north of Flemington," he reminded her. "We're planning to meet in the parking lot of FitzRandolph Academy at ten on Saturday morning and return at three. Lunch will be provided."

Now she remembered. Not too long ago, Professor Gilroy had described in great detail the large railroad display, with its intricately carved canyons, thousands of handcrafted buildings, suspension bridges, and of course, the trains, more than a hundred of them, running through villages, tunnels and mountain passes.

"Thank you, Professor," Abbie said. "It's very kind of you to want to include Ben. Unfortunately, he has baseball practice on Saturday. And you know that nothing will make him miss that." She didn't add that although Ben found the professor's gifts "cool," he wasn't that big on trains anymore, and would have probably turned down the trip to Northlandz.

The professor was clearly disappointed. "Another time, then," he said curtly.

Not wanting to commit herself, or Ben, Abbie said goodbye and moved on to the next table.

Twenty-Three

John sat at his desk with his lunch in front of him—a cup of coffee and a cheese sandwich, both from the vending machine out in the lobby. Between bites, he read over the various lab reports that had been brought to his desk earlier.

The tire casts taken at the crime scene had been matched with tread files furnished by various tire manufacturers. They showed that the tires were Goodyear, the kind commonly found on sport-utility vehicles, and had been manufactured in the last couple of years.

Officer Wilcox had been right about the shoe prints. Those found throughout the parking area did not match the victim's. They were much larger. And since the footprints and tire tracks seemed to have been going in the same direction, it was safe to assume that someone other than Ian McGregor had had a confrontation with the SUV.

John took another bite of the sandwich and chewed it slowly as his mind worked out several possibilities. Had the driver surprised the killer and tried to stop him? Or had the killer spotted the truck and attempted to kill a potential witness? Either way, the driver of the SUV should have come forward and reported the incident. So why the hell hadn't he?

He brushed the crumbs off the page and flipped to another. Several sets of fingerprints lifted in McGregor's motel room had been identified as belonging to Arturo Garcia, a convicted felon who had served an eight-year sentence for running a drug distribution center in Toledo, Ohio, and whose residence was listed as El Paso, Texas.

Upon being questioned earlier, the maintenance man at the Clearwater Motel had remembered seeing a battered green pickup truck with Texas tags in the motel parking lot on the afternoon of the murder. That statement, combined with the manager's admission that a man answering Arturo Garcia's description had been looking for the victim, left John no doubt that the owner of the green pickup was Arturo Garcia.

He leaned back in his chair. After ten long years, it appeared as if Garcia had finally caught up with the snitch he had sworn to kill. Whether or not he had kept his word still had to be proven. Evidence, though circumstantial, pointed to him as the killer, but there were still too many questions that remained unanswered. Such as why had the two men walked over to Lake Carnegie in a downpour? Why not kill McGregor at the Clearwater, with no witnesses to worry about? And for that matter, why had the two men hung around in the motel room for hours, eating pizza and drinking beer as if they were the best of pals? The teenager who had delivered the pizza had identified Ian as the man who had opened the door and paid him, but Arturo must have been there too, unseen by the delivery boy.

Earlier, at John's request, Detective Otis Bloom of the Toledo Police Department had sent mug shots of Arturo, a copy of his rap sheet and an El Paso address and phone number.

A call had confirmed what John already suspected. Garcia wasn't there. According to a woman who said she was his mother, Arturo had gone west to visit some friends. No, she had told John a little pointedly, she didn't know where he was staying or how to get in touch with him, adding that her son was forty years old and had stopped accounting for his whereabouts long ago.

After hanging up, John had put an APB out for Garcia and his truck, making sure his ugly mug appeared on the front page of every newspaper in the area and was shown on every TV newscast. At the 7:00 a.m. briefing this morning, Captain Farwell, who headed the PTPD with an iron fist, had speculated that Garcia and his truck were probably hundred of miles from Princeton by now. John, however, wasn't dismissing the possibility the man was still in the area.

Setting the lab reports down, John picked up the autopsy folder and read the dead man's statistics along with a list of old injuries. Those included a healed shoulder fracture, a broken nose, most likely sustained in a fistfight, surgery on the left knee and four fairly deep punctures on the left forearm, made by what Dr. Wang believed was a fork. There was also a more recent wound—a scratch on the throat, possibly made by a sharp blade, and deep enough to have bled.

The time of death had been narrowed down to between 9:00 and 11:00 p.m. Cause of death: massive internal bleeding brought on by multiple stab wounds. Killer was left-handed, a detail he was pleased to note excluded Abbie DiAngelo as a suspect, even though she had never been one. The lady was right-handed.

He was going over what the victim had been wearing, when Tina walked in. Fatigue and disappointment were etched into her fine features. In the space of ten days, she seemed to have aged ten years. She walked straight to his desk, dropped into a chair and took his coffee cup.

"You don't mind, do you? I badly need this."

"Rough morning?"

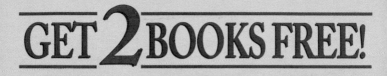

GET 2

HOW TO GET YOUR
2 FREE BOOKS AND FREE GIFT!

1. Peel off the MIRA sticker on the front cover. Place it in the space provided at right. This automatically entitles you to receive two free books and an exciting surprise gift.

2. Send back this card and you'll get 2 "The Best of the Best™" novels. These books have a combined cover price of $11.98 or more in the U.S. and $13.98 or more in Canada, but they are yours to keep absolutely FREE!

3. There's <u>no</u> catch. You're under <u>no</u> obligation to buy anything. We charge nothing – ZERO – for your first shipment. And you don't have to make any minimum number of purchases – not even one!

4. We call this line "The Best of the Best" because each month you'll receive the best books by some of today's hottest authors. These authors show up time and time again on all the major bestseller lists and their books sell out as soon as they hit the stores. You'll like the convenience of getting them delivered to your home at our special discount prices . . . and you'll love your *Heart to Heart* subscriber newsletter featuring author news, horoscopes, recipes, book reviews and much more!

SPECIAL FREE GIFT!

We'll send you a fabulous surprise gift, absolutely FREE, simply for accepting our no-risk offer!

5. We hope that after receiving your free books you'll want to remain a subscriber. But the choice is yours – to continue or cancel, anytime at all! So why not take us up on our invitation, with no risk of any kind. You'll be glad you did!

6. And remember...we'll send you a surprise gift ABSOLUTELY FREE just for giving "The Best of the Best" a try.

Visit us at
www.mirabooks.com

® and TM are trademarks of Harlequin Enterprises Limited.

BOOKS FREE!

Hurry!

Return this card promptly to GET 2 FREE BOOKS & A FREE GIFT!

The Best of the Best™

YES! Please send me the 2 FREE "The Best of the Best" novels and FREE gift for which I qualify. I understand that I am under no obligation to purchase anything further, as explained on the back and on the opposite page.

385 MDL DH5Y   185 MDL DH5Z

FIRST NAME	LAST NAME

ADDRESS

APT.#	CITY

STATE/PROV.	ZIP/POSTAL CODE

▼ DETACH AND MAIL CARD TODAY! ▼

(M-BB3-02) ©1998 MIRA BOOKS

The Best of the Best™ — Here's How it Works:

Accepting your 2 free books and gift places you under no obligation to buy anything. You may keep the books and gift and return the shipping statement marked "cancel." If you do not cancel, about a month later we will send you 4 additional novels and bill you just $4.74 each in the U.S., or $5.24 each in Canada, plus 25¢ shipping & handling per book and applicable taxes if any.* That's the complete price and — compared to cover prices of $5.99 or more each in the U.S. and $6.99 or more each in Canada — it's quite a bargain! You may cancel at any time, but if you choose to continue, every month we'll send you 4 more books, which you may either purchase at the discount price or return to us and cancel your subscription.

*Terms and prices subject to change without notice. Sales tax applicable in N.Y. Canadian residents will be charged applicable provincial taxes and GST.

If offer card is missing write to: The Best of the Best, 3010 Walden Ave., P.O. Box 1867, Buffalo, NY 14240-1867

BUSINESS REPLY MAIL

FIRST-CLASS MAIL   PERMIT NO. 717-003   BUFFALO, NY

POSTAGE WILL BE PAID BY ADDRESSEE

THE BEST OF THE BEST
3010 WALDEN AVE
PO BOX 1867
BUFFALO NY 14240-9952

NO POSTAGE
NECESSARY
IF MAILED
IN THE
UNITED STATES

"Frustrating. I thought I had a lead on the pedophile but it turned out to be a false alarm."

"Still no clue, huh?"

She shook her head and took another sip of coffee. "The bastard knows what he's doing."

"Have you questioned everyone on your list?"

She gave a weary nod. "Questioned and requestioned— from the widowed uncle who visits once a year to the gardener who has known Eric Sommers since he was a baby. All have been cleared."

"The man's not going to stay incognito forever, Tina. Sooner or later, he's going to make a mistake. And when he does, you'll be there to catch him."

Dark, probing eyes caught his. "Let's hope I don't have to wait until another boy is killed before that happens."

"Ours is a tough business."

"I know, I know, and if we don't have the stomach to take the bad with the good, we should get the hell out and give a chance to somebody who will do the job right."

He hated it when she felt that way. "You're doing the job right, Tina," John said sincerely. "Don't let anyone tell you different. This case is a little more grim than most and this guy's slippery as a snake." He shut the file on McGregor. "Anything I can do?"

Tina put the cup back down on his desk. "Yeah. Why don't you guys spring for a coffeepot? This stuff is awful."

At two-fifteen that same afternoon, the desk sergeant on duty brought a copy of the *Mercer County News* to John's desk. "Is that what you were waiting for?" he asked, handing him the paper.

"Yup. Thanks, Luke." John nodded approvingly as he saw Arturo Garcia's mug shot on the front page. The accompanying article included a detailed account of his life of crime, his suspected whereabouts and a description of the pickup truck. Princeton was a small town and Princetonians peace-loving citizens. The news that a dangerous criminal was roaming their fair city would be enough to make everyone who read the article alert and willing to help.

John glanced at his watch. Abbie DiAngelo would be closing her restaurant just about now. If he hurried, he might catch her before she left. After all, he had told her he'd keep her informed of the progress on the case and he was nothing if not a man of his word.

He found a parking space in front of the restaurant and was feeding quarters into the meter when a good-looking young man in jeans and Allen Iverson sneakers walked out, a duffel bag swung over his shoulder.

To John's surprise, the man grinned at him. "Hi. You're Detective Ryan, aren't you?"

"That's right." John flipped the handle on the meter. "And you are?"

A hand shot forward. "Brady Hill. I'm Abbie's sous-chef. I was here when you stopped by yesterday."

John liked him right away. He was direct and friendly and not at all intimidated, as some people were when speaking to a homicide detective. He tucked the newspaper under his arm. "I was hoping to catch Abbie before she left."

"Then you're in luck. She's still in the kitchen." A bright light danced in his eyes as he pushed the door open with his elbow. "Good to see you again, Detective."

John wondered if Abbie would feel the same way, or if his visit would put her on the defensive again.

Well, there was only one way of finding out. He said goodbye to Brady Hill and walked into Campagne.

* * *

"Hi, there."

Startled, Abbie turned around and felt a flush creep up her neck at the sight of John Ryan standing just inside the kitchen's swinging doors.

He gestured toward the dining room. "I ran into your sous-chef."

She reached for a dispenser on the edge of the sink, pumped a small amount of lotion into her palm and rubbed it into her hands. "And I suppose he told you to come right in."

"Do you mind?"

What was she supposed to say to that? *Yes, I mind, because I could let my guard down and tell you something I shouldn't.* She smiled instead. "No, of course not."

She walked into the utility room to discard her apron. When she returned, John Ryan was leaning against the counter, his observant eye moving from one end of the room to the other, taking in every detail. He looked perfectly at ease—but then, why shouldn't he? She was the one who was being put under a microscope.

She leaned against the island, facing him, trying to appear just as relaxed. "What can I do for you, Detective?"

He took the folded newspaper tucked under his arm and handed it to her. "I was wondering if you had seen this?"

She took the paper, and had to make a tremendous effort to keep her face blank. Staring at her, looking every bit as nasty as he had the first time she had seen him, was her attacker, the man she had left for dead at the lake and who had later disappeared.

"Arturo Garcia," she said softly. "The man you told me about."

"He's beginning to look more and more like a prime suspect."

She listened as he brought her up to date about the lab results, Arturo's early association with Ian in Toledo and the drug distributor's vow to kill Ian when he got out of prison.

"What I haven't figured out yet," John continued, "is why those two spent several hours in Ian's motel room on the day of the murder, ate pizza, drank beer and then walked together to Lake Carnegie in the pouring rain." He paused. "Unless they were meeting a third party."

Abbie felt as if a mule had kicked her in the stomach. "A third party?"

"You know, a buddy, maybe even an accomplice."

"Are you saying that Arturo and Ian somehow made up and were planning something together?"

"That's a possibility, don't you think?"

She gave what she hoped was a semi-disinterested shrug. "This third party. You have any clue who it might be?"

She wondered if his slight hesitation was calculated, or totally innocent. "Not yet. I was hoping some of the residents along that stretch of road saw or heard something. They didn't."

Thank God for small mercies. Maybe her luck was holding after all. Not sure she could maintain her poise much longer, she picked up a stack of empty vegetable crates from the floor and was about to take them to the back room, when John rushed forward.

"Here, let me help you with this," he said, taking the load from her.

She felt his arm accidentally brush against her breast, and for and instant she couldn't speak. She even forgot he was the enemy and saw him, perhaps for the first time, as a man who had managed to stir up her senses in a way she hadn't experienced in a long time.

"Where do you want them?" he asked, apparently unaware of what had just taken place.

"Uh…" It took her a second or two to remember. "The utility room. Over there," she added, pointing. She cleared her throat. "Against the wall."

He walked back into the kitchen, plucking a piece of lettuce from the lapel of his jacket and setting it on the counter. "Anything else I can do for you?"

She laughed, pleased to feel some of her tension melt away. "Are you looking for a side job, Detective?"

"No. Just an excuse to spend a little more time with you."

His candor caught her off guard and she felt herself blush again. "Why?"

"Because you and I started on the wrong foot yesterday. In my eagerness to be efficient, I came off as a bully. I'd like a chance to make it up to you, show you I'm not such a bad guy after all."

She knew exactly where he was going with that approach. She may be out of practice when it came to the fine art of flirting, but she wasn't stupid. She could see a come-on as clearly as anyone else. The thought of indulging in a little flirting of her own vanished quickly. No matter how tempting that concept may be, she could not allow herself to be charmed. What if she was wrong about him and all he wanted was to trip her up?

"I never thought you were a bad guy," she said cautiously.

"Then would you do me the pleasure of having a late lunch with me?"

That, she hadn't seen coming. "Now?"

"I thought you might be the impulsive type. Don't tell me I was wrong about that."

Abbie sighed. He wasn't an easy man to say no to, and

he was much too good at analyzing people, which was the reason she had to stay clear of him. "I'm sorry, Detective. I have a half-dozen errands to run before my son gets home."

"Tomorrow, then."

Charming *and* persistent. "I'm afraid not. You see, I—"

"Are you afraid of me, Miss DiAngelo?" he asked with a smile.

That was a little too close for comfort, but she managed to skirt around the question fairly convincingly. "Why would you think that?"

He folded his arms and leaned forward, gazing deep into her eyes. "You didn't answer the question."

His proximity threatened to break down the barrier she had carefully erected. For safety's sake, she pulled back just a little. "No, Detective. I am not afraid of you. I have no reason to be," she added, boldly holding his amused gaze. "The truth is that I'm too busy to socialize." She almost said "date" and stopped herself in time. "I have a son to raise, a business to run and a mother who needs my attention. Believe me, there are times when twenty-four hours are not enough to fit it all in."

He gave a graceful bow. "In that case, I'll have to catch you one day when you're not so busy."

And with those words, he turned and walked away, leaving her standing there with her mouth open.

Twenty-Four

Tony slapped the newspaper on Arturo's lap. "Take a look at this."

Arturo took his eyes off the TV screen, not bothering to look at the newspaper. "What's the matter with you?"

Exasperated, Tony gave the front page a backhand slap. "This is what's the matter with me. Because of your stupidity, your face is in all the papers. And on every TV station."

Arturo glanced at the screen. "I didn't see nothin'."

"If you watched something other than those asinine cartoons, you would have seen it."

Arturo picked up the paper and read. "Shit," he said when he was finished. "How did that happen?"

"How do you think it happened?" Tony bellowed. "You parked the truck outside McGregor's motel room and left it there for the whole world to see. And if that wasn't enough, you left a half-dozen set of fingerprints behind. Why didn't you just leave a note to the cops, telling them what you had done and where they could find you?"

His brother gave him a blank look. Tony rolled his eyes. Sarcasm was wasted on Arturo. "Are you happy now?" he continued. "There are APB's all over the tristate area. It's only a matter of time, maybe only hours, until they find you."

Arturo kept looking at the paper with its blaring headlines, its details of a massive manhunt for the driver of a green pickup truck with Texas plates. There was also a photo and a description of Arturo, ex-con, age forty, armed and dangerous.

"All right, so they made me." Arturo shrugged. "That means shit, man. They don't know where I am."

"People in the neighborhood have seen the truck."

"You said Enrique had agreed to hide it."

"I don't know if we can trust Enrique."

"Why wouldn't you trust him all of a sudden?"

"Because you killed a man and Enrique isn't going to want any part of that."

In a fit of anger, Arturo crumpled the newspaper and flung it onto the floor.

"That was mature," Tony remarked.

"Shut up, will ya? I'm tryin' to think."

Tony gave him a steely look. "There's nothing to think about. You've got to give yourself up."

Arturo's face turned red. "Are you fuckin' crazy?"

"McGregor tried to kill you, which means you acted in self-defense. A good lawyer will prove that and get you off."

Arturo sneered. "You know a good lawyer, Tone? One who works for free?"

This time, Tony remained silent. Arturo had a point. Other than the few hundred dollars they had brought with them, they had nothing. Tony walked over to the window overlooking Second Street, wondering how long it would take for the cops to find his brother. His first impulse, after seeing the newspaper, had been to take the next bus out of town and head back to Texas. The hell with Arturo. Let him fend for himself for once. It's not as though he hadn't been warned. But by the time Tony reached the front door of the apartment they now called home, he had changed his mind.

How could he abandon his brother at a time when Arturo needed him the most?

As always when the two best teams in the league met, the stands at Carl Ripken Ball Field were packed, not only with parents but grandparents and neighbors as well, all of whom had come to cheer the Falcons and the Cardinals.

On the field, the players were warming up, their faces bright with excitement, their eagerness to get the game started almost palpable.

Sunday was Abbie's only day off, twenty-four blissful hours she always set aside for Ben. Although most of that time was spent at the ballpark these days, she didn't mind. Watching Ben have fun was one of her greatest pleasures.

Today, Abbie was in charge of post-game treats. The battle for first place warranted something special, so instead of bringing the usual ice-cream bars, she had baked chocolate-fudge cupcakes, each decorated with a ball and bat.

"Can you make enough for the other team, too?" Ben had asked as he licked chocolate frosting from his finger. "I've got lots of friends on the Cardinals."

Rather than disappoint him, Abbie had let him ride with one of the players' mothers, and had quickly whipped up another batch.

The bleachers were already full when she arrived, so she went to stand by the fence, directly behind Jimmy Hernandez, Ben's best friend and the Falcons' first baseman.

It was the bottom of the fifth inning, score tied 4–4, when she heard a man's voice next to her. "Giving the ump a hard time already?"

Embarrassed to have been overheard criticizing the umpire's last call, Abbie turned to see John Ryan standing beside her. He had changed into casual khaki pants, a gray T-shirt with some sort of police logo on the front and a New York Yankees baseball cap that had seen better days. Behind the aviator sunglasses, his expression was still as unreadable as it had been the first time she'd met him, but the amicable smile was genuine. If he felt any resentment over her refusal to go to lunch with him yesterday, he didn't show it.

"Hello, Detective Ryan." The words sounded stiff to her, and she reminded herself to work on her attitude before he started wondering why she was being so defensive. "You're not coaching today?"

"I just got off duty." He stopped to follow the course of a fly ball that the Falcons' center fielder caught easily. "Jordan has been talking about this game all week," he said.

"So has Ben. I couldn't get him to eat any lunch."

They watched as Ben, playing second base, rushed to catch a fast ground ball the pitcher had missed. The crowd roared, drowning Abbie's cheers. Leaning toward her, John said, "Think my team is in trouble?"

"Time will tell." Although his presence made her uneasy, she couldn't help glancing at him from time to time, struck by how different he was from the man who had questioned her on Friday. It was easy to see why the single mothers she knew were lusting after him. There was something both dangerous and reassuring about him—a quiet strength that made you instantly aware that should trouble occur, John Ryan was the kind of man you wanted in your corner.

"How long has Jordan been playing ball?" she asked.

"Since he could walk. He used to watch me play for the township police team. By the time he was three, he knew the name of every player and the position they played. He had his first home run when he was six and last year he made MVP. He also plays soccer in the fall and basketball in the winter.'' He grinned. ''Are you sorry you asked?''

She returned the smile. ''Not at all.''

A man proud of his son. She liked that. Jack had never shown much interest in Ben's accomplishments. He had barely reacted when she had told him he had missed Ben's first steps. ''There'll be plenty more where those came from,'' was his reply.

The sudden silence that fell over the field made her snap back to attention. It was the last inning and the Cardinals' last batter was getting into position. Aware so much rested on his young shoulders, the boy swung the bat a few times, slashing through the air, then, finally ready, he sank his feet into the sandy ground and gave a nod to the pitcher on Ben's team.

The sharp crack of the bat brought the crowd to its feet. The ball took off like a rocket, while nearly two hundred people jumped and cheered for the Cardinals as the ball landed well beyond the fence. Grinning, the batter took his time running the bases, and was nearly swallowed up by his teammates as they ran out of the dugout to congratulate him on his home run.

The Falcons' winning streak had just been broken, but not their spirit. Though momentarily stunned by the un-expected home run, they recovered quickly, and, in a show of good sportsmanship that made Abbie proud, each player went to congratulate their rivals. Abbie could already see Ben going from boy to boy and pointing in her direction. Within minutes, she was surrounded by a sea of happy faces as she passed the cupcakes around.

''Great game, Jordan,'' she said as she handed John's son one of the treats.

"Thanks." He beamed at his father. "We're tied for first place now. Aren't we, Ben?"

Ben's tongue came out to lick some of the frosting. His eyes shone with friendly mischief. "Yeah, but for how long?"

The teasing forgotten, they were soon chatting away about the all-star picks that would take place in a couple of weeks. Jordan was a handsome boy, a head taller than Ben and athletic-looking, like his father. He also had his father's mischievous grin and dark hair. Only his eyes, a clear green, were his mother's. Abbie had seen Clarice Ryan once or twice, always perfectly dressed and rather distant, as though a Little League ball field was the last place on earth she wanted to be.

"I tell you what," John said, taking Abbie by surprise. "Since neither of you boys had lunch, why don't I take everyone out for pizza?"

Jordan squinted against the sun. "The whole team, Dad?"

"No, smarty-pants, just the four of us." He looked at Abbie. "If that's all right with Ben's mom."

Excited at the prospect, Ben turned imploring eyes toward Abbie. "Oh, Mom, can we?"

Abbie was already trying to come up with a graceful way to say no. A casual conversation at the ball field was fine, but anything more than that was asking for trouble. "I'm not sure we have time."

"Sure we do. The restaurant is closed on Sundays," Ben told John as if that explained everything.

"I was thinking more in terms of your homework, Ben. You didn't finish it, remember?"

"I can finish it tonight. Please Mom, let's go for a pizza. I'm *staaarving*." As if the emphasis on the word wasn't enough of an attention getter, he pressed his hand to his stomach and made a face, mimicking what she assumed was a starving boy.

Abbie laughed. "All right, all right. I know when I'm beat. We'll go."

John gave a nod. "Good. Want to ride with us?"

"I have my car. I can take both boys. Just tell me where we're going."

"Conte's Pizzeria, next to the police station. Know where it is?"

"Sure we do," Ben said excitedly. "We go there all the time."

John watched Abbie walk away, momentarily mesmerized by the gentle sway of her hips. He was shaken from his lusty thoughts when she stopped by her car to let the boys in.

Abbie DiAngelo drove an SUV. The same type of vehicle the police lab suspected had been at the crime scene. John's gaze drifted down to the tires, and although he couldn't read the make from where he stood, he was ready to bet a month's salary they were Goodyear.

But so what, he reasoned as he walked toward his own car. In the last five years, the number of people driving SUV's in the United States had nearly tripled. And Princeton was no exception. The fact that Abbie drove a sport-utility vehicle was no indication she was involved in the murder. Especially since she had told him she hadn't left the restaurant until *after* eleven.

Because he was a cop twenty-four hours a day, he was still thinking about Abbie's truck when he walked into Conte's Pizzeria five minutes later. But the moment he saw her and the two boys waving at him from a back booth, he put his thoughts aside and went to join them.

After finding out they both had a fondness for anchovies,

Abbie and John shared a pie, while the boys, who had made disgusted faces at the word *anchovy,* ordered a plain pizza.

As expected, the conversation centered around professional baseball, their favorite teams and players.

"Hey," Ben told Jordan as he slurped the last of his Coke through a straw. "Want to see my baseball card collection?"

Jordan's eyes lit up. "When?"

"How about now?" He turned to Abbie, who clearly did not see the next question coming and had no time to hide her dismay. "They can come to the house, right, Mom?"

As much as John would have loved to prolong the afternoon, he felt obligated to come to Abbie's rescue. "I think your mom probably has other plans for today, Ben."

But Ben was relentless. "No, she doesn't. Do you, Mom?" He didn't let her finish. "Sundays are our 'do nothing' days. We just hang around the house and swim, or play games. You like to swim, don't you, Jordan?"

"Jordan doesn't have his swimming trunks, Ben," John said quickly. "Maybe another time?"

But like Ben, Jordan didn't let obstacles stand in his way. "You could stop home and pick up a pair, couldn't you, Dad? And I could ride to Ben's house with Ms. DiAngelo."

This time John couldn't come with an answer and apparently neither could Abbie.

"Oh, why not?" she said with a laugh. "Clearly, this is one battle we're not going to win."

Twenty-Five

John stood in Abbie's kitchen watching her feed fresh lemons into a juicer. Sunlight poured through the open French doors, settling on the counter and streaking her hair with fiery highlights. Outside, the boys splashed in the pool, practicing their cannonballs with great exuberance, judging from the noise they were making and the soaked concrete deck.

The house, a rambling, revamped farmhouse, had been as much of a surprise to John as its owner. Set on a slight rise, it offered a spectacular view of the rolling hills that surrounded the property. The interior was all log walls and wood floors polished to a soft patina that gave the DiAngelos' home a unique country charm. But it was the kitchen, snugly tucked beneath an open loft, that was the focus point. It reminded John of Abbie's restaurant. Colors were everywhere—on the blue-tiled island with its well-used copper pots hanging from a wrought-iron rack, on the walls where bunches of garlic, red peppers and various wildflowers hung, and on the counter where a huge blue bowl held an assortment of green, yellow and red peppers. Against the wall, a stone fireplace was flanked by two deep chairs in a rusty shade and a mosaic coffee table where the boys had left their baseball cards.

As for Abbie herself, she was even more beautiful in casual clothes than she had been in her elegant outfit a few days ago. She wore white cotton shorts that showed spectacular legs, a rather distracting aqua T-shirt and white sandals. He tried not to think of the way his arm had brushed against her in Campagne's kitchen yesterday. Or how the feel of that firm round breast had sent his blood pumping. It wasn't easy.

Reluctantly, he tore his eyes away from her and looked around him. "This is quite a place you have here."

"Thank you. It didn't always look that way."

"I know. Most people in the department are familiar with this property. Mrs. Ramsey used to call us on a regular basis, either to rescue her cat or to help her with a fallen tree."

Abbie laughed. "Did she really?"

"We didn't mind. In fact, we used to fight about who would answer the call, because there was always a homemade lunch waiting for us and a plate of cookies to take back to the station. Not to mention that her donations to the police athletic league and numerous other charities were unequaled."

"Catherine is a very generous woman."

"I was surprised to find out she had sold the property, though. She was very attached to it."

Abbie selected another lemon and inspected it carefully before cutting it in two. "She held on to it as long as she could, but it had become too much for her. She had help, of course, but you know how she was, always wanting to do everything herself."

"I thought a developer would have jumped at the chance to build a handful of luxury homes on this tract."

"Oh, they wanted to, believe me." She reached across the counter for a glass pitcher and he caught a whiff of her perfume again—a light, feminine fragrance he had smelled at the restaurant. "Developers had been courting her for years, offering her insane amounts of money for the land. But Catherine, as you know, was a wealthy woman. She didn't care about money. All she wanted was for someone to maintain the beauty of the area. When she heard I was looking for a piece of land to build my house on, she came to see me. At first I just laughed, because I knew I'd never be able to pay her what I assumed she wanted. She surprised me by making me an offer I couldn't refuse. All she wanted in exchange was my promise—in writing—that I would never sell a single acre to developers.''

John gazed at the high open-beamed ceiling, which hadn't been here before. He had always been fond of wood. "Has she seen what you've done with the place?"

"Catherine is a frequent guest here. She loves every nook and cranny. Sometimes she teases me, claiming she wants to buy the property back."

"Isn't a place like this hard to maintain?"

She looked amused. "You mean, do I manage to cut the grass, clean the pool, change the lightbulbs, all those manly things men do around the house?"

He laughed. "Something like that."

"The same young man who cuts my mother's grass cuts mine. And he plows in the winter. The big jobs are done by a handyman, and the rest I do myself, with Ben's help."

"You seem very self-sufficient."

"You sound surprised."

"A little, but not in the way you think. I was simply wondering why someone with your looks, and brains, never got remarried."

"I guess I haven't found the right man."

"Are you looking?" The question was out before he could stop it, and it surprised him as much as it did her.

She recovered quickly, though, and slanted him a mocking look. "Do you have someone in mind?"

"You never know."

"What about you? Why didn't you remarry?"

"Too busy, too fussy." He grinned and borrowed her phrase. "Never found the right woman."

Maybe he had. Maybe she was standing right here. Suddenly that big word—*commitment*—didn't sound so threatening anymore. He watched her pour the contents from the juicer into the pitcher, admiring her quick, precise movements as she added a few tablespoons of sugar, a handful of ice cubes and water.

"I didn't know anyone made lemonade that way anymore."

"In this house, it's the real thing or nothing at all." She set the pitcher on a waiting tray. "One of my mother's mottoes I still live by."

He remembered reading how her mother had influenced her life and the choices Abbie had made. He suddenly found himself wanting to know everything about her, and those around her. "You and your mother must be very close."

"We are." She pointed to a cabinet. "Would you please get me four glasses from the top shelf? The tall ones with the blue shells?"

He took the glasses down and set them on the counter. "Do you see her often?" he asked.

"Who?"

"Your mother."

"Yes, I do," she said a little curtly. She handed him the tray. "You can take this out. I'll bring extra ice."

Surprised by her abrupt tone, he started to say something, then stopped himself. Something had ticked her off. Maybe she didn't like people prying into her private life. Or maybe her mother's illness made her uncomfortable.

Even though the disease had been around for some time now, some people still found it difficult to talk about it.

But no matter how he tried to justify her sudden change in behavior, he had a nagging suspicion it was somehow related to her stepbrother's murder. He didn't know how, but he couldn't shake off the thought, especially after he had seen her get into her SUV earlier.

Abbie wasn't sure when the conversation turned from polite chitchat to something more personal, or who had initiated the sudden change. She had been on her guard at first, all too aware of the risks she was taking having this man in her house. She had soon realized that her fears were unfounded. John Ryan was not only easy to talk to, his candor was quite refreshing. At least when he was off duty.

John was more interested in hearing about her ex-husband than Abbie was in talking about him, but after cutting short his questions about her mother earlier, discussing her failed marriage wasn't that difficult.

"Jack was always a driven man," she explained, glad she no longer felt any rancor toward him. "Unfortunately, most of that drive went into his law practice. When I complained he wasn't spending enough time with Ben and me, he kept telling me the reason he worked so hard was so I could have everything I wanted."

"So his job was the reason the two of you split up?"

"No, not his job. Mine. Jack didn't want me to work. He said it made him look bad vis-à-vis his colleagues, whose wives spent their time playing tennis or golf, and sponsoring scores of charities. The problem was, I wanted to work. I took pride in what I did. And since my catering job made it possible for me to be home with Ben, I didn't see any harm in doing what I loved to do. But Jack saw it differently."

"How long have you been divorced?"

"Four years."

"His idea or yours?"

She smiled. "Are you always this nosy? Or is your curiosity a professional hazard?"

He threw his head back and gave a hearty laugh. "Touché. I'm sorry."

"I was just teasing." She watched the two boys race across the pool in a furious crawl. "Jack and I realized we no longer had a marriage at about the same time. The difference was that I wanted a divorce and he didn't. To him, divorce meant failure, and he hates failure of any kind. When he realized I wasn't budging, he tried to get me to change my mind by filing for full custody of Ben. The judge's decision to rule in my favor was another slap in his face. Outside the courthouse, he actually threatened to kidnap Ben. I had to get a restraining order against him."

"Does he ever see his son?"

"Yes, but not very often, even though I lifted the restraining order long ago." She picked up her glass and twirled the ice cubes around. "Jack moved his law practice to Edison and claims he doesn't have time to come down, even though he's less than an hour away. He keeps in touch through phone calls and e-mail."

John gazed toward the pool where Ben and Jordan had started a splashing fight. "That's got to be tough on your son."

"It was, at first. Jack may not have been the greatest father in the world, but Ben looked up to him, and when he left, his little world collapsed."

"How did you handle it?"

She had always been fiercely protective of her private life, but here she was, opening up to a man who was practically a stranger, and not feeling the least bit awkward about it.

"I kept him busy. And then later, when I decided to open the restaurant, I made him an integral part of that decision. He loved that, being consulted, being made to feel important. I know I'll never be able to take the place of a father, but we're very close. And he has Brady when he's in need of some serious male bonding."

"Your sous-chef?"

She nodded and drained the last of her lemonade. "He's good for Ben."

Afraid they'd start talking about her mother again, she skillfully guided the conversation toward John's own family. She discovered that he had a wonderful sense of humor, especially when he told her about a recent visit he'd had—the second this year—to the headmistress at FitzRandolph. All wit disappeared, however, when he mentioned his ex-wife's intentions—intentions he had quickly put an end to—of sending Jordan to military school.

"I wish I could have him with me full-time," he said seriously. "I know that's what Jordan wants."

"Then why don't you talk to your ex-wife? Tell her how you feel."

"If I was doing anything else but police work, I would have made my move long ago. But with my hours..." He shook his head.

Abbie felt sorry for him. This was a man who truly wanted to be a full-time dad and couldn't. Or thought he couldn't. "I felt the same way when I decided to open Campagne," she said, hoping he'd find her experience helpful. "In fact, I almost gave up my dream. I told myself the hours would be too long, the stress too high, the profits nonexistent—at least at first."

"But you made it work."

"It wasn't easy, but yes, I worked it out, with a little help from my friends—Claudia, who pitches in and baby-sits occasionally, and Tiffany, the college girl who takes over for me when I'm not home. For a long time, my mother was also able to help, but..." She bit her lower lip, realizing that this time it was she who had brought her mother into the conversation.

His expression softened. "How severe is your mother's illness?"

Abbie gave a fatalistic shrug. "Not too—yet. Some days are better than others. She's hard to predict."

"She lives alone?"

"Not anymore. I hired a wonderful woman to stay with her. They get along beautifully." She smiled. "Until they find something to disagree on. Then watch out."

She caught him looking at her in a funny way and let out a nervous laugh. "What?"

"You're quite a remarkable woman, Abbie DiAngelo."

Abbie felt herself blush. She had never been good at accepting compliments, especially when they were made by a man as attractive and magnetic as John Ryan. She was searching for a witty reply, when the boys jumped out of the pool to announce they were hungry again.

Twenty-Six

"Today was great, wasn't it, Dad?"

John had just pulled into Clarice's driveway. At his son's question, he threw the gearshift into park and turned around in his seat. "Yes, it was, son. You and Ben had a lot of fun together."

"Yes, we did, but...I like spending time with you, Dad. I wish..." He stopped, but John knew what he had been about to say. Like him, Jordan wished they could have more time together.

"And I like spending time with you." Anxious to bring a smile back to his son's face, John tousled the boy's hair. "I tell you what. The Phillies are playing at the Vet next Sunday. Why don't I see if I can get a couple of tickets?"

Jordan's face lit up. "That would be neat, Dad. Do you think you could? It's kind of late."

"Hey, I'm a cop, remember?" Slapping his hand on one hip, he did his awful impression of John Wayne, which never failed to make Jordan roar with laughter. "And if I can't buy the darn tickets, I'll get my six-shooter out and shoot our way in."

Jordan laughed. "You're funny, Dad."

"And you'd better run. Your mom said you still had homework to do."

"Okay." He gave John a quick hug. "You'll be at the game on Tuesday? Now that we're tied for first place?"

"I wouldn't miss it."

He watched Clarice's front door long after Jordan had closed it, thinking about his earlier conversation with Abbie, and how impressed he had been at the way she had managed to combine home and career. Had he been too insensitive to Jordan's feelings? Too quick to assume he couldn't take care of his son because of a demanding career? After another minute, he put the Plymouth in gear again, backed out of the driveway and headed straight for his father's house in Lawrenceville.

Two years ago, when John had thought of filing for custody, Spencer Ryan had been very supportive, going as far as suggesting John hire Percy, Spencer's butler, to help take care of Jordan. The Scotsman had run the Ryan household ever since John's mother had died twenty-two years earlier. Dignified as well as efficient, Percy wore many hats around the house. He was a cook, a chauffeur, a housekeeper and a confidant. He also happened to worship Jordan.

His father's offer had been tempting, but John had felt guilty taking Percy from Spencer. The two men were like brothers, and so tuned to each other's idiosyncracies, it was impossible to imagine one without the other.

Maybe there was a way to make everyone, including his ex-wife, happy, but before he spoke with Clarice, he wanted to run the idea by his father.

Percy, a small round man without a single hair left on his shiny, pink scalp, opened the door, greeting John with his usual affability.

"Good evening, John." A long time ago, he had tried to call him *Master* John, as he had with his previous employer, but John had quickly put an end to that, threatening to call him Percival in retaliation. The word *master* had never passed Percy's lips again. "How are you this evening?"

"Actually, Percy, I'm in a terrific mood."

Percy smiled. "I'm glad to hear it. And so will your father, I'm sure. He's in his study."

The highly decorated, four-star former army general was in his favorite La-Z-Boy, and although John couldn't see him, the familiar smell of pipe tobacco delicately laced with chocolate told him that Spencer Ryan was indulging in two of his favorite pastimes—smoking and watching the History Channel. Today, the Battle of the Bulge was unfolding on a large-screen TV, detail by detail.

"Hi, Dad."

Spencer shut off the TV set and swiveled in his chair. Unlike Percy, John's father had a full head of silver hair and a physique that would have made a thirty-year-old green with envy.

"John. Did I know you were coming?"

John laughed and sat down. "I doubt it, since I didn't know myself until a few minutes ago."

"Good. You had me worried for a moment." He took a puff of his pipe. "How did Jordan do today?"

"The Cardinals won. They're now tied for first place."

"Excellent. I'm sorry I missed the game. An old army buddy of mine stopped by and I lost track of time."

"You'll catch the next one." John waited until his father had taken another puff before speaking again. "Dad, I've decided to ask Clarice to let me have Jordan—on a permanent basis."

The statement drew a startled look from his father. "I thought you had given up on that idea."

"I've reconsidered." Jack told him about the incident at school and Clarice's decision to put Jordan in military school. At the mention of Jordan's "killer hook," John thought he saw a smile twitch at the corner of his father's mouth.

"I don't blame you for standing firm on this, son," he said when John was finished. "Military school is no place for a nine-year-old. But if Clarice has already made up her mind, she'll put up one hell of a fight."

"She might. But I have a feeling that, although she loves Jordan very much, this full-time mothering is more than she bargained for, especially now with all those additional responsibilities."

"Does that mean you're willing to hire Percy?"

"Yes, but only on the condition that I don't take him away from you completely." He told him the plan he had come up with, and he could see from the grin on his father's face that he had his full approval.

"The question is," John continued, "will Percy agree?"

Spencer stood up. "I don't know. Why don't we ask him?"

Captain Matthew Farwell wasn't a big man—five foot six and a hundred and fifty pounds, if that—but in his seven years as head of the Princeton Township PD, his size had never been a handicap. His assertive personality and clear judgment had earned him the respect of the men and women in the department—except Tina. She felt, and John didn't entirely disagree, that Farwell was more of a politician than a cop, and would bail out on them to run for office if the opportunity ever presented itself. He was also a hopeless male chauvinist and she resented the fact that she always had to prove herself to him.

The still-unsolved rape and murder of eight-year-old Eric Sommers was a huge thorn in the captain's side. Parents were scared for their kids, the mayor was worried about his job and putting pressure on the chief of police, and the chief was putting pressure on Farwell.

Yesterday, a nervous teacher at Eastbrook Elementary had reported a car parked behind the playground and had been concerned enough to jot down the license plate number before it drove away. No child had been abducted from Eastbrook, but the tension around town had escalated dramatically over the last twenty-four hours.

So it was not surprising that the atmosphere in the captain's office on this Monday morning was charged. Because John and Tina were technically still partners, Farwell had called them into his office together.

"You can both brief me about your respective cases," he said from behind his messy desk. "You first, Wrightfield. What have you got?"

"There may be a small break in the case," she said, looking a little more hopeful than she had in recent days. "The car that was spotted in front of Eastbrook Elementary yesterday was reported by a Barbara Michaels as stolen. Mrs. Michaels lives on Hunt Drive and owns a gray Ford Taurus with New Jersey plates MSC 5438."

Farwell's expression brightened. "Stolen? That's the same MO we had when Eric Sommers was abducted."

"That's right."

"Where is the Taurus now?"

"It was found abandoned on Rosedale Road this morning with another set of tags on it. That's why it took so long to locate. I've had it towed to our garage. The lab techs are going over it now."

Farwell seemed to deflate like a punctured balloon. "That's your break, Wrightfield? You're hoping our killer left a calling card?" He made an exasperated gesture. "Forget it. It's not going to happen. The man is too clever."

"Not so clever after all, Captain." John hated it when Farwell used his rank as an excuse to talk in that tone, especially to an officer as dedicated and methodical as Tina. "Why don't you hear Tina out?"

Farwell raised an eyebrow at his only female detective. "Sorry, Wrightfield. Go ahead."

Tina, who was thicker-skinned than John realized, threw him one of her "thanks, but I fight my own battles" looks and forged ahead. "Barbara Michaels has insomnia. She was awake when her car was stolen, heard the engine being cranked and ran out in time to have a glimpse of the driver."

"Have you talked to her?"

"Not yet. The information was relayed to me from the stolen-vehicle division a short while ago." Her voice chilled slightly, enough for Farwell to notice. "I was on my way out the door when you called me in."

"Oh. Well…" Farwell cleared his throat and drummed his fingers on his desk, a sign that he was flustered. "In that case, go to it, Wrightfield. And bring me some good news."

As soon as she had closed the door, he looked at John. "Maybe you should go with her."

Good thing Tina hadn't heard that or there would have been fireworks. "What for? When it comes to interviewing witnesses, there's none better than Tina."

Farwell thought about that for a moment, then nodded. "All right." He leaned back in his chair, crossing his fingers over his flat stomach. "Where do you stand on the McGregor murder?"

John brought him up to date, carefully omitting any reference to Abbie, and informed him he'd be leaving for New York to talk to Liz Tilly in a few hours.

Twenty-Seven

Liz Tilly lived on McDougal Street, in a neighborhood of coffeehouses, jazz clubs and ethnic restaurants. John had no problem imagining the former wife of Jude Tilly living there. The various newspaper articles he had read on the Internet had described her as a free spirit who was often seen attending some of the more avant-garde plays that were still a staple in and around Greenwich Village.

Liz had moved to New York in the early eighties, but hadn't become part of the Manhattan celebrity scene until her marriage to the rocker and consummate bad boy. The famous couple had been two of the most photographed people in New York, entertaining their friends in their lavish Manhattan penthouse, attending movie premieres and flying to the four corners of the world. The charmed life, however, hadn't been without its problem. Jude had been hopelessly addicted to drugs, a habit that had put a strain not only on his marriage, but on his career as well.

The rock star's divorce ten years later had attracted almost as much attention as his wedding, but when Jude's career started to take a nosedive following the breakup of his band, public interest had quickly faded. Unable to cope with this latest failure, Jude once again tried to find comfort in booze and drugs, but only managed to kill himself with an overdose.

In an interview with *Rolling Stone* some years ago, Liz

had admitted that the divorce had nearly destroyed her. If it hadn't been for her weekly therapy sessions, she was certain her life would have ended just as tragically.

It wasn't until three years ago, in a "Where are they now?" column in a fan magazine, that an overzealous reporter had found out Liz tended bar at the Manhattan Towers in New York.

Her photograph, although a few years old, showed a noticeable resemblance to Ian McGregor. Both had the same dark eyes, the same angular features, although Liz's were softer, and the same pronounced widow's peak.

When John had called her the day before, she hadn't sounded surprised or reluctant to talk to him. In a pleasant, rather sexy voice, she had given him her home address and told him to meet her there on Monday evening at seven.

True to his MO, however, he had gone to the Towers first, choosing a table in the back of the lounge so he could observe her, much as he had done with Abbie that day at Campagne. Liz moved behind the bar with the ease and efficiency born of years of experience, smiling as she poured, and handling the occasional pass like a pro.

At six o'clock sharp, she had taken her drawer out of the cash register, tossed a few good-nights to her customers and walked out. John had settled his tab and done the same.

It had taken him longer than he'd expected to get his car from the valet, and even longer to maneuver through the traffic that made South Manhattan such a nightmare.

This was John's first trip to downtown New York since the tragic events of September 11, 2001. He had come to Ground Zero as part of a special relief team, but also as a counselor for the surviving families of the many victims who had perished in the collapse of the Twin Towers.

The area had changed in the last two years. The debris and chaos were gone and the shops thrived once again, but the memories were still there. One could not drive down Broadway and not remember.

He had almost given up on finding a parking space, when a delivery van pulled away from the curb just two blocks from Liz's building. Moments later, he was ringing her doorbell.

She still wore her bartending uniform, although she had shed the black vest and the shoes, and had undone the first two buttons of her white blouse.

A light smile flitted across her lips. "Lost your way from the Towers, Detective?"

He laughed. "You spotted me?"

"This may be news to you, but men with your looks don't exactly go unnoticed—even in New York." She opened the door. "But I'm embarrassing you. Come on in."

He followed her into a living room furnished with attractive contemporary furniture and a white baby-grand piano in the center of the room that he assumed had belonged to her late husband. Several photographs stood on it, and although hard rock had never been John's music of choice, he easily recognized Jude Tilly, of The Boys From Hell fame, in most of the shots.

"Would you care for something to drink?" Liz asked. "Another club soda? Or would you prefer something stronger?"

"A beer will do fine, if you have one."

"I may even have two." She started for the postage-stamp-size kitchen. "Glass or bottle?"

"Bottle, please."

Two minutes later she was back, with two bottles of Heineken in one hand and a bowl of peanuts in the other. She put the latter on the coffee table and handed him one of the beers before taking a long drink.

"They don't let you drink booze on the job. Can you believe that? We can have soda until we burst, but a lousy beer?" She shook her head. "Isn't that the dumbest rule you ever heard?"

Not crazy about rules himself, John agreed. "How long have you been working at the Manhattan Towers?"

"Too long." She took another sip. "Going on ten years," she added, gazing into the distance. "I wouldn't have to work at all if I had invested Jude's life insurance money instead of blowing it on therapy sessions." She shrugged. "But I was never the idle type anyway. Sooner or later I would have looked for a job."

"This one seems to suit you."

"I guess. It's easy enough. And bartending was all I could find at the time." She laughed. "Being a roadie for a rock band doesn't exactly prepare you for a corporate position."

She scooped up a handful of peanuts and popped one in her mouth. "So, what do you want to know, Mr. Princeton Township Detective?"

"To start with, the obvious. Do you have any idea who would want to kill your brother?"

"Well, let's see now. There was Nick Valenti in sixth grade. He hated Ian for stealing his girlfriend. And the lady next door, who claimed Ian ran over her cat with his dirt bike." Lifting the bottle to her mouth, she gave John a teasing look. "But you'd rather have something a little more current, right?"

"If you don't mind."

"That's not hard either. My brother, you see, had a knack for making enemies. He lied to people, he stole from them and he double-crossed them. Most men would have learned their lesson after the first payback. Not Ian. If he thought he could get away with a scam, he dived in and worried about the consequences later.''

''Can you give me names?'' He took his notebook out. ''Other than Arturo Garcia.''

''Ah, you've heard of big bad Arturo.''

''Rose filled me in. She told me Ian was scared of him.''

''That's an understatement.'' She shook her head. ''Why Ian crossed that man is beyond me. Personally, I would have done the time rather than rat on a man like Arturo Garcia, but as I said, Ian always thought he was smarter than everyone else.''

The lady wasn't pulling any punches, nor did she seem overcome with grief. ''Did he mention any other enemies besides Arturo?''

''No. Unless, of course, you count Abbie DiAngelo.'' Holding the bottle by the neck, she swung it gently. ''She did tell you Ian was blackmailing her, didn't she?''

Damn, he hadn't seen that one coming. So that was what Abbie had been keeping from him. He should have guessed it. He might have, if he hadn't been so taken by her.

''No,'' he said quietly. ''She didn't.''

''Hmm, I wonder why.'' Her tone had turned sarcastic. ''Could it be she was afraid you'd suspect her of murdering my brother?''

He didn't see any reason to tell her Abbie had never been a suspect. ''Why was Ian blackmailing her? I thought they hadn't seen each other in twenty-eight years.''

''That's true.''

''So what did he have on her?''

''Not on her. On her mother.''

Another surprise. ''Irene DiAngelo?''

''I'm assuming you know about the fire that destroyed our Palo Alto house and killed my father.''

''Abbie mentioned it.''

She held the beer bottle at eye level and seemed to study it as she spoke. "Shortly after being released from prison two weeks ago, Ian learned that the fire wasn't an accident after all."

"What was it?" But he already knew what her answer would be.

"Arson." She glanced at him to check his reaction, which he managed to keep neutral. "Irene had decided she no longer wanted to be married to my father, you see, so she hired a professional killer and paid him to set fire to the house."

John took a moment to digest the news, studying the woman across from him and trying to determine if she was lying. It was obvious she wasn't fond of the DiAngelos, but would she make such an outrageous accusation just to get Abbie and her mother in trouble?

He settled deeper into his chair. "Why don't you tell me what you know."

She chewed a few more peanuts. "Sure, but remember, all this is secondhand. Until a couple of days ago, I believed my father's death was accidental."

"I'll keep that in mind."

She got out of her chair and, bottle still in hand, walked over to the window overlooking the noisy street below. Even from the fourth floor, the cacophony of horns and police sirens was deafening. It made John appreciate the serenity of his Princeton neighborhood.

"While Ian was in prison," Liz began, keeping her back to him, "a man on death row at another Ohio prison saw Abbie on TV. Apparently, she had just won an award important enough for one of the major networks to do a piece on her. He remembered that Irene's former name was DiAngelo, and when he heard the broadcast, it reminded him of the woman who had hired him and her connection to Ian.''

''What's the inmate's name?''

''Earl Kramer. He and Ian met years ago when both were involved in some scam. Through the grapevine, Earl found out Ian was about to get out of prison and sent word that he wanted to see him. When Ian got there, Earl told him that twenty-eight years ago, Irene McGregor had paid him five thousand dollars to kill her husband and make it look like an accident.''

It took all of John's training to keep his voice on an even keel. ''I find that hard to believe.''

Liz turned around. ''I was surprised, too. Irene never struck me as the cold-blooded-killer type, but then, she was an abused woman. Not physically abused—my father didn't believe in hitting women. He preferred to fight them on an emotional level. There were times when she seemed so…beaten, so desperate, I felt sorry for her. It was probably despair that drove her to write that letter.''

John sat up. ''What letter?''

''Irene was very close to her father and used to write him long letters. Ian intercepted one of them and was using it to keep Irene from telling Patrick that Ian smoked pot.''

''What was in the letter?''

''Various grievances. And her admission that she had thought of killing her husband.''

''Did you see the letter?''

''No, but Ian told me he gave Abbie a copy.''

John was silent, digesting the information. Ian had not come to Princeton to reunite with a long-lost sister and hit her up for a loan. He had come to blackmail her. Had he been successful? John's instincts were at odds with his growing feelings for Abbie. On one hand, he couldn't imagine her giving in to blackmail. On the other, he knew she loved her mother and would want to protect her at any cost.

"What was Kramer's reason for admitting to the crime three decades later?" he asked at last.

"Ian said the man had become some kind of religious fanatic. Apparently many inmates do once they get on death row."

"He could have confessed to the police instead of your brother."

"He thought Ian could put the information to good use. My brother's words, Detective," she added, raising her hands, "not mine."

"What exactly does Earl claim to have done?"

"Torched my father's house. Again, Ian's words. My brother was never big on subtleties."

"What kind of proof is he offering?"

"His confession, which he seems to think counts for something. He also gave Ian the exact location of the house, the placement of each bedroom and a description of the master bedroom, where my father slept."

"That only proves he knew the layout, which your brother could have given him."

She looked surprised. "Are you implying my brother made up the story for the sole purpose of blackmailing Abbie?"

"Isn't that conceivable, considering Ian's background?"

She seemed to consider the question. "I would agree with you, except for one thing."

"What's that?"

She took her time answering, as though savoring the moment. "Abbie agreed to pay my brother one hundred thousand dollars for his silence."

Twenty-Eight

Tiffany had only been gone a few minutes when Abbie heard the sound of footsteps crunching on the graveled driveway.

Walking quietly, she approached the front door and peered through the long, narrow window alongside it, ready to hit the panic button on her security system if she didn't like what she saw. The outdoor sensors had been activated and the driveway was bathed in bright light, confirming her suspicions. Someone was out there. Someone who apparently wasn't trying to hide, judging from the car that had been left in plain sight.

Taking a closer look, she let out a sigh of relief as she recognized John Ryan's black Plymouth. But what was he doing here at this hour? And why hadn't he come directly to the front door and rang the bell instead of sneaking around like a thief?

She opened the door. "You have something against doorbells, Detective?"

He seemed surprised at the question, as though walking around her property in the middle of the night was the most natural thing in the world. "I thought you might be out by the pool."

She looked at the flashlight in his hand. "At eleven-thirty at night?"

"I need to talk to you."

He was different, she thought, feeling a sudden chill, not as friendly as he had been the previous day. And she didn't believe he had expected to find her relaxing by the pool at this time of night.

A dreadful apprehension started to build in her gut. He knew something.

"May I come in?" he asked, ending her speculation.

She wanted to tell him no. It was late and she was exhausted, not to mention completely unprepared to answer whatever he had come to ask. But something about the way he stood there, with that serious look on his face, told her he wasn't going anywhere until he had talked to her.

Managing a nervous smile, she let him in and walked ahead of him in silence, until they had reached the kitchen. She knew she probably should invite him to sit down, but since this visit had such an official feel to it, instead she leaned against the counter and waited.

He took off his jacket, as if he was planning to stay a while, and draped it over the back of a chair, taking his time. Her gaze stopped on the leather holster strapped to his shoulder and the gun tucked inside. Both—which she hadn't seen before—seemed to fit the occasion.

When he finally spoke, his voice was filled with mild disappointment. "Why didn't you tell me you were being blackmailed?"

Her heart lurched in her chest. She thought of answering the question with a swift denial, accompanied by a shocked expression. She had become such a master manipulator these last few days, she could probably pull it off and he'd never know the difference. Obviously someone had tipped him off, but so what? It would be that person's word against hers.

She couldn't do it. She couldn't lie to him anymore.

Reluctantly, she met his unblinking gaze. "How did you find out?"

"So it's true."

She nodded, slowly, to give herself a little time to get her thoughts together.

"Would you be more comfortable if we sat over there?" He surprised her by motioning toward the two easy chairs in front of the fireplace.

Since he seemed to be calling the shots, she followed him to the cosy corner. Unable to relax, however, she sat on the edge of the chair and clasped her hands on her lap.

"Go ahead," he said gently.

The soothing sound of his voice helped her calm down. She talked for more than ten minutes, her voice growing stronger and more confident with each word, as if the simple task of finally telling the truth had removed a huge weight from her chest. She told him everything, starting with the death of her biological father when she was five and the fire that had burned the McGregors' house down, to her attempt to deliver the blackmailing money to Ian at Lake Carnegie and the letter she had burned along with its copy.

John didn't interrupt her, not even when she mentioned taking the PPK with her to the lake. She half expected a stern lecture, a reminder that carrying a concealed weapon was a serious offense as well as a dangerous practice. Instead he asked, "Can you describe the man who attacked you?"

There was no hesitation there. The man's face would be engraved in her mind forever. "It was Arturo Garcia."

John nodded. "I figured that much."

"Have you uncovered what he and Ian were doing at the lake together?"

"From the information we have so far, I gathered Arturo

found out where Ian was staying and went there to collect his money. Ian had to make a choice—tell Arturo about the forty-eight thousand dollars and offer to give it to him or be killed.''

''Then why would Arturo kill Ian before he could get the money?''

''My hunch tells me Ian had no intention of handing the money to Arturo. That's why he lured him to the lake. He felt he had a better chance to kill him if—''

''Kill him?''

''We found a garrote, made from a coat hanger, near the body. It looks as if Ian may have tried to use it on Arturo.''

''And instead, he got himself killed.'' Abbie fell back against the cushion and was surprised when John leaned forward and took her cold hands in his, warming them instantly.

Their stare locked and held. ''Why didn't you tell me sooner, Abbie?''

As his gaze skimmed her face, she was suddenly acutely aware of him, of his masculinity, the way he looked at her with eyes that had turned warm and caring, and especially the way he held her hands with a grip that was both strong and gentle. ''I was afraid you'd call the Palo Alto police and turn my mother in.''

''You thought I would take the word of a con man— *two* con men—instead of yours?''

''I wasn't thinking rationally.''

''Not too many people would in the same circumstances.''

She gave him a hopeful smile. ''Are you saying that you believe my mother is innocent?''

''I can't answer that until I've checked Earl Kramer's story, but I won't turn your mother in on such flimsy evidence, Abbie. I'm not that kind of cop.''

Claudia had tried to tell her that but she hadn't wanted to listen. "What about the letter I burned? Isn't that destroying evidence?"

"If your mother didn't commit a crime, that letter has no meaning."

If. Suddenly, finding out the truth about that horrible night twenty-eight years ago had become her prime focus. Until then, there could be no peace of mind for her and for her family.

She looked down at their joined hands, remembering he had not told her everything. "John?"

"Yes?"

"What were you doing walking around the back with a flashlight earlier?"

"I was looking for your truck."

"My truck?"

"The lab report indicates that the tire prints found throughout the lake parking area were made by Goodyear tires, found mainly on sport-utility vehicles. When I realized you drove an SUV, I had to check out your tires." He pointed at the flashlight on the table. "I was about to take a peek through the garage window, when you walked out."

"So I am a suspect, after all."

"Not a *murder* suspect, just a witness withholding evidence."

Gently, she pulled her hands away, but not because she was upset with him. Why should she be, when he had just volunteered to help her? "How did you find out that Ian was blackmailing me?"

"That's not important."

"It is to me. I have a right to know," she added when he didn't answer.

He seemed to give that statement a moment's consideration. "Liz Tilly told me."

Liz. So her fears had been justified after all. And Liz was still the same bitch she used to be.

John stood. "I think I've kept you up long enough. Why don't I let you get some rest. We'll talk more about all this tomorrow."

At the door they both stopped. She looked up and saw the change in his eyes, the way his gaze drifted to her mouth, lingered there for a moment before returning to her eyes. The effect was as potent as if he had touched her.

He spoke first, breaking the spell. "I'll see you at the funeral?"

"Yes." For some reason, she couldn't manage much more than that.

She waited until the Plymouth's red taillights had disappeared before going back in and closing the door. She listened to the silence, surprised at how empty the house felt now that John was gone.

She slept that night for the first time in over a week.

Twenty-Nine

The unseasonable weather that had plagued the Delaware Valley these past couple of days had been replaced by blue skies and a brilliant sunshine that burned through the trees and turned the pond in front of Wilbert Pharmaceuticals into glass.

The building where Clarice Ryan worked was located in Princeton Forrestal Center, a lush seventeen-acre park owned by Princeton University and occupied by research facilities and corporate offices of internationally known companies.

Wilbert was the park's most recent addition, having moved its headquarters from Bordentown to Princeton two years ago. The three-story glass and stone structure, with its enclosed atrium and its own corporate art gallery, had already become a landmark every Princetonian talked about with great pride.

Clarice had been surprised to hear from John in the middle of the week, and even more surprised when he had refused to put off the meeting.

Although he knew Clarice had been promoted to vice president six months ago, nothing had prepared him for the size and elegance of her new office when her secretary ushered him in. With one quick glance, he took in the bank of windows overlooking the pond, the antique desk that held center stage and the oriental rug beneath it. There was even a Van Gogh painting on one wall that couldn't possibly be the real thing. Knowing Clarice, though, it probably was.

"Wow," he said when she rose from behind her desk. "This is some digs you've got here. No wonder the price of meds is going through the roof."

The remark, which he had intended as an icebreaker, brought him a cool stare. "What do you need to tell me you couldn't discuss over the phone?" she asked.

In other words, the lady was busy and he should get on with whatever was on his mind. Fair enough. "May I sit down?"

She waved toward a green brocade chair. "All right. But I must warn you. I'm in between meetings."

"This won't take long." He propped one ankle over his knee. "I'd like you to rethink our arrangement about Jordan."

She sat down, a puzzled look on her face. "*Rethink* our arrangements? What does that mean?"

"It means that I would like to have custody of Jordan. *Full* custody."

She leaned back in her chair, a shocked expression on her otherwise impassive face. "Are you out of your mind?"

"Not at all. Actually, it's a very sound decision, and the more I think about it, the more it makes sense."

"To you, maybe, but not to me."

"I admit I have erratic hours, but since you became vice president, you have even less time with Jordan than I do. You travel more than ever before, sometimes out of the country and for several days. During that time, Jordan is shuffled from one household to another and that isn't good for him. The neglect is beginning to affect his grades and his behavior."

"Are you accusing me of neglecting my child?"

He shook his head, annoyed at himself for sounding so critical. That had never helped him before. "That was a poor choice of words. I'm sorry. The fact is—and this is Mrs. Rhinehart's own observation—Jordan may *feel* neglected, and he's reacting the only way he knows how—by forcing us to pay attention to him."

"Jordan is not a devious child. He wouldn't do that."

"Maybe not consciously." He gave her a second to think those last words through before adding, "He's just nine years old, Clarice. You keep saying he needs discipline and focus. I say he needs continuity and familiarity. He needs a home he can come to every afternoon and he needs the same person to be there, day in and day out, baking cookies, making his dinner, helping him with his homework."

Clarice let out a sarcastic laugh. "*You're* going to do that? Bake cookies and make his dinner?"

"Not me. Percy."

She folded her arms. "Percy." She said the name with a certain degree of cautiousness, perhaps because Percy was one of the few people in the world who Clarice actually respected.

"Why not? Jordan and Percy already have a great relationship, and Percy, I'm sure you'll agree, is one of the most reliable persons you and I know."

Clarice allowed a smile to touch her lips. "I can't imagine him with Jordan on a permanent basis. The boy can be quite a challenge."

"Percy can handle him. He's already proven that."

"And he would be willing to leave your father to care for a nine-year-old?"

"He wouldn't be leaving my father entirely. We came up with an arrangement that will suit everybody. A few hours a week, while Jordan is in school, Percy will go to my father's house to do all the things that need to be done and—"

"No."

John brought his leg down. "I beg your pardon?"

"The answer is no. I won't give up custody of Jordan."

"Why not? You can see him whenever you wish."

"I'm his mother, John. I shouldn't have to see him whenever I wish. The boy should be with me. A judge apparently thought so, too, or he wouldn't have granted me custody."

"That was before you became vice president of this company. He might feel differently now that you—"

"Stop throwing my position in my face," she said heatedly. "Yes, my job takes me away occasionally, but so what? A lot of parents have obligations that include business trips. You don't see them giving up their children."

"You could put your career on hold for a few years." That wasn't the smartest thing he had ever said, but he couldn't help it. She was pissing him off.

"And have you support me?" The way her mouth puckered told John what she thought of that idea. "No, thanks."

"You don't have to look at it as support. I've never touched a penny of my grandfather's trust fund. You say the word and I'll turn the whole thing over to you and Jordan."

"I don't want your damn money, dammit." Her composure was starting to crack and that was never a good sign. "I want to work!"

"Fine then. Work. Move up the corporate ladder. Just let me have Jordan."

She jumped out of her seat. "I can't believe your arrogance, John. Walking in here, making demands, accusing me of neglecting my child, claiming he'd be better off with a...butler than he is with me.''

"Percy would give him the attention he needs when I'm not there.''

"Your father put you up to this, didn't he?'' she asked almost viciously. "He's never liked me.''

"My father had nothing to do with it.''

She continued to gaze at him, her arms folded across her chest.

"Clarice,'' he said, leaning forward and softening his tone. "Do you actually believe that putting Jordan in a military school is in his best interest?''

"Yes. The boy needs—''

"Discipline and focus. Yes, you've told me. I can provide that, too, Clarice, along with all the things a boy needs from a father.''

"Jordan belongs with me,'' she said stubbornly.

"But he wouldn't be with you if you enroll him at Brandywine. He'd be fifty miles away, in a school that would only allow him to come home on weekends and holidays. You'd be willing to do that, but you won't let him stay with his own father?''

He had saved his trump card for last. "Summer vacation is coming up. How will you manage caring for Jordan during those long three months, while still fulfilling your professional obligations?''

Obviously she hadn't thought of that, because she averted her eyes and started to play with a pencil on her desk. He waited her out until she looked up.

"Have you discussed this with Jordan?''

"No. I wanted to talk to you first.''

"What if he's against it?''

"I don't think he will be.''

"How do you know? Has he said he wanted to stay with you?"

"No. He knows that would hurt you, and he could never do that."

"You think you know him so much better than I do, don't you?" Her voice had an odd quality to it, a mixture of bitterness and resignation.

He couldn't find anything appropriate to say, so he kept quiet. He had said everything there was to say. The next step wouldn't be so pleasant. For all their sakes, he hoped she wouldn't force him to take it.

The intercom on her desk buzzed, breaking the awkward silence. Clarice leaned over it. "Yes, Sonia?"

The receptionist spoke in a soft, British-accented voice that seemed to blend with the decor. "Mr. Campbell and his associates have arrived."

"Very well. Get them something to drink, will you? I'll be right out."

She released the button, and looked at John for several seconds. "I'll agree to a *trial* arrangement only. After a couple of weeks, if Jordan is not happy, you'll have to send him back."

"What if he wants to stay with me?"

She picked up a stack of paper and tapped it on the desk surface until it formed a neat rectangle. "I don't want to commit myself to anything. Let's see how those two weeks work out first."

"All right."

"When were you planning on doing this?"

"At the start of the summer recess. I see no reason to disrupt his routine now."

She nodded and rose at the same time he did. "Just one

thing," she said as they walked to the door together. "I'd like to be the one to tell Jordan about this new arrangement."

"Fair enough."

Thirty

In spite of her decision to attend Ian's funeral, Abbie had come awfully close to being a no-show. Now that she knew how quickly Liz had turned on her, the prospect of facing her stepsister sounded as appealing as mud wrestling. Nor did she look forward to paying her respects to a man—a blackmailer—who had tried to destroy her family.

Brady, with his usual common sense, had brought her back on track. "Do it for Rose," he had told her. "She's a good person."

Brady was right. Rose had played no part in Ian's nefarious scheme. Her only sin was to have loved a man who probably didn't deserve her. Keeping that in mind, Abbie had put her doubts aside, donned her favorite black dress— a sleeveless Donna Karan number she had bought for Campagne's grand opening three years ago—and left to pick her mother up for the funeral.

As she drove, she kept glancing at her, searching for signs of distress, but Irene sat calmly, gazing out the side window and saying an occasional word to Marion, who sat in the back. There was no telling how Liz, who apparently believed Irene was a murderer, would react when she saw her. Would she make a scene? Come over and spew accusations? Abbie had no idea what to expect, which was the reason she had tried to discourage her mother from coming along, but Irene had refused to change her mind.

Rose was already there when they arrived. She was dressed in black and stood close to the casket, looking sad and lost. Abbie walked over to where she stood and introduced her to Irene and Marion.

John Ryan was a few feet away, scanning the area. He gave Abbie a nod, but remained at his post. She had heard that homicide detectives routinely attended the funerals of murder victims in the hope the killer would show up, but she was doubtful. What killer would be foolish enough to show his face here?

On the other side of the casket, standing alone and not looking at any of them, was Liz. Abbie wouldn't have recognized her any more than she had recognized Ian. The long, mousy brown hair had been colored a muted shade of blond, and styled in a sleek page boy, with one side tucked behind her ear, allowing the other to spill forward and obscure part of her face. She was heavier than Abbie remembered, more voluptuous and not without a certain sex appeal.

She showed no emotion as the minister began talking about redemption and eternal peace. Yet, for reasons she couldn't explain, Abbie felt sorry for her. For all the dreams Liz had entertained as a teenager, and the exciting life she had led for a brief time with Jude Tilly, she had ended up all alone.

Beside her, Irene gripped her arm. "Is that Liz?" she asked in a whisper.

"Yes," Abbie whispered back.

"She's very pretty."

"Yes, she is."

"Should we go talk to her? After the service?"

God, no. That was the last thing Abbie wanted. "She doesn't want to talk to us, Mom."

"You don't know that."

Abbie didn't reply, but Irene persisted. "I don't think it's right, coming to her brother's funeral and then ignoring her. She was family once."

There was no point in arguing with her. Nowadays, when Irene made up her mind about something, she fought relentlessly until she got her way. "I tell you what," Abbie said diplomatically. "After the service, you and Marion go wait in the car and I'll go say hello to Liz and see if she wants to chat for a few minutes. If she does, I'll bring her over. How's that?"

Looking satisfied, Irene gave a short nod and returned her attention to the minister.

The service was brief and unemotional, except for Rose's soft sobs. As Liz started walking toward the minister, apparently to thank him, Abbie asked Marion to take her mother to the car, told John and Rose she would see them later, and walked around the open grave. When Liz turned around to leave, Abbie stepped up.

"Hi, Liz," she said quietly. "I'm Abbie."

Hostile dark eyes met hers. "I know who you are, Abbie." Her voice was deep and scratchy. "And quite frankly, I'm surprised to see you here. Unless you want to make sure Ian is really dead."

"I'm here because Rose asked me to be."

Liz's chin jutted forward a little, reminding Abbie of the rebellious teenager she had once been. "Did you kill him, Abbie?"

"You know I didn't."

"I know you hated him, and wanted him dead."

"I wanted him out of my life," Abbie snapped, and then forced herself to relax. An outright confrontation was not what she had in mind. "You know my mother could never do what Ian accused her of. He and his sick friend made it all up so they could extort money from me."

"Is that your version?"

"That's the truth."

Liz's hard gaze softened. "Look, if you're worried I'll make a scene, or say something to Irene, relax, okay? I'm not going to do that. I know about her condition. I'm angry, yes, but I'm not a monster."

"How do you know about my mother's condition?"

"Ian told me."

"How did *he* know?" But the answer to that was clear. He had been snooping.

Liz shrugged. "I have no idea how he knew. Docs it matter? It's the truth, isn't it? Irene has Alzheimer's?"

"Yes, it's the truth."

"I'm sorry."

Something in Liz's almost gentle tone made Abbie wonder if the woman was really as tough as she tried to appear. People who lived alone often developed a thick, protective outer layer that enabled them to cope with life's many inconsistencies. Considering the ups and downs Liz had encountered over the years, was it any great surprise she kept her true feelings to herself?

Encouraged, Abbie asked, "Are you staying at the Clearwater with Rose?"

"I was. I checked out."

Abbie did some quick thinking. Would there be any harm in inviting her and Irene to the house for a while? She could make some sandwiches and pretend they were all a big happy family. How hard could that be?

"Look," she said, "I know it would be unrealistic of me to expect us to be friends after all this time, but…could we at least be civil to each other? We were family once," she added, borrowing the line from her mother.

Liz let out a brittle laugh. "You're still a dreamer, aren't you, Abbie? Just like you used to be."

A gust of wind blew across the wide expanse of grass, lifting Liz's hair. At the sight of the ugly scar on the right side of her face, Abbie couldn't suppress a wince.

Liz caught the look and quickly smoothed her hair back in place.

"I'm sorry," Abbie said. "I didn't mean to stare."

"That's okay. Everybody does."

"Is that from the fire?"

"What else?"

"I thought you had plastic surgery."

"I did. This side of my face was the most seriously burned and couldn't be taken care of at the same time as the rest. When the time came to do the surgery, I decided I'd had enough."

"I'm so sorry, Liz. You have a right to be angry, even bitter, but not at my mother. She didn't cause this."

Liz looked suddenly flustered, as if Abbie's show of compassion had caught her unprepared and she didn't know how to handle it. "I've got to go." She started to turn away.

"Liz, wait. I thought…I mean, I was wondering…" She glanced toward the Acura again and saw her mother watching her. "I thought we could all go to my house for a light lunch."

"Thanks, but I need to get back. I'm working tonight."

But Abbie wasn't ready to let her go just yet. She planted herself firmly in front of her. "Don't you want to know anything about me?"

"Ian told me everything I need to know. You're a famous, successful chef. You have a lovely home, a son."

"His name is Ben. He's nine years old, and he loves baseball."

"You're very lucky."

Relieved that Liz no longer showed signs of hostility, Abbie decided now was a good time to find out more about her stepsister. "You and Jude didn't want children?"

Liz glanced toward a gray sedan, the only car left except for the Acura. For a moment, Abbie thought Liz was simply going to walk around her and leave. She surprised her. "Not at first. We were having too much fun. When we finally decided the time had come to start a family, I found out I couldn't have children."

News of Liz's sterility came as a shock. "I'm sorry," Abbie said softly. "I had no idea."

"No one did. Both Jude and I agreed to keep that part of our lives to ourselves. It was just too painful to share with others."

At the little catch in Liz's voice, Abbie was filled with an incredible sadness. No matter how little she and Liz had in common, Abbie was certain her stepsister would have made a good mother. She wasn't sure what made her ask the next question. "Would you like to meet Ben?"

"There you go again, trying to be a pal. I told you it won't work."

"How do you know until you try?"

"Give it a rest, Abbie, will you?" Liz glanced toward the car again, hesitated for a moment as though she was reconsidering the offer. Then, with a shake of her head, she walked past Abbie and headed for the sedan.

When Abbie returned to Campagne following the funeral, Brady was standing outside the restaurant, which hadn't opened for lunch yet.

"Ken Walker showed up again," he informed her, casting an angry glance across the square.

"He came into the restaurant?"

"No, he stayed outside. He walked up and down the sidewalk first, then went to sit on that bench over there." He pointed toward the Green.

"Did he say anything? Cause any problems?"

Brady's voice grew impatient. "Not this time, but Abbie, come on, the man is unstable. There's no telling what he'll do next."

Abbie scanned the square, but Ken was nowhere in sight. "I'll talk to Lainie. Maybe she can reason with him."

But when she called Ken's wife, Lainie's news was disconcerting.

"Ken moved out last week," she said. "I told him not to come back until he stopped making everyone around him so miserable."

"Is he gambling again?"

"No, but his negative attitude was starting to get me down. And Robbie's a mess. He loves his dad, but he doesn't understand why he's acting this way."

"What exactly is Ken doing?"

"He's blaming everyone for his problems, moping around the house instead of looking for a job. Maybe now he'll realize what he stands to lose if he doesn't make some changes." She paused. "I'm sorry if he's taking his frustrations out on you, Abbie. You've been more than fair to him, considering what he did."

Abbie hung up, still unwilling to call the police as Brady had suggested. Ken was going through a rough time, and adding to his troubles by calling the authorities would not be very effective. She would just have to be on her guard, and make sure there was no repeat of the incident of a few days ago.

Thirty-One

Wkhen John arrived at the station on Thursday morning, he found two Federal Express envelopes on his desk. One was from his new friend, Detective Otis Bloom in Toledo, and contained a copy of Earl Kramer's court transcripts. The other contained Rose's cell phone records.

He picked up the transcripts first and started to read. Kramer's trial for the murder of a police officer had lasted only five days, and for the prosecution, it had been a slam dunk. Although the defendant had pleaded not guilty and repeatedly claimed he was the victim of an elaborate police frame-up, two witnesses had seen him shoot Officer Daniel Moyarty point-blank, as the young policeman lay wounded on the sidewalk.

The incident had begun a half hour earlier, when Kramer's neighbor had called the police to report a domestic disturbance next door. When Moyarty and his partner, Kevin Luthcomb, had arrived, they had found Kramer's girlfriend badly beaten and unconscious. Alerted by the police sirens, Kramer had escaped through the fire escape and taken off in his car.

After a fifteen-minute high-speed chase through the streets of Toledo, he had crashed his car and tried to run just as Moyarty and Luthcomb were getting out of their vehicle. Kramer had shot them both, hitting Luthcomb in the chest and Moyarty in the shoulder. According to the two witnesses, Kramer had stood over Officer Moyarty and shot him in the head, execution style, before fleeing in the cruiser.

He was found a day later, hiding in a bordello. Luthcomb survived the shooting but Moyarty had died on the spot, leaving behind a wife and a six-month-old baby.

As expected, Kramer had a rap sheet longer than the Delaware River, but his attorney had not allowed any of his priors to be introduced in court. Nevertheless, a jury of seven men and five women had found him guilty on all five counts: assault and battery, fleeing from the scene of a crime, first-degree murder, attempted murder and grand theft.

After two appeals, both of which had been denied, Kramer's chances of escaping the death penalty were slim to none.

John read every word of the sixteen-page transcript twice, searching for something he could use as leverage against Kramer, something his attorney or the prosecution had missed.

He found nothing.

Disappointed, he picked up the rap sheet again. The man's felonies over the past twenty-five years ranged from misdemeanors to more serious charges, such as the molestation of his seven-year-old stepdaughter when he was twenty-three, and the aggravated assault on a Chinese immigrant. He had served time for both before being charged for the killing of Officer Moyarty.

As the germ of an idea began to worm its way into John's head, he picked up Rose's cell phone records and went down the list. Since the day she and Ian had arrived in Princeton, six calls had been made to numbers in the 609 area code—four to take-out restaurants and two to Campagne. There was also one long-distance call to Toledo. Judging from the date and time, John guessed that was the call Ian had made to Earl Kramer's wife from Abbie's restaurant.

Only one call had been made *after* Ian's murder. That call could only have been made by the person who had stolen Rose's phone. If John was lucky, that person and McGregor's killer would be one and the same.

His eyes on the number, John dialed it.

"Enrique's Garage."

John didn't miss a beat. "I need to bring my car in," he said. "Where exactly are you located?"

"In Trenton. Corner of Center and Bridge Streets. You can't miss it." The man had a faint Hispanic accent. "What's the problem with the—"

But John had already hung up.

The man who had answered the phone had been right. John couldn't possibly have missed Enrique's Garage, not with the colorful sign in the shape of an old Edsel and the American and Puerto Rican flags flying side by side just above the entrance.

A man's upper body was hidden under the hood of a beat-up Chevy Impala. John approached it. "Excuse me. Are you Enrique?"

The man straightened up, inspecting him with sharp brown eyes. "Yeah, I'm Enrique. What can I do for you?"

John took out his badge and gave Enrique a few seconds to inspect it before putting it away. "For starters, you can tell me where I can find Arturo Garcia."

There was no change of expression in the man's face. "I don't know any Arturo Garcia," he said with a shake of his head.

"Are you sure? He called this garage four days ago."

Enrique shrugged. "Lots of people call here, Detective. They don't always give a name."

John took out Arturo's mug shot and held it up so Enrique could have a good look. "Maybe this will refresh your memory."

The man leaned forward a little, going to great pains to carefully study the picture. "Sorry." He shook his head again. "I never saw him before."

"He drives a green pickup truck with Texas plates."

"There are lots of pickup trucks in this neighborhood, but they all belong to locals, people I know. And none have Texas plates."

John looked around. "You work alone?"

"Yes, sir, I do it all." Enrique looked proud. "The repairs, the towing, the bookkeeping." He pointed at a sign advertising used tires, starting at nine ninety-nine. "I even do my own promotion."

John had no reason not to believe him. The man seemed sincere enough, and apparently he was a hard worker. However, John was suspicious by nature, so rather than take the mechanic at face value, he handed him his card. "Call me if you suddenly remember something, will you? Or if you see Garcia around."

Enrique took John's card. "What's he done, Detective?"

"He's wanted in connection with a murder. The victim is a man Garcia knew back in Toledo—Ian McGregor. You may have read about it."

This time there was a change in Enrique's cool demeanor. His mouth opened slightly and his complexion turned gray. He could have been worried about the possibility of a murderer running loose in his neighborhood. Then again, it could be more than that. John decided it might not be a bad idea to keep a discreet eye on Enrique.

As John turned to leave, he bumped into a young man

who bore an amazing resemblance to Ricky Martin, the singing sensation the girls in Jordan's class were so wild about. Giving him a curt nod, John walked out.

Tony waited until the man had disappeared from sight before letting out the breath he had been holding. He had heard enough to know he was a police detective, and was looking for Arturo. So his hunch had been right after all. The cops had traced his brother through that stupid phone call on McGregor's cell phone.

Tony ran shaky fingers through his hair. Jesus. This situation was getting more dangerous with each passing minute, and the worst part was that he was the only one who had enough sense to worry. Now that Arturo had hidden the truck in the garage of a Latina woman he had met a few nights ago, he didn't give a damn about anything, except Abbie DiAngelo's money and how to get his hands on it.

Enrique had picked up an oily rag from a workbench and was walking toward him. "Is it true?" he asked, nervously wiping his hands on the rag. "Your brother killed a man?"

Admitting the truth would be like signing Arturo's death sentence. Tony gave a vigorous shake of his head. "That's crazy, Enrique. Arturo didn't kill anybody."

"That's not what that detective said. He even showed me Arturo's picture. And he gave me a description of the truck." He threw the rag back on the workbench. "You told me your brother ran away from a state trooper because his driver's license had expired, but if it's more than that—"

"It's not, Enrique, I swear." Sweat ran down Tony's back, soaking his shirt. "That cop made a mistake. Or he's looking for a fall guy. It happens all the time. It's called ethnic profiling. You know how those *gringos* are.''

Enrique must have experienced his share of discrimination over the years because he pondered that remark for a moment, looking torn. Tony prayed he wouldn't ask them to move out. Where would they go?

"Look," Enrique said after a while. "I don't mind helping a couple of brothers. God knows I've needed help in my time, too. But I run a legitimate business now. I want no trouble."

"You won't have any. I give you my word. All I ask is that you let us stay here a few more days."

"And then you go, okay?"

"I promise."

The Hispanic community in Trenton's south side was a small, close-knit nucleus. It comprised, for the most part, hard-working and law-abiding citizens, many of whom owned businesses, like John's good friend, Manuel Cabrero.

John had met Manuel four years ago, when a Princeton Township liquor store had been robbed at gunpoint and its owner killed. One of the robbers had been identified as Manuel's sixteen-year-old son, Freddy.

Despite his emphatic denials, Freddy, who had been in trouble with the law before, was arrested. But John had liked the youth. He came from a good family and was trying to put his life back on track. Not satisfied he had the right man, John continued his investigation. A week later he had apprehended the real killer. Manuel and his wife were so grateful that, on the day Freddy was cleared, they told John he had a standing invitation at their home and at the Cabreros' bakery on Lalor Street.

Manuel was behind the counter, making change for a

customer, when John entered the bakery. He was a sturdy, well-built man with dark curly hair and dazzling white teeth. The moment he saw John, he let out a loud greeting in Spanish, and called his wife, *"Pilar, ven a ver quien está aquí."* Come and see who's here.

He circled the counter and came to shake John's hand, pumping it vigorously. "How are you, my friend?"

"I can't complain, Manuel. How about you?"

"Life is good. Freddy is in college and working with us part-time. He wants to go into the FBI," he added proudly.

"Then I'm sure he'll succeed."

Before Manuel could reply, Pilar was running out of the back room, moving as fast as her short legs would allow, and gave him a warm hug. "What a nice surprise. Manuel, get John a chair. Are you hungry?" She spoke rapidly and with a pronounced Spanish accent. "I could make you a sandwich. I have some of that cassava bread you like. Or a nice bowl of conch chowder? Maybe you'd prefer a pastry?" Her gaze turned mischievous, as though she knew his weaknesses. "How about a thick slice of piña colada pie?"

Laughing, John put up his hand. "I don't need a thing, Pilar, honest." He grabbed hold of her wrist and held her still. "And stop fussing over me. I'm fine."

"You're not fine, you're too thin." She shook a finger under his nose. "I'm going to give you some good home-made food to take with you. And I won't take no for an answer."

He wouldn't have dreamed of offending her by turning her offer down. Besides, he loved Pilar's cooking. "Thank you, Pilar." He took out Arturo's picture from his pocket. "But what I really came for is information." He handed Manuel the mug shot. "Have you seen this man around here?"

Manuel and Pilar both studied the picture. "No," they said in unison. Manuel looked up. "Who is he?"

John told them and described the truck. Pilar pressed a hand to her chest. "Murder. *Madre mia.*" Worry filled her eyes. "You really think he's hiding in this neighborhood?"

"That's a possibility. What do you know about the owner of Enrique's Garage on Center Street?"

Pilar shook her head, but Manuel apparently knew the man. "That would be Enrique Soledad. He's a good man, and a hard worker. He got himself in a little trouble a few years back, but he's straightened up since then."

"Would he harbor a fugitive?"

"Never." Manuel gave a firm shake of his head. "Not Enrique." He handed the photo back. "You want me to keep my eyes and ears open, *amigo?*"

"I'd appreciate that, Manuel."

Half an hour later, John was back in his Plymouth. In his back seat was a bag filled to the brim with an assortment of breads, soups and pastries, all of which would take a week to finish.

The real payoff from his visit would come later, hopefully. After twenty years in the area, Manuel and his wife had strong ties to the community and knew just about everyone within a ten-mile radius. If Arturo was in their neighborhood, or anywhere close to it, the Cabreros would find out.

Thirty-Two

John waited until he had left the outskirts of Trenton before calling Tina on her cell phone. As the father of a young boy, he was as anxious to have that horrific pedophile caught as any parent in the Princeton area.

"How did it go with Barbara Michaels?" he asked when she answered.

Her grumble spoke volumes. "Not as well as I had hoped. She only saw the driver from the back and the only thing she's sure of is that it was a man and he wore a big, light-colored hat, tan or gray. It may have been one of those large-brimmed straw hats you see at the beach, but she wasn't positive."

"Isn't that the same description the Eastbrook teacher gave you?"

"Pretty much. Miss Foley said the hat was definitely a fedora, which is why I spent the morning going from one department store to another to see how many fedoras had been sold in the last week. The result is none. Hell, most stores don't even *carry* fedoras!"

"Look at it this way," he said, trying to cheer her up. "Now you know the perp is a snappy dresser."

He kept his tone light for Tina's sake, but he knew this was serious business—serious enough that he, Clarice and Jordan had sat together two weeks ago to discuss new safety rules. John and Clarice disagreed on a lot of things, but Jordan's safety was something neither took lightly.

His remark made Tina chuckle. ''A snappy dresser. Let's see, in a town like Princeton that narrows it down to a couple of thousand men.''

''You'll flush the right one out,'' John said with absolute confidence. ''You always do.''

He hung up. Then, on impulse, he dialed Campagne.

''Are you allowed to take coffee breaks?''

At the playful sound of John's voice, Abbie glanced at the clock, which read two-ten, and switched the phone to her other ear. ''Have you sworn to wear me down?''

''Is it working?''

Oh, it was working, but she wasn't about to tell him that. ''I've been known to take an occasional break. I'm not all work and no play, you know.''

''I'm glad to hear that.'' His low chuckle sent a little shiver down her back. ''Can you come out and play right now?''

''What did you have in mind?''

''Nothing too serious. Coffee at Winberie, right here on the square.''

''I think I can arrange that. Give me two minutes.''

She hung up and turned to find Brady watching her, his eyes gleaming with curiosity. ''Going somewhere?''

''To Winberie, for a coffee break.''

''Who are you meeting there?''

''Oh, for God's sake.'' She tossed her apron on a chair. ''Can't a girl have a little privacy around here?''

Brady waited until she had reached the swinging doors before yelling, ''Give my regards to Detective Ryan!''

J. B. Winberie, in the heart of Palmer Square, was a typical Irish pub, with thick burgers, a large selection of beers and, according to Brady, the best Guinness in town. Abbie smiled at the hostess, whom she knew, and let her eyes roam the busy room, searching for John. She found him in a back booth, looking terrific in a tan jacket and a brown shirt opened at the neck. He rose when he saw her.

"What?" she asked at his expression. "Why are you looking at me that way? Do I have chocolate mousse on my face or something?"

"No." He continued to gaze at her as he sat down. "You're just perfect."

She let out a self-conscious laugh. "That's nice to hear, even if it is an exaggeration." A waitress stopped at their table and they both ordered coffee. When she was gone, Abbie spoke again but in a lower voice. "You know something, don't you? I can tell." She was learning to read him, when he let her.

He nodded. "We're making progress, thanks to an unexpected source—Rose's missing cell phone. Ian had been using it, and when we didn't find it at the crime scene, we assumed the killer took it."

"Did he?"

"*Someone* took it. And did something very stupid."

"He made a call."

"Bingo. I traced the call to a garage in south Trenton that belongs to an Enrique Soledad. Unfortunately, Enrique claims he's never heard of Arturo Garcia."

"Did you believe him?"

"Let's just say Enrique was not totally comfortable having me there."

"So you think he knows Arturo?"

"He may know where he is, and is afraid to talk. Can't say I blame him."

She listened as he told her about Arturo's long list of felonies, the most serious of which had ended with him in prison for eight years. His angry outburst in the courtroom, where he had shouted obscenities at Ian and sworn to gut him like a fish, made her realize just how close a call she'd had that night at the lake. Had Arturo been able to get to her, he would have killed her without a moment's hesitation.

Their coffee arrived and Abbie poured a container of dairy creamer into hers. "How will you find him if he stays hidden?"

"According to Detective Bloom, Garcia is a restless creature. Most men who have done time are. My bet is he won't be able to remain totally out of sight. A man like Arturo needs to get out, move around, drink a few beers. A friend of mine in the Trenton area is keeping a lookout for him."

The thought of a massive search for Arturo Garcia failed to reassure her. As badly as she wanted her attacker caught and put behind bars, she would have preferred to hear he had fled the state and was a thousand miles away.

"I know you're worried about him," John continued. "And I wouldn't presume to tell you not to be. Just remember that although Garcia is not too bright, he's not a complete idiot either. I doubt he would try anything while being the object of a statewide manhunt."

"He seemed pretty determined to get that money from me."

"I know. That's why you should be careful. Be aware of what's going on around you, but don't lose any sleep over him."

She nodded. "Brady already said he'll stay until closing time from now on. He's always wanted to do that anyway. Now is his chance."

Her attention was suddenly drawn to the bar, where a man was sitting at the far corner and watching her reflection in the mirror behind the counter. It wasn't until their eyes met that she realized the man was Ken Walker. She was almost certain he hadn't been here when she'd arrived. She tried to tell herself his presence at Winberie was perfectly innocent, nothing more than an annoying coincidence. If he had as much time on his hands as his wife claimed, he was bound to get bored and thirsty.

As she debated what to do, John glanced over his shoulder. "Someone you know?" he asked, turning back.

"No. I mean yes." She pulled her gaze off Ken and picked up her cup. "He's a former employee."

"He makes you nervous. Why? Has he been bothering you?"

She smiled. "Is that your psychology training showing? Or am I that easy to read?"

"Maybe a little of both." He turned again and this time his study of the man lasted a few seconds longer. Walker's gaze quickly focused on his beer.

John returned his attention to Abbie. "What's the story with him?"

"Brady caught him stealing money from me and I fired him. A few days ago, he came to the restaurant, said he was no longer gambling and asked for his old job back."

"The man is not lacking in nerve."

"No. The situation quickly escalated to the point where Brady had to throw him out. Yesterday, while I was at the funeral, he came back. He didn't make a scene, but he was there, walking around outside the restaurant and annoying Brady."

"You could request a restraining order."

"I don't want to do that. Ken is angry right now. It'll pass. See?" she said when she looked up and found the bar deserted. "He got bored and left."

John didn't look convinced, and neither was she, but she didn't say anything more on the subject. Instead, she concentrated on John's second reason for wanting to see her. The warden of Stateville Prison had agreed to let him visit Earl Kramer. John was flying to Ohio first thing Sunday morning. The news made Abbie both elated and nervous. What if Kramer decided to play hardball? Or if the truth was not what she expected. What then?

Pushing aside her morbid thoughts, she smiled and raised her cup. "Here's to a successful trip."

John leaned forward as he raised his own cup. "And to new beginnings."

"New beginnings?"

"As in, you and me."

Abbie laughed. "My God, you are persistent."

"You didn't think I'd let you off the hook so easily, did you?"

She had been hoping he wouldn't. In fact, she had been thinking about him a lot lately, about the way he had looked at her the other night at her house, how her hands had felt in his, how badly she had wanted him to kiss her...

"To tell you the truth," she said, unable to resist a little teasing, "I haven't given it much thought. With all that's been happening—"

"Liar."

Abbie pretended to be shocked. "I beg your pardon?"

"You're a lousy liar, Abbie DiAngelo. You enjoy my company every bit as much as I enjoy yours. The difference is that I'm willing to admit it and you aren't."

"Well, well," a female voice said, cutting short Abbie's response. "Is that what our tax-paid police force does during duty hours? Cavort in local bars."

John's smile faded and he straightened in his seat. "Mary Kay." Ignoring her previous remark, he added, "Do you know Abbie DiAngelo?"

The woman gave Abbie a phony smile. "I don't believe I've had the pleasure."

Abbie took the extended hand, quickly noting the slender shape, elegantly clad in white slacks and a fitted black jacket, the pronounced cheekbones, the keen hazel eyes that were openly assessing her.

"Mary Kay Roder is a reporter for the *Mercer County News.*" His expression stony, John took a ten-dollar bill from his pocket and dropped it on the table. Then rising, he added, "You'll excuse us, won't you? We were just leaving."

Her eyes remained on Abbie. "Not on my account, I hope."

"You flatter yourself, Mary Kay."

Bewildered, Abbie scrambled to her feet, felt John take her arm and followed him out the door, running to keep up with him.

"Wow," she said when they reached the sidewalk. "What was that all about?" She glanced back toward the pub. "If looks could kill, I'd be six feet under by now." She looked at John. "And so would you."

"Mary Kay is a royal pain in the butt. And a vulture in more ways than one."

Abbie smiled. "In other words, she has the hots for you."

"Whatever she has, I didn't want any of it and told her so. She's had it in for me ever since."

"Is she dangerous?"

"She only likes to think she is."

They walked together to the restaurant. The walk seemed to calm John down. "I'd love to pick up our conversation where we left it off," he said when they reached Campagne's front door, "but I know you have to go home." Unexpectedly, he kissed her cheek. "Rain check?"

If it hadn't been for her promise to take Ben shopping for new cleats, she would have cashed in John's rain check this very minute. Instead, she let out a small sigh of regret. "I have a wedding reception on Saturday and I'm going to be awfully busy until then, but...would you like to call me when you get back from Toledo?"

His grin lit up his face. "I'd like that very much."

"What's the matter with you?' Arturo asked when he walked in. "You look like you're gonna puke."

Tony, who had been sitting in the front room, waiting for Arturo, looked up. "I ran into that detective in charge of McGregor's murder."

Arturo gave him one of his blank looks. "Where?"

"At Enrique's Garage. He was questioning him, showing him your mug shot and giving a description of the truck."

Now he had Arturo's attention. "How did he find out about Enrique?"

Tony gave him an icy look. "Would it really kill you to use your brains once in a while, Arturo? How do you think he found out? From that phone call you made on McGregor's cell phone! That's how he found out. The cops traced the call."

"I hope Enrique kept his fucking mouth shut."

"He did, but he's scared. He doesn't want any trouble with the police."

"Shit." Arturo scratched his bald head.

"He wants us out of his apartment, Arturo. I convinced him to let us stay a few more days, but after that, we'll have to go."

"I ain't goin' nowhere until I get my money from that bitch."

Tony expelled a frustrated breath. "When are you going

to get it through your thick skull that McGregor's sister is not going to hand you forty-eight thousand dollars just for the asking.''

"Maybe she won't. Maybe she will."

Tony stood up. "What the hell does that mean?"

"I've been checking out on her, where she lives, where she works. Did you know she had a kid? A boy."

"So?"

"Now who's the dumb one, huh?" He laughed, obviously proud of himself. "That kid could come in handy, Tone."

Even though Arturo towered over Tony by at least a foot and outweighed him by a hundred pounds, Tony grabbed him by the collar and backed him against the wall. "The only thing you're going to do is keep out of sight, do you hear me? I'm going to do what I can to get you out of this mess you made for yourself, but I warn you, if you screw up again in any way, I'll make you regret it." He gave him another shove. "Did you hear me, Arturo?"

The two brothers stared at each other for a long minute, then Arturo shoved Tony aside. "What the fuck is with you, man?"

"I've had it. The only reason I didn't bail out on you after you killed McGregor was because I believed you killed him in self-defense. I still do, but I don't want to hear any more whining about Abbie DiAngelo's money. For the next few days, I expect you to stay cool and out of trouble." He caught Arturo's dark, angry look but didn't flinch. "I mean it."

Sitting on a stool, Abbie watched Claudia chisel a block of ivory marble she claimed would soon be transformed into a rendition of a mother and her child.

"How did the funeral go?" Claudia asked.

"Better than I thought. Liz was there. She was the same old Liz, aloof and sarcastic, but for all her efforts to appear heartless, I don't think she's that at all."

"Then why did she tell John Ryan that Ian was black-mailing you?"

"If your brother convinced you someone had killed your father, wouldn't you turn them in?"

"Does she really believe that?"

"I don't think she knows what to believe."

"Did Irene talk to her?"

"Liz never gave her the chance. Needless to say, my mother was disappointed. She wanted to tell her about the letters she had written to both children after we left California, letters I now know Liz's aunt never gave them."

Claudia adjusted her protective goggles and continued to chip away. "Why are you so concerned about Liz? Let her believe what she wants. And if she doesn't want a relationship with you and your mother, well, maybe you're better off."

"That's not what Ben thinks."

Claudia stopped in midmotion. "He's still talking about her?"

"He wants a real aunt." She smiled. "Sometimes I wonder if he and my mother are conspiring behind my back."

"What does he want you to do?"

"Are you familiar with the saying, 'If Mohammed won't come to the mountain—'"

"The mountain will come to Mohammed." Claudia ran her hand over the rough finish. "You're planning on going to see her, aren't you?"

"Yes. I'll call her first and give her an opportunity to tell me to go to hell." She leaned against the broad back of the still-untitled reclining woman and watched her friend work. "She won't, though."

"How do you know?"

"She's all alone, Claudia."

"Maybe that's the way she wants it."

"Nobody sets out to live a lonely life."

"And you are setting yourself up for a fall, Abigail." Claudia sometimes resorted to Abbie's full name when she was dispensing advice.

"Maybe so, but at least I'll be able to tell Ben that I tried." She glanced at her watch. "In fact, I think I'll call her right now. According to Rose, Liz should be home, getting ready for work."

She reached inside her purse and took out her cell phone, along with the number Rose had given her.

"Liz," she said when her stepsister answered. "It's Abbie."

Her stepsister's tone was only a shade warmer than it had been on Wednesday. "I recognized your voice."

"I won't keep you. I know you're getting ready for work, but…I had a thought."

"Just as long as it doesn't involve me."

Abbie didn't let Liz's cool tone deter her. "As a matter of fact, it does. I was thinking about taking Ben to New York on Sunday. It's been ages since we've been to the city and—"

"Don't tell me—you'd like to stop by my place so Ben can meet me. We could even go somewhere for brunch, talk about old times, swap a few photos, act nice and cozy, like any normal family."

Abbie could have done without the sarcasm, but she let it go. "Something like that."

"I work on Sundays."

"All day?"

There was a slight hesitation. "No."

"Well, when *do* you have to go to work?"

"At two."

"Then that's perfect. Ben and I could come up early, meet you at your place and then go somewhere for breakfast. Afterward I could take him to the Central Park Zoo, which I know he'll love. How does that sound?" She braced herself for a turndown, but kept her tone jovial. "It's not too much to ask, is it?"

"Why are you doing this?"

"Because Ben feels bad that he doesn't have aunts and uncles, like all his friends. He wants to meet you, Liz. I just couldn't tell him no. I know you and I have never been close, and maybe we never will, but won't you do it for Ben? Please?"

A long silence fell over the line, stretched into another. Abbie didn't dare break it.

At the sound of the resigned sigh, Abbie allowed herself a smile. She had won the first round.

"All right," Liz said. "Sunday morning. Ten o'clock. Don't come any earlier, because I'll be in a cranky mood if I don't get my eight hours' sleep. And don't expect me to be a chatterbox either. That's not my style. Tell Ben that."

"I will. Thank you, Liz."

Her only answer was a grunt.

"I'll need your address."

Abbie wrote it down, and hung up, feeling a little like the cat who had swallowed the canary.

Thirty-Three

It was a few minutes after ten on a glorious, sunny June morning, when Abbie and Ben arrived in New York City. Because it was still early, the traffic was light and Abbie quickly found a parking space half a block from Liz's apartment building. Ben could barely contain his excitement while they rode the elevator to the fourth floor. His remark when she had told him Liz had agreed to see them had been a confident "I told you so."

Liz opened the door, dressed in black slacks and a white blouse, and gave them a lukewarm smile Abbie assumed was meant for Ben rather than her. She ignored the cool reception, confident Liz would eventually warm up to that sweet little boy.

To Abbie's satisfaction, she did, even laughing at some of the stories Ben was telling her about his friends and his school principal—the one with the fuzz above her upper lip.

As they walked to a Caribbean restaurant Liz was fond of, Ben continued to fill her in on the events of the past year. Over giant pineapple-coconut pancakes, which he never would have eaten at home but devoured here, he told Liz about his team's battle for first place and how much he was looking forward to summer vacation.

Although she had expertly dodged his questions about her private life, he looked so hopeful when he mentioned her late, famous ex-husband that she was more or less trapped into saying a few words about him, his rise to fame and his eventual fall.

"Why don't you have any kids?" Ben asked at one point. At his blunt question, Liz simply replied. "We can't all be as lucky as your mother."

As they parted, an hour and a half later, Abbie invited Liz to visit them in Princeton, adding that Irene would love to see her, but her stepsister wouldn't commit to a date, even when Ben chimed in. Abbie didn't push her. Liz had made a huge concession today. The rest would have to be taken one step at a time.

"You think Aunt Liz liked me?" Ben asked as they drove up Sixth Avenue.

Abbie smiled at him. "I think she's crazy about you, sport. How can she help it?"

Thanks to Otis, who had put in a good word for John, the warden at Stateville Prison had been quick to provide information on his less-than-model prisoner.

"Earl Kramer isn't one of our favorite people around here," Timothy Paulson said as he escorted John down a dank, depressing corridor. "At least not with prison administrators. He instigates riots, he bribes guards, which forces us to fire them, and he goes on hunger strikes, attracting more attention to our facility than we'd like."

"Do you remember Ian McGregor's visit last month?"

The warden sighed. "I certainly do. For the record, I was against it from the start, but Kramer's wife vouched for McGregor, claiming he was an old friend, practically a family member. She was so vocal and loud about letting him in, I thought she was going to start a riot all by herself. So I made a judgment call and allowed McGregor to visit his friend. According to the guards, they didn't do anything but talk. Knowing what I know now, I wish I had stuck to my guns." He let out another sigh. "Making decisions in a place like this isn't always as easy as one thinks."

"I don't suppose their conversation was recorded."

Paulson gave a regretful shake of his head. "Conversations between inmates and visitors used to be recorded. Then came the uprising of '92, and a list of demands that included inmates' right to privacy on visiting days. They were holding two of our guards hostage and we had no choice but to go to the bargaining table and allow them a few concessions. The demand for privacy was one of them."

John's hand went to his breast pocket where he had tucked a small tape recorder earlier. The warden caught the movement as they started down another corridor. "Of course, as I said earlier, you have my permission to record your own conversation with Kramer. Whether or not he'll let you do it is another matter."

John smiled to himself. Kramer would have no problem with the recorder. Or any of John's requests. He could almost guarantee it.

Condemned men all looked the same, John thought. On the surface, there was this cockiness, this swagger as they shuffled into the room, chains clinking. But to the discerning eye, fear—and sometimes, hope—were visible, for a new visitor could only mean good news. What else could a man on death row expect? Occasionally, you could see something else—a deep-rooted anger. In their eyes, the system had let them down. It wasn't their fault they were screwed up. It was the fault of the drunken father who had walked out on them, or the mother who had brought a new man home every night, or the beatings they had suffered as kids. Sometimes, sadly, the claims were legitimate, other times they were manufactured. Whatever worked. Sorting out truth from fiction was a task John gladly left to others.

Earl Kramer was no different. Not only was he a con artist, he was also a ruthless killer. The bible he carried in his hand as he approached the glass booth did nothing to change John's opinion of the man.

They picked up the receivers hanging from the wall at the same time.

"Hello, Kramer."

Wary eyes studied him. "Who the hell are you?"

"Didn't they tell you?"

"They said some cop wanted to see me, but I've never seen you before."

"Then this is your lucky day." John gave him a cool smile and was rewarded by a flash of hope in those beady little black eyes.

"It is?"

"You bet. But first, let me offer my condolences."

Kramer's eyes narrowed slightly. "Who died?"

"Your buddy. You know. Ian McGregor."

Kramer's expression turned blank. "Don't know what you're talking about."

"Sure you do. He's the guy who came to see you a couple of weeks ago with this little plan that would put the two of you in the money—a hundred grand, to be exact. All you had to do was confess to a crime you didn't commit."

Kramer laughed. "Now why would I do a dumb thing like that?"

"Because you liked the idea of collecting fifty grand without lifting a finger, and because you knew that admitting to a new crime would open a new investigation, thus delaying your execution indefinitely." John flashed him a grin. "How am I doing so far?"

Kramer's expression didn't change. For the time being, he seemed supremely confident. That would soon change. "You're nuttier than a fruitcake," Kramer said.

"I don't think so. You see, we have proof that McGregor called you on June 4 from Princeton, New Jersey, asking you to call his sister, which you did, that very same day." He paused to study Kramer's reaction. "Is your memory coming back?"

The man was quick on his feet. "Oh," he said, tapping his forehead as though his memory had indeed miraculously returned. "*That* McGregor. Why didn't you say so? Yeah, sure, I know Ian. He's an old buddy of mine." His gaze lowered to the bible in front of him. "I'm sorry he passed. I'll pray for his soul."

What a load of crap, John thought, but said instead, "Why did he come to see you?"

"Because I asked him to. I had heard he was getting out and I wanted to talk to him."

"About what?"

"About me torching his father's house, and I wanted to ask for his forgiveness. But I don't know nothin' about no hundred grand." He placed one hand on his chest. "I did what I did out of the goodness of my heart."

"You're lying, Kramer."

Kramer let out a thin laugh that grated on John's nerves. "You cops are all the same, you know that? You think just because you got a badge and a gun you can push people around and make them admit things that ain't so." His lips pulled into a sneer. "Well, guess what? You ain't gonna push *me* around. So rave all you want about that half-baked story of yours and get the hell out of my face."

John leaned forward. As much as he felt like reaching over and squashing Kramer's face against the glass, it was important to keep his temper under control. "Then I'm going to keep it nice and simple for you," he said quietly. "Before I came here, I did my homework. It's a little passion of mine, learning all I can about cons like you. You're not going to like what I found out."

Still no reaction. Either the man was stupid or he was one hell of a poker player.

"You've done some nasty things in your lifetime, Kramer. But one of them is especially disgusting. You know what I'm talking about, don't you?"

Kramer didn't bother to acknowledge the question. He continued to watch John, both hands on the bible.

"I'm talking about molesting your little stepdaughter. How old was she, Kramer? Five? Six?"

This time Kramer flinched. "Seven, and I paid for that crime, so what the fuck are you bringing this up for?"

"I'm bringing it up because it wasn't mentioned during your last trial."

"The prosecutor tried to, but my attorney stopped him before it could go on record. It's called 'motion to exclude evidence.'" He puffed up his chest and gave John a smug smile. "You see, I know a little about the law, too."

"That was a lucky break for you, wasn't it? Otherwise the information may have leaked out, maybe right into this prison."

For the first time, there was a glimmer of fear in Kramer's eyes. He had finally gotten the message.

"How do you think your fellow inmates would feel if they knew the nasty things you did to that little girl? I don't think they'd like it, do you? Some of those men may be hard-core criminals, but they have one rule they all abide by—you don't hurt a child. In fact, they get so worked up when they find out a child molester is in the same prison, they often take the law into their own hands and administer whatever punishment they feel is right. One case I remember had an entire cell block attack the man and beat him within an inch of his life. I heard one of the inmates bit off his dick." John gave a sad shake of his head. "Poor bastard never did walk right after that."

Kramer's face had turned as gray as the dingy walls behind him. "You can't release that information. You'll be held in contempt."

Apparently Kramer *had* had time to learn some legalese. "I don't think so. Last time I looked, freedom of speech was still alive and well in this country. All I have to do is drop a few words into the right ears, and by tomorrow you could be a dead man. Or you might wish you were."

Kramer stared at him for a long time, under hooded eyes. John figured he was weighing the odds and not liking how they added up. John didn't rush him. He just returned the stare.

"What do you want?" Kramer asked at last.

John took his tape recorder from his breast pocket and put it on the table.

"Tell me what really went down between you and McGregor."

Thirty-Four

Abbie could barely control her emotions when John called on Monday morning to tell her about his successful trip to Stateville Prison and Earl Kramer's confession, which had been signed and witnessed before John left Ohio.

"I can't believe you got him to confess," she said excitedly. "If you were here right now instead of halfway across town, I'd plant a big kiss on that handsome face of yours."

He laughed. "Hold on to that thought then, because you're going to get your chance."

"Is that so."

"How does a little dinner sound? Say, around nine?"

"It sounds wonderful. And I can do nine. Mondays are slow."

"I know. Brady told me."

She cast a glance toward her sous-chef, who looked as if he knew exactly who she was talking to. "He did, did he?"

"Only because I threatened him with bodily harm if he didn't fess up."

"That's right, stick up for him."

"Aren't you going to ask me where I'm taking you?"

Actually, she was wondering how she'd last until nine tonight. "Where are you taking me?"

"Church Street Bistro."

"It's one of my favorite places."

"Good. Shall I pick you up at Campagne? Eight forty-five?"

"I'll be ready."

She hung up and turned to Brady. "So, you've been discussing me with John."

"Just a little."

"What did you tell him?"

"Only enough to help him choose a restaurant—things like the foods you like, the kind of restaurants you prefer, the best time to ask you out."

"Best time to ask me out?"

"You know, how mornings are good because you're up-beat, relaxed, excited about the day ahead. Evenings are not so good. You're punchy and frazzled."

She laughed. "In other words, you've divulged all my secrets."

"Not all of them. I left out a couple so he could discover them on his own."

A deliveryman walked in, wheeling a cartful of French baguettes, and handed Brady a clipboard. Brady glanced at the cart before scrawling his name on the invoice. "So," he said when the deliveryman had left, "where is he taking you?"

"Church Street Bistro in Lambertville."

Brady nodded his approval. "Good choice. The food is simple but excellent, the service friendly without being overpowering." He winked. "And the romantic atmosphere can't be beat."

She snatched a dishtowel from the counter and swatted him on the rear with it. "You're incorrigible."

He gave her a silly grin. "I am, aren't I?"

Abbie was too busy over the lunch hour to think about her upcoming date with John Ryan. But when she and

Brady walked out of Campagne at two-thirty everything changed. She felt like a teenager preparing for her first date, dropping things, staring off into space and half listening to what Ben was telling her.

At four-thirty, she went upstairs and subjected her closet to the worst abuse in years as she rummaged through her clothes in search of an appropriate outfit. After trying on a half-dozen different combinations, she settled for a gauzy skirt in a muted shade of purple, a simple, sleeveless white tank and high-heeled mules the same color as the skirt. She was probably overdressing, but it was getting late and she had run out of clothes to try.

After kissing Ben and telling Tiffany she'd be home at the usual time, she left.

John arrived at Campagne fifteen minutes early and ended up waiting outside the restaurant's back door, worried his eagerness would make him look stupid. Showing up early for a date had never been a concern before. On the contrary. He was usually late.

When he finally went in, his first thought as he stood on the threshold was that Abbie looked absolutely luscious. Under the white apron, he caught a glimpse of an airy, purple fabric, the hem of which seemed to float around her ankles as she moved. She looked taller tonight, and when he glanced down again, he saw why. Though she wore high heels, she moved about the kitchen as easily as if she were wearing sneakers.

"You look beautiful," he managed to say when she finally walked over to him.

She looked down at her stain-splattered apron. "You think so?"

"Stop teasing the man and get going," Brady said as he took an order slip from a waiter. "You're in the way here."

"All right, all right." She was untying her apron when Marsha, Campagne's lovely hostess, rushed in, her cheeks pink, her eyes bright with excitement.

"You'll never guess who's here," she said.

"I don't know and I don't care." Abbie tossed her apron aside and picked up a small clutch purse from the chair. "I'm out of here."

"Archibald Gunther."

The room went silent. Everyone, including Abbie and Brady, seemed to have gone into a trance. It was as if a magic wand had touched them all and frozen them in place.

Abbie was the first to recover. "Are you sure?" she asked, already rushing to the double doors and peering into the dining room.

"He gave me his name and said he didn't have a reservation."

"I don't see him."

"I sat him at table two."

John leaned toward Brady and whispered, "Who is Archibald Gunther?"

"Only the most famous restaurant critic in the country," Brady whispered back. "He used to write exclusively for the *New York Times,* but he now freelances and has a weekly syndicated column that appears in more than two hundred newspapers. He travels all over the country and only reviews restaurants he deems worthy of his attention, never those recommended by enthusiastic readers." He punctuated his remark with a snort. "He's full of himself, scathing when he doesn't like a particular establishment, and incredibly rude. Some say his goal in life is not to inform the public about outstanding restaurants but to destroy them."

"Why would anyone want to be reviewed by this wind-bag?"

"Because if he likes your restaurant—which happens, occasionally—he can propel you to stardom as quickly as he can sink you into oblivion. For many, Abbie included, it's worth the risk."

"I don't think I like him."

Brady laughed. "I *know* I don't like him, but in spite of that, it's taking every ounce of self-control I have not to jump with joy at the thought that the great Archibald Gunther is here and about to eat the food *I'll* cook tonight. I'm excited and scared out of my wits at the same time. Isn't that crazy?"

John glanced at Abbie and saw that her reaction reflected the same mixture of dread and elation. Her cheeks were flushed as she grabbed the arm of a waiter who had just returned from the dining room.

"Jim, you have table two, right?"

The waiter nodded. "Marsha told me who just came in. Gosh, Abbie, I can hardly believe it. Archibald Gunther." He said the name with such reverence that John almost laughed. Good sense told him not to.

"Don't make him wait," Abbie said, waving him back outside. "Be natural, okay? Address him by his name, since he gave it to Marsha, but don't gush. Treat him the same way you would anyone else."

"But he's not anyone else. He is—"

"Archibald Gunther, yes, I know. Nonetheless, we treat him like a mere mortal, not a god. Now go."

After a few seconds, she turned to John, who was watching his romantic evening go down the toilet, thanks to Archibald Gunther.

"John—"

Gallantly, he bailed her out. "I know. You have to stay. I understand."

"You don't mind?"

"I didn't say that. In fact, I'm about this far—" he held his thumb and forefinger close together "—from walking into that dining room and punching the great Archibald Gunther in the nose."

The corners of Abbie's mouth pulled into a smile. "He weighs close to three hundred pounds."

John gave a smirk. "Like I would let that stop me."

She laughed and the tension seemed to ease off her shoulders. "I'll make it up to you. I promise."

"I'll hold you to that."

Jim walked back into the kitchen, looking haggard.

"What's wrong?" Abbie asked. "He didn't leave after reading the menu, did he?"

"No, but…" He glanced at the slip of paper in his hand. "I don't think you're going to like this." He started reading. "He ordered the basil and garlic soup, the lentil salad with duck breast, the veal shank in cider, and for dessert, the roasted figs with crème fraîche."

"I hope he brought his own stretcher," John murmured to no one in particular, but when he saw the panicked expression on Abbie's face, he realized this was no laughing matter. "Problems?" he asked.

"No, not really. It's just that the dishes he ordered are complex and time-consuming. And I let Sean leave early."

"Who is Sean?"

"One of our kitchen helpers."

"So call him back."

"I can't. He's halfway to Baltimore by now. By the time he got back, the dinner would be over."

John did some quick thinking. "Obviously, you need

another pair of hands, so give me an apron and tell me what to do.''

Abbie gave him a blank look. "What?"

"You heard me. I'm offering my services."

"But you don't cook."

"No, but I can peel and I can chop and in a pinch I can even whip." He had already removed his jacket, glad his .38 was strapped to his ankle and well concealed under his pants. He didn't think that the nervous staff could have taken the sight of a gun at the moment.

Abbie was biting a fingernail. "I don't know about this. By the time I've finished explaining—"

"Take the offer, already," Brady muttered as he pulled a crate of assorted vegetables from the refrigerator. "Archibald's waiting."

Abbie's hesitation lasted but a second. "All right." She pointed at the crate Brady had put on the counter. "The onions and potatoes have to be peeled and diced. The green beans cut in inch-size pieces. Those beans," she said, pointing, "have to be shelled and rinsed. Let me know when you're done and I'll give you something else to do."

For the next hour and a half, the kitchen hummed like a busy beehive as Abbie and Brady sautéed, stirred, strained and poured with a speed and efficiency that made John dizzy. He did his part, half hoping for a smile and a pat on the back for his effort, although he wasn't offended when he got neither. When he was not needed, he stayed out of the way, content to watch Abbie, who led her team with the hand of a master, encouraging, praising, even laughing occasionally to break the tension.

Whenever Jim came in, all eyes would turn toward him, but each time, the young waiter shook his head. Archibald had not made a single comment. After his dessert was carried out on a special Limoges plate Abbie had taken out of what she called her "treasure chest," she collapsed on a chair.

"What now?" John asked, handing her a glass of water, which she took gratefully.

"We wait, a week, two, three, until he decides whether or not he'll write the review."

"You mean you went through all this without being sure you'd be reviewed?" John was aghast.

"That's a chance you take. And of course, there's always the possibility that he hated everything, *will* review the restaurant and totally destroy you."

"Can't you go and ask him if he enjoyed the meal?"

She gave him a horrified look. "My God, John, that would be the kiss of death."

"But you'll be able to tell when you make your rounds, right?"

"I'm not making my rounds tonight. If I did, at this late hour, it would look crass, as if my only purpose was to impress him." She took another sip of water. "I'll only go if he asks to see me."

It was soon clear that he didn't. The entire kitchen staff huddled at the double doors and watched as Archibald stood up, with the help of his cane, and gave a curt nod to Jim, who was holding the door open for him.

Then he was gone and Abbie almost fell apart. "He hated it," she said, looking utterly defeated. "He hated everything."

"I doubt that." Jim had reentered the kitchen. "He didn't leave a single morsel of food. And you know what he does when he doesn't like something, Abbie. He takes one bite, maybe two, and he leaves the rest."

"He said nothing at all?"

"Not a word. But he gave me a nice tip, not huge, but

nice.'' He showed her the credit card receipt. ''That's got to be a good sign, don't you think?''

''That proves he liked the service, not necessarily the food.'' With a resigned sigh, she glanced at the wall clock. ''It's late, people. Go home.''

''Not until we've cleaned up,'' Brady said.

''I'll take care of the cleanup.'' She looked at John and forced a smile. ''Maybe my very understanding date will give me a hand. What do you say, Detective Ryan?''

John bowed. ''I'm at your service, Chef DiAngelo.''

Within moments, all four employees were gone and John and Abbie were left to deal with a stack of dirty pots and pans. Abbie walked over to the coffeemaker, which had sustained them all throughout the evening, and poured a cup for John.

''You've been a good sport about this.''

John took a sip of coffee, watching her as he drank. ''And you were awesome,'' he said. ''It was like watching a choreographer leading a group of talented performers. Everything was so perfectly synchronized and so beautiful to watch, I'm no longer surprised you've become such a success.''

Abbie felt herself blush. ''Thank you. And by the way, I was kidding about the cleanup.''

''I wasn't.'' To her surprise, he walked over to the sink, the sleeves of his shirt still rolled up at the elbows, and turned on the faucet. ''Come on,'' he tossed over his shoulder as she just stood there, not knowing what to say. ''You don't expect me to scrub all those pots by myself, do you?''

She laughed, snatched another sponge from the counter and joined him at the double sink. They worked fast, chatting about the night's unexpected turn of events, while in the background, an Andrea Bocelli CD continued to play some of the tenor's most famous ballads.

When the first strings of *Conte Partiro* began, John dropped his sponge, dried his hands and turned to Abbie. "Do you tango, Ms. DiAngelo?"

She met his gaze, and in that instant all signs of fatigue seemed to wash away from her. "Is that an invitation to dance, Detective Ryan?"

He opened his arms. "It most certainly is."

Without a word, she slid into his arms, fitting her body against his, feeling his heat radiate through the thin fabric of her tank top. She no longer felt tense, or worried about Archibald Gunther. The food critic could have been on another planet for all she cared. At this very moment, all that mattered was John, the way he held her, so tightly she could feel the pounding of his heart. Or was it hers?

Eyes closed, Abbie let herself be swept by the music, aware that John's hand had let go of hers and slipped around her waist. Instinctively, she slid her arms around his neck and looked up. His proximity made her dizzy, but it was the expression in his eyes, a mixture of playfulness and lust, that had her insides turning to mush.

"You're doing it again," she said with a small catch in her voice.

"Doing what?"

Looking at me and not kissing me. "Scrutinizing me."

"I was just noticing something." His hand brushed a strand of hair from her face. "Do you know that your eyes actually change color when you're nervous?"

"What would I have to be nervous about?"

"You tell me."

Her gaze locked on his mouth and she felt all her will-power dissolve. If he doesn't kiss me this very instant, she thought, I'll scream. Or I'll kiss him myself. And then we'll see how Mr. Cool handles—

She never had a chance to finish her thought. Wrapping one hand around her neck, he pulled her to him. She met him halfway, lips parted. Oh, God, she needed this. She needed that strong, hard body pressing against hers, that warm mouth kissing her and murmuring her name, those hands moving up and down her back, pulling her closer, as though he wanted her inside of him.

She wasn't sure how long the kiss lasted. She felt as though she was in another time zone, where nothing mattered but the feelings and sensations she was experiencing in this man's arms.

"Come home with me, Abbie," he whispered against her mouth.

Every fiber of her body wanted to scream yes, and nearly did. She let out a small sigh instead. "I can't. My baby-sitter needs to go home."

However close he had come to losing control, he was equally quick in regaining it. "All right." He hooked a finger under her chin, forcing her to look at him. "But we're not finished, you know. Not by a long shot."

She held his smoldering gaze. "I hope not."

Thirty-Five

"Oh, Abbie, I feel so guilty about this," Rose said. "Here you are, a famous, busy chef, and I've got you carrying my bed."

"I'm glad to help." Panting, Abbie put her end of the twin bed down at the bottom of the stairs and took a few shallow breaths. Now that Rose was moving in with Kat, she had needed a bedroom set, bedding and a few accessories. Knowing she didn't have much money, Abbie had taken her to a thrift shop she knew on Route 1, where Rose had bought a bedroom set, a lamp and a mirror. To the purchase, Abbie had added a couple of items she no longer needed—curtains for the window, a spread for the bed and a rug to throw over those cold tiles.

And since the thrift shop didn't deliver, she had also volunteered the Acura.

Although Rose was still mourning Ian, she had rebounded remarkably well, partly because she kept busy at the diner, taking shifts no one else wanted, and partly because the poor woman was all cried out. It was silly, but in a way, Abbie felt responsible for Rose. Ian's death had left her high and dry, and if she hadn't found a job she apparently liked, Abbie had been ready to offer her one. But what she felt for Rose went a step beyond responsibility. She actually liked the woman. And it made her feel good to see her excited about her new home.

The small duplex sat on a shaded street in Lawrenceville and consisted of two small bedrooms, one bath, a living room and a kitchen that had made Rose squeal with delight. Her roommate wasn't much of a cook, but Rose admitted to being somewhat of a gourmet buff, which gave her and Abbie one more thing in common.

Apparently rested enough, Rose glanced at Abbie. "Ready?"

Abbie looked up at the dozen or so steps remaining and wondered why they hadn't taken the bed apart and brought it up to Rose's room one piece at a time. Then, chiding herself for being such a wimp, she gripped the rail. "Ready," she replied.

Once the bed was in place, Rose looked around her. "I wish I could have brought more with me," she said. "But Ian was in such a hurry to leave Toledo, I sold all I had, including a practically new TV set."

"I know one or two reputable places that sell used television sets," Abbie said, brushing the dust from her T-shirt. "Say the word and I'll take you there."

Rose's eyes filled with gratitude. "I'm glad we've become friends, although to tell you the truth, you feel more like a sister to me than a friend. Do you feel the same way?"

Abbie smiled. The woman's candor was downright refreshing. "Yes, Rose, I do."

They walked back down to the car, but as Abbie started to reach inside the truck for the mirror, Rose went still.

"What's the matter?" Abbie followed Rose's gaze and saw she was staring at a maroon vehicle parked across the street. Behind the wheel, so tall he had to hunch over, was a man wearing dark sunglasses and a cowboy hat.

"Someone you know?" Abbie asked.

Rose seemed paralyzed. "Not really, but..." She turned back, her face pale. "Abbie, I think that's Arturo Garcia."

Abbie threw the man a sharp glance. He looked big enough to be her assailant, but with that hat and the glasses, it was impossible to tell for sure.

"It can't be," she said. "He wouldn't be stupid enough to come here, in broad daylight, with every cop in the state looking for him. And anyway, he doesn't have a goatee."

Rose didn't take her eyes off the car. "He could have shaved it."

"Rose, you're being paranoid."

"I'm telling you it's him. The cards said so this morning. Call the police."

"You've never even met him. All you know is what Ian—"

"Call the police!"

She had shouted those last words loud enough for the man in the car to hear them. Suddenly, he threw the newspaper aside, gunned the engine and left in a squeal of tires.

Abbie scrambled for her cell phone, but it was too late. The man Rose was certain was Arturo Garcia was long gone.

John arrived ten minutes later and took a description of the car.

"I didn't get a chance to get the tag numbers," Abbie said, wishing her reflexes had been quicker. "But the car had New Jersey plates, with the same *Shore to Please* logo as I have on the Acura."

John made note of that before calling in the info to the police dispatcher.

"A couple of squad cars are on their way," he said after he hung up. "If the man you saw is Arturo and he's headed back to Trenton, they'll catch him."

"And if he's not going to Trenton?" Rose asked.

"The fact that he was here shows he's beginning to take chances. If that's the case, we'll get him."

"But why is he taking chances?" Rose's fears had not ebbed. "And why is he following me? I don't have anything."

"But I do." Abbie said quietly.

Rose gave her a curious look. "You? Why would you say that?"

Abbie hadn't planned on telling her about Ian's black-mailing, but with Arturo hanging outside Rose's new home, she felt she owed her an explanation. She had put her in the line of fire, so to speak, and she had a right to know why. Abbie looked at John, who understood what she was about to do and nodded.

Rose listened intently, but instead of being upset at Abbie for lying to her initially, she gave her one of her mighty hugs. "You poor thing," she said. "Carrying that burden all by yourself. You should have told me." She released her. "I knew Ian was up to something when I found that letter, but I wasn't sure what." Her cheeks were white with anger. "I'm sorry for what he put you through, Abbie. And sorry I ever loved that rotten son of a bitch." A sad smile worked its way to her lips. "I guess there's no accounting for taste, huh?"

Abbie wrapped her arm around Rose's shoulder. "We've all been there at one time or another, so don't be too hard on yourself, okay?"

But Rose had already forgotten her woes and was focusing on Abbie. "You really think Arturo wants your money?"

"It's the only thing that makes sense. He was a madman that night at the lake, yelling at me over and over to give him the money. I'm certain he would have killed me just to get his hands on the forty-eight thousand dollars.''

''Abbie is right.'' John looked up and down the quiet street. ''The money is the reason he hung around after killing Ian.''

''But what was he trying to accomplish by following us here?''

''He may have been trying to find out where I lived.'' At the thought of finding that animal hidden behind her bushes, ready to attack her again, Abbie broke into a cold sweat.

The look of worry on Rose's face grew. ''If Abbie is in danger, shouldn't she be under some kind of police protection?''

John took his cell phone out. ''Definitely.''

''No way,'' Abbie protested. ''I won't have my life disrupted and my son unnecessarily frightened by the presence of a police officer around our home.''

But John was already dialing. ''Ben won't even know he's there.''

Any further objections would have been useless. John was already talking to someone named Officer Wilcox and making the necessary arrangements.

Although Abbie had turned down John's offer at first, knowing that she and Ben would have around-the-clock protection brought her peace of mind. She may not have wanted to admit it, but the sight of Arturo Garcia outside Rose's new home had spooked her. If he was crazy enough to come out of hiding and follow Abbie around, who knew what he was capable of?

The lunch hour at Campange was over, and she and her staff were cleaning up, when Sean handed her the phone. ''It's your baby-sitter.''

"Ms. DiAngelo," Tiffany said when Abbie took the phone. "Did we get our signals crossed? Was I supposed to come later today?"

Abbie glanced at the clock. It was exactly two-thirty. "No, why would you think that?"

"Because you picked up Ben from school, and I didn't know anything about it."

For a second, Abbie had no reaction. What was Tiffany talking about? She hadn't—

Her heart gave a powerful thump in her chest. "Tiffany, Ben is not with me."

"But…you picked him up!" There was an edge of panic in the young woman's voice that matched the panic Abbie felt rising inside her. "I called Ben's friend, Jimmy Hernandez, and he said you did. He saw Ben get into your truck."

"But that's impossible! I haven't left the restaurant!"

A sudden hush had fallen over the kitchen. In two long strides, Brady was by her side. "What's wrong?"

"Ben d-didn't go home," she stammered.

"There has to be a logical explanation."

Tiffany was talking again, her voice more agitated with each passing second. "I don't understand. Jimmy said your car was there, parked at the curb. He saw it. You honked the horn and Ben ran to it."

"Didn't you hear a word I said?" Abbie shouted, on the brink of hysteria. "I wasn't there! It wasn't me. And it wasn't my truck!"

Brady touched her arm. "Abbie, calm down. Let me talk to Tiffany."

"I won't calm down. I want to know where my son is!"

Brady took the phone from her hand, but kept her close, one arm around her shoulder. Fear was engulfing her, choking her. She was aware of someone pressing a glass of water into her hands. She pushed it away and shut her eyes, as if shutting out the light would also shut out the horrible images that were beginning to form in her head. Over the last six months, there had been three cases of child abduction in central New Jersey . All three children had been raped, then strangled. One of them, Eric Sommers, was a Princeton boy, whose body had been found only a month ago in Herrontown Park.

The darkness threatened to pull her in, but she fought it. No matter how raw her fear, she needed to stay alert, and strong, for Ben.

She took a breath, and another, until she was able to think rationally. Ben hadn't been on the bus, but Brady was right. There had to be an explanation. Maybe one of the mothers that routinely picked up their son from school had given Ben a ride home, and Jimmy had gotten the two trucks mixed up. Or maybe Ben had gone to a friend's house, not Jimmy Hernandez, but someone else, and had forgotten to tell Abbie.

"Stay where you are, Tiffany," Brady said, still talking to the baby-sitter, "in case Ben calls. When he does, let us know immediately."

He hung up. Then, holding Abbie's arm, he led her toward a chair but she wouldn't sit down. "Jimmy Hernandez is certain that it was your SUV parked outside the school," he said, looking concerned. "He recognized the Little League decal on the side window."

The kitchen was silent as a tomb. Whatever task each worker had been involved in prior to the phone call had been forgotten as all eyes focused on Abbie. Sean hadn't moved. He still stood in front of Abbie, the glass of water in his hand.

"Jimmy is wrong," she protested. "My truck has been

right here in the parking lot since I came back from Rose's house.''

To prove it, she marched out of the kitchen, Brady behind her.

Outside the restaurant, she stopped dead in her tracks.

The Acura was gone.

Thirty-Six

"Oh, God." Her heart pounding, Abbie leaned against the wall and closed her eyes. New images flashed across her mind—a stranger driving her SUV, joining the dozen or more vehicles already parked in front of the school, Ben spotting the truck, waving the way he always did, unsuspecting.

Arms wrapped around her middle, Abbie bent over. "Oh, God, oh, God, oh, God."

She was barely aware of Brady leading her back inside. "I'm calling John," he said. "What's his number?"

She motioned toward the utility room. "His card is in my purse."

Somehow, while Brady was dialing John's cell number, Abbie managed to find her address book. Trying to ignore her growing panic, she called every mother she knew, becoming more terrified with every call. No one had seen Ben or given him a ride. Most of the women she talked to assured her they wouldn't have picked up Ben without being certain Abbie knew about it. While no one mentioned it, the kidnapping of little Eric Sommers, and his ultimate death, was still very fresh in their minds. To put a mother through the nightmare of not knowing where her child was was unthinkable.

Jimmy Hernandez, who had walked out of the classroom with Ben, only repeated what he had already told Tiffany.

Abbie's SUV had been parked at the curb, a little ahead of the other cars. Whoever had been behind the wheel had honked the horn once, and Ben had shouted a quick good-bye to his friend and rushed toward the waiting truck.

Abbie was about to dial the school's administrative office when John arrived. He rushed to her, took her hands in his and forced her to look at him.

"Abbie, listen to me. More often than not, reports of missing children turn out to be false alarms. You know how boys are."

He spoke in a quiet, calming voice, and for an instant she was tricked into thinking all was well. She bobbed her head in agreement, desperate to believe him. But deep down she knew Ben was too level-headed to go anywhere without asking permission first or at the very least, calling to let her know where he was.

"A forensics team is on its way," John continued. "They'll comb every inch of the parking lot." She gave another stiff nod. "I'll need the names and addresses of Ben's classmates, and of his teacher."

"I've already talked to all his friends," she said dully. "They couldn't tell me anything more than what I already knew."

"It won't hurt to ask again. Give me the information, Abbie."

She handed him the address book she had used earlier, directing him to the first name on the list.

"I'll also need a recent picture of Ben. And the Acura's license plates."

Brady must have anticipated the request because he was already searching through her purse.

Tears ran down her cheeks as she pulled out Ben's latest school picture, the one where he had insisted on wearing his baseball uniform. He was grinning as he looked directly into the camera. A stubborn little cowlick stuck out at the back of his head. He had coaxed it down that morning with gel, but it had popped up again.

She ran her thumb over the smiling face and clamped her teeth over her lower lip, wondering how many mothers had gone through that same ritual of handing their child's photograph to a police detective, praying he or she would be returned to them safe and sound.

Her hand shook when she handed John the picture. "This was taken at the beginning of the school year."

John took the picture. "What was he wearing when he left the house?"

Abbie thought for a moment, recalling the frantic morning, the rush to get breakfast on the table, the hunt for that special shirt Ben wanted to wear, then a quick check of his backpack to make sure his homework was in it, the hasty peck on the cheek.

"Blue jeans," she said in a voice that sounded foreign. "A navy polo shirt with white stripes, black sneakers."

"Did he have a school bag?"

"A Harry Potter backpack, blue and black. Ben's name is on the inside." It had been a morning like any other, except that Ben had missed the bus and she'd had to drive him to school. She blinked back tears. "Where…will you start looking for him?"

"I'm going to talk to his teacher before I do anything. And his classmates. One of them may have caught a glimpse of the driver."

She knew they hadn't, because she had already asked, but she didn't say anything. John was an expert investigator, and if there was a way to get those children to remember something vital, he would find it.

"Abbie." He hadn't put his book away. "I have to ask

you about your ex-husband. You said he threatened to take Ben once.''

She closed her eyes. Jack. He had completely slipped her mind. She would have to call him. ''That was a long time ago. He wouldn't do anything now. His career is going well. He's serious about someone. Ben would only be a hindrance to him.''

''I'll still need to talk to him.''

She gave him the number and watched him jot it down.

''Can you think of anyone else who could have taken Ben? Someone who might want to get back at you about something? Torment you?''

She shook her head. She had no enemies. Or at least she didn't think she had. That possibility had never been a preoccupation before.

Brady walked over, a frown on his face. ''You mean… someone with a grudge?''

John turned around. ''Yes, someone with a grudge could do this. You know such a person?''

Brady gave Abbie a knowing look. ''Ken Walker comes to mind.''

John's attention snapped back to Abbie. ''That former employee you saw at Winberie?''

Brady's eyes widened. ''He followed you to Winberie? You didn't tell me that.''

''Because it wasn't important,'' Abbie said impatiently. ''Nothing happened. And Ken would never kidnap Ben.'' But Brady's intervention had put enough suspicion in John's mind to make him question her further about her former employee.

''I'll check him out,'' he said when she was finished. ''In the meantime, it's probably best if you stay here a little while longer, in case Ben calls.'' He glanced at Brady. ''I don't want her to be alone, though.''

Brady gave a quick nod. "I'll stay with her."

Ken forgotten, at least in Abbie's mind, she gripped John's arm. "Find him," she whispered. "Find my son."

"I will."

Find my son. Find my son. Find my son. She kept repeating those three little words in her mind, over and over, like a mantra.

"I'll call you as soon as I know something." John put his notebook away.

As soon as he left, Abbie called her ex-husband's office, only to be told he was attending an American Land Title Association conference in Honolulu and wouldn't be back until Thursday.

"I'll be glad to tell him you called," his secretary said.

"This is an emergency, Jen. Please ask him to call me immediately."

She hung up and hugged herself, feeling suddenly very cold.

John waited until he was out of earshot before calling the dispatcher at the station.

"Helen? John Ryan. I need a bulletin out on a young Princeton boy. Name's Ben DiAngelo. Someone in a red Acura SUV, license plates MER 2316, took him from outside his school—Princeton Elementary—at about two o'clock today."

He looked down at Ben's photo. "He's nine years old, about four foot three, seventy-five pounds. Blue eyes and red hair, freckles on his nose. Last seen wearing blue jeans, a navy polo shirt with white stripes and black sneakers. He's carrying a blue and black Harry Potter backpack."

"Got it. Shall I notify the state troopers, too?"

He hesitated, still hoping the boy was going to turn up at someone's house, but agreed, just to be on the safe side.

"Please. Tell them to still be on the lookout for that green pickup with the Texas plates. And Arturo Garcia." At this point he didn't have any reason to believe Garcia had taken Ben, but he wasn't taking any chances.

He hung up and got inside his car, the knot in his gut tightening. Although he hadn't said anything in front of Abbie, his first thought when Brady had called was that Tina's pedophile had struck again. He still considered that a possibility. And if he was right, the chances of finding Ben DiAngelo alive were very slim.

From time to time, as he drove, he glanced at the photo on the dashboard, remembering Ben's laugh, the sounds he and Jordan had made in the pool as they showed off their respective diving skills. The thought that that same happy boy could now be in the hands of a madman filled him with fury and helplessness.

Then, because he still couldn't get those dark thoughts out of his mind, he dialed Clarice at work.

"Yes, John?" As always, she sounded rushed and stressed.

He felt a little impatient himself, so this time he dispensed with civilities.

"Where's Jordan?" he asked abruptly.

His sharp tone seemed to bring her down a peg or two. "At his friend's house. Why?"

"Which friend?"

"Philip Goertz. John, for God's sake, what's wrong with you?"

"Do me a favor," he said, ignoring the question. "Call the Goertzes' house and make sure Jordan is there, and that he'll stay inside until you pick him up."

"*What is wrong?*"

"Do it, Clarice, now." Realizing he had spoken sharply, he softened his tone. "Please. I'll hold."

He heard a soft bang as she put her phone down. It was followed by a rustle as she searched for her cell phone, the muted sound of keys being punched, then her voice, which now sounded strained.

"Hi, Nancy. It's Clarice. I just wanted to make sure Jordan was with you." She laughed. "Did he really? No, no, no need for that. I forgot to remind him he should go home with you today and I just had to make sure he was there." Another laugh. "I know. Thanks, Nancy. See you at about six."

She came back on the line. "Everything's fine. The boys are downstairs, playing with Philip's birthday present— PlayStation 2."

"You didn't tell her to keep them inside."

"I didn't have to. She said they had already turned down a street-hockey game with their friends. They're not going anywhere." Too smart not to have picked up on this urgent line of questioning, she asked, "Has another boy disappeared, John? Is that what this is all about?"

He could hear the tension in her voice and decided to level with her, for Jordan's sake. "Yes, but don't tell Jordan. The missing boy is a friend of his and I'd like to tell him myself. Is it okay if I stopped by after dinner?"

"Of course. You could eat with us, if you want. I'm picking up some Boston Market chicken on the way."

His hesitation was brief. It would be good to spend an hour or so with Jordan, and prepare him for what he had to tell him. "I'll do that. Thanks, Clarice."

"John?"

"Yes?"

"Are you really worried about Jordan? I mean... Do we need to take extra precautions?"

"It won't hurt to keep a close eye on him for a few

days, until I know exactly what happened to that other boy. If that's a problem, I can—"

"No, no problem," she said quickly. "I'll make the necessary arrangements."

"I'll see you this evening, then. About six-thirty?"

"That will be fine."

He hung up and pulled into the parking lot of Princeton Elementary.

Brady had called Claudia, who arrived at the restaurant a half hour later. "I don't know what to say." She held Abbie in a tight embrace. "Except have faith in John. He'll find Ben." She put a kettle of water on the stove and turned on the burner. "Did you hear from Jack?"

Abbie nodded. "He said he was leaving Hawaii on the first available flight."

Claudia made tea, her remedy for just about anything from a sore back to anxiety, and the two of them sipped in silence, jumping every time the phone rang. Brady had elected himself telephone operator, taking calls from mothers anxious to hear if Ben had been found, or heard from. He even took a couple of last-minute reservations.

At some point, he turned to Abbie. "What do you want to do about tonight? We're almost fully booked, but if you want me to, I'll call our customers, tell them we had an unforseen emergency. They'll understand."

The restaurant. She had been sitting here, in this familiar kitchen, but had hardly paid attention to what was going on around her. She forced herself to focus. "No, let's stay open. If you don't mind handling everything without me."

"Of course not."

Later, in the bathroom, where she had gone to splash cold water on her face, she caught sight of her reflection in the mirror. She looked as if she hadn't slept in days. Her hair was a mess, her face chalk white, her lips bloodless, and her eyes had a wild, haunted expression in them. She just stood there, holding on to the edge of the sink as the seconds stretched into an eternity.

Ben is gone. Ben is gone. Ben is gone.

The mantra had changed. Despair was setting in. Any moment now, the strings that had held her together for the last hour would snap. And then what? How could she help Ben if she fell apart?

As she returned to the kitchen, she glanced out the window and saw two men wearing gloves and holding plastic bags walk around the parking lot, their eyes on the ground. She wanted to go out there and ask if they had found anything helpful, but knew it would be pointless. She would only be in the way. And they wouldn't tell her anything. So, she just stood at the window and watched them until they left in their township police van.

At five o'clock the staff returned. In a whisper, they asked Brady if there had been any news, and when he shook his head, they quietly began their evening chores.

Abbie was pacing back and forth between the kitchen and the utility room, when John came back. It was all Abbie could do not to scream the question "Did you find him?"

Instead, she stared at him intently, praying for good news, a small lead, a description of whoever had taken Ben, anything she could hang on to. Anything that would make the task of finding her little boy easier.

The grim look on John's face put an end to her fantasies. "Ben's teacher and his friends concur with what Jimmy Hernandez told Tiffany," he said. "Whoever was behind the wheel of your car—and they all assumed it was you—tooted the horn. Ben heard it, saw the SUV and ran to it."

"And he got inside?" Abbie said, aghast. "After he realized it wasn't me."

"It doesn't sound as if he had much time to do anything. According to Jimmy, the Acura sped away quickly."

"No one saw the driver?"

"Not through those dark windows, no."

She had a sudden vision of Arturo Garcia, the look on his face as he had shouted at her. A man with so much rage and determination wouldn't give up easily. And he would be resourceful, knowing exactly how to get the information he needed, such as the location of the restaurant, Abbie's home and Ben's school.

"Could Arturo have done this?" she asked.

"I doubt he'd have the guts to—"

"But what if he did?" Abbie's voice rose. "Ben could be anywhere by now. My son could be hundreds of miles away, with a maniac."

"He couldn't have gotten far, Abbie. We had APB's out within a half hour."

"You'll never find him!" Abbie shouted. "Why don't you say it? Why do you keep tiptoeing around the obvious?"

"Because I stopped relying on the obvious a long time ago. We're doing everything in our power to find Ben. Squad cars from several adjoining communities have joined in the search. They have a description of your truck, along with the licence plates."

Under the unsurmountable weight of despair, she felt her shoulders sag. "This is all my fault." There, she had said it. She had finally voiced the thought that had been on her mind all afternoon. "If I had gone to the police when Ian approached me with his crazy scheme, Ben would be home right now."

"You were protecting your mother," Claudia reminded her. "You had no way of knowing it would go this far."

Claudia's remark brought her no comfort. She twisted and untwisted her hands. "What about that forensic team you sent to check the parking lot?"

"They didn't find much, and it's doubtful the kidnapper left any evidence behind, but they're examining every scrap they picked up. They'll keep me informed."

John gripped her shoulders. "We'll find him, Abbie. No matter who took him, we'll find him."

She wanted to believe him. Oh, God, how she wanted to believe him. But what if it was too late? Like it had been too late for Eric Sommers. She scolded herself for having such thoughts. She had to keep faith.

"Why don't you let Claudia take you home," John said gently.

"I can't. I need to be here when Ben…"

"Brady will be here if he calls. You need to go home, Abbie."

She nodded obediently and let Claudia take her hand.

Thirty-Seven

It almost seemed like old times, John thought, the three of them sitting around the dining-room table—Clarice didn't like eating in the kitchen—and Jordan doing all the talking. He was thrilled to have John home, and totally unaware that this unscheduled visit came with a heavy price—the disappearance of his friend.

The Boston Market chicken, with all the trimmings, was good, a lot better than the burrito John would have grabbed on the way. At Clarice's insistence, he took seconds, then waited until all three were finished with their cherry pie before standing.

"Why don't we go in the family room," he told Jordan. "I need to talk to you about something."

Already halfway out of his chair, Jordan stopped. "Did I do something wrong?"

John laughed. "You'd better not have, because I couldn't take another scolding from Mrs. Rhinehart. The woman scares me out of my wits."

Jordan laughed. "She does not. Nothing scares you, Dad."

"That's what you think."

One hand on Jordan's shoulder, he walked him into the tidy family room with its navy upholstered furniture and brick fireplace, and made him sit down on a cushiony footstool while John took the chair. There was no easy way to break the news to him, so he said it straight out. "Ben is missing."

Clarice, who had followed them, let out a short gasp. "Are you talking about Ben DiAngelo?"

John nodded.

Jordan's expression was a mixture of concern and confusion. "What do you mean, he's missing?"

"He's been kidnapped."

Jordan sprang up. "No way! It's not true."

"I'm afraid it is, kiddo. There's a statewide search for him—"

"But why? Who took him?"

Clarice came to sit on the footstool next to Jordan, and wrapped a protective arm around the boy's waist. "My God, John. How could something like that happen?"

It was easier to answer Jordan's question first. "According to his teacher and a couple of classmates, someone driving Ms. DiAngelo's SUV was waiting outside Ben's school. When Ben came out, he recognized the Acura, ran to it, thinking his mother was behind the wheel, and got in. He hasn't been seen since. Or heard from."

"But you're looking for him, right, Dad? You're going to find him."

"We're doing everything we can."

"Is he being held for ransom?" Clarice asked.

"No one has come forward with a demand yet, but I suspect they will." He wasn't about to tell them that if Eric Sommers's killer had taken Ben, ransom would not be a concern.

Suddenly, Jordan broke free of his mother's hold and ran out of the room and up the stairs. John heard the slam of a drawer, then Jordan was racing back down and into the room.

"I was saving this for a new skateboard." He handed

John two ten-dollar bills and a five. "But I'd rather give the money to Ms. DiAngelo." He blinked, fighting back tears. "Tell her I want to help with the ransom."

John had a hard time keeping a dry eye himself. He took the money, folded it carefully and put it in his wallet. "That's very nice of you, son. I know Ms. DiAngelo will appreciate it."

He drew Jordan close to him and held him, wondering what Abbie would give to be able to hold her own son in her arms. "But now you've got to do something for your mom and me."

"Sure."

He could tell from Clarice's slight nod that she knew what he was about to say, and for once they were in agreement. "I want you to be extra careful for a while. Don't talk to strangers and don't go near anyone's car, even if you think that it's mine or your mom's. If it is one of us, we'll get out of the car so you can see us plainly. Understood?"

"You think I'm going to be kidnapped, too?"

"No, because your mom and I will do what needs to be done to make sure that doesn't happen. But you've got to do your part, too. Okay?"

"Okay."

Satisfied Jordan would keep his promise, John stood up to leave. As he did, his gaze fell on the end table, where something caught his attention. "What's that?" he asked, pointing.

Jordan picked up the model-railroad car. "It's a refrigerator car from the Santa Fe Railroad."

"Where did you get it?"

"The professor gave it to me."

"Professor?"

"Professor Gilroy. You remember him, don't you, Dad?

He took my class to a field trip to Northlandz last Saturday to visit the railroad display.''

"Yes, I do." John took the small car from him and looked at it closely. Where had he seen it before? Not the identical car but something similar. Then he remembered. Abbie. One of her customers had given it to her the day he had gone to Campagne with Tina.

"He builds them himself, out of tiny pieces of wood." Jordan sounded excited, and for a moment his friend's kidnapping was forgotten. "He has several sets of trains already built in his house. One is a garden display. He said I could go see it one day after school if I wanted."

"Did he really?" John turned the miniature car in his hands, remembering the well-dressed man who had sat alone. "Tell me about this professor."

Jordan shrugged. "Tell you what?"

But Clarice seemed to know exactly what John wanted to hear. "I met him when I drove Jordan to the school parking lot. He seemed very nice. He's a former professor of English literature. I believe he taught at Wesley College. He retired a few years ago and now builds model railroads."

"What's his connection to Jordan's school?"

Though visibly shaken, Clarice did her best to sound unfazed by the questions. "I'm not sure. I think he just contacted FitzRandolph, told them about Northlandz, and offered to escort the children there. He seems to be well known and highly regarded by the teachers I spoke to that morning."

"Describe him for me."

"He's about fifty-five, maybe sixty, slender, with short gray hair, a thin mustache. He speaks with a British accent."

John didn't need to hear any more. Clarice had definitely

described the man in Abbie's restaurant. But so what, he thought, knowing how his suspicious mind worked. Why couldn't a respectable former professor have a hobby he wanted to share with young boys? FitzRandolph Academy didn't seem to have a problem with that, so why should he?

Because you're a cop. Suspecting people is what you do.

"Why do you want Professor Gilroy's description, Dad?" Jordan was watching him intently. "Did he do something wrong?"

"No." John cupped the back of Jordan's neck. "I thought I knew him, that's all. Now I realize I don't."

Jordan and Clarice walked him to the door. Both were looking at him anxiously, though for different reasons.

Jordan was the first to speak. "You'll let me know when you find Ben, right, Dad?"

"You bet." He kissed Jordan on the cheek. "Now go finish your homework. I want to talk to your mom for a second."

He waited until he had disappeared before turning to Clarice. "I don't want Jordan within five hundred feet of Professor Gilroy. Not until I've run a thorough check on him."

"My God, John." She threw a quick glance toward the kitchen to make sure Jordan wasn't listening. "You can't possibly think he's the one who took Ben. He seems so…unthreatening," she added.

"They usually do," John said grimly.

"Should I alert the other mothers?"

John shook his head. "There's no need to alarm them until I know more about the man. I think the news of Ben DiAngelo's disappearance will be enough to make parents take a few additional precautions. You do the same, Clarice."

Thirty-Eight

As always at this time of night, Jose's Tapas & Bar on Lalor Street was filled with smoke, sweaty bodies and the sound of salsa music blaring from the jukebox. Tony sat at the end of the bar alone, sandwiched between a burly construction worker and a gabby blonde. He had hoped to stay home and keep an eye on Arturo, but his brother had left the apartment in the middle of the afternoon and told Tony not to worry. He was keeping a low profile, and the people he hung around with could be trusted. By people, Tony knew Arturo meant women. How much they could be trusted was debatable.

There hadn't been any more talk on Arturo's part about Abbie DiAngelo, and for that Tony was grateful. Maybe talking tough to him was just what his brother had needed.

When the TV sitcom Tony had been watching on and off was suddenly interrupted by a special announcement, Tony looked up at the screen. He immediately froze, his beer halfway to his mouth.

On the upper right corner of the screen was the photo of a young boy. Underneath was his name: Ben DiAngelo. Tony set his bottle of Dos Equis down as the announcer began to speak.

"Nine-year-old Ben DiAngelo of Princeton, New Jersey, was abducted from his school earlier today. He was last seen getting into a red Acura SUV, which was later reported stolen by the child's mother, Abbie DiAngelo. Police have refused to comment on the possibility that this latest incident is connected to the abduction and consequent killing of young Eric Sommers, also of Princeton. The township police has scheduled a press conference for seven o'clock this evening. Stay tuned for further developments. In sports…''

Tony felt as if a fifty-pound weight had suddenly lodged itself in his stomach. Not even the beer, which he badly needed right now, would go down. He kept staring at the broadcaster while Arturo's words replayed in his head.

''Did you know she had a kid?''

That bastard. He had kidnapped the boy! In broad daylight. Was he crazy? Did he have some kind of death wish?

Tony reached into his pocket, took out a few dollar bills and dropped them on the counter. He had to get out of here. He had to find Arturo and make him return the boy, or both he *and* Tony would find themselves behind bars.

After sending Tiffany home and forcing Abbie to sit in one of the chairs by the fireplace, Claudia had busied herself in the kitchen, pulling food out of the refrigerator and pots from the cupboard. She was making soup, another of her cure-alls, even though Abbie had told her she wasn't hungry.

''It gives me something to do,'' Claudia had replied.

Abbie hadn't fought her. She needed every bit of energy she had to stay calm. It wasn't easy, not with reminders of Ben in every nook and cranny of this house. Her gaze fell on the coffee table where a stack of baseball cards lay, the same cards Ben and Jordan had oohed and aahed over not so long ago. Abbie spread them out and found Ben's favorite—Scott Rolen, with the third baseman's signature scrawled on the bottom. She remembered Ben's excitement last year when Brady had taken him to a Phillies game and, through a friend he knew, had managed to get an introduction to Ben's hero. Ben had talked of nothing else for weeks.

Abbie took the card and touched it gently, remembering the last time Ben had looked at it, touched it. This morning. This morning, when everything had been so normal and wonderful.

The ringing of the phone broke through her thoughts. She ran to it, practically yanking it from Claudia's hand. "Hello?"

"Abbie, it's John."

"Did you find him?" she blurted out.

"Not yet." She heard the sound of traffic, a burst of static, then he was back. "I need to ask you a couple of questions about Professor Gilroy."

The question threw her. "Oliver?"

"Are you on a first-name basis with him?"

"He's a regular customer."

"How regular?"

"He's been coming to the restaurant every day for the past two years. Why are you interested in him?"

"Does he know Ben?"

"Ben has met him, yes."

"When?"

The intense questioning sent a wave of unease throughout her system. "What's going on, John?"

"Answer the question, Abbie. Please."

"They met a couple of months ago."

"Under what circumstances?"

Abbie took a shallow breath and released it. "When Oliver found out I had a son, he started bringing Ben model-railroad cars he built himself. One day, when Ben had a half day of school, I brought him to the restaurant to thank Oliver in person.''

"Has he ever asked to take Ben somewhere? Alone?"

Now she was frightened. She may not have known John very long, but she knew he wouldn't be asking all those questions without a good reason. "No," she replied. "Although…"

"What?"

"Last week, after Oliver learned of Ian's death, he told me he was escorting a group of boys from FitzRandloph Academy to Northlandz to see a train display. Fitz-Randolph," she repeated. "That's Jordan's school, isn't it?"

"Yes, it is. Go on."

"Oliver wanted to take Ben, but Ben had baseball practice that day and couldn't go."

"How did Gilroy take it?"

Abbie was aware that Claudia had come to sit in the other chair and was listening intently. "All right, I guess. No, that's not entirely true. He was disappointed. He sounded almost…insulted."

"Did he say something to make you think that?"

"No, it was just a feeling I had, but it went away when Oliver said he understood and would make it up to Ben some other way." She locked eyes with Claudia. "What is it, John? Do you know something about Professor Gilroy I should be aware of?"

"I don't know anything yet except what you and my ex-wife told me. Jordan took part in the field trip to Northlandz. Sometime during the bus trip back, the professor gave Jordan a railroad car and invited him to his house to see his own display. Call me paranoid, but that invitation didn't sit right with me. Especially after I realized Gilroy was the same man I had seen at Campagne last week, giving you a railroad car.''

He faded away for a second or two, then came back. "What do you know about him, Abbie?"

She was almost glad for the questioning. It made her feel useful and took her mind off her fears for a while. "Not much, except what he told me. He came to this country fifteen years ago and taught English literature at Wesley College until his retirement four years ago. That's when he turned his passion—building model trains—into a full-time hobby.''

"What does he do when he's not building trains?"

"I don't know. I only speak to him when I make my rounds at the restaurant.''

"He's not married?"

"He's a widower. He has a daughter and a grandson whom he visits in London every Christmas.''

"Anything else?"

She shook her head. "That's all I know. Someone at Wesley might be able to tell you more.''

John thanked her, told her he'd be in touch and said goodbye.

Claudia waited until Abbie had put the phone down before speaking. "Did I understand correctly? John thinks Professor Gilroy took Ben?"

"He didn't come right out and say that, but..." She shook her head. "He's got to be wrong, Claudia. I can't picture Oliver as a kidnapper. Much less a rapist and a killer.''

"Oh, I don't know. Personally, I never cared much for the man. From the moment I saw him at the restaurant, I thought he was just a shade too smooth.'' She gave an unladylike snort. "This habit he has of coming to Campagne every day, at the same precise time, requesting the same table, drinking the same wine, is just plain creepy. And why *your* restaurant, Abbie? No offense, Campagne is one of the best, but...don't you think a normal person would want a little variety?''

''I'm not disagreeing with that—''

The sound of the doorbell interrupted her reply. Abbie jumped and ran to answer it.

Brady stood on her doorstep, his face ashen. He handed her a sheet of paper. ''I think you'd better see this.''

Abbie willed her hand not to shake as she read the words that sent ice through her veins.

''How do you want your boy, bitch? Dead or alive?''

Thirty-Nine

As expected, Captain Farwell assigned the disappearance of Ben DiAngelo to Tina, but at her request he agreed to let John assist with the investigation, since he was a friend of the family and had already done the preliminary work.

Farwell looked preoccupied as he stood at his desk being briefed, and John couldn't blame him. Ever since Ben's disappearance had been made public, the captain's phone had been ringing almost nonstop.

"You said you learned nothing useful from this Walker character," he said, addressing John.

"He claims he was home at the time the boy was abducted, but can't prove it. His wife kicked him out of the house, and home is now a small room in Hopewell Township."

"First impressions?"

John sighed. "The man has a temper, and he holds a grudge against Abbie DiAngelo, but..." He shook his head. "He doesn't strike me as the type of man who would kidnap a child just to get back at a former employer."

"Keep an eye on him anyway." He pulled at his bottom lip. "What about the parking lot? Forensics got back to you on that?"

"Just now. They found the usual stuff—a cigarette butt, a gum wrapper, the cap from a soda can. They're checking each item for fingerprints, but I doubt they'll find anything."

"What about the other store owners on Palmer Square? A few of them back onto that parking lot, don't they?"

"I've questioned them. No one saw anything."

"Amazing. A car is stolen in the heart of Princeton, in broad daylight and at the height of the shopping hour, and no one sees a thing." He started to pace. "The mayor isn't going to like it. He credits himself for keeping Princeton one of the safest towns in the state. Now, with two murders and the disappearance of another boy, all in the space of a month, the man is foaming at the mouth. His reelection depends on how quickly we apprehend the perp."

He came to stand in front of John and Tina. "Which brings me to the press. As you know, they've been particularly vocal about this case. Hopefully, you'll be able to appease them at the press conference."

John and Tina exchanged a look. "I thought *you* were holding the press conference," Tina said.

"I can't. I have a meeting with the mayor at seven-fifteen. The two of you will have to handle it."

Not giving them a chance to reply, he headed for the door, and gave John a friendly slap on the shoulder. "Good luck with the vultures. Both of you," he added, nodding at Tina. "Don't let them smell blood."

"That rat," Tina muttered when he was gone. "He could have made the press conference. I happen to know that his meeting with the mayor is not until seven-thirty. He just doesn't want to be put in a bad light with the press. Looking stupid is our job."

The area in front of the police station was jammed when John and Tina stepped out. Reporters poured out of news vans and rushed toward them, elbowing each other for a front-row spot. All had the excited, hungry look typical of reporters who had just found out something big had broken in their pristine community and the hell with good manners. This was every man for himself. This was war.

"Detective Ryan!" As though she couldn't wait to repay him for his brush-off at Winberie the other day, Mary Kay Roder came to stand in front of him. Her eyes glinted with shrewd speculation as she went straight for the jugular. "Is there any connection between the disappearance of the DiAngelo boy and the death of Eric Sommers?"

"It's too early to jump to conclusions," John replied smoothly. "While we're not overlooking the possibility that Eric Sommers's abductor struck again, it's important for the investigators, as well as the public, to focus on Ben DiAngelo and what can be done to find him."

The man beside Mary Kay raised a hand. "Do you have any suspects yet?"

John let Tina field that one. "We're working on a couple of possibilities," she said easily. "Nothing we can discuss."

At those words, angry protests broke out as the reporters clamored for more information. Tina ignored them and started passing out copies of Ben's photograph. "Please tell your readers to stay alert for any sightings. And to report those sightings to the police quickly."

John tried to take another question, this time from a man in the back, but Mary Kay wasn't finished with him yet. "How confident are you you'll find Ben DiAngelo alive?"

John hoped Abbie wasn't listening to this. "We were fortunate to have been notified within the first half hour of the abduction. That allowed us to put a bulletin out right away, before the perpetrator could get out of the area—if that was his intention."

"But it's been almost seven hours and the boy hasn't been found."

Before he could reply, Bill Gasier, of the *Princeton Journal,* fired another question. "You're homicide, aren't you, Detective Ryan? Mind telling us why you're assisting Detective Wrightfield with this case, considering the department is currently short-staffed?"

"Detective Ryan was assigned at *my* request," Tina cut in.

"But isn't it true, Detective," Mary Kay shouted loud enough for everyone to hear, "that the true reason you're on this case is because you're a friend of Ms. DiAngelo's? A *very* close friend," she added with a little smirk.

So that's what she was after—a little sleaze to spark up her prose. "My relationship with Ms. DiAngelo has no bearing on this case," he said dryly. "A child has disappeared. I would think that tragedy would be your primary focus, Mary Kay, not some rumor you may have heard about my private life, which, incidently, is none of your business."

She smiled sweetly, totally unfazed by the sharp rebuttal or the snickering of her colleagues, who knew her as well as John did.

His cell phone rang as Miss Congeniality was about to throw another question at him. Cutting short the conference, John thanked the reporters and stepped aside to take the call. It was Abbie. She had just received a note from Ben's kidnapper.

On the way to Abbie's house, John called his father. "Do you still play golf with the dean of admissions at Wesley College?" he asked when Spencer answered.

"Every Tuesday morning at ten." Spencer chuckled. "And I'm still whipping Lyman's ass. Why do you ask?"

"I need a favor, Dad."

"Shoot."

"A professor by the name of Oliver Gilroy taught English lit at Wesley until four years ago. He came here from England in the late-eighties, is a widower and has a daughter and a grandson in England he visits every year. I need to know anything else you can find out about him."

"Does this professor have anything to do with the press conference I just saw? And the disappearance of that young boy?"

"He could."

"In that case, I'll call Lyman right away."

"Thanks, Dad," John said as he approached his destination. "I appreciate it."

Abbie must have been watching for him, because her front door opened before he'd had a chance to get out of the car.

The ordeal had taken its toll on her beautiful face. There were shadows of fatigue circling her eyes, and the corners of her mouth were turned down, making her look tired and defeated.

He held her for a moment, stroking her hair, aware that a little more than twenty-four hours ago, he had held her much in the same way. Her heart had beaten just as fast, though for different reasons.

After another few seconds, he released her. "Let me see the note."

Without a word, she handed it to him. He read it as he walked down the hall and toward the kitchen. A young woman with frizzy red hair and small rimless glasses, whom Abbie introduced as her friend Claudia Marjolis, shook his hand.

"How did you get this?" he asked Abbie, holding up the note.

"Brady brought it. It came through the fax at the restaurant. Apparently it had been there for some time, but with what's been going on, no one paid attention to the fax machine.'' She pointed at a name near the top of the page. "It came from a place called Cyber Café."

John read the chilling message again. "There was no follow-up phone calls? No e-mail?"

"Nothing." She nodded toward the open laptop on the coffee table. "I've had this on since I came home. A beep lets me know when I have a new message."

She ran an unsteady hand through her hair. "Arturo Garcia used the word *bitch* several times that night at the lake."

John nodded. "The rough language could be a deterrent, a way for the culprit to steer the investigation away from him and toward someone else."

"What's being done to find Ben?" Claudia asked.

John met her steady blue gaze and liked her instantly. She would be a soothing influence on Abbie, whose nerves seemed as brittle as glass. "Besides the APB and repeated TV announcements, I've made arrangements for someone to come here and wire the phones. They'll explain the procedure when they get here." He glanced at the sheet of paper in his hand again. "In the meantime, I'll check out this Cyber Café. I know the place. It's in New Brunswick. Last I heard, it was open twenty-four hours a day."

Abbie lay a hand on John's arm. "John, tell me the truth. Why that angry message? Why didn't the kidnapper ask for a ransom?"

"I don't know. It could be that he wants to toy with you, rattle you, so that when he does ask for a ransom, you'll take the request seriously."

"I'm taking it seriously now! I'll give him everything I own, my house, my restaurant, my car, everything! All I want is my son back."

He wrapped his arms around her and held her, waiting

for the trembling to stop and her breathing to return to normal. He wanted so much to make everything right for her, but for the first time in all his years in law enforcement, after all the cases he had solved and the dozens of criminals he had put behind bars, he was having doubts about this one.

The sound of the front doorbell put an end to his gloomy reflections. Claudia went to answer it, and a moment later there was an abrupt exclamation, followed by Claudia's angry voice.

"I thought Abbie made it clear you should stay away from her. What will it take for you to—"

In a few fast strides, John had joined her at the door. Standing on the porch was Ken Walker, the man he had questioned only hours ago. "What are you doing here?" he asked sharply.

Abbie pushed John aside. "You've chosen a lousy time to come and harrass me, Ken." Her voice was thin and angry but the man gave an emphatic shake of his head.

"I didn't come here to harass you, Ms. DiAngelo, I swear. And I'm not mad at you for sending the police after me. In your place—"

"That's enough. Get out of here." John took the man by the arm. "Before I haul your ass off to jail."

"You don't understand! Ms. DiAngelo, please, listen to me! I know who took your boy!"

Forty

Abbie barely gave him time to finish his sentence. Pushing John aside, she grabbed Ken by the shirtsleeve and pulled him inside. "Who is it? Who took my son?"

"Abbie, let me handle this," John said.

"No! Let him talk." She didn't take her eyes off Ken. If he was lying, if this was another of his "get back at Abbie" games, she would know and then God help him. "Who took my son?" she repeated.

"Arturo Garcia." He looked at John. "After you left, I had to get out, so I went for a walk and then later, I stopped at Winberie for a beer. That's when I saw that man's face on TV, and I remembered him."

"What do you mean, you remembered him?" John asked. "From where?"

"Princeton Elementary. I saw him there yesterday." He looked away and spoke in a quieter tone. "I went there to see my boy. Yesterday was Robbie's tenth birthday and I didn't want him to think I had forgotten." He looked up again and met Abbie's gaze. "I guess you know Lainie kicked me out.

"I went there to give him his present," Ken continued when Abbie nodded. "I was waiting for Robbie to come out, when a car—a maroon sedan—pulled up along the curb, maybe three or four car lengths ahead of me. That's the reason I noticed him, because he could have parked closer to the school but didn't. And he looked uncomfortable being there, you know, like he didn't belong. I never thought anything of it, though. Not until a little while ago, when I saw his face on TV.''

The man outside Rose's apartment had been driving a maroon car. "Are you sure you got a good look at him?"

"Good enough to know it's the guy on TV."

"What did he do when Ben's class came out?"

"I don't know. Robbie came out first and I had to hurry and give him his present before he got on his bus. Then I left.''

"And the man stayed behind?''

"I guess so. Like I said, I wasn't looking for anything out of the ordinary at the time, so I didn't pay much attention to him after that first look.''

"He didn't talk to anyone?''

"Not that I saw.''

Abbie leaned against the console. In spite of her differences with Ken and the recent incident at Campagne, she didn't think he would make up such a wild story, especially in the presence of a police detective. He was telling the truth. Arturo had been outside Ben's school yesterday afternoon. Maybe he had gone there to familiarize himself with the surroundings. Or he had meant to take Ben yesterday and for some reason had changed his mind and decided to do it the following day. Whatever the reason, it didn't change anything. While they now knew the identity of Ben's kidnapper, Arturo remained as elusive as ever.

"I'll need you to come to the station and take a look at Garcia's mug shot.'' John's car keys were already in his hand. "Can you do that now?"

"Yeah, sure. I'll be glad to.'' Ken ran his hand across his mouth, hesitated, then said to Abbie, "I'm real sorry about Ben, Ms. DiAngelo. I hope you find him soon.''

"Thank you. And thank you for coming here. I know it wasn't easy for you."

"You would have done the same for me."

With Claudia's hand holding hers, Abbie watched John and Ken drive away in their respective cars. There were still so many questions, but only one mattered.

Where was Ben?

After John had placed Garcia's mug shot on the desk, it had taken Ken Walker only a few seconds to positively identify him as the man he had seen outside Princeton Elementary the previous day. According to his description, Arturo had apparently shaved his goatee since McGregor's murder, but that didn't change Ken's conviction.

Tina took his statement, typed it and handed it to him for his signature. She had just left to request a warrant for Arturo's arrest, when John's phone rang. It was Manuel.

Although John wasn't superstitious, he crossed his fingers that Manuel's call would bring him good news. He could use some right about now. "What's up, my friend?"

"I have a customer by the name of Henrietta who likes to brag about her conquests, not to me, but to Coletta."

"That's your niece."

"*Sí.* She helps around the store when Freddy is in school. She and Henrietta have been friends since the fourth grade. Henrietta came in today and started to tell Coletta about that man she met a few days ago. Normally I wouldn't have eavesdropped, but when I heard Henrietta describe him, I made a point to listen."

"What did you hear?"

"I think her new boyfriend is the man you're looking for, John. She didn't call him Arturo. She said his name was Mike, but the way she described him—big, bald and with tattooes of mermaids and dragons all over his arms, I knew it had to be the same man."

John pulled a yellow pad toward him. "Where can I find this Henrietta?"

Manuel chuckled. "She's a lap dancer at night, so she's home during the day, catching up on her sleep. From what I heard, her new boyfriend spends a lot of time there, too."

"Do you have an address?"

"Yes—113 Olden Avenue."

"Thanks, Manuel." John tore the sheet on which he had scrawled the address. "I owe you one."

No sooner had he hung up than Tina walked back in. "The judge wasn't in, but his clerk told me he'd be back within the hour. I'll—"

"No time for a warrant." John told her about Manuel's call and handed her Henrietta's address. "We need to get there fast." He grabbed his jacket from the back of his chair and slipped it on. "We'll call for back-up from the car. I don't think our friend is going to come in willingly."

They approached the door quietly—John, Tina and three uniformed officers, guns drawn. They knocked twice, yelling 'Police! Open up!,' then, when the door remained shut, they kicked it down.

The girl was sitting on the sofa, hastily pulling a short robe around her. The man, naked except for a black T-shirt, already had a knife in his hand and was in an attack position.

John stopped him short. "Don't even think about it, Romeo, or you're a dead man."

Arturo looked at the five guns aimed at him. He didn't seem to be oozing with intelligence, but he was no dummy either. Quickly assessing the situation, he dropped the knife and put his hands up. He had been through the drill before.

"Okay if I put my pants on?" His tone turned sarcastic as he gave Tina a lewd grin. "Unless Rambo chick here wants to take another look."

Tina gave a disinterested shrug. "Nothing much to look at, shorty." Then, as Arturo's grin faded, she turned to one of the officers. "Toss him his pants, Joe, but check them first. And bag the knife."

The girl, a brunette with a Kewpie doll face, sat huddled in a corner of the sofa, watching the exchange and looking terrified. "What's going on?" she asked in a small voice. "Why did you have to break my door? How am I going to explain that to my landlord?"

"We'll do the explaining," Tina said. "Are you Henrietta?"

The girl nodded.

"We'll need you to come with us."

"Why? I didn't do anything."

"It's just routine. It won't take long."

Arturo hollered all the way to the station, demanding to talk to an attorney and threatening to sue them for arresting him without a warrant. He was still shouting obscenities when they shoved him into an interrogation room.

"Let him stew for a while," he told Tina. "I have to call Abbie and hope she can pick him out of the lineup as the man who attacked her at the lake. Once we have him for murder, he'll cooperate with the rest."

Abbie arrived fifteen minutes later, her cheeks flushed. "Did he talk? Did he tell you where Ben is?"

"Not yet. I want to make sure he's the man who attacked you. That will give us some leverage."

Even without the goatee, she took only five seconds to identify him. "That's him," she said, recoiling slightly as Arturo complied with John's request and took two steps forward.

"Are you sure, Abbie?"

She kept nodding. "Yes, yes. It's him. I've never been more sure of anything in my life."

At John's suggestion that she let Claudia take her back home, Abbie let out a dry laugh. "I'm not going anywhere, John, not until Arturo tells you where Ben is."

"It could take a while."

Her gaze did not waver. "I'm staying, John."

In the interrogation room, where Arturo had returned after standing in the lineup, Tina perched a hip on the corner of the desk and pushed a phone in his direction. "You can do this two ways," she said sweetly. "The hard way or the easy way."

"How 'bout I do it to you up your ass, Rambo chick? Would you like that?" He snickered. "I bet you would. You look the type."

John watched Tina closely, knowing she had a short fuse, but her expression didn't change. "You can shut your mouth, and call your attorney, or you can do your yapping in a cell and hope I don't get one of my memory lapses and forget you're in there."

Garcia sneered. "You ain't so tough. And what about you, copper?" he said to John. "You ain't got the balls to interrogate me, so you're letting a broad do it? What kind of man are you?"

Tina yanked the phone back. "That does it." She nodded to the uniform standing by the door. "Lock him up."

"Wait!" Arturo sat up. He glared at Tina, but knew when he was beat. "All right. I'll do it your way."

Without a word, Tina pushed the phone back toward him and motioned for the officer to uncuff him. "Keep it short."

More subdued now, Garcia dialed a number. John noted

with satisfaction that he punched the keypad with the index finger of his left hand. The noose around the man's neck had just gotten a little tighter.

"Hey, Tone," Arturo said, his eyes on Tina. "I've been arrested, man. Murder." He let out an oath in Spanish. "Shut up, Tone, and listen, okay? I need a lawyer. Right away, okay, Tone? 'Cause I ain't spending one stinkin' night in this place."

He listened for a few seconds and looked at Tina. "Where the fuck am I?"

John answered. "Princeton Township P.D. on Witherspoon." He said it loud enough for "Tone" at the other end to hear.

"You got that, bro?" When Garcia had his answer, he hung up and let the officer cuff him again. "I ain't sayin' a word until my lawyer gets here. You got that?"

"Who's Tone?" John asked.

Arturo thought for a while and must have figured there was no harm in answering the question. "My brother, Tony."

"Your brother traveled with you from El Paso?"

Arturo's eyes narrowed. "How do you know I'm from El Paso?"

"Oh, we know a lot of things about you, Arturo. We know you tried to attack a woman at Lake Carnegie moments after you stabbed Ian McGregor to death."

"Don't know any Ian McGregor."

"What about Ben DiAngelo? That name ring a bell?"

He frowned as though deep in thought. "That the kid that was kidnapped?"

"That's right."

"Why ask me?"

"Because you were seen parked outside his school yesterday. Why were you there, Garcia?"

"Checking out the female teachers. Some of them broads are hot, man."

"I wouldn't be such a smartass if I were you." Tina leaned toward him, wincing slightly when she caught a whiff of his breath. "We've got you for murder, assault with a deadly weapon and kidnapping. I'm no judge, but offhand, I'd say that's worth about a hundred years in the can. You've been around, Garcia. What do you think? Am I in the ballpark?"

"You're bluffing. You can't make those charges stick."

"Tell him I'm not bluffing, John."

"She's not bluffing. Abbie DiAngelo just identified you as the man who attacked her at the lake on June 6. We also have two witnesses who swear you were at the Clearwater Motel on the afternoon of Ian McGregor's murder. And then you did something that wasn't very bright, Arturo. You left your fingerprints all over McGregor's room. As for your knife, I haven't heard from forensics yet, but I'm fairly certain your switchblade will turn out to be the same kind that killed your old buddy. Now, do you still think we can't make those charges stick?"

When Arturo didn't answer, John said casually, "We're ready to make a deal with you, Garcia. Want to hear it?"

Arturo stayed silent.

"We're willing to drop the assault charge and let you plead down from murder one to self-defense. All you have to do is tell us where Ben DiAngelo is."

"Are you guys deaf? I don't know where Ben DiAngelo is! I didn't take him!"

They were interrupted by a knock on the door. The officer closest to it opened it, and a man who looked as if he was barely out of school stood in the doorway. He wore a gray pinstriped suit and carried a leather briefcase without a single trace of wear and tear on it. He looked nervous, as if this case was too big for him. His expression when he saw his client would have been amusing if the moment hadn't been so serious. The thought the attorney might bolt at any time crossed John's mind for a moment, but to the man's credit, he gave a shaky smile and stepped into the lion's den.

Behind him was another nervous-looking young man John recognized instantly as the Ricky Martin look-alike he had seen in Enrique's garage.

"Who are you?" he asked, but had already guessed his identity.

"Tony Garcia. I'm Arturo's brother."

"And I'm Jason Hardell," the man in the sharp suit said. "From legal aid."

John made the introductions and all three shook hands. Hardell gave Arturo a nervous look. "Is that my client?"

"In the flesh," Tina replied. She briefed Hardell on the various charges. When she mentioned kidnapping, the young attorney's eyes bulged. He turned to Tony Garcia. "Kidnapping?" He swallowed. "You didn't tell me that. Who is he supposed to have kidnapped?"

"Ben DiAngelo," Tina offered. "And since time is of the essence, I suggest you talk to your client and convince him to tell us where the boy is. We have a deal on the table I think is fair, but he's playing hardball and our patience is wearing thin."

Hardell stole another glance in his client's direction, and looked as if he was about to pass out. John always considered inexperienced attorneys a gift from heaven, but not today. Hardell might lack the firmness needed to convince Arturo to cooperate. He glanced at Tony, wondering if he might have better luck with the brother.

"May I speak to my client in private, please?" Hardell asked.

"Certainly." John, Tina and Tony waited outside until the attorney reopened the door ten minutes later. He looked pale, but otherwise calm.

"My client can't accept your offer." Hardell looked from Tina to John. "I'm sure you know why."

John had a sinking feeling he did, but shook his head.

"Arturo didn't kidnap Ben DiAngelo. He thought about it, because he figured that was the only way he could get his hands on Ms. DiAngelo's forty-eight thousand dollars, but there were too many people at the school, too much chaos. He couldn't pull it off."

John saw Tina's shoulders sag a little. "You believe him?" he asked.

Some of the attorney's confidence had returned. "Yes. Just as I believe that he killed Ian McGregor in self-defense."

"So he admits it."

"My client wants to cooperate, Detective."

"Is he ready to make a statement?"

"Yes."

"Then let's go."

By the time John returned to his desk, Abbie and Claudia were still there. Abbie stood up, but this time she didn't say anything. She just looked at him expectantly, as though he should be the bearer of good news.

He hated what he was about to tell her. "Arturo didn't take Ben."

"What do you mean, he didn't take Ben? Of course he did. You heard what Ken said. Arturo was at the school."

"He didn't do it, Abbie. There was too much going on and he got scared. He confessed to killing Ian, in self-defense, and of attacking you, but that's all he did."

"He's lying! He knows what the penalty for kidnapping is and he's lying."

"He didn't do it, Abbie. I talked to the people at the Cyber Café. They didn't see anyone who even remotely resembles Arturo. And Henrietta swears he's been with her since two o'clock this afternoon."

"And you believe her?" Abbie let out a dry laugh and walked around in small circles, like a caged animal. "What's the matter with you, John? A couple of hours ago you believed Arturo had kidnapped Ben as much as I did. Now you don't." She let her arms drop by her sides. Her eyes were dark with disappointment and resentment. "Would you give up this easily if it was Jordan who was missing?"

"I'm not giving up. I just don't believe in wasting time and energy on the wrong suspect."

"And who would be the *right* suspect?" she asked sarcastically. "Professor Gilroy?"

"He's a possibility."

"You're wrong. Oliver stopped by the restaurant earlier. Did you know that? He came to ask Brady how I was holding up and if there was anything he could do. When Brady told him to pray for Ben's safe return, he said he already had but he would again. Now tell me, does that sound like something a psychotic killer would do? Would he be so bold as to come to my restaurant and say those things if he had kidnapped my son?"

John's experience told him yes, that was exactly what a clever psychotic killer would do, but explaining his philosophy to Abbie was pointless. She was too upset with him right now to see things in a logical manner. She had wanted the kidnapper to be Arturo. She had *counted* on it, and now the letdown was like an ice-cold shower.

He turned to Claudia, who had stayed discreetly out of the way. "Please take her home, Claudia. See that she gets some sleep."

Abbie gave him a withering look and walked out.

Forty-One

At eight o'clock the following morning, after only three hours' sleep, John called Abbie's house. She had been upset with him yesterday afternoon, and while he understood her frustrations, he didn't want to let this wall build between them at a time like this.

Rose Panini answered on the first ring.

"Rose. What are you doing there?"

"Claudia needed to catch up on her sleep," she said in a low whisper, "so I came to relieve her."

"Is Abbie there?"

"She's sleeping, John, right here in the kitchen easy chair. I don't think I should wake her up, unless you've got good news."

"I wish I had. And you're right to let her sleep. Sergeant Tyler showed up okay?" he asked, inquiring about the police technician who had been sent to install a tracer on Abbie's phone.

"Yes, but no one called yet, just friends and neighbors."

Promising he'd call back later, John hung up. No sooner had he put the receiver down than his father called with startling news.

"Seems your man is a bit of a fibber, son."

John's ears perked up. "In what way?"

"To begin with, he's not a widower. His wife divorced him about a year before Gilroy moved to the U.S. She is alive and well and living in a little cottage somewhere in the Cotswolds. Secondly, he doesn't have a daughter, or a grandson.''

''You're kidding!''

''No. The Gilroys were childless. And your professor has never been back to England.''

''Is Lyman sure about that?''

''As sure as a close associate can be. To his knowledge, Professor Gilroy hasn't set foot in England since the day he landed in the U.S. He spends his vacations either in the Caribbean, which he loves, or here at home, where he likes to tinker with his trains. That's a hobby of his—trains.''

''I know.'' John was stunned. Why would the man claim to have a bogus family he visited every year when he didn't? And why had he chosen Abbie to tell that lie to?

''I don't suppose you thought of asking where Gilroy lives by any chance?'' he asked his father.

He heard the smug chuckle at the end of the line. ''Have you ever known me to do a half-assed job?''

John smiled. ''Not to my recollection.''

''Professor Gilroy lives in Princeton Township, 7 Ridge View Road.''

Gilroy's Tudor-style house stood poised at the top of a hill, clearly visible from the road, yet far enough from neighboring homes to afford complete privacy. John had taken a chance the professor would be home and was prepared to wait if he wasn't. Fortunately he didn't have to. A black Town Car in the driveway and movements in one of the front rooms told him the good professor was home.

Gilroy opened the door himself, looking as dapper as he had the day John had seen him at Campagne.

''Professor Gilroy?''

''Yes?''

"I'm Detective John Ryan of the Township P.D.—Jordan's father."

"Jordan." Small white teeth clamped over a thin lower lip, as though he was trying to place the name.

"Black hair, blue eyes. You escorted his class to Northlandz last week and gave him a railroad car."

"Ah, yes, I remember now." He smiled. "The young man with all the questions. I'm sorry it took me a while to match the name with the face. I meet so many youngsters."

"I can imagine." John raised an eyebrow. "May I come in?"

The request seemed to catch the professor by surprise. "Well, actually, I was about to leave."

"This won't take long, Professor. I just need to ask you a few questions."

The professor's cool demeanor dropped a notch, but he moved aside to let John in and quickly closed the door. "What kind of questions?"

"It's in regard to the disappearance of Ben DiAngelo. I understand you know his mother quite well?"

"Yes, indeed I do. I'm one of Abbie's most loyal customers, as well as a friend." His expression clouded. "What happened to her son is a calamity. What sort of monster would put a child, and a mother, through such an ordeal?"

"That's the question many people would like answered." John glanced around him, taking in the heavy, elaborately carved furniture, all polished to a high shine. "How did you hear about the kidnapping?"

"I was in my car and heard it on the radio." He gave a bewildered shake of his head. "I couldn't believe it. A missing child is a terrible thing, but it affects you differently when it's someone you know."

He sounded so sincere, so genuinely troubled, John wondered if he could have been wrong about him. It wouldn't be the first time he had chased the wrong suspect. "You haven't seen Abbie since then?" he asked. "Or communicated with her in any way?" *Sent her a fax, perhaps?*

If the phrasing of the question puzzled him, Gilroy gave no indication of it. "No. I stopped at Campagne last night to offer Abbie my support, but she wasn't there. I left word with her sous-chef. I hope he gave her my message."

"He did. She's not in much of a mood to return calls at the moment."

"I understand. I just wanted her to know I was there for her."

The man was too calm, John thought. Time to shake things up a bit. "Abbie told me you have a grandson."

He took a moment to answer. "That's right."

"Henry, isn't it? He lives in England with your daughter?"

"You and Abbie discussed my family?"

"It's all part of the investigation. People don't like it, but when a child disappears, everyone is put under scrutiny."

The shrewd eyes narrowed. "Have you been investigating me, Detective?"

"Nothing formal, just a few questions here and there."

"And what have you deduced so far from those questions?"

John knew that if he was wrong about the man, there would be hell to pay with the captain, but he went for it anyway. "That dishonesty fits you like a second skin."

Gilroy gave a short, harsh laugh. "Excuse me?"

"You told Abbie you were a widower. In fact, you are divorced and your ex-wife is very much alive. Then you went a step further and told her you had a daughter and a grandson that do not exist. You care to explain why you did that, Professor?''

He seemed more disappointed than upset. ''Abbie shouldn't have repeated something I told her in confidence.''

''Is it true? Did you lie to her?''

''Yes, it's true! I lied. There, are you satisfied now? Have I broken any laws?''

''No, but you can't blame me for wanting to know why you did it.''

''Because I despise pity!'' His voice shook with indignation. ''And if I want to invent a family in order to avoid being pitied, that's my business, no one else's.''

''Are you sure you didn't make up a phony grandson to get close to Abbie DiAngelo? Or was it Ben you wanted to get close to?''

The professor's complexion got a shade paler. ''What are you saying? What are you accusing me of?''

''Answer me this—did you ever invite Ben DiAngelo to come to your house to see your train displays?''

He blinked rapidly and repeatedly. ''Why would I do that? I hardly know Ben.''

''You didn't know my son, either, yet you extended an invitation to him to come to your house.''

''I don't recall—''

''My son remembers the invitation very clearly, Professor. In fact, he was quite excited about it.''

''If he's so certain, then perhaps I did. As I said earlier, it's difficult to keep track of whom I meet.''

''What about Eric Sommers? Do you ever remember meeting him? Or inviting him to your house?''

John couldn't decide what he saw first in the man's eyes—fear or fury. The two emotions were so well intermingled, it was impossible to separate one from the other. Or to tell if the latter was an act.

"This is an outrage," Gilroy said in a low, menacing voice. "You have no right to come to my home and throw accusations you can't back up. Get out before I report you to your superiors. I have connections in this town, you know."

"Why won't you answer the question, Professor?"

"You want an answer?" he shouted. "Fine, I'll give you one. No, I did not invite Eric Sommers to my house. I had never heard of Eric Sommers until he was kidnapped. Nor did I kidnap Ben DiAngelo." He smoothed down his necktie with a hand that was remarkably steady for a man who appeared to be so shaken. "And now, if you're finished, I'm late for an appointment." He opened the door. "Good day, Detective."

Forty-Two

Abbie awoke with a start. She sat up, eyes wide open as she looked around her. Why had she slept in the kitchen? And why was Rose standing at the counter, making coffee?

Abbie blinked once before the fog of sleep lifted and reality hit her.

Ben was gone.

Ben had spent the night away from home, in some unknown place, in the company of a ruthless stranger. Had he finally succumbed to fatigue, as she had, and slept? Was he cold? Was he hungry? Was he scared?

Was he wondering why she wasn't coming to rescue him?

The tears came, scalding her cheeks, blurring her vision as she tried to focus on Rose. "Where is Claudia?"

Rose turned around and smiled briefly. "I sent her home to get some sleep. She'll be back later."

"What about you? Didn't you just finish a shift at the diner?"

"I'm not tired. And I wanted to be with you." She came to sit in the twin chair, across from Abbie. "I'm glad you slept. You needed it."

Abbie brushed her hair back from her face. "Anyone call?"

"John. He just wanted to check on Sergeant Tyler. He said he'd call back later. Your ex-husband also called," she added. "He had just landed. Said he should be here in a couple of hours."

Abbie wasn't looking forward to seeing him. He would probably blame her for Ben's disappearance and she wasn't in the mood to hear his accusations right now. On the other hand, he had a right to be here.

"Your mom also called," Rose said.

Telling her mother about the kidnapping had been an ordeal in itself. Irene had been devastated, and so fearful, it had taken Abbie and Marion over an hour to calm her down. "How is she doing?"

Rose smiled and stood up. "Worried about you. She's going to stop by later, too."

That was the part Abbie was dreading. Not necessarily her mother's visit, but the calls, the endless parade of well-meaning friends and neighbors, all eager to offer comfort and sit with her when all she wanted was to be left alone.

"I made coffee for Sergeant Tyler—he's in the next room. Would you like some?"

She glanced toward the doorway. She had forgotten about the police technician. He had arrived late last night to install a tap and a tracer, and explained that Abbie or someone of her choosing had to be here to answer the phone in the event the kidnapper called. He had hooked up the equipment to the living-room extension in order not to be in Abbie's way, and told her he'd be monitoring the phones for the next twelve hours before someone else came to relieve him. Her job, if the kidnapper called, was to keep him on the line as long as possible.

"Here—" Rose pressed a mug into her hands "—I hope you like your coffee strong, because I don't know how to make it any other way."

"I do like it strong." She drank, taking small sips,

watching the clock, then the phone, willing it to ring. Why weren't they calling? Why were they being so cruel?

What did they want from her?

She hadn't noticed that her fingers had curled tightly around the mug, now empty, squeezing it so hard, her knuckles had turned white.

"I tell you what." Rose gently pried the mug from her hand. "Why don't you go up and take a shower, and while you do that, I'll make you some scrambled eggs."

"I'm not hungry."

"You've got to eat."

Not until Ben came home. She felt guilty enough to have slept. She hadn't wanted to sleep. She hadn't wanted to lose the mental thread that connected her to Ben. No, she wouldn't eat. The mere thought of food made her nauseous anyway. The shower, on the other hand, and some fresh clothes, wouldn't hurt.

She stood under the pelting water for a long time, with her eyes closed, as the heat penetrated through her skin and the steam cleared her mind.

After she dried herself off, she walked into her bedroom, pulled a pair of jeans and a sweatshirt from her dresser and got dressed. She went through each motion automatically, without thinking, painfully aware of how different this morning was from all the others. There was no running up and down the stairs, no scrambling to get breakfast on the table, no "Mom, where is my red shirt?," no mad rush to catch the school bus.

How did other parents do it? she wondered. How did they survive the loss of a child and go on with their lives, when she could barely get through the morning?

Against her better judgment, she walked out of her bedroom, down the hallway and into Ben's room. The shock as she stood, holding on to the doorjamb, was almost too much. She let her gaze sweep across the room, lingering on the neatly made bed, the closet that had been left open, the desk where Ben had left his Game Boy and Harry Potter books.

The sight of his bat propped against the foot of the bed and the glove hooked over it reminded her he had missed yesterday's practice—a first for him. She wasn't sure how her eyes managed to stay dry. Maybe she was stronger than she thought. Or maybe she didn't have any tears left.

The next hour brought a succession of calls, all from concerned mothers who wanted to know if there had been any news of Ben. Some offered to come over, but Abbie gently talked them out of it, promising she'd call as soon as Ben was found.

She had just finished talking to Jimmy Hernandez's mother when she heard the faint ring of her cell phone inside her purse.

"What's that?" Frowning, Rose looked around her, trying to identify where the ringing was coming from.

"My cell phone. It's probably John." She took it out, pushed the talk button, ready to apologize to him for being so rude yesterday. "Hello?"

"How are you holding out, bitch?"

Abbie gasped, half in fear, half in relief as she tried desperately to place the male voice and couldn't. Nor could she find the words she had waited so long to speak.

"Listen to me very carefully," the voice went on. "If you have someone monitoring your other phone, I suggest you don't alert him. Don't alert anyone or your kid dies. Do you understand?"

"Yes," she said in a strangled voice.

Rose had put the glass carafe back on the counter and was watching her. Abbie gave her a nervous smile, trying to appear casual, but knew she wasn't fooling her.

"Whether your son lives or dies is entirely up to you," the caller went on, "and how well you follow my instructions. Get a pen and paper."

Abbie almost knocked over her laptop trying to get to the hutch's drawer where she kept odds and ends. Rose quickly got out of her way, but didn't take her eyes off Abbie.

"Who is it?" she mouthed.

Abbie signaled her to be quiet and set a spiral-bound notebook down on the kitchen counter. "I'm ready," she said into the phone.

"Do you know how to get to Route 80 West?"

Route 80 West was the major highway that led to the Pocono Mountains, where she and Ben skied every winter. "Yes, I do," she said. "But please, let me talk to Ben. Let me make sure he—"

"In due time. Follow 80 West until you reach Route 715 North, which parallels Pocono Creek, and take the Camelback exit."

Abbie wrote frantically. "What do I do at the exit?"

"Follow 715 until you come to a crossroad and a wooden sign that says Private Road, No Trespassing. Be warned, the road has been cleared, and every twist and turn is visible from the house up on top of the hill. In other words, I'll see you coming."

"You'll see me coming," Abbie repeated, anxious not to upset or contradict the caller. "And then what?"

"What will you be driving? Since I have your truck."

Abbie thought quickly. The only cars out there now were Sergeant Tyler's and Rose's. "An Oldsmobile," she replied, drawing a startled look from Rose. "I'll be driving a green Oldsmobile with Ohio plates."

"Fine. At the bottom of the private road, you'll stop and turn the car around so that the back faces the house. You can't miss it. It's the only one up there. After you stop, you'll get out of the car and open the trunk.''

''Why do I have to open the trunk?''

''I want to make sure you didn't decide to do something cute, Abbie, like bringing the cavalry with you.''

''I won't bring anyone. I promise. I'll do everything you say, just let me talk to Ben.''

''Not until you get here. That should be about two hours from now, if you leave right away. And Abbie, not a word of where you're going to anyone. Remember, I can see you as you come up the private road. If you're not alone, the boy dies. If I *think* you're not alone, the boy dies. Are we clear on that?''

''Yes.''

The line went dead.

In one quick motion, Abbie switched off the phone, tore the page from the notebook and jammed it into her purse.

Rose grabbed her arm and spoke in a low but firm voice. ''You're not doing what I think you're doing—meeting some lunatic without knowing if he's legit or not.''

Abbie jerked her arm free. ''Rose, for God's sake, he has Ben.''

''How do you know? How do you know the call wasn't from a serial killer who heard about the kidnapping and is using that to lure you somewhere?''

''Because a serial killer wouldn't have my cell phone number.''

''Who does?''

''I don't know! It doesn't matter. All that matters is that if I don't do as he says, Ben will die. Is that what you want, Rose? For my son to die?''

''Of course not. All I ask is that you don't go alone. Call John.''

"No. The instructions were explicit. No police. No one. Just me. Or Ben dies."

"How do you know the kidnapper won't kill you both?"

"That's a chance I have to take."

Leaving Rose to mull over that last remark, Abbie ran upstairs, opened the armoire, unlocked the top drawer and grabbed the gun, which she had unloaded after her botched attempt to kill Arturo. Her mind focused on the task, she reloaded the PPK, slipped some spare cartridges into her pocket and tucked the weapon in her waistband, pulling the loose sweatshirt over it.

Back in the kitchen, she checked her purse to make sure she had money, then looked at Rose. "I need your car, Rose." Her voice turned imploring. "Please."

Rose folded her arms across her chest and assumed a stubborn expression. "What if I refuse?"

"You won't. Because you don't want my son's death on your conscience."

With a sigh of resignation, Rose walked over to her own purse on the kitchen table, took out the keys and handed them to Abbie. "I know I'm going to regret this."

But Abbie was already out the back door.

Forty-Three

"John!" Rose sounded frantic. "You've got to come to Abbie's house right away."

John, who had started to take off his jacket, stopped in midmotion. "What happened?"

"She got a phone call and tore out of here like a bat out of hell, with my car."

"Where the hell is Tyler?"

"Right here. The call came on her cell phone. He never heard it ring."

"Where did she go?"

"She wouldn't say. Apparently the kidnapper—if that's who it was," she added doubtfully, "threatened to kill Ben if she didn't follow his exact instructions."

"Damn!" John dragged his hand through his hair. He hadn't thought of her cell phone. "How long ago was that?"

"She just left. She made me swear not to call you, but…I'm scared, John. That call could have been from anyone—a rapist or a serial killer. They do that, you know, they prey on—"

"Stay where you are, Rose. I'll be right over."

Sitting at her desk, Tina was watching him anxiously. "What's wrong? Did something happened to Abbie?"

"Come on," he said, running ahead of her. "I'll tell you in the car."

Sergeant Tyler and Rose were in the kitchen when they arrived. The technician immediately started to apologize.

"I'm sorry, John. She left through the back door. I didn't realize what was happening until I heard the car. I ran after her but it was too late."

"It's not your fault." He turned to Rose. "Did she say anything at all, give any clue while she was talking on the phone as to where she was going?"

Rose repeated some of the comments Abbie had made, including the apparent warning that whoever was waiting for her would see her coming. "The rest she wrote on that pad over there." She pointed to a spiral-bound notebook.

John picked it up and held it at eye level. There were impressions on the blank page left by Abbie's writing. He took the pencil that lay beside the notebook and started rubbing with the side of the point over the entire page in a light, zigzag motion, right to left, left to right, until the entire page was covered with gray and the words stood out in white relief.

John jotted down what he read. "Looks like she's heading for the mountains."

"We'll need backup." Tina took her cell phone out. "And a chopper if we want to stop her."

But the only police helicopter had been dispatched to a multivehicle accident on the I–95 and wouldn't be back for hours.

Tina clicked off her cell. "Shit."

"That's okay. I may know where to find a chopper." John tucked the directions in his pocket. "Let's go."

"What about backup?"

"We'll call it in later." From the car, he called his father and told him what he needed.

On the way to his father's house, John stopped to buy a topographic map of the Pocono Mountains; according to the directions on the notebook, that's where Abbie was headed.

Spencer hadn't wasted any time either. A map similar to the one John had brought was already spread out on his desk. An avid skier, he knew all the resorts—Camelback, Shawnee, Big Boulder, Jack Frost—as well as the less traveled back trails.

"Did you get the chopper?" John asked.

"It's gassed up and ready to go."

John let out a sigh of relief. When he had talked to his father earlier, Spencer hadn't been sure if Colin Birghman, his old army buddy, was even in town. Now CEO of a small but successful airline, Birghman traveled from one meeting to another in the same type of aircraft he had piloted in 'Nam—a helicopter.

"What about a pilot?"

"He'll be waiting for you at Princeton Airport. By the way, I don't know how many people you're planning to take with you, but the bird can only accommodate five passengers, including the pilot."

Tina was already on her cell phone, requesting a two-men SWAT team, M–16's and bulletproof vests. Before hanging up, she gave the dispatcher directions to Spencer's house.

"Look here, son." John and Spencer bent over the map. "According to your directions, this is the route she'll be taking." He picked up a highlighting marker and traced the winding road in bright orange all the way to a red X. "And this, to my estimation, is where the house sits." He tapped another, smaller X. "That's Big Sky Airfield. Colin uses it occasionally when he goes to the mountains."

"How far is the airfield from the private road?"

"A couple of miles. There'll be a car waiting for you."

He had thought of everything. "Thanks." And now for the hard part. "Is there any way to get to the house without being seen?"

Spencer's finger moved a fraction of an inch. "I remember a trail in that area. It should lead you all the way to the west side of the house, but I warn you, it's three hundred feet up."

John turned to Tina. "How's your climbing, Wrightfield?"

"Every bit as good as yours, Ryan." She laughed. "Which, come to think of it, probably ain't that good."

The temperature cooled off considerably as Abbie got into the mountains, leaving urban civilization and congestion far behind. The last time she had traveled this route had been in February, when she and Ben had gone to Camelback for a ski weekend.

Pictures of years past flashed by as she drove—the hesitant toddler, who had stared at the snow-covered mountain with a look of apprehension, the more daring five-year-old, who had been filled with confidence and bravado, the excited kid, gliding down the slopes like a pro, stopping on a dime at the end of his run and grinning at her, saying, "So, Mom, you think I'm good enough for Steamboat Springs now?"

But darker thoughts kept intruding—the Acura parked outside Ben's school, the look on Ben's face when he had realized it wasn't his mother behind the wheel, Ben being dragged out of the car and into a strange house, maybe unconscious, maybe fighting.

Ben tied down.

Her hands gripped the Oldsmobile's steering wheel. *I'm coming, Ben. Just hang in there, baby.*

Whenever she moved, she could feel the reassuring pressure of the PPK against her back. This time she would not freeze. This time it wasn't her life she would be trying to save, but her son's.

She continued in a northwestern direction, driving through familiar territory—Stroudsburg, Bartonsville, Tannersville. Vacation homes that ranged from modest cabins to luxury mansions were sprinkled along the mountainside. Two miles past the Camelback exit, she saw the sign for the private road. On the top of the mountain sat the house, made entirely of redwood and glass, glinting in the sunshine.

As instructed, she backed down the road, got out of the car and went to open the trunk. Except for a spare tire and a crowbar she wished she could smuggle into the house, there was nothing anyone could object to.

Twenty or thirty seconds went by. Nothing happened. A chilling thought hit her as she remembered Rose's warning. What if this was some sort of a setup? The brainstorm of a psychopath who had only wanted to lure her to his isolated mountain retreat?

At last, her cell phone rang.

"Proceed," was all the voice said.

It took Abbie a little over fifteen minutes to reach the house. The Acura was nowhere in sight. She turned off the engine and got out.

The massive redwood door was halfway open. The moment Abbie walked through it, she heard a hiss and spun around. The door had closed. Remote control, Abbie thought. She stood still for a moment, looking around the large foyer with its shiny hardwood floor and huge antler chandelier. Bright sunshine poured in from the twin skylights above.

Her heart pounding, she started down the long hallway. "Hello?"

There was no answer, but the first door on her left was open, so she walked through it. The first thing she saw was a bank of tall windows overlooking Big Pocono State Park and Camelback Mountain.

It wasn't until she saw the person sitting in a high-backed chair, with a gun pointed at her, that she let out a soft cry.

It was Liz Tilly.

Forty-Four

"Hello, Abbie. Did you have a nice trip?"

Confused and speechless, Abbie looked around her.

"There's no one else here, Abbie. We're alone."

"But the voice on the phone," Abbie murmured when she found use of her own voice again.

"Was male. Yes, I know." Looking pleased with herself, Liz picked up an instrument from the table beside her, which, at first glance, resembled a small answering machine. "This little gadget is an absolute marvel. It can make you sound like a robot, it can lower or raise your tone, or it can change your voice from male to female and vice versa. Clever, isn't it?"

Abbie stared at her, trying to control the rage tearing through her. "You? You did this? You kidnapped my son?"

Now it was Liz's turn to look surprised. "You mean my performance was so brilliant you never had a clue?" She threw her head back and let out a laugh. "Wow. And to think a Broadway producer once told me I had no acting talent. It goes to show you how much they know, doesn't it?"

"Where is Ben? What have you done with my son?"

"First, be a good girl, Abbie, and put your gun on the floor—slowly, or I might get nervous and shoot you. Then kick it over to me, very gently."

Abbie didn't move. "What gun? What are you talking about?"

"The gun that activated the metal detector when you came through the front door. This house belonged to Jude, you see, and he was paranoid about security. Not that he didn't have any reason to be. With all the hate mail and death threats he received over the years because of the offensive songs he wrote, I would have been scared, too." She waved a pistol Abbie recognized as a Glock. "Come on, Abbie, the gun."

Abbie did as she was told, watching Liz bend over and pick up the PPK and put it on the end table. "Now do the same with your purse."

Once again, Abbie complied. After inspecting the purse's contents and turning off Abbie's cell phone, Liz set the bag on the floor.

"Now can I see my son?"

Liz picked up a remote control on the table beside her and pushed a button. A panel on the left wall slid away to reveal a window overlooking a room with a minimum of furniture.

Ben sat on a sofa, dressed in the same clothes he'd had on the morning he had disappeared, looking more bored than frightened. Abbie couldn't believe that only a little more than twenty-four hours had passed since she had last seen him. It felt as if he had been gone a year.

"Ben!" She ran to the glass panel and started pounding on it. "Ben! I'm here! Ben, look at me!"

"He can neither hear you nor see you." Liz's voice was calm and even. "The room is completely soundproof. Jude and his band used to rehearse in there."

Abbie let her arms fall to her sides and turned around. "I want to talk to him. Let me in there, Liz. I've done everything you asked. Now it's your turn to keep your word."

Liz laughed. "You're hardly in a position to make demands, Abbie."

"I'm not making demands. I'm pleading with you. Keep me if you want, but let Ben go. He's just an innocent little child. Just let him go."

"I can't do that, not now that we're all reunited." She snapped her fingers. "I keep saying that, but we're *not* all reunited, are we? One is missing—Irene. Actually, I had planned to include her in our little powwow, but I changed my mind. She's living in her own hell, a hell worse than any I could have engineered for her."

Abbie glanced toward the room where Ben was being kept, grateful for those few glances. He hadn't moved. He was just sitting there tapping his foot and staring out the window. *I'm here, Ben. Don't be afraid, baby. I've come for you.*

"Why did you bring us here?" she asked, turning back to look at Liz.

"Justice, Abbie. You do believe in justice, don't you?"

"For God's sake, stop talking in riddles. Justice for what?"

"For all the injustices *I* have suffered." Liz pressed the remote again, and to Abbie's dismay, the wooden panel slid back. "Starting with this." She tucked her hair behind her ear, exposing the scar Abbie had glimpsed at the cemetery.

"Are you still blaming my mother for what happened in Palo Alto? Is that it? I told you, Irene had nothing to do with that fire—"

"I was not only disfigured that night," Liz continued as if she hadn't heard her, "I also lost two people—two people I loved more than anything in the world."

Two people? To Abbie's knowledge, Patrick McGregor had been the only casualty. "I thought you hated your father. You told me once you wished *he* had died instead of your mother."

"I wasn't talking about my father." She stroked the barrel of the Glock along the side of her face and smiled. The gesture was almost sensual, as if the feel of the cold metal against her puckered skin brought her intense pleasure.

"Then who?"

"Glen Fallon. The first and only man I ever loved. We were going to get married, did you know that?" She didn't wait for an answer. "Then the fire happened. A week later, when the doctors removed the bandages, Glen saw my face and ran." Her eyes went flat. "I scared him, Abbie. The man I loved with all my heart and soul, the man I thought loved me just as much, couldn't bear to look at me. He called me a freak—not to my face, but you know how kids are. My so-called friends made sure I knew all the nasty things he had said about me—word for word."

Abbie remembered Glen Fallon, who had spent a lot of time at the McGregors' house. She wasn't aware, however, that they had split up because of her scars. How could she have known? She was just eight years old.

"I'm sorry for all you went through, Liz, but you have to stop blaming my mother. She didn't do this and now I can prove it. Detective Ryan went to Stateville Prison to talk to Earl Kramer. He confessed to having lied, Liz. It was Ian who went to see him with that fabricated story about my mother, not the other way around."

Liz's angry fist hit the chair's armrest. "Don't you get it? It doesn't matter how the fire got started. Your mother is still responsible for what happened to me. Your mother and you."

"*Me?*"

"Yes, you. If Irene hadn't been so intent on saving you first—"

"What was she supposed to do?" Abbie cried. "I was her daughter! I was screaming for her to come and get me."

"She should have gotten me out, too. My room was just two doors down."

"She tried. She couldn't find it. The hallway was filled with smoke. She tried to go back for you after she handed Ian and me over to the neighbors, but by then the firemen had arrived and they stopped her."

Liz's eyes were filled with hatred. "Your mother left me to die. She didn't like me. She was scared of me because I was always sneaking up on her, or taking the jewelry my father gave her, jewelry that should have been *mine*. She kept telling my dad I was nasty, that I had a dangerous streak. She even suggested I see a shrink. Can you believe that?"

"I know you two had problems, but—"

"She hated my guts! That's why she left me there to burn." She fell back against her chair, almost gasping for breath. "And in so doing, she killed my baby."

Abbie stared at her. "Baby? What baby?"

"Glen's baby. I was three months pregnant. I miscarried in the ambulance."

"My God." Abbie searched her memory, trying to remember the conversation that had taken place in the hospital when she and her mother had visited Liz. She couldn't remember hearing about a baby. Or a miscarriage. So, that's what Liz had meant when she'd said she had lost two people. She was talking about Glen and her unborn baby.

"Did my mother know?" Abbie asked in a whisper.

"No." Her voice had turned dreamy, and the sound of

it was so disturbing, so eerie, it sent an icy shiver down Abbie's spine. There was something terribly wrong with Liz. Something...unnatural. Why hadn't she seen it before?

"I wanted that baby so badly," she continued. "It would have helped me get over Glen. And who knows? It might even have helped me get Glen back."

"Why didn't you tell him you had lost his baby? Maybe he would have come back to you if he had known."

"I did. He didn't give a damn. And he already had another girlfriend." She turned the barrel of the gun toward herself and gazed into it, shutting one eye. "That's why I killed him."

Abbie went still.

Liz brought the gun down. "Why the shocked expression, Abbie? You don't think Glen deserved to die?"

"I don't believe you killed him. You're just trying to scare me."

"Oh, be scared, Abbie, be very scared, because I'm telling the truth. I killed Glen Fallon."

"But how could you? You just finished telling me you loved him more than anything."

"That was before I realized that love wasn't being returned. Do you know he and Joanna were an item before I even left the hospital?"

"No."

"I tried to accept it. I tried to tell myself he didn't deserve me. That Joanna, who had the reputation of a harlot, would make him miserable. Nothing helped. So I killed him. It really wasn't that hard."

"I thought he had a car accident."

"An accident *I* caused by draining the fluid from his brakes. Glen's father was a mechanic, if you recall. In order to be with Glen as much as possible, I hung around his father's garage, where Glen worked part-time. I even helped out on occasion, and learned a lot.'' Her chin tilted up a little. ''Mr. Fallon even said I had potential.''

Abbie was aghast. ''My God, Liz, you killed a man. How can you live with yourself?''

''Actually, I killed two men—if you count my ex-husband.''

''You killed Jude Tilly?''

''He deserved to die just as much as Glen did. I had just found out I couldn't have any children, you see. Apparently, something had gone wrong with the D & C the doctors performed after my miscarriage, and as a result, I was sterile. So Jude dumped me. Do you know what that feels like, Abbie? To be thrown away like yesterday's garbage? No, of course not.'' She waved the Glock in the air. ''How would you know? You have everything your little heart desires—a mother and a son who love you, a successful business, a beautiful home, good friends. And judging from the way that hunky cop was looking at you at the cemetery, you'll have him too before long. Do you think it's fair, Abbie? That you should have so much and I should have so little?''

How could she have believed there might be some good in this woman? Abbie wondered. Why hadn't she at least gotten a tiny glimpse of that twisted, maniacal mind? A small sign that would have warned her to back off.

''You have your job at the Towers, which, from what you told me, you seem to enjoy.'' Maybe if she made her talk, she would have time to think of a way to get herself and Ben out of here. ''And this house.'' She cast a quick look around the room, noticing for the first time the simple but expensive furniture, and a second piano, even grander than the one she had seen in Liz's New York apartment. ''That has to be worth something.''

She made an impatient gesture. ''Those are all material

things. I don't care about material things. Jude did, but I don't. The only reason I fought to keep this house was because Jude hurt me and I wanted to get back at him by taking something from him that he loved. But I really don't give a damn about the place. All I ever wanted was a family, children of my own, a guy who loved me—really loved me. I wanted the little house in the suburbs, complete with the white picket fence, the station wagon in the garage and the kiddie pool in the backyard. It would have been enough.''

Every time Liz glanced away, Abbie threw a furtive look around her, searching for a weapon, something she could use against her captor. The vase on the piano seemed to be the only possibility right now, although Abbie wasn't sure how much damage it would do, or how she could use it without getting killed.

"I tried to make you part of our family. You didn't want anything to do with us."

"You threw me a bone, Abbie. How grand of you."

She had to get her gun back, Abbie thought. That was her only way out of here.

"What do you want from me?" she asked quietly.

Liz let both of her hands dangle between her legs and leaned forward. Her eyes had a shiny, almost feverish expression to them. "I want you to feel the pain I experienced when my baby died. I want you to know the wrenching despair, the hopelessness, as you lay there and death takes *your* child."

Abbie's heart kept hammering in her chest. Liz was insane. Whatever act of revenge she had planned for Abbie and Ben had been ruthlessly, maliciously mapped out, step by step.

She would not make a mistake now. Unless Abbie forced her hand.

"What are you going to do with us?"

Nothing could have prepared her for Liz's answer. "I'm going to reenact the events of that night twenty-eight years ago. I'm going to set fire to this house with you and Ben trapped in it. I often wondered why I kept this place, when all it did was remind me of that bastard. Now I know." She smiled sweetly. "I was saving it for you, Abbie, dear."

Abbie's legs almost buckled under her. "You're going to burn us alive?"

"Bingo." Liz picked up the remote and Abbie heard a click.

The dead bolt on the door behind her had slid shut.

Liz's smile was absolutely chilling. "Clever, don't you think? Death by fire. Talk about sweet justice."

"You're mad!"

"Maybe. Maybe your mother was right after all. I should have gotten help." She shrugged. "No need worrying about it now, is there?"

Abbie thought she'd make one more attempt to sway her. "Why are you doing this, Liz? Ben and I aren't guilty of—"

"Oh, stop whining! Don't you get it yet? If it hadn't been for you, if your mother hadn't tried to save you first, she would have saved *me*, and my baby would have lived. You're guilty of having been born, Abbie. You're guilty of having had the opportunities I never had. You're guilty of being everything I wanted to be, everything I *deserved* to be."

Inch by agonizing inch, Abbie had moved closer to the piano—and the table where the gun lay. She tried to gauge her chances of overpowering Liz, assuming she wasn't stopped by a bullet first. They were both approximately the same size, although Liz outweighed her by maybe ten pounds. Abbie's class in self-defense would come in handy, but before any hand-to-hand combat came into play, Liz had to be disarmed.

"You'll never get away with this." Abbie moved another inch. "John Ryan will find out who this house belonged to and he'll come after you. Is that what you want? To be a criminal like your brother? To spend the rest of your life in prison?"

Liz gave her a condescending smile. "Oh, Abbie, for a rather successful businesswoman, you aren't very bright, are you? I have no intention of getting away with anything. And I'm definitely not the type to sit in a prison cell for forty or fifty years. I'm going to be right here with you, Abbie. I'm going to burn my way into hell, just as you and Ben will."

The chill that had settled in the pit of Abbie's stomach spread throughout her entire body. A murder/suicide. That's what she had been planning all along. Whatever thin hope Abbie had had of changing Liz's mind was now gone forever. There was nothing she could offer to a woman who no longer wanted to live. "Why do you want to die?"

Liz's eyes suddenly glinted with moisture. "Because I'm alone and unhappy and hopelessly screwed up. Because I'm tired of going from one day to the next longing for something I'll never have. Because I'm sick of inspiring pity and even disgust whenever someone takes a good look at me. Because I'm simply tired of living, Abbie."

Reaching under her chair, she took out a long handled butane lighter. with no sign of emotion on her face, she held up the lighter and clicked it a few times, watching the flame go on and off. A cruel smile pulled the corners of her mouth.

"Got any last wish, Abbie?"

Forty-Five

John, Tina and the two SWAT officers had touched down at Big Sky Airfield without a hitch, and were now climbing steadily up the steep mountain.

The trail Spencer had pointed to on the map was no longer there. Rather than waste precious time looking for it, the foursome had simply chosen an area directly across from the house, and started climbing, hoping no one would decide to look out one of the many windows on that side of the house.

All four of them were equipped with bulletproof vests, and the three men, all sharpshooters, carried M–16 rifles. Tina had preferred to hang on to her trusted 9mm Smith & Wesson. Although shafts of bright sunlight filtered through the trees, at this elevation the temperature was a good fifteen degrees cooler than it was down below, making the climb easier.

A quick reconnaissance flight over the house earlier, where they had sighted the Oldsmobile, had confirmed that Abbie had arrived, although there was no sign of the Acura. When she hadn't answered her cell phone, John had radioed the Pennsylvania authorities, given them the location of the house and requested information on its owner. He was still waiting to hear from them.

Behind him, Tina had stopped to catch her breath. John turned around.

"Everything all right?"

"Just dandy." Too proud to complain, she started climbing again. John did the same, not talking, but conserving his energy.

His mind was on Abbie. He had thought of little else since leaving Princeton, and even though he was furious at her for not calling him before taking off, he understood why she had done it. She was a mother, and she had reacted as any mother would—by flying blindly to her child's rescue.

He tried not to think about the unthinkable—that Abbie had fallen into the hands of a maniac who intended to kill her and her son. Even his feelings for Abbie, the way she had burst into his life and made him rethink his opinion of women, had to be sidelined for now. He had to keep focused on only one thought—to get Abbie and Ben out of that house alive.

His cell phone rang and three pairs of eyes snapped in his direction. John patted his chest, searching for the phone, found it and answered it as it rang a third time. "John Ryan."

"Detective Ryan, this is Lieutenant Bernard of the Tannersville P.D. You called a while ago about the house on Evergreen Road?"

"Yes. Do you know who owns it?"

"Sure do. It belongs to Elizabeth Tilly. It was part of her divorce settlement from that rock star—Jude Tilly."

Liz. Son of a gun.

"Hope this helps, Detective."

"It does. Thank you, Lieutenant."

His three companions were still watching him. "The house belongs to Liz Tilly," he said, flipping his phone shut.

Tina's eyes widened. "McGregor's sister? The woman you went to see in New York? She's Ben's kidnapper?"

"Apparently."

As if spurred on by new energy, all four of them rapidly climbed the last remaining feet.

Liz shot out of her chair. "What was that?"

"I didn't hear anything," Abbie said quickly. But she had. She had heard a dull sound she couldn't quite identify. Someone was out there.

Liz tucked the butane lighter into her waistband. "Against the wall!" she ordered. "Now!"

Abbie flattened herself against the wall, desperately trying to find a way to take advantage of this unexpected situation.

No longer so cool and calm, Liz ran from window to window, peering outside, muttering to herself, but never taking her eyes off Abbie long enough for her to do anything.

"Are there wild animals around here? Maybe that's what it was." As Abbie talked, she kept glancing at the PPK on the side table. If only she could get to it without being seen.

Liz had picked up another remote control and aimed it at a monitor Abbie hadn't noticed before. Almost immediately, the screen was filled with a section of the outside perimeter. There didn't seem to be any suspicious activity, until Liz turned on a second monitor and Abbie saw four people, three men and one woman, climbing up the mountainside, moving quickly and carrying rifles.

Rage contorted Liz's face. "You brought the cops!"

Abbie tried not to look at the gun pointed at her midriff. "No! No, I didn't. I swear."

"You did. That's John Ryan out there," she shouted, pointing.

Abbie threw a frantic look at the monitor. She was right. That was John. And Tina Wrightfield. They had found her.

"I didn't tell him a thing, Liz, I swear." She shouted the words, hoping the people outside would hear her. "You've got to believe me, Liz."

"Shut up."

As the four people kept gaining ground, Liz reached behind the chair she had occupied earlier, pulled out a red can and twisted off the cap.

"Oh, God, Liz, no!"

"You don't think the arrival of your boyfriend is going to change anything, do you?" She gave her a hard-eyed, cynical look. "You're still going to watch your son die, Abbie. I promise you that. We're just going to have to move a little faster than anticipated, that's all."

She started walking around the room, dousing everything with gasoline—the chairs, the rugs, the tables—everything, until she had emptied the last drop.

Abbie was frantic. She had to do something. She couldn't let this lunatic burn them alive. She stepped away from the wall.

The sound of a gun exploded in her ears. Abbie let out a scream and grabbed her left arm as spears of fiery pain shot through it. She had been hit. Liz had shot her.

"Another stupid move like that," Liz said, "and I'll put a bullet in your other arm, but I won't kill you, if that's what you're hoping." She waved the gun. "Back against the wall."

Abbie didn't have to put much effort in the moaning and groaning that came next. Blood had soaked her sleeve, probably making the wound look worse than it was. Good. That's exactly what she wanted Liz to think.

Her arm hurt like hell, but she could move it, and she could flex her fingers, which meant there was no nerve damage.

"My arm." Eyes closed, Abbie rocked back and forth. "I can't feel it, Liz. I can't feel my arm."

Liz was running around, checking all the locks. "Shut up, dammit. I can't hear myself think."

"I'm bleeding," she said, making her voice sound faint.

"Tough shit."

Outside, the sound of heavy footsteps running across the deck could be heard.

"Police!" someone shouted. "Open the door!"

Liz let out a cry of frustration, and yanked the lighter from her waistband. In doing so, she took her eyes off Abbie for a couple of seconds. It was enough for Abbie to lunge for her gun. And this time she made it.

From a kneeling position, she gripped the weapon with both hands, barring her teeth against the pain. "Liz!"

The commanding sound of her voice made Liz look up.

"Why, you bitch," she hissed.

She raised her Glock and pulled the trigger a split second after Abbie pulled hers.

For a moment, Liz just stood there, one hand holding the lighter, the other her gun. There was a look of total shock on her face. If it hadn't been for the neat black hole in the center of Liz's forehead, Abbie might have doubted she had hit her.

A fraction of a second later, her arms dropped by her sides. The gun and the lighter slipped from her hands and she fell to her knees, like a woman in prayer, before hitting the floor, facedown.

Abbie heard the sound of gunfire and crashing glass. With a strangled sob, she crawled to the table and took the remote control. Ben. She had to get Ben.

Loud, forceful pounding rattled the door. "Abbie, are you in there? Abbie, answer me!"

"John! I'm here." Why couldn't she talk any louder? Why couldn't she find the strength to get up? What was wrong with her? "I'm here," she whispered.

"Get away from the door!"

Another burst of gunfire filled her eardrums, then John rushed into the room, Tina behind him.

"Christ." He ran to her, gently took hold of her arm. "You've been shot."

"Oh God, John," Abbie heard Tina say. "She's losing a lot of blood."

"I know." He started to tear at her shirtsleeve, exposing the wound. "Call the hospital in Tannersville. Tell them we're bringing in a gunshot wound. Could be serious."

"John..." Abbie handed him the remote, pointing at the panel behind him. "Ben...in there..."

Her eyelids felt heavy. She had to fight to keep them open. "Must get him. Must get Ben..."

Tina took the remote from her hand. "I'll do it, Abbie. Keep still."

Abbie was vaguely aware that John had taken off his own shirt and wrapped it tightly around her arm. "Ben...I need...to see Ben."

"Shh." John held her as two more men rushed in, carrying a first-aid kit. "Ben is going to be all right. Don't talk, darling. For God's sake, don't talk."

She tried to stay awake, but darkness had wrapped itself around her, blotting out all sound, shutting out all the light, taking away all her willpower.

With a sigh, she surrendered to it.

Forty-Six

Abbie woke to find Ben sitting at her bedside, holding her hand and looking worried but unharmed.

She felt groggy and vaguely remembered a nurse giving her a sedative. When was that? Yesterday? The day before? Bits and pieces found their way through her hazy mind—the drive to Tannersville, the confrontation with Liz. The shooting.

She looked down and saw that her left arm was bandaged and in a sling. "Ben," she murmured. *Thank God.*

The pressure on her hand tightened. "Hi, Mom."

"Where am I?"

"Memorial Hospital in Tannersville. That's in the Poconos. You lost a lot of blood, but the doctors say you're going to be okay."

"What about you?" With her good hand, she reached for his precious face and touched it. "Are you all right?"

"Yeah, I'm fine. Mr. Ryan and Claudia have been taking good care of me. They're outside, waiting to see you."

"How long have I been here?"

"Since yesterday afternoon. They let me spend the night. They didn't want to at first, but Mr. Ryan talked to the chief of staff and they gave me a bed." He pointed behind him. "Right there next to yours."

She closed her eyes. "Tell me what happened between you and Liz."

"Mr. Ryan said to wait."

"I want to hear it now, Ben. From you."

He nodded, looking grave. "I know I shouldn't have gone with Liz. I should have remembered that only three people are allowed to pick me up from school—you, Claudia and Brady. But when I saw her driving your car and she told me to hop in, I didn't think, Mom. I just did it."

Of course he had. After all, hadn't they just visited her in New York? Had breakfast with her? Hadn't she promised to come down to see him?

"Once I was in the truck," Ben continued, "she changed. And then she held an awful-smelling handkerchief over my face and I must have blacked out, because when I woke up, I was in that room, all alone. I kept pounding on the door and the windows, but they were locked and no one answered."

"Did she feed you?"

"Just some bread and cold cuts."

"Did she hurt you?"

He gave an emphatic shake of his head. "I only saw her once, when she brought the food in, but she didn't talk. She just left the tray on the table and left." Eyes downcast, he added, "I was scared, Mom. I thought Liz was going to leave me in that room to die and no one would ever find me."

"Come here." He snuggled close and she held him tight with her good arm. "There's no shame in being scared, sport. I was, too."

"Mr. Ryan won't tell me what happened when you got to the house. He said you and I would talk about it later, but..." Anxious eyes searched her face. "How did you get shot, Mom? Did Liz do it?"

At least he was no longer calling her Aunt Liz. "I'll tell

you everything when I feel a little stronger, okay, Ben? Right now all I want is to hold you."

That was how John and Claudia found them a few minutes later, in each other's arms.

"Hello there, lazybones." Claudia walked over to Abbie's bed and kissed her on the forehead. "About time you woke up."

"You are disgustingly chipper," Abbie muttered.

"Could be the fresh mountain air. Speaking of fresh mountain air," she added, turning to Ben. "I'm starving. Why don't you and I go to the cafeteria for some breakfast. I hear they whip up a mean omelette."

"I'd rather have pancakes."

"You've got it, Bud. Let's go."

John waited until they were gone before taking the chair next to Abbie's bed. "How do you feel?"

"As though I was ninety years old."

"Would it make you feel better if I told you you don't look a day over twenty?"

"Only if you mean it."

"Oh, I mean it. You are beautiful. And you are alive." He took her hand and brought it to his lips. "You gave me one hell of a scare, lady."

"Did you spend the night here, too?"

"Yup." He thumbed toward the door. "I wasn't as charming as Ben, so all I could get from the staff was permission to sleep in one of those chairs outside your room. With Claudia as my companion. Did you know she cheats at poker?"

Abbie smiled. "How much did she take you for?"

"Forty-five bucks."

"Consider yourself lucky."

He kissed her fingertips again. "When I found you, nearly unconscious and bleeding so badly I thought you weren't going to make it. I thought, here I am, a police officer, trained to serve, protect and save lives, and I can't save the woman I love.''

The woman I love.

She wanted to tell him she loved him, too, but her eyelids were getting heavy again and she couldn't quite get the words out. So she just lay there, smiling foolishly as words she hadn't expected to hear from him so soon came pouring out of his mouth like a fountain.

He was still talking when she drifted off to sleep.

Forty-Seven

One week later

Not surprisingly, Jordan had jumped at the chance to move in with his father. Thanks to Percy, who had taken care of every detail, the transition from one household to another was made quickly and effortlessly. At first John had feared the town house might be too small to accommodate two men and an active boy, and give each the privacy they were accustomed to. But with three bedrooms, two full baths and a den John had insisted Percy use as his office, space was not a problem.

Clarice called every afternoon, and in the five days since the move, she had already stopped by twice to make sure her son's living conditions were acceptable. But even her discriminating eye hadn't found a single reason for disapproval. For the first time in two years, John's house was spotless, free of clutter and the refrigerator fully stocked.

"Dad?" Jordan stood in front of him, his baseball glove and ball in his hand. "Is it time to go to Ms. DiAngelo's house yet?"

"Not for another fifteen minutes. She's not expecting us until two, remember?"

"She won't mind if we get there early."

John smiled at the boy's impatience, although, to be

truthful, he was getting pretty antsy himself. Except for the time he had spent with Abbie at the hospital and in the district attorney's office where she had given her statement, he hadn't seen much of her these past few days. He had been too busy moving Jordan and Percy in and wrapping up the McGregor case. As for Abbie, she had taken some much-needed time off to rest from her ordeal and to be with Ben. Today's little gathering at her house was her way of thanking her friends, old and new, for standing by her during those difficult couple of weeks.

"You know something," John said, glancing at the three boxes marked Books, "the next fifteen minutes will go much faster if you keep busy."

"Doing what?"

"You could start by taking those boxes to your room and unpacking them."

"But Percy said he would do it when he came back from Grandpa's house."

A typical kid, Jordan hadn't wasted any time getting used to being waited on. "Percy can't be doing everything for you, Jordan. We talked about that, didn't we?"

The boy swung his head from side to side in that familiar "yeah, yeah" motion, grabbed one of the boxes and walked up the stairs, stomping his feet, not hard, just enough to let John know he wasn't happy.

Not one to let a situation get out of control, John followed him. He stood in the doorway for a moment, watching Jordan unpack his books and put them in the new bookcase John had bought him.

"You're not having second thoughts about living here, are you, kiddo?"

Jordan spun around. "Gee, no, Dad. I like being with you, and seeing you every day." He grinned. "Doing guy stuff."

"So do I, Jordan, and I know we're going to have a great time together, but you're still going to have to do chores, just as you did at your mom's house."

Jordan nodded.

"As for Percy, he did us a huge favor by agreeing to move in here. Your mom would have never gone along with this arrangement if it wasn't for him."

"I know that."

"Then you understand why he should not be treated like a servant."

"I didn't mean to do that, Dad. Percy is the one who always wants to do things for me."

That was true. In fact, John himself had tried to take advantage of the butler's thoughtfulness years ago until Spencer had given John the same speech he was now giving to his own son. "I guess I'll have to talk to Percy as well."

As Jordan took the last book out of the box, John glanced at his watch. "Well, what do you know? It's time to go."

After keeping Abbie at Tannersville Memorial one more night, the doctors had released her with a clean bill of health. The bullet had gone right through, causing significant blood loss but not damaging any nerves or major muscles. She would regain complete use of her arm as soon as she healed.

Feeling nervous, even with John at her side, Abbie gave a formal statement to the Tannersville D.A., who chose not to bring charges against her. John explained later, that, had she wanted to, Sandra Zolov could have charged Abbie with second-degree murder and let her plead self-defense in the killing of Liz Tilly. But this was an election year, and given the exceptional circumstances of this case, Zolov thought it wise to let Abbie go.

By the time they all returned home, Abbie's former husband was waiting for them. Father and son had spent the entire day together, catching up. Before leaving, Jack had promised to come down more often. Abbie had no idea whether or not he would keep his word, but Ben seemed to think he would, and for now, that was enough.

The Princeton district attorney, Abbie learned, had been busy, not only with Arturo Garcia, who would be standing trial for Ian's murder, but with another bizarre development—the arrest of Professor Oliver Gilroy.

Dissatisfied with his inconclusive talk with the professor, John had contacted Scotland Yard in London, and learned that in 1987, Gilroy's twelve-year-old neighbor had accused him of touching him in an improper manner. The boy later recanted his story, claiming he was angry with the professor for not buying a tin of vanilla wafers during a Boy Scouts' fund drive.

Although the charge was dropped and the boy made a public apology, Professor Gilroy was quoted as saying that the damage done to his reputation was irreparable. Six months later, in a surprising move, his wife divorced him, ending their eighteen-year marriage.

While Gilroy was never asked to resign his teaching position at Middlesex College, he no longer felt comfortable working there. Shortly after handing in his resignation, he applied for a U.S. visa and moved to the States.

A search of Gilroy's house uncovered a locked room, where one wall was almost entirely covered with snapshots of young boys the professor had photographed, some with their knowledge, some without. Eric Sommers and the other two murdered boys, as well as Jordan and Ben, were included in the display. In an upper shelf in his bedroom closet, the police had also found child-pornography literature and one other interesting item—a cream-colored fedora Gilroy swore he hadn't worn in years.

Although Gilroy was arrested, he refused to admit to the raping and killing of the three New Jersey youths, insisting the photographs proved nothing other than a harmless fondness for the dozens of boys who shared his passion for trains. As for the pornographic material, he claimed to have no idea how it got there. It wasn't his. His refusal to cooperate had prompted Captain Farwell to send Tina to England for further investigation.

It was a brilliant Sunday afternoon, and for the first time in a little over a week, Abbie felt alive again. John and Jordan had arrived moments ago, and the boys were already in the pool, laughing and playing as though the events of last week had never taken place.

She, John, Claudia, Rose and Brady sat on Abbie's patio, the remains of Irene's strawberry cheesecake on the table in front of them. Her mother had stopped by earlier to deliver it in person, but hadn't wanted to stay. Abbie hadn't pressed her, knowing she felt uncomfortable when surrounded by too many people. But at the door, Irene had surprised her by whispering in her ear, "I like that Detective Ryan very much. He's everything Claudia said he was."

Rose's voice pulled Abbie out of her reverie. She was talking to John. "What happens now? With the professor, I mean."

"It all depends on how Tina makes out in England."

Brady helped himself to another cup of coffee. "Will she be talking to Gilroy's ex-wife?"

"And Peter Brice, the boy—a man, now—who made that initial accusation against the professor sixteen years ago. The idea is to make Gilroy crack. Hopefully that will do it.''

"But if you have enough to charge him," Claudia said, "shouldn't you have enough to convict him? With or without his confession?''

"I wish we did. Unfortunately, the evidence against him is all circumstantial. We can prosecute, and still present a strong case, but whether or not we'll get a conviction is debatable. We're hoping that when the truth about what happened in England comes out, Gilroy will agree to plead guilty in exchange for a lighter sentence—life imprisonment instead of the death penalty—and save the county the expense of a trial."

"What about that cute guy? Tony Garcia?" Claudia assumed an innocent look. "Any chance they'll let him go?"

Brady roared with laughter. "Oh, no, here comes groom number four! The Runaway Bride strikes again!"

She slapped his arm. "Shut up, Brady."

"Actually," John said, "Tony appears to be a good guy who tried to get his brother to turn himself in and failed. He was wrong to protect a man he knew had committed murder, but they'll probably go easy on him, as they will on Enrique."

He looked at Abbie, who had remained silent during the exchange. "You haven't said much. Everything all right?"

Abbie gazed down at her sling and flexed her fingers, just to make sure they were working as they should. "I was thinking about Liz. I still can't believe how I allowed myself to be so completely fooled by her. Or how she could have planned such a horrible fate for a little boy who only wanted to love her."

"We'll never really know what was in that head of hers, but it's not unusual for someone who has suffered a severe loss to want revenge on the people he or she believes caused that loss. In Liz's case, her hatred for you and your mother had lain dormant for many years. It might never have resurfaced if Ian hadn't shown up and convinced her of Irene's guilt.''

"But at the cemetery, when I told her my mother wasn't responsible, I felt as though she believed me.''

"Whether she did or not doesn't matter. She still blamed Irene for saving you first. In her mind, that's what caused her to lose her baby, then Glen, and to become sterile and eventually lose Jude as well.''

Abbie thought of that last conversation with Liz, and the woman's conviction that what she had done in the name of justice and revenge was warranted. "She killed two people,'' she mused. "And each time, she went on with her life as if nothing had happened.''

"She was a sick woman, Abbie.''

"And I made it so easy for her, calling her, practically begging her to become a part of our lives.''

"If you hadn't sought her out, she would have sought you. After Ian approached her, she had it all planned.''

Rose reached over to take her hand. "Don't think about it anymore, hon, okay? Just be glad you and Ben are safe and s—''

They were interrupted by the frantic, repeated sound of the doorbell. "Abbie!'' a voice shouted. "It's me, Sean. Open up, quick!''

Abbie's heart sank as she ran to the door ahead of the others, wondering what catastrophe was hurtling toward her now.

Sean stood on the front porch, his face red. In his hand was a single sheet of paper. "I left my tennis racket at the restaurant yesterday and had to go back to get it. When I walked into the utility room, this was just coming through the fax.'' Beaming, he handed Abbie the sheet of paper. ''It's from Archibald Gunther.''

''The review?'' Brady's arm shot forward and snatched the paper from Sean's hand. ''Oh my God,'' he said as his eyes coursed over the page. ''Jesus Almighty!''

''Is it good?'' Abbie's heart began to pound. ''How good? Darn it, Brady, read it!''

Brady cleared his throat, held the paper at arm's length as if preparing to read the Declaration of Independence, and began:

''Much hype had been raised in recent weeks about Campagne and its owner, Chef Abbie DiAngelo. We knew she had trained in France, that she had made quite a name for herself as a caterer, and oh, yes, she did win the Bocuse d'Or, last month, a prize bestowed on only the very best and that no American had ever won before, let alone an American *woman*.

Curious to see if all that fuss was justified, I broke my cardinal rule of never listening to rumors, and made the trek to Princeton, New Jersey, on a balmy Monday evening.

If you are tired, as I am, of French-theme restaurants with Edith Piaf ballads in the background, Belle Époque posters on the walls and phony French accents, then you'll find Campagne refreshingly different.

With its clever blend of colorful tablecloths, understated china, inexpensive glassware and impeccable service, Campagne has created a warm country atmosphere that is comfortable, pleasant to the eye and totally relaxing.

I began my meal with a humble soupe au pistou, which was one of the best I've ever had, although the vegetables could have been cut a shade smaller. The pesto, which can often be overwhelming, was the perfect combination of basil, garlic, pine nuts and olive oil, all pounded to a smooth consistency and lightly blended into the soup.

The second course was a warm lentil salad with magret de canard—thin, rare, crisp-edged slices of duck breast—served on a mound of tender frisée. There couldn't have been a better prelude for the main course, a fall-off-the-bone veal shank, slow-cooked to perfection and fragrant with thyme. This Normand version—new to me—included hard cider, a touch of cream and egg yolk to thicken the sauce.

The steamed asparagus that accompanied the meat tasted as if they had been picked from a local farm that very day, and the potatoes au gratin were crisp and golden brown on the outside, creamy and delicately laced with nutmeg on the inside.

The many other delectable items on the menu made me wish I had ordered more. Alas, I only had room for a light, savory dessert of red ripe roasted figs and crème fraîche, the memory of which still brings a smile to my face.

To my earlier question, is Chef DiAngelo worth all the fuss, my answer is a resounding yes. What now remains to be seen is if this level of excellence can be maintained over the next twenty or thirty years."

Brady lowered his arm just as Abbie let out a whoop of victory. "I'll never say a nasty word about that man ever again," she vowed, hugging Brady. "From now on he *is* a god."

"Personally," Brady said with a straight face, "I always knew the man had good taste."

"Liar. You hated him as much as the rest of us did."

"What was that remark about the vegetables?" Claudia wanted to know.

The happy chatter stopped as two pairs of eyes turned toward John. "You," Abbie said, pointing a finger. "*You* are the one who chopped the vegetables."

John put up his arms in mock self-defense. "Now just a minute. You were all pretty damn happy to have me pitch in, if I recall. For the better part of an hour, I tolerated your temper tantrums, your barking orders and your fits of depression. And this is what I get for my efforts?"

"Okay, okay," Brady said. "We'll let you off the hook—this time."

Eager to celebrate, Abbie brought out a bottle of Dom Pérignon and the next hour was spent discussing the glowing review, what it meant for the restaurant and the best way to use it.

Later, when everyone had left, John pulled Abbie into a corner of the kitchen and took her in his arms. "Alone at last." He glanced outside where the boys were playing catch in the field beyond the pool. Satisfied they weren't paying attention to them, he kissed her. It was a long, burning kiss Abbie returned with all the passion a one-armed woman could muster.

"Well," she said when he finally let her go. "I was wondering when you'd get around to doing that."

"I would have done it sooner, but I have this thing about kissing women in front of an audience."

"In that case, why don't you do it again?" She coiled her good arm around his neck. "To make up for lost time."

When they finally parted, John walked over to the chair where he had draped his jacket and took out a flat, brightly wrapped package from the seat. "I got you something."

She beamed. "A present? What's the occasion?"

"Your safe return. And I never did get a chance to thank you properly."

She was already untying the ribbon, tearing the pretty paper. "Thank me for what?"

"For inspiring me. Without your little pep talk, I would still be wishing I had Jordan with me. Now that wish has become a reality and I owe it all to you. You made me realize that anything is possible, if you want it badly enough."

"I'm glad everything worked out so well for you and Jordan, but you certainly didn't have to..." She opened the box. "Oh."

Inside the box was a five-by-seven card with a logo at the top she recognized immediately. It belonged to l'Auberge du Midi in Avignon, France. A reservation for dinner for two had been made in John's name.

Abbie looked up, absolutely stunned. "L'Auberge du Midi is where I spent my apprenticeship."

"I know. You told me all about it the day Jordan and I were here. I also remember you saying how much you'd like to go back there someday. Well, lady, the day has come."

Choked up with emotion, Abbie pulled out the card with the confirmed reservation written in her former boss's familiar handwriting. It was the sweetest thing anyone had ever done for her, and it touched her deeply.

"François called a couple of days ago, after he found out what happened," she said when she could trust her voice again. "He never mentioned this."

"I asked him not to."

She let out a bewildered laugh. "You talked to François? Who doesn't speak a word of English? Wait, don't tell me. You speak French."

He brought his thumb and index finger together. "*Un*

peu. Enough so François understood what I wanted. He's thrilled by the way. He can't wait to show you to his customers, some of whom remember you."

"You're full of surprises, aren't you, Detective Ryan?"

"You ain't seen nothin' yet, Chef DiAngelo."

"How did you know where to find François?"

"Brady helped."

She laughed. "Brady the conspirator. Why am I not surprised?"

"By the way, I've already talked to Percy. He said he'd be delighted to have Ben stay with him and Jordan for a few days, if that's all right with you. I would have taken the boys with us, but…" He pulled her to him again. "I wanted this to be a special time for us."

The thought of being in that magical part of the world, with this very special man, prompted her next question. "When do we leave?"

"July 12. That should give us enough time to talk to Ben and Jordan about us, get them used to the idea of you and me together."

You and me together. She liked the sound of that.

"And as you see," he added, sounding very proud of himself, "I made the dinner reservation for July 14—Bastille Day. François said there would be lots of fireworks at the inn."

"I love fireworks."

"I know that, too." Very gently, he backed her against the wall and kissed her again, murmuring against her lips, "Who knows? We might even make some fireworks of our own."

CHRISTIANE HEGGAN

66870	MOMENT OF TRUTH	___ $6.50 U.S.	___ $7.99 CAN.
66783	BLIND FAITH	___ $6.50 U.S.	___ $7.99 CAN.
66577	ENEMY WITHIN	___ $5.99 U.S.	___ $6.99 CAN.
66536	TRUST NO ONE	___ $5.99 U.S.	___ $6.99 CAN.
66466	DECEPTION	___ $5.99 U.S.	___ $6.99 CAN.
66305	SUSPICION	___ $5.99 U.S.	___ $6.99 CAN.

(limited quantities available)

TOTAL AMOUNT $_____
POSTAGE & HANDLING $_____
($1.00 for one book; 50¢ for each additional)
APPLICABLE TAXES* $_____
TOTAL PAYABLE $_____
(check or money order—please do not send cash)

To order, complete this form and send it, along with a check or money order for the total above, payable to MIRA Books®, to: **In the U.S.:** 3010 Walden Avenue, P.O. Box 9077, Buffalo, NY 14269-9077; **In Canada:** P.O. Box 636, Fort Erie, Ontario, L2A 5X3.

Name:_____
Address:_____ City:_____
State/Prov.:_____ Zip/Postal Code:_____
Account Number (if applicable):_____
075 CSAS

*New York residents remit applicable sales taxes.
Canadian residents remit applicable GST and provincial taxes.

MIRA®